Ezra Grayson arrives in the small town of Edgewood, following a clue that will hopefully lead him to the men responsible for the deaths of his parents. His desire for revenge, the only thing keeping him going after five years of trailing the midnight twelve.

Colleen Warren was not like the other girls working at the Lady Luck Saloon in Edgewood. It was not easy to explain to her customers that the soft, feminine Colleen was also the hard, masculine Cole.

A miscalculation throws them together as they run from the law and the bounty on Ezra's head, but it is fate that guides their journey across the land; bringing them closer to the answers they both seek and to each other.

# THE MIDNIGHT TWELVE

Outlaw Seven, Book One

*Hairann*

A NineStar Press Publication

Published by NineStar Press
P.O. Box 91792,
Albuquerque, New Mexico, 87199 USA.
www.ninestarpress.com

# The Midnight Twelve



Printed in the USA
First Edition
May, 2018

Print ISBN: 978-1-950412-75-4

Also available in eBook, ISBN: 978-1-950412-74-7

Warning: This book contains sexually explicit content, which may only be suitable for mature readers, death of secondary characters, and mention of rape and off-page rape of a child.

This book is dedicated to any reader who grew up unable to see themselves in the characters they read about. Who hid away their deepest secrets for fear of not being accepted. For any member of the wonderful LGBTQA+ community that I am proud to be a part of. We see you. We accept you. We love you.

And to my wonderful husband for putting up with me through this entire process. It's not easy to love someone who's mind is constantly in a land of their own creation.

# Prologue

WEST OF SHADYNOOK 1818

Long after dusk settled over the desert, the landscape veiled in darkness as there was no moon to illuminate the night sky, a boy of nine years was awoken from a deep sleep. He was dreaming of hunting rabbits with his father when a strange feeling gnawed at the edge of his mind. Confused by the sudden intrusion, he wiped the crusted sleep from his pale green eyes, before he glanced around the dark room and waited for them to adjust. His only source of light was an almost dead fire that burned its last log in the hearth; its embers barely gave off a red glow, let alone any real source of light.

On many a night such as this, the swaying shadows caused him to tremble in fear, unable to discern what they were, as he woke from an unsettling dream or for the need to relieve himself. Eventually he outgrew those fears, but tonight they managed to unnerve him once more as the strange sensation that awoken him still weighed on his mind.

As the feeling grew stronger, he glanced toward where his parents slept unaware, before turning his attention to the window on the far side of the room. For a moment, he hesitated—the floor beneath his bed would be cold, and he didn't want to risk waking his parents as the old, worn wooden planks creaked beneath his feet. Things never ended well for him whenever a misstep caused his father to wake.

Try as he might, the sensation refused to release its urgent grasp on his mind. His lone blanket tossed aside, he crawled out of bed, breath held as though that might prevent the boards from their inevitable betrayal and made his way over to the window. Hands pressed firmly on the ledge, he pushed himself up and looked through the condensation. Even though the fire no longer heated the small home, it was still warmer within than it was outside during a cold, desert night.

With only the stars shining above him, he saw little more than the silhouette of cacti and the outline of the fence that surrounded his family's lone mare. Staring out into the cold, dark night, he watched as a star twinkled out of existence. An ominous chill crawled its way down his spine—a shiver that had nothing to do with the cold. As he glanced once more out into the land that surrounded his modest two-room home, he saw nothing but the dusty ground and the darkened sky that was always present. Whatever had caused the strange feeling refused to make itself known to him, and the young boy frowned in annoyance.

Perhaps he simply imagined the entire thing; his sleep-laden mind was prone to play tricks on him. About to give up the feeling as having been his imagination and head back to bed, the boy caught a flare of light from beyond the edge of their property.

Confused, he watched the small flame dance around a few feet off the ground as it grew ever closer to his home. Soon he realized what it was he was seeing—a torch. Its small flame was as dim as the one in his own hearth, no doubt caused by the distance. Its movement was almost rhythmic as it seemed to rise and fall in sync with his breathing. It dawned on him that whoever carried the torch did so from the saddle.

He wondered who might wish to call on them at this late an hour, especially when visitors during the day were a rare occurrence. The torch's singularity was proved to be short-lived as flame after flame appeared behind it, their bearers now close enough for him to see. A knot formed in his throat.

The boy let go of the window ledge and made his way to where his parents slept unaware. "Papa," the boy called out as he gently shook him, his shaky voice betraying the fear that rose within him.

His father shooed him off with a wave of his hand, not bothering to open his eyes. "Get back to bed, Ezra. It was just a nightmare." He rolled back over and appeared to fall asleep once more.

Not wanting to suffer his father's wrath in case he decided to bring out the switch, the boy was about to give up and go back to bed when he remembered how many torches were on a journey toward his home at that moment.

There was no innocent reason he knew of for men to be headed toward their house that late at night and in such large numbers. Once he decided it was worth the punishment if he turned out to be wrong, he pushed on. "Papa, men are comin'."

His father growled even as he turned to glare at him in the dim firelight. The boy shivered in dread at how his father might punish him, but he refused to let his apprehension deter him. "Riders are comin', Papa. With torches. I lost count at ten torches."

His father threw back the covers, jumped out of bed, and rushed toward the window.

His mother, awoken by the commotion he made, sat up in bed. "Benjamin, what is it? Who is outside at this hour?"

His father didn't answer.

Unsure of what to do, Ezra stood in silence as his mother, a young woman of twenty-eight years, climbed from the warm bed, and silently made her way over to the window. She glanced out into the front yard, and her breath hitched in her throat, audibly enough for him to hear.

He moved closer toward his parents in order to see outside, barely able to make out the torches as they cast an eerie glow on the hardened faces of the men who bore them before his mother stepped in front of him to block his sight.

"He found us, Benjamin. After all these years, he finally found us," she whispered as she trembled in fear; the vibration even noticeable in the dark braid that fell on her back. In that moment, he knew with certainty that nothing good would come from meeting with the visitors outside. If his mother had ever felt anything other than happiness, she took great care to ensure he never realized it. How frightened must she have been to not even bother with pretenses.

"Aye, my love, but we have shared ten more years of freedom than we were ever meant to have. We knew he would find us eventually. No one leaves alive, we knew that in the very beginning. We both can't escape from our fate, but it is not too late for you and the boy, Lisette. Take him and make your way out the back before they have the chance to surround us. They will surely kill him if they find him here, but as none knew your pregnancy was the reason we left, they will not know of his existence. I will convince them you died years ago. Hide in the large bushes and wait until they leave to do so yourself. Do not risk being heard."

*No one leaves what alive?* Ezra thought. *Why are they here to kill any of us? How was my mother being pregnant with me the reason they left whatever it was that they ran from?* Ezra knew not to question his parents at that moment and instead continued to watch them in silence. Watch as his mother shook her head defiantly, tears forming in her eyes. Watch as his father leaned down and placed a kiss upon her lips.

Watch as the fight slowly faded out of her eyes, and she nodded before she cupped his father's cheeks, resting her forehead against his. It was a gesture he saw many times in his short life, usually when his father returned from being gone overnight, but he had never before seen it seem so sad.

His mother grabbed his arm and led them through the small room they occupied and into the kitchen. Without releasing her grip, she gathered his overcoat, shoes, and a loaf of bread, before ushering him to the back door. She did not bother to grab anything of her own. "Take these and follow your father's instructions. I wish more than anything to go with you, but I cannot risk your father's assumptions that they will believe me dead.

"If they don't, they will not stop until they find me, but they have no way to know of your existence. We left them before they realized I was pregnant. Hide in the bushes and do not move from that spot until long after the riders have gone. They may leave a rider behind for a little while, and if they find you, they will kill you. Now listen to your mama and go." Before he had the chance to speak once again, his mother placed a quick kiss upon his confused brow and pushed him out the back door.

A moment later, he heard the bar come down, locking him out and preventing him from trying to go back inside. He made his way around the small house, not bothering to put on his coat or shoes—he had no chance to outrun them anyway.

He pushed his way into the bushes, making sure he was close enough to see the riders when they arrived out front, but far enough out of sight they would be unable to see him. He was less than ten feet away from where his parents were standing inside his home, but he might as well have been a half a world away. Though the four walls that made up his home had never been quite enough to keep out all of the winter's chill, they were enough to keep the sounds trapped within so he could not hear what they were saying. Were they arguing about his mother's decision? Would his father agree, or would he try to send her out again?

The riders arrived, stopping a few feet in front of the porch. The men fanned out behind the first one to stop—Ezra counted a dozen of them. Unsurprisingly, each carried a pistol or two in holsters at their hips. Two of them, the riders who were at the ends of the group, held rifles across their laps. Each one's clothing differed slightly, either through the color and pattern on their shirts or that some wore vests while the others wore jackets, but it was not hard for even a boy as young as him, who had never seen an outlaw in his entire life, to figure out that was exactly who they were. Something about the dark look in their eyes, the grimaces set on their faces, convinced him they were not men of law.

"Come out, Grayson, I know you're in there!" the man in the front called out, startling Ezra and causing him to shake the bush slightly. Holding his breath, he froze as he watched for any sign of the men hearing him, before finally exhaling in relief when they continued to glare at the front of his house. A moment later, he heard the telltale creaking of the front door opening and his parents' footsteps making their way across the threshold. He was not able to see them from his position, but he did hear his parents stop at the top of the stairs.

"Took y'all long enough. Was startin' to think you turned coward and ran again, Benjie. It's good you finally show some courage at the end. Won't stop what's comin' but won't have to make it worse in spite neither. Mister De Voe sent'cha a message I'm supposed to deliver before you die." The man spat, his dark eyes never leaving his parents.

"He said to tell you that ain't nobody leaving the Pine Box Crew except for in one. Your fate is already sealed, Benjie boy, but Mister De Voe said he would be more than happy to let Lisette warm his bed in exchange for her life." Ezra didn't completely understand the odd grin the man was giving his mother, but he knew whatever he was suggesting was not something his mother would approve of, even if he had not seen the man's mouthful of rotten and blackened teeth. One of the other men, who was out of his line of sight, let out a creepy laugh.

Judging by the man's next words, he was correct. "Your choice, but it ain't like it would have been the first time you laid with the boss man." The man smirked before gesturing over his shoulders at the men behind him. "I'll let the Johnson brothers send you on your way." The man turned his horse around and headed back in the direction they came from only a few minutes before. As he passed his men, he nodded to them. Two broke away, moving closer to the porch as the others followed after their leader. Not daring to move, Ezra clenched his fists so tightly his nails bit into his palms as the men raised their six-shooters at his parents.

He knew without being able to see that his parents stood there unarmed, their only rifle currently sitting on the table in the gunsmith's shop as it waited to be repaired. They were unable to defend themselves as a loud noise thundered around them. The deafening sound filled the air repeatedly as the men continued to fire, their horses whinnying in protest to the sudden noise. It was not long before the sound was drowned out by his parents' screams, confirming at least a few of the bullets hit their targets.

Time seemed to slow to a crawl as he shut his eyes and waited for it to stop, unable to bear watching any longer. Eventually, the men ran out of bullets, and the noise stopped as suddenly as it began. Ezra opened his eyes to find them already making their way toward their comrades. They stole his father's horse and left without looking back.

That was how little taking the lives of his parents mattered to them. They were not even worth a second glance, a confirmation that they were no longer suffering. He bit into his bottom lip to prevent himself from making a sound while the men were still close enough to overhear him. The fire from their torches grew farther and farther away. Each step their horses took provided him with a little more protection.

He heard his parents wailing in pain, apparently still alive for the moment, but he was unable to force himself to move. The gunshots echoed through him, each one piercing his heart a little more than the last. The brave face he put on for his mother was now all but forgotten as he shivered in the foliage, his heartbeat pounding louder in his ears with each passing moment. He would have to come out of hiding eventually—every second he wasted was another moment he would never get back with his parents, but he was still too scared to move.

He would have remained there, unaware of the passing time, had he not heard the soft, frail voice of his mother calling out to him: "Ezra."

His head shot up, searching around for what must have been her ghost speaking to him when he remembered she was still alive. His eyes flitted around, searching for a sign of any dangers lurking nearby, but still, he was frozen in place even after he was unable to find any.

"Come to me, baby. You are safe," his mother's voice called out again, assuring him. This time, the pain in her voice was enough to get him to rise to his feet once more.

He rushed toward the front of the house and skidded to a halt at the sight before him. Mere feet away, his parents lay on the porch, bleeding badly from wounds even he knew would prove to be fatal. His father's hauntingly empty eyes stared off into the distance even as his chest continued to rise and fall ever so slightly. His mother's gentle eyes turned toward him, unfocused, as her hand raised barely an inch off of the porch toward him.

Once more, he froze, unable to will himself to move as he took in all that was before him, burning it forever into his memory. Every drop of his parents' spilled blood. Every painful gasp for air. The frighteningly hollow look in their eyes. He would memorize every last bit of it, even knowing it would haunt his dreams for the rest of his life because he knew this would be the last time he would ever see them. As much as he wanted to remember them as they were the night before when he went to sleep, a peaceful, loving memory of his parents would not serve him well if ever he wished to avenge their deaths.

No longer would this be a porch where his mother used to read him stories as the bright summer sun sank below the horizon, continuing until the words were no longer legible in the dimming light. Now it would be the place his parents were gunned down for reasons unknown to him. No longer would the stairs before him be where his father taught him how to clean his gun and skin a rabbit properly. Now they would be the final steps he took toward his living parents.

No longer would it be a place that held so many of his favorite childhood memories. Now it held the bodies of his dying parents; their blood seeping into the grain of the wood and forever staining it. Hearing his mother weakly calling out his name once more, he tentatively took a few steps toward her. He scanned the scene before him but refused to look on either of their faces. With each step that brought him closer, he made out more of the details that were missed before, opting to concentrate on them instead of the actual people before him.

The sticky, red blood continued to gush from their wounds, staining their clothes and pooling beneath them. He listened to the raspy breathing of his mother and the wet, gurgling breaths his father struggled to take. "Mama, Papa," he gasped before collapsing beside them, finally turning his attention to their paling faces. Grabbing her raised hand in his smaller, chubbier ones, he barely managed to whisper, "Mama," once more before the tears burst from his eyes and he collapsed against her bloody form.

"Listen to me, my sweet baby boy. Papa and I ain't long for this world, and there is nothing to be done about it. You cannot stay here, it ain't safe without us. Pack only what you can manage and make your way toward the rising sun. It will lead you straight into town and to Sheriff Jarrett. He can take you to your grandmother's. You will be safe there, my dear Ezra." She paused for a moment, struggling to take a breath as she cupped his cheek. Both of them ignored the smudge of blood she left there as her strength drained away, and her arm fell back to her side.

"This world is full of good, honest people, but there are also those more evil than you ever imagined. If you ever hear the name Godfrey de Voe, run as far and as fast as you can, for you will find none worse than him. He is the man that has murdered us and is far more dangerous than you can believe. Be safe my child and know that you were loved more than life itself by your Papa and me." Her words tapered off as she lay back and closed her eyes. Apparently, even the simple task of keeping them open required more strength than she had.

Laying down beside her, undaunted by the pool of blood beneath him, Ezra wept as he curled up in her loving arms. It wasn't until the sun rose on the horizon that he finally lifted his head once more and glanced toward the bodies of his dead parents. The uncertainty of his future path was all but forgotten the moment his parents breathed their final breath. He was an orphan now and one day, though he didn't know where or how, Godfrey de Voe would pay for what he had done. He rose to his feet with determination and set about the long, exhausting task of burying his parents.

AS SOON AS Ezra finished adding the last shovelful of dirt on to his mother's grave, he collapsed in exhaustion on top of her final resting place and remained there all night.

When he awoke the next morning, the events from the night before were forgotten by his sleepy mind for a moment, and he imagined he was in his warm, lumpy bed.

But as a crow cawed in a tree no more than a few yards away from him, he quickly realized he was sleeping outside. With that realization, the memories came flooding back all at once, and it became clear to him that the lumpy blanket he thought he was sleeping on was, in fact, the mound of dirt that covered his mother's lifeless body.

He leaped to his feet and nearly tripped over the shovel he discarded beside him, squeezing his eyes closed against the horrifying sight of his parents' graves. Wiping his dirty palms on his pants, he tried not to think about what the crusty substance that stained his arms and clothes was. Without looking back at the small graveyard he'd dug himself, Ezra made his way into the silent home that used to be filled with the happy, loving sounds of family.

The sound of his mother giggling when she caught his father staring at her when he thought she hadn't been looking, was gone. The sound of his father's voice calling him over to sit in front of the fire and instructing him on how to whittle a chunk of wood into a tiny bird would never echo within the walls again. His own laughter when his mother would tickle him as she tucked him into bed at night, saying every day should start with a smile and end with a laugh, would ring out no more.

Now the house was empty, void of all sound other than the loud beating of his heart as it echoed in his ears and the sniffles he tried to fight. Boys didn't cry, not according to Papa, and he did not want disobeying his father to be the last thing he did in his childhood home. That would wait until he was safely in his grandmother's arms. Even though he had never met her before, he knew he would be safe and welcome with her. She was his only living relative now, and you took care of family, right? But, as he had no other choice at the moment, he decided it did not matter how he was received when he arrived. First, he needed to get there.

Making his way around the small home he was sure he would never see again after that day, he gathered up what he was able to take with him; what he couldn't bear to leave behind. His father's whittling knife. His mother's necklace. The train his father whittled for him for his ninth birthday a few months back.

Grabbing the pillowcase off of his parents' bed, he added the items he collected, along with the loaf of bread his mother gave him the night before. He went to the kitchen and grabbed what food he found, adding it to the makeshift sack before throwing it over his shoulder and making his way outside once more.

As his mother instructed him, he headed due east, toward the sun that was still rising, already forcing away the previous night's chill. He had only been there a few times since they bought the homestead when he was a baby, but he knew the trip into town would take him a good while since he was walking.

As he thought about their last trip into town, the image of his mother laughing at something his father said on the way home flashed through his mind. He did not understand what had been so funny, but just the thought of his mother's beautiful laughter was enough to cause a sob to escape his lips without warning, startling him. Stopping for a moment, he shook his head, steeling his shoulders defiantly, and then continued walking toward his destination. Each hour, each mile passed by in a blur as the tears threatened to fall. He paid them, and the passing scenery, little mind.

One foot, then the other. One step, then another. Over and over, he whispered these instructions to himself until he was no longer sure if he was actually speaking out loud or if it was all in his mind. He had no way to know how long it took him to walk the distance from his home to the small town where they bought their supplies, the journey completely forgotten the moment his eyes landed on the sheriff.

How long or how far the journey had been was irrelevant as he had no wish to remember the last time he ever walked away from his family—from his home. He did not want to think about the unshed tears that stung his eyes or the throbbing of his feet that had him wanting to call out for his mother. He became a man the night before, the moment his father took his last breath.

Making his way over to the small sheriff's office, its old porch creaking as a man with a gold star on his chest paced back and forth. Two other men, each sporting a silver star, seemed unconcerned by his behavior as they rested their heads against the wall behind them. Ezra gave the lawmen a once over to assure himself they were not there the night before, even if he hadn't really gotten a good enough look at any of the men to confirm either way. It didn't seem likely. There was something in the way they carried themselves, not to mention how they were dressed that seemed as if it was the exact opposite from the twelve men from the night before.

Turning his attention to the man with the gold star—Sheriff Jarrett, his mother had called him—he couldn't help but notice how his soft eyes reminded him of his mother's. Though where hers were green, much like his own, the sheriff's were blue. His short, dark hair reminded him of his father's.

He seemed shorter than his father even as he stood on the porch above him, but Ezra wasn't entirely sure if that wasn't his memory making his father seem larger than life. As Ezra approached, the sheriff froze, no doubt startled by the sight he must have made covered in dried blood. He rushed toward Ezra. "What has happened to you, boy? Whose blood is this?"

The sheriff's sudden movements startled the deputies, causing them to jump to their feet and join him before Ezra. "Ma and my Papa were killed last night. Men came to the house and shot them dead. Ma said you would lead me to my grandmother's home. You know how I can get there, right?" He looked up at the sheriff with tired, watery eyes. He managed to keep the tears in so far, but they were always on the edge and ready to fall as soon as he let his guard down.

"Don't you worry about that none, boy, your parents made arrangements with me in case anything were to happen to them. Said they needed to be careful living that far out of town, and in all honesty, I always thought they were worried for nothing. Guess your parents knew better than I did. I'll take you to your grandmother's." The sheriff turned his attention to the two silent men standing beside him. "Head out to the homestead west of here. See if you can pick up their trail. I'll be back before dark." Barely noticing their nods of agreement, Ezra kept his eyes trained on the sheriff as he made his way toward the small one-horse wagon that was tied up beside his office.

"Let's go, boy. It's not a long trip by wagon, but far too long to walk."

Nodding, Ezra allowed himself to be picked up, along with his bag of meager belongings, and placed in the front seat of the wagon. The sheriff climbed in beside him, signaling for the horse to go. Much like the men the night before, he never looked back to make sure the deputies were following orders, but Ezra did, for a moment wondering if he should have told them about burying his parents.

Before he made up his mind, the sheriff was already guiding the horse toward the northeast, and Ezra did his best to ignore the hot sun that was now bearing down on them. The sheriff turned his attention to him once more, giving his appearance a closer inspection, a sad, sympathetic expression on his face. Clearly, he pitied him. What else was there to be feeling at that moment? It was bad enough his parents were killed, but to add having to bury them himself on top of that, it was a wonder he had not gone into shock—or perhaps he already did. In truth, Ezra had no idea how it felt to be in shock so, for all he knew, maybe he was.

"Have you ever met your grandmother?" the sheriff ventured after a few minutes passed in silence. Ezra continued to stare off into the distance. Though he did not see anything that was in front of him, he was unable to pull his eyes away to focus on something else. "Priscilla Mandel is a bit rough around the edges, but I'm sure being around her only grandchild will soften her. Met her a few times myself, but it has been a while since I've been out this way."

Ezra didn't fault the man for his attempts to draw him out, but he could form no reply—his body had already given up listening to what he wanted. As time passed by slowly, Ezra wondered if the silence was causing the minutes to draw on even more than they usually did. How long would it take them to reach their destination? One hour? Two? Would he regain control over himself before they arrived and he was expected to move again?

"If you don't like it with your grandmother, there is always the Mayview Orphanage south of Shadynook. I've taken a few children there over the years. Seems like a decent enough place," the sheriff continued, undaunted by his silence. Judging by the heavy sigh that came from the sheriff, he was not completely unaffected by Ezra's inability to respond.

Ezra tried to smile but couldn't manage it. If he had, it would have been a shadow of the smiles he used to grace his mother with when the men came back from a day of hunting and found her waiting there with open arms. A pale reflection of the grin that nearly split his face when he managed to trap his first rabbit and turned toward his father to find him beaming with pride. He was certain, in that moment, that he would never truly smile again.


EVENTUALLY, THE SILENT trip came to an end as the sheriff pull the wagon to a stop a few yards before a small, two-story home made from warped wood that had seen better days. It wasn't much to look at, even if it was bigger than his parents' house was, and the dingy windows and tattered curtains that surrounded them showed their owner either cared little for their upkeep or was unable to handle the work they required by herself. Ezra was not at all surprised to find an old woman, slightly hunched from age, make her way slowly out onto the porch to greet them.

The shotgun she aimed at them, however, was completely unexpected. Ezra managed to find the strength to hide behind the sheriff, moving for the first time since their journey began. The older man's body shielded most of the exchange from him, but he still saw him raise his hands in surrender. "It is Sheriff Jarrett, Mrs. Mandel. We have met a few times already. Must you point that gun at me every time?"

Ezra was startled when the sheriff chuckled at the seemingly dangerous woman, but he did not dare question his reaction. That would draw her attention to him, and that was the last thing he wanted at that moment.

The sheriff continued. "Remember? I came out to help rebuild your roof last year after that huge storm?" As he spoke, he tilted his head back to show her his face unobstructed by his hat. She lowered her gun, but continued to hold it tightly and did not look the least bit welcoming to Ezra.

"It's all right, boy," the sheriff assured him. "She's not going to hurt you."

Ezra did not move. Instead, he took the opportunity to examine his only living relative more closely. Her long gray hair was pulled up into an unkempt bun, her stiff fingers no doubt unable to pull the strands tight anymore. Her dull, brown dress was covered in patches.

"Funny, I don't remember promising no such thing," she said. "You best be explaining what you are doing on my property before I decide to forget who you are again."

For a moment, Ezra wondered if he would not be better off going to the orphanage the sheriff mentioned on the way there. Just as quickly as it crossed his mind, Ezra pushed the thought away. No matter how strange the first meeting with his grandmother was going, she was the only family he had left. If his mother was there, he knew she would be telling him first impressions were not always a true reflection of who somebody was. He shouldn't blame her for her reactions since they showed up on her property without warning. And worse than that, he realized, he was still covered in his parents' blood. With the sight that they must have made, it was no wonder his grandmother behaved as she did.

"Sorry to have to tell you this, Mrs. Mandel, but Lisette was killed last night along with her husband. This is their boy. Years back, I was instructed to bring him to you if anything were to happen to his parents. I am simply fulfilling my obligation to her." Catching the sheriff's attention turn toward him, Ezra finally took his eyes off of his grandmother long enough to look up at the sheriff and find him nodding in her direction. "You should greet your grandmother. Wouldn't want her thinking your mother hadn't raised you right."

Ezra reluctantly did as he was instructed and nodded to her in silent greeting. "You got a name, boy?" she demanded, her voice devoid of any compassion or familiarity. Try as he might, he found himself unable to answer her. "Spit it out, boy, I ain't got all day. Either tell me your name, or I will call you boy from now on."

Her warning went unheeded as Ezra remained silent, but not because he was unable to force himself to talk still, but because he decided it probably wouldn't matter either way. Something told him she would be calling him that whether he told her his name or not. And honestly, it didn't really matter what she called him anyway. The only people he wanted to hear calling his name never would again. Perhaps once they had gotten to know each other and grown closer like a family should, he would tell her, but for now, he held his tongue.

"Very well, boy it is. Well boy, get on down out of the wagon. There are plenty of chores to be done before supper tonight." She went inside without waiting to see if he would follow. Ezra barely made out what she grumbled under her breath. "Idiot child running around and getting herself knocked up." Ezra bit his lip to prevent himself from calling after her and demanding she take back what she said about his mother.


"GRANDMOTHER!" HE CALLED out as he rushed toward where she was sprawled out across the bottom of the stairs, dropping to his knees as he rolled her onto her back. Brushing her gray hair out of her face, he was startled by the cool touch of her skin. Gasping softly, he forced himself to look into her eyes, finding what he feared he might. Her eyes stared into nothingness. She passed alone while he was out doing his hunting and chores. If he had returned, checked in at some point in the day, he might have been able to have been there for her in the end, but Ezra knew with certainty that she would not have wanted him by her side.

She hadn't wanted him for a single moment in the four years he lived with her, and he knew her heart would not melt in the end. She would not have called out for him or reached for his hand to hold as she passed. Four years they lived beneath the same leaky roof and not once did she ever call him by his name. She never spoke to him like a grandmother, only ever as an unfeeling taskmaster. Never a gentle hand upon his head, instead she turned to the well-used rod.

Resting back on his heels, Ezra stared at her lifeless form in silence as the tears fell down his cheeks. He did not cry for the woman he lost, as she never gave him a single reason to, but because he was completely alone once again. This time, he did not have a long-lost relative to stay with, no other family to take him in. As he sat there, unconcerned by the passing time, he wondered how any of this was fair. Why had so much been against him when he always did as he was told?

What had he done to cause himself to be punished so? For the second time in his short life, Ezra was being forced to bury a member of his family without any help. At least this time, he decided as he dragged his grandmother's body outside, there would be nothing to run from. But there was also nowhere for him to run to even if there was. He had no one—nowhere to go.

He was completely and utterly alone in the world. Ezra could do anything he wanted, go anywhere he wanted, but the only thing he wished for in that moment was to be in his mother's loving arms once again. Instead, once his grandmother was laid to rest, he walked into an empty house and sank to the floor. Hugging his knees to his chest, he rested his head upon them and allowed the tears to fall freely. He would no longer worry about what his father would say if he saw him crying.

It no longer mattered that he was the man of the family and needed to be strong, be brave, as he was the family now. As he sat there, his tears more for the parents he was never able to mourn properly than for the grandmother who never wanted him, he thought about nothing else than their smiling faces as he allowed his exhaustion to catch up to him once again.

THE SOUND OF dry leaves crunching under boots echoed around Ezra as he removed a rabbit from one of his traps and made his way back home. Although the trees near his home did not cover much of the land, they were quite dense and more than once blocked the sounds from the outside world from reaching his ears.

So it came as no surprise to him when he crossed the threshold of his tiny forest and found Sheriff Jarrett waiting for him on the steps of his porch. He did not know if the sheriff figured out his grandmother passed away because she did not greet him with a raised shotgun or because he passed her three-week-old grave on the way in, but the sympathetic expression marring his face was enough to assure Ezra he already knew. He would have liked nothing more than to ignore the look, but unsurprisingly, the sheriff had other plans.

"I am sorry for your loss, son. I think it is time for you to move on to the Mayview Orphanage. A boy your age should not be alone. You should not have to deal with everything by yourself," the sheriff insisted instead of giving him a proper greeting as he usually did when he visited.

Assuming he was simply startled by returning to find so much had changed since his last visit, Ezra decided not to hold his lack of greeting against him. However, that did not mean he would agree with what he was asking for either.

"Sheriff Jarrett, I am doing fine here by myself. I have been taking care of myself for far longer than the three weeks she has been gone. The only real difference is now I have to cook for myself. I am not going to an orphanage. I am old enough to take care of myself, and I already have a place to live. If you force me to go there, I will run away and come back here where I belong." Ezra sat down on the porch and skinned the rabbit without waiting for him to reply. No matter what the sheriff decided to do about him tonight, they still needed to eat before the sheriff got back on the road.

"Tell you what—I will give you a month to prove yourself to me. If, when I return, you are well fed, in good health and able to take care of the house—if I can find nothing here to make me worry about your safety, I will allow you to remain on your grandmother's land. I suppose it is your land now. Is there anything you want to talk about, Ezra?" Even if he did not come right out and say it, it was not hard for Ezra to figure out that he was referring to his grandmother's passing. As much as he wanted to forget everything that happened, he knew it would be better to talk to the sheriff for now.

He would have no one else to talk to for another month other than the birds he whittled and hid up in the trees after his grandmother threw his first one into the fire, and they weren't very good conversationalists. "There isn't much to tell, to tell you the truth. She fell down the stairs one day, and by the time I found her, she was cool to the touch. I don't even know if she died and fell down the stairs or fell down the stairs and died. No way to know, but it don't matter none either. She's gone, and she would not be my choice to bring back even if it was possible. Till the day she died, she still never once called me by my name.

"I finally told her one day hoping it would help bring us closer, finally make us seem at least somewhat family, but she acted as if she didn't hear me and continued to call me 'boy.' That is all I ever was to her, some random boy that showed up on her doorstep and became an unwanted burden for her. I don't miss my grandmother, Sheriff, I don't miss who she never was, who she never wanted to be for me. I miss my mother and my papa. I miss the life I lost with them. Going to an orphanage would never bring that back, it would only make me miss it even more.

"At least here, even if I am alone, I feel connected to them. This was the house my mother grew up in. I sleep in the same room she did when she was younger. I sit at the same table and eat from the same dishes she did as a child. I climb the same trees for apples. I chop the same trees for wood that she did once she was old enough." He paused for a moment as he tried to imagine his mother up in the trees as a child; instead, he was plagued by a vision of his grandmother yelling at her from the front porch to stop dawdling like she had done to him many times. "This may not be where they are buried, where they lived the happier years of their lives. I do not know if my father ever stepped foot on this land, but this is where I feel them the most. Back home, I would only feel their deaths and not their lives.

"I would not go back there, even if I was certain it was safe from those men, and I would no sooner leave here. This is home now, and for the first time since I met the unfortunate woman who was supposed to be my grandmother, I feel like I am home. That I am wanted and welcome. The chickens have never looked at me with disdain. The horse has never slapped me across the face for something my father did many years ago."

Having already said far more than he planned on to the sheriff, Ezra grabbed the skinned rabbit, and leaving the fur to be dealt with later, he began making his way inside when he was stopped by the sheriff's words. "If things were so bad with her all this time, why did you never say anything when I came to visit? I might have helped things between you two."

Instead of answering, Ezra continued making his way into the kitchen and rebuilt the dying fire in the hearth even as the sheriff followed in after him. As he prepared the rabbit to roast over the fire while he dealt with the fur, he explained over his shoulder, "You would have tried bringing me to the orphanage if you realized how bad things were with my grandmother and me. Most of the time, I kept hoping that tomorrow would be the day when things finally became better between us, but each new day left me disappointed. Truthfully, I would debate asking you to take me away the next time you visited each night as I laid down to sleep, but each morning somehow brought me renewed hope that things would be different.

"I kept telling myself that I would regret it if I gave up on the only family I had left, never knowing how things might have changed the day after I left. Even with my foolishness, at the very least, I was here to bury her instead of her body being left there to attract animals. But none of that matters anymore as she is gone, and I am not." As he added the rabbit to the fire, he turned back to the sheriff, who had a strange expression on his face. "What is it?" he questioned as he moved over to wash his hands in a nearby pail of water.

"Sometimes you sound far older than you actually are. Perhaps you are correct, with this wisdom you seem to have even at such a young age, and you will be okay by yourself. If I do agree to let you stay here after I have returned in one month and see that you are able to live on your own, I will start coming by once a month instead of every two, but I do not see why there would be any problem with it. At the very least, without your grandmother here, you will have more fur and vegetables to trade with the townsfolk."

Ezra nodded in agreement and led them back outside and tended to the rabbit fur while the sheriff told him stories of what happened in town since his last visit. Since it was a quiet town, very little was worth mentioning. Ezra was certain he only updated him simply to give them something to talk about, but he admitted, at least to himself, he looked forward to his visits and what little he learned about the outside world. It may not have been the whole world, but it was certainly a world away from the small existence he lived in here even before his grandmother passed away.

ONE DAY EZRA headed out to check on the traps again as the sun was setting. They were empty, and with a sigh, Ezra made his way back toward his home. Before he crossed the tree line, he heard voices drifting on the wind. His disappointment was quickly forgotten and replaced by apprehension. The sheriff was not due to return for a couple of weeks, and no one else ever came to visit in the almost six years he had lived there.

Doubting their arrival would lead to anything good, Ezra quietly crept closer and hid in the thick underbrush to eavesdrop on the trespassers. As he crouched there, watching as a group of five men tore apart his home in search of anything worth stealing, the night his parents died played in the back of his mind. Though these were not the same men who were there that night and, as far as he knew, they were not there to kill anyone, he still found himself shivering despite the warm air.

The man who appeared to be the leader called out, "Take anything of value. Bring any pretty ladies you find hiding in there to me. Y'all can keep the ugly ones." Ignoring his crude joke, Ezra turned his attention to each of them he saw moving around and committed their faces to memory. They were far too young to have been the men there the night his parents died, far closer to his own age than theirs, but they were dressed in the same fashion as the men had been.

Not that he needed any other proof of their nefarious nature, considering how they were currently treating his property. He was not too worried about the fact that they were ransacking his home, as long as they didn't burn it to the ground after they were done. Anything they took was replaceable. There was nothing of value for them to steal since the money he was able to save up was buried out in the yard. It was a habit he developed after his grandmother stole his earnings for the third time, and he kept it even after she passed. The only object he cared about was his mother's necklace, which was safe around his neck.

He reached to touch it, but it was not there. Patting his neck inside his shirt in case it was hidden, he realized his worst fear was coming true. He forgot to put it back on that morning after he bathed. It was still inside the house. Silently he prayed the men would not find it, but his prayers went unanswered as one of them came stomping down the stairs with the necklace dangling from his closed fist.

Ezra felt an overwhelming urge to go and get it back from him, but knowing his mother would not want him to risk dying over it was enough to hold him in his place. He was vastly outnumbered by men and guns, as the shotgun at his side only had two bullets loaded, and he would need to be extremely lucky for those to hit their targets. He only ever used the gun to chase off coyotes that were trying to get to his chickens. He had never even pointed it at another human being, let alone attempted to pull the trigger. Biting his lip at the thought of losing his last connection to his mother, Ezra turned his attention from the necklace to the man holding it. "No one's home, boss. Looks like only one old biddy lives here judging by all the useless crap in there. Lots of her mending supplies about. Not much jewelry neither, just this one."

Holding his breath as the man held it up for his leader to inspect, Ezra felt a quick flash of hope that they might leave the necklace behind, believing it to be worthless. He had no idea if it was worth anything or not, but he doubted it was expensive considering the simple life his parents led.

"Another dud? Why did McKinley stick us with this section anyways? These houses are miles apart and not worth the trip," the leader grumbled, drawing Ezra's attention back to him.

He was so focused on memorizing their appearances to give the sheriff a description of the men that he almost missed what he said next. "Surely we'd serve Pine Box better by hitting wealthier houses and earning our spots faster. At this rate, we won't even make it into their lowest ranks. Gather up the food and animals, then saddle up. This pile of junk is depressing me." The realization that they were taking his horse or that they had indeed kept his mother's necklace would not dawn on Ezra until much later.

At that moment, there was only one thing on his mind as the man's words unknowingly sparked a long-forgotten memory. He suppressed the memories of that night as much as he was able, but now a single thought flooded back to the surface, refusing to be ignored any longer. Almost as if the man was standing in front of him once more—Ezra once again nine-years-old hiding in the bushes—he heard the words the man spoke to his parents all those years ago.

*"Ain't nobody leaving the Pine Box Crew except for in one."*

Pine Box. Pine Box Crew. Surely, they must be referring to the same thing. What were the chances they weren't? No, they had to be referring to the same gang, but how far must their reach have been to kill his parents back home and rob his grandmother's home almost six years later? And with a much younger group? These men were not responsible for his parents' deaths, he was already certain of that, but what if their leader was? What if McKinley was there that night?

There was nothing to even suggest he might have been—simply being in the same crew did not automatically make him guilty, but could Ezra give up a possible lead to the men responsible for killing his parents? Did Ezra want a lead that sent him anywhere near a man possibly surrounded by robbery and murder? But even as he thought this, he realized he would not let the man who ordered the death of his parents get away with it. He did not know how or when, but he would find the Midnight Twelve, and they would lead him to his ultimate goal: Godfrey de Voe.

# Chapter One

EDGEWOOD 1830

Ezra shook his head to clear his mind of years long past; reminiscing about his devastating childhood would do no good. For the past three days, he had traveled westbound, following the trail his encounter with Morton, one of the Midnight Twelve, had led him to. It had taken him five years of searching to get him to this point, the men who were there that night having spread out over the years. When he did manage to track one of them down, they never seemed to have the exact location of one of their companions—wouldn't give up more than one name.

Instead, he would be led to one of their lackeys, and he would have to follow the chain of command to the top. So far, his plan, though slow in execution, led him to two of the men from that night. The third was said to frequent the saloon in Edgewood, and though Morton himself was not able to give him that information, he informed him of a town his target once lived in. A couple of his lackeys still called it home and gave him another piece of the puzzle—the town he traveled to when he left the year before.

Town after town, he followed his trail. At last, someone told him about the woman his target had been visiting for years. Why no one else seemed to know about her, if he was coming around for so long, irked Ezra to no end. Did the others truly not know of this relationship or they simply kept the useful information to themselves?

Perhaps before this was over, he would be able to ask the man himself once he found him in this small, rundown town of Edgewood that was in the middle of nowhere and had seen better days. As he slowly led his horse down the only real street in the whole town, the dirt beneath the animal's hooves being kicked up with each step and causing a dust cloud to rise, he took stock of the nearly empty town around him. On the left side of the road, there was a general store, a five-table diner, and a one-teller bank.

On the right, there was a one- or two-cell jailhouse, a telegraph office, a few scattered houses and, of course, his destination—the saloon. Up on a small hill overlooking the town, was an old church that looked like it too had seen better days. The warping wood planks and jagged edges of what remained of the broken windows showed it had not been used in a very long time.

Turning his attention back to the rest of the town, he found the other buildings weren't in much better shape. Though their windows were still intact, the long, wood planks the structures were made of were bending and warping from age and abusive weather. They were in desperate need of repair, and he would not be surprised if they were to buckle under the pressure if they were not tended to soon.

He pulled back on the reins of his jet-black stallion as he closed in on the hitching post outside the saloon, and he wiped the back of his hand across his forehead to remove the sweat that accumulated during his travels. Though he stole the horse from a prisoner a few years ago, the animal had been a loyal friend.

The two-story building before him was in slightly better shape than the rest of the town. The wide front porch looked as if it had been completely redone recently. The windows on the bottom floor looked as if they had just been installed, and even the swinging doors looked new. Such an establishment would likely make quite a bit of money in a small town like this where there was nothing else for the men to do after a hard day's work. He doubted the repairs had anything to do with the owner wanting to make the place more aesthetically pleasing.

He would be willing to bet every dollar he had to his name, all forty of them, that the repairs were done out of necessity. No doubt a combination of out-of-control brawls and warping wood had caused major damage, and the owner was forced to make the repairs or shut down. If there was anything Ezra learned from the few times he went into a saloon, it was that they never shut down.

Dismounting his horse, he tied the reins to the leftmost post, as there was one on each side of the stairs leading up to the front door. As he climbed the three steps leading to the entrance, he heard the hustle and bustle of the clientele coming from inside. When he was younger, he would hesitate before entering a saloon. He didn't anymore.

All eyes were on him as he pushed open the swinging saloon doors. Each man and woman present gave the stranger a once over. Ezra let them stare—he knew he cut an impressive figure. At six foot three, he towered over most men. His short, dark hair and pale green eyes led some to call him handsome, although he never paid them much mind. His well-toned and muscular physique remained covered by his long tan sleeves and buckskin pants.

His eyes scanned the dim room. The room was about half full with men of many different walks of life, including gunslingers, bank tellers, ranchers and the like. A few women scurried about. Judging by their revealing dresses, they were no doubt saloon girls who were trying to part the men from their money. Some succeeded, others did not, judging by one of the girls who was suddenly punched by the man she was talking to. About to step in to say something, Ezra decided against it when the girl turned toward him and smiled, appearing unbothered by the rough treatment. Figuring if she didn't need saving, he would not force it upon her, Ezra turned his attention toward the layout of the room. To his left was a long bar, a few scattered, worn down stools placed before it. A rather small selection of alcohol in dusty bottles littered the shelf behind it. An older man, hair long since turned gray, stood behind the bar as he wiped the water from a glass and took the order of one of the ranchers. Though they glanced up at Ezra when he walked in, they quickly dismissed him and turned back to what they were doing. On the left of the bar was a single door—most likely the owner's bedroom. On the right, a darkened hallway led to two doors; one he saw from his position and one he couldn't.

Assuming the first led to a supply closest or perhaps a cellar for the liquor bottles currently not on display, he paid it as little mind. He spotted the back door that led to the outhouse and marked it as a possible escape in case the need arose. Straight in front of him, on the far wall, was a set of stairs.

One of the saloon girls led a man up the stairs by the hand, giggling at something he said. It was not hard to figure out that upstairs was where the girls did business. That was one place he never bothered to visit when at a saloon. On his right, in the furthest corner away from where he was standing, was an old piano. Judging by the thick layer of dust that covered it, it had not been played for quite a while. Littered throughout the first floor were card tables, three or four of which were occupied by men playing poker. At a few others, men were simply sitting around drinking and hitting on the working girls.

Apparently deciding he was uninteresting, they turned their attention back to what they were doing before the interruption, and Ezra crossed the threshold into the room. The barkeeper was serving a bushy looking trapper at the end of the long wooden bar, so he took a stool at the other end. Ezra gave him a quick once over as he had with the rest of the men upon entering the saloon and decided the over-six-foot-tall bear of a man, who was probably well over fifty, was not the man he was looking for.

None of them were, and Ezra began to worry that his latest clue would prove to be a dead end. It wouldn't be the first time his luck ran out, and he needed to backtrack to find another clue. Doing so was easier said than done as the clue holders tended to be dead before he moved on. Usually, they ended up doing something stupid, but it wouldn't matter as Ezra refused to risk them getting the word out that he was looking for De Voe.

He removed his five-dollar Stetson felt hat and carefully placed it on the bar beside him before flagging the barkeeper down. "Whiskey neat," he ordered. The barkeeper grabbed a glass and poured his drink without so much as a nod of acknowledgment. A moment later, the glass was placed before him.

"Fifteen cents," the barkeep said.

Ezra reached into the coin purse at his side. Fishing out a couple of coins, he placed a dime and a nickel on the bar.

He raised the glass to his dry lips, barely noticing the barkeeper picking up the money and making his way over to his next customer and scrunched up his nose at the taste. The whiskey was obviously watered down, and the water was most certainly not fresh, but at only fifteen cents for the glass when his last, and equally bad, drink had been a quarter, Ezra decided it wasn't worth causing a stink over. There was no reason to draw unnecessary attention to himself before he was even able to find his mark.

Setting the empty glass back down on the counter, Ezra swiveled on the stool and was about to search the crowd again, for any new faces that might have arrived while his back was turned. One of the saloon girls sat down on the stool beside him, placing a dainty hand on his thigh. "Are ya looking for a good time tonight, Sugar?" she purred, giving him a sultry smile even as she traced slow circles on his leg, each one moving her closer toward his inner thigh. His gaze traveled up her body, starting at her crossed legs. Her green dress fell to her ankles in the front; poofy, black cloth made up the bustle in the back. His eyes continuing further upward, to her green corset, which pushed her small assets higher than gravity intended.

Though bright in color, her dress was devoid of accents and embellishments, such as lace and embroidered flowers, which were present on the other girls' clothes. Their dresses he found to be overly frilly, extremely low cut, leaving him to wonder why they even bothered to cover themselves at all, and hiked up in the front. Whereas hers was the length of a proper lady's dress.

Even covered, he caught a glimpse of her stockings every now and then when her legs moved. Her fiery red hair was pulled up into a rather large bun, and her eyes were a soft violet. He noticed the bruise already beginning to form on her cheek. Before it registered in his mind what he was doing, he reached up to brush his thumb across the offending mark. Startled by the unconscious gesture, he quickly removed his hand and glanced away and spotted the girl's secret.

# Chapter Two

EDGEWOOD 1830

Ezra sat transfixed, staring at the spot on her neck that attracted his attention. It bobbed each time she swallowed. Finally, he pulled his eyes away and returned his gaze to hers, barely managing to catch the flash of disappointment in her violet eyes before it disappeared. It was instantly replaced with a friendly expression and a soft smile. "Not interested in a good night tonight, Sugar? Perhaps there is something else I can interest you in. A hot meal or room for the night?" she offered sweetly. Her hand left his thigh and went to rub her neck, hiding her Adam's apple from his sight.

He looked her over again. Nothing else was amiss. She looked the part of a saloon girl perfectly with her slim, delicate figure, pale skin, and abundance of fiery hair.

But now that he realized she was different, he picked up on subtle differences between her and the other girls. While they were endowed with large bosoms and rounded hips nearly equal in size, showing their hourglass figures, her corset barely managed to pull her waist in slightly.

Where they were curvy, she was nearly shapeless with her shoulders, waist, and hips falling in an almost complete line. Cocking his head to the side, he turned his attention back to her seemingly small breasts, finally realizing that they were, in fact, her pectoral muscles that were pushed up by her corset. Thoroughly confused, he returned his gaze to her, finding her staring at him expectantly as he had yet to answer her question.

What reason did she have for not only dressing the part of a woman but also performing the job of one? Though he heard tales over the years of men who preferred the company of other men, even a few women who preferred their own gender, he never heard of one doing it so openly. Surely there was not a huge calling for such a preference in such a small town, no doubt preventing her from making much money.

It was in that moment that it dawned on Ezra this was the exact reason why her clothing lacked the embellishments of the others. She simply did not make enough money to pay for them. Judging by the fact she gave him no indication that she anything other than what she first appeared to be, he doubted she told any of her other potential customers. More than likely, the discovery was what caused her to be punched by the last man she approached. How she expected to lay with the men without them discovering she was, in fact, one of them, he had no idea.

It didn't matter. He was not there to unlock the mysteries of a random, albeit strange, saloon girl. If it did not relate to his mission, he needed to ignore it, no matter how intriguing it might be. About to dismiss her second offer of a room to stay in for the night, he was interrupted when one of the other girls shrieked excitedly before jumping off a man and rushed toward the entrance of the saloon. The abandoned customer called after her, angrily voicing his outrage of being dismissed until another girl came down the stairs and quickly whispered in his ear. Whatever she said seemed to have the desired effect as he rose to his feet and followed her back upstairs.

"Dowes!" The girl jumped into his arms. His large hands grasped her backside and squeezed the plentiful mounds, raising her high enough to return his eager kiss with fervor. Ezra clenched his hand as he heard the man's name, even as he silently reminded himself that he would need more than just a name to confirm the identity of the man he sought.

They went at each other, seemingly about ready to screw right there in the saloon's doorway. He ignored their actions and instead turned his attention to the man's form. If he had to guess, he would estimate he was about two inches short of six feet tall, two hundred pounds, in his late forties. Everything matched the description he was given, but it was still not enough. After all, how many men in their late forties had his exact build? No, it would take more than an average-sized body to confirm his target.

Thankfully he did know of one distinguishing mark and, much to his relief, he spotted a small, aged scar in the middle of his left cheek. According to his information, the man he was looking for was once shot by a sheriff before the rest of his gang was able to ambush and kill him. It was only a graze, but it was enough to assure him that this was his target—Gill Dowes. He was one of the men that were there the night his parents were killed; though Ezra never actually got a good look at him, his previous target was good enough to give up his name.

He may not have been the one to order his parents' deaths or pull the trigger himself, but he was guilty all the same. He was there. He did nothing to stop it. And, whether he did so willingly, he would relinquish the next clue for Ezra to follow before very long. Dowes would lead him to the next name to check off of his list; bringing him another step closer to the man truly responsible for all of this—Godfrey de Voe. The man that ordered his gang to kill his parents and for what? What reason would he use to justify murdering them in cold blood? Ezra swore he would have the answer before his mission was finished and he ended De Voe's reign of terror.

Ezra shook his head to his clear thoughts. Dowes and the girl finally separated, and she led him upstairs to continue what they'd started.

Ezra turned back to the strange girl beside him. "I will take a room for the night and a hot meal to be served upstairs." He stealthily retrieved a quarter from his purse and place it in her hand. "Put me up next to him. I like to listen." Whether she believed his reasoning or not, she nodded her head before making her way to the other side of the bar.

The saloon girl spoke to the barkeeper. He gave Ezra a strange look before handing her a brass key and shaking his head as she made her way back over.

"Follow me, Sugar," she instructed. Ezra rose, following her toward the stairs and taking the same path his target took only a few moments before. As they passed, a few of the men and most of the girls turned to him with strange looks; apparently, they knew about the girl's secret and found it odd he'd chosen her. Or maybe they thought he didn't know.

Either way, it was irrelevant. The only thing that mattered was that Dowes wasn't alerted to his presence. Following her upstairs, Ezra took in the surrounding area. The faded brown carpet that covered the stairs was no doubt there to prevent them from squeaking during the night and disturbing the guests.

Along the wall to his right, there were scattered paintings of different sizes; each one depicting women in various stages of undress. The first was a saloon girl in full dress—stockings, boots and all. She held a delicate fan to hide her face. The last was pretty much the same with one exception—everything was removed save for the fan.

Once they reached the top of the stairs, they made a slight left, and the room opened up to a long hallway, with a row of doors on each side. From the first door on the left, he heard splashing and girlish giggles—

the communal bathing room, probably. Unsurprisingly, as that room would need to be larger than the sleeping rooms, its door was much further apart from its neighbor than the others were on that side of the hall. Looking at the five doors on the left side, he realized there was no keyhole on any of them.

Figuring they were the cheap rooms, the saloon owner choosing to keep them unlocked either to protect his girls or his income, he turned his attention next to the row of doors on the other side of the hall. Where on the left side there were five small doors, there were three larger ones on the right. They were spaced much farther apart, and each door looked far sturdier than their counterparts did. They even sported a keyhole beneath their handles. Though he had not seen Dowes' girl get a brass key, like the one leading him did, he was sure the other man was plenty rich enough to pay for one of their better rooms. His crisp, clean clothing was able to tell him that.

Walking past the first door, Ezra picked up nothing from inside. As they passed the second, he heard a woman giggling within. Judging by her voice, he was certain it was the girl he saw with Dowes downstairs. Turning his attention from them, he glanced up to find his guide stopped in front of the third door, a large red one with the number three scratched directly into the wood. She inserted the key into the lock and pushed the door open. He followed her inside.

On the left-hand side of the room, there was a large wardrobe and a shaving mirror. Across from the mirror, in the far-right corner was a king-sized bed. A door to the balcony was straight ahead. On the right were a dresser and a closed door.

"This is one of our expensive rooms since it has its own adjoining bathing room equipped with a hearth for heating water. It is the only possible room to take if you want to be next to Dowes. Well this one and the one on the other side of him, but the other room doesn't allow for you to overhear their carnal activities as well as this one and it will be much quieter in here since you are further away from the noise downstairs.

"Right now, you are above the bar keeper's room, but he's usually only in there to sleep and break in new girls so there will be almost no noise here. All the better for eavesdropping." She winked before making her way across the room and opening the other door. "This is your bathing room," she continued, lowering her voice.

He walked through the door. Inside was the largest tub he had ever seen sitting in the middle of the room. It was currently a third full of clean water. On the left was a single chair and trunk which he was certain would house the linen for the room. On the right were a small stool and a bucket of water, for washing yourself before entering the tub. Beside them were a couple of folded washcloths. Across from where he stood was a large hearth that already had a small fire burning within it.

"The rate is five dollars a night, paid upfront," she informed him, startling Ezra out of his musings. He followed after, scoffing as what she said registered in his mind.

She looked back over her shoulder. "Like I said, it's one of our expensive rooms. The smaller rooms across the hall are only a dollar a night, but they only include a room with four beds and nothing else. Each bed is a dollar, so you would end up sleeping near a few strangers who may or may not pay for one of the girls.

"If they do, you might have to leave while they conduct their business or be charged for watching. Only other option would be to pay for all four beds if they are even available, but neither meals nor the girls are included in the price, so you are already looking at over four dollars a night. More important than that, you would not be able to eavesdrop on him from there. Though you would have a great view if you would rather watch the girls in action rather than just listen to them." She gestured to the main room. "This room comes with the private bed and bathing rooms, all meals are included along with drinks and full service from me.

"Since you are not interested in my full services, that would leave preparing your bath, seeing to your meals and helping with any other daily necessities. Laundering or mending clothes, tending to your horse if you have one, shaving you and any other grooming needs. Usually, we split the tasks up when someone orders these rooms, but seeing as you don't want full service, I should be able to handle it alone. Unless, of course, you wish to request a different girl or room?" While Ezra mused over the offer, she worried her bottom lip.

The pleading look in her violet eyes and the way her fingers picked at the key in her hand was enough to tell him she was worried he would take her up on the suggestion of wanting someone else. No doubt most of her patrons did once they realized the truth about her if they didn't assault her like the man earlier did. He would not be surprised to learn she was barely managing to scrape by; going most days with nothing more than water to drink. Naturally, she would not want to lose him as a client as he already gave her an entire quarter just to keep quiet about his 'interests.'

Though she would have no idea how much money she'd make off of him before Ezra left, he was certain she would not find a more generous customer, especially without actually having to satisfy him. If the saloon owner was anything like the others he met in his travels, she probably received a dime per dollar he made off of her. No point in him sending for another girl when this one already had the most compelling reason to stay quiet about his actions—poverty.

"One girl or another doesn't make a difference to me as I am only interested in your most basic services," he said. "If you keep your hands to yourself, do as I ask without question and not mention my interests to anyone you will be paid nicely. I cannot afford to be distracted or attract unwanted attention right now. Can you handle the secrecy required?" Once she nodded, he headed back into the bathing room and pressed his ear up against the far wall near the hearth. Though he was able to make out some giggling coming from the saloon girl on the other side, it was too quiet to hear anything else.

"When they open the door to their bathing room, you will be able to hear them much better," she assured him. "Just be careful the two hearths share the same vents to let out the smoke, so if they are in their bathing room, they will be able to hear you as well. Always shut your door to the bedroom when you are not trying to listen in. They will most likely light the hearth in the evening when it starts getting colder, so do not be surprised if you are unable to hear anything most of the time."

Nodding, Ezra stepped away from the hearth and made his way back out into the bedroom, making sure to close his own door behind her so they wouldn't be overheard.

"See to our meals for now. I am probably in for a long wait." Ezra mumbled the last part to himself as he scanned the room, searching for a safe place to hide his coin purse once she left. Ezra knew better than to leave it on his person and risk anyone hearing the jingling of coins and being alerted to his presence. Plus, he would have no use for it for the rest of the night. He removed five dollars from his purse and handed it to her.

"Use this to pay for tonight and our meals. We will dine in the room. Can't have anyone wondering why I paid for this room and yet did not keep you close by," he explained at her startled look. Whether it was because she did not expect him to pay for her meal or welcome her company while he ate, he was unsure but dismissed his curiosity. Her expression changed to one of appreciation, and Ezra was about to usher her out when a sudden thought crossed his mind. "What is your name?"

"It's Colleen, Sugar," she introduced herself with a smile before leaving the room. After a moment, he heard the lock turning once more before her footsteps moved further away. He stared at the closed door, wondering if he made a mistake. What was to stop her from going next door and telling Dowes about him? Even if all she thought at the moment was that he wanted to overhear the sounds of them going at each other. Reaching down to his holster, he put a hand on his gun in preparation. As the seconds ticked by without anyone coming barreling into his room, Ezra's paranoia lessened, and he eventually turned his attention back to the task at hand.

Scanning the layout of the room, it did not take long for him to decide on the wardrobe. Though inside it would probably be the first place a thief would look, it would still be able to protect his money under the right circumstances. He pushed his gun belt to the side and pulled off his coin purse before laying down on the floor. Reaching under the wardrobe, he searched for a loose floorboard, giving each one a hard tug as he dug his fingers into the grooves between them.

Finding none, which he took as a good sign as it meant that no one knew of a possible loose board and the hiding spot it would make, he reached back and carefully slid a small knife from the sheath on his inner calf. Though it was hard to reach through his boot, it was never meant to be used in defense, but as a backup, in case he was ever tied up. Awkwardly pushing its tip into the furthest groove, barely able to angle his hand into the right position in such a confined space, he pried up the floorboard, careful not to make any noise that might alert others to what he was going.

Once it was up high enough, he dropped the coin purse inside and pressed the board back down into place, making sure no sign remained that it had been tampered with. As it was hard to see from his current angle, he was certain no one else would be able to spot anything to alert them to a possible hiding spot, at least not without moving the wardrobe completely. Replacing his knife, he climbed back to his feet and dusted his hands off. Turning his attention to the next, and more crucial, part of his plan, he made his way over to the balcony door.

Pulling back the floor-length, dark blue curtains, he unlatched the small metal hook and pulled it open, blasting himself with a hot, burst of air. Shielding his eyes from the bright rays of the setting sun, he stepped out onto the small balcony and glanced down at the quiet town below. Though it was not visible from his vantage point, he knew his horse was tied up on the other side of the saloon on his left and the exit to the outhouse was on the far right. It would make getting out of here quickly that much easier and gave him an easy backup escape plan, or two, if the need arose.

He glanced to his right and found an identical balcony to his own, which led to his target's room. Though the curtains were drawn as his own were, he saw a sliver of the room where it curved slightly from too many years of being bound by a cord. Inside he saw enough of the bed to find the room's occupants currently engaged in the woman's more than basic services. With everything looking to be identical to his own room, he knew it might prove to be problematic for his plan.

If it was exactly the same as he found his room, other than its bathing room being on the opposite side of the suite in order to be beside his, it meant that there was a good chance the balcony door would be locked; no doubt a habit of the girls. He would not risk himself failing in his mission because of a single lock. He had come too far, there was still too far left to go, to let things end here. Turning back to his own balcony door, he softly closed it while still outside before examining the lock only to realize he would not be able to learn how to lift the latch while it was unlocked.

Stepping back inside, he examined the lock more closely. Latching it once more, he retrieved his knife and slid it between the edge of the door and the wall beside it. It was an easy enough feat to slide the blade up, pulling the hook with it, but the only way to be absolutely certain was to have himself locked outside. He needed to ensure the space on the outside was wide enough for his knife as it was on the inside. If he was lucky, he would be able to lock it from the outside, much in the same way that he intended to unlock it.

If he wasn't, he would have to ask Colleen to lock him outside. That would, of course, mean having to come up with an excuse for him wanting to be next to Dowes that had nothing to do with his supposed kink of listening to others having sex, or the truth, wanting to eavesdrop on him to find the others he was connected to. There was always offering to pay her more money to keep silent, but he knew the offer of money would simply lead to one wanting more. Either way, he decided to not bother worrying about the ramifications of telling her his secrets until he was certain he would actually have to confide in her.

As it turned out, he worried over nothing as he stepped back onto the balcony once more and closed the door behind him. Slipping his knife in the crack, not bothering to figure out an excuse in case he managed to lock himself out, he lifted the latch up with his blade. Ezra was certain that if he was able to lift the latch into place from the outside, then he could remove it as well.

The latch slipped free from his blade before it was able to rise above the lock. He growled in frustration before trying again. The second, and third, times failed as the first did. As he was beginning to worry, he would have to enlist the help of the strange woman he only just met, the latch slid into place, and he found himself locked out on the balcony. Sighing in relief, Ezra smiled at his reflection in the dingy windowpane before positioning his knife once more beneath the metal latch.

Without making a sound, he effortlessly lifted it up and found the path to his temporary room open once more. Making his way back inside, he closed and relocked the door before heading toward the wardrobe. He hung his hat and gun and kicked off his boots before adding those as well, making sure the sheath and knife were well hidden under his pant leg. As much as he was certain he would not be needing it anytime soon, he was not about to take the chance when he didn't have to.

Since he had nothing else to unpack, having left the rest of his few belongings in his saddle bag to make it easier for him to escape quickly, Ezra made his way over to sit down on the bed.

# Chapter Three

EDGEWOOD 1830

Colleen locked the door and pressed her back up against it, sighing in relief. Though she would not let it show in front of him, by agreeing to stay as her client, he pretty much saved her life. She was already to the point where she was surviving most days with nothing more than water to drink, and if things continued this way for much longer, she would not even be able to pay for that. When the barkeeper agreed to let her stay here, even after he found out the truth when he tried to bed her as he did all of his new, nonvirginal girls, she was promised a dime off of every man she bedded.

She knew some of the other girls made fifteen cents, with the most popular girls earning an entire quarter, per clients who played a dollar each. When they ordered more uncommon requests, it was possible to make a bit more, but either way, most of the money they earned went into the barkeeper's purse. Which would not have been so bad, in Colleen's opinion anyway, if working there included meals and a bed to sleep in. Instead, she was forced to dip into her own meager earnings to eat and only managed to find a bed when her customer paid for one. And they almost never let her share the bed with them if she actually managed to find one with the money.

In fact, she only remembered one occasion where she was allowed to share the bed with one of her customers, but even then, he had not been an actual customer, and she paid for the bed herself. Though she dressed the part of a saloon girl, in truth, most of the money she earned came from doing odd jobs around the saloon. It was a very small town, and most of the men there already avoided her. The rebuilding of the porch after a rather nasty brawl destroyed a lot of the wood, kept her fed for a little while, but there wasn't enough of those jobs for her to survive off of for very long. And certainly not enough for her to save up enough money to leave this place eventually. For the first time, her luck finally started to change for the better.

This man, this gorgeous specimen, booked a five-dollar room, and even if it was only for one night, it gave her an easy half dollar. He agreed to let her continue to take care of him, even if it meant she was unable to try him out sexually. He was even willing to pay her for her silence, which he would have gotten anyway. Colleen didn't buy the idea that he wanted to be close to Dowes to hear the grunts and moans coming from his room, not when it would have been cheaper to buy one of the beds in the shared rooms and pay to watch the girls work in there.

Whatever the real reason for his interest in Dowes was, she had no intention of telling him or anyone else about his odd request. She did not have enough clients to risk losing possible future ones by being a gossip. And more than that, tonight she was going to eat a real, hot meal for the first time in what felt like forever, and she didn't have to spend a single penny on it. Unable to prevent the smile from forming on her face, Colleen held her shoulders high as she made her way downstairs, ignoring the mocking looks and giggles the other girls sent her way for returning so soon.

Apparently, they assumed she had been turned down even after bringing him up to the rooms, and though they were technically correct, she was not about to give them the satisfaction of knowing that. More than that, except for perhaps Katherine, she would make more money tonight than the others would even with him only wanting her basic services. Anyone who ordered a five-dollar room besides Mr. Dowes was rare and, if her math was correct, they would have to have at least five customers tonight in order to make the seventy-five cents she already earned for doing nothing, seven for the girls who were paid as little as she was.

Gracing the others with a smug smile, Colleen sauntered over to the bar. "Need two meals for room three. Lady luck shines on me tonight." She flashed a smile, making sure to raise her voice, and the five-dollar bill, high enough to get the others' attention. She risked a backlash by taunting them, but she would not push things too far. A little humility would do them some good after the way they treated her. She only hoped it did not come back to bite her in the ass later. Handing the barkeeper the five, and taking her two quarters in return, she waited silently as he headed over to the register and deposited the money. When he made his way back over, Colleen was handed two tickets.

"You'll have to pick up the meals yourself as all the girls are busy. The diner should have them ready by now." Even before he finished speaking, the barkeep went to help another customer. Though she was a bit annoyed—if it had been any other girl coming to pay for a meal, he would have sent someone else to retrieve it so she was able to get back to her customer quicker. Colleen dismissed the annoyance. At least with her going to get them, she was certain the others would not spit in her food or steal from her plate.

She decided she would not let the slight ruin her mood and pocketed the coins before making her way outside into the setting sun. Ignoring the looks she received from those she passed on the street, already having grown used to the disapproving glances from the women who didn't work in the saloon—mostly wives of the men who worked in the mines and other jobs around town—and the lustful glances of the men who either didn't know or care at that moment who she was, she headed toward the diner.

Pushing open a squeaky door that was in desperate need of repair, she nodded politely to the two women who were working vigorously to prepare for the dinner rush that would be coming in soon. Most of the miners and other workers in town ordered from them, as the saloon did, since the businesses acted as the employee's homes, but were not big enough to have kitchens as well. Originally, long before Colleen arrived in town, there was nothing more than a large campfire set up in camp for the couple dozen people who founded this mining camp, where their wives would prepare meals for everyone.

Then, as too many new settlers started arriving, the women found themselves unable to keep up with the demand on nothing more than a campfire. Eventually, two sisters settled in town with their husbands, and seeing the need, opened up a small diner equipped with a two-hearth kitchen and slowly added tables as the need arose. They were up to five now but were only at three when Colleen dined there the first time. Now the tables usually remained empty as most prefer to eat their meals where they worked.

Their small diner became overcrowded every day with people waiting for their meals, and the sisters eventually set up the ticket system. It allowed them to save time and get the customers out of their way while they cooked. They gave out the tickets to anyone who paid in advance, and you simply needed to show up with a ticket and grab one of the already prepared meals. Only those who wanted to eat at the diner had to wait more than a few moments.

Catching the attention of the sisters, Colleen waved her tickets in the air before placing them in a bowl on the end of the bar, which contained a couple dozen tickets already, before adding two meals onto a wooden tray. She nodded her head in thanks and went back outside and toward the saloon. As before, she ignored the stares she received from those she passed; she was not about to let them ruin her good mood. There was no telling when she would be so lucky again, and she was going to enjoy every moment that she was.

Reaching the saloon doors, she turned around and backed across the threshold since her hands were full. Ignoring everyone that glanced up as she entered, barely able to make out more than their silhouettes as her eyes had yet to adjust to the dimly lit room, she headed back upstairs. Walking past the room she knew Katherine would be in, she tried to pick up any sounds coming from inside but was met with silence. Shrugging her shoulders, careful not to spill their food, she continued on toward room three.

Having no way to unlock the door with her hands full, Colleen knocked at the base of it with her boot. The movement she heard as she walked up stopped, and she waited for it to be opened. Instead, she found herself waiting in the silence as seconds passed without a response from within. "It's me, Sugar. Hands are full, so I can't open it myself," she called out, making sure to be loud enough that he heard her.

After a few moments, she heard the lock turning from inside the room before the door was pulled open. Smiling in greeting, Colleen stepped passed him once he backed away to give her enough room and set the tray down on the bed. "Come and get it while I'm hot." She glanced over her shoulder at him with a flirty smile.

He may have told her he didn't want her to touch him, but he never said she wasn't allowed to flirt. Ignoring the way he rolled his eyes, Colleen waited until he moved to sit down on the bed before removing the lids from the dishes. Setting them aside, she handed Ezra his plate before taking her own. Though the enticing aroma of the food caused her to salivate, Colleen took small, slow bites to prevent herself from looking like a starving beggar, even if that was practically what she was.

Needing some way to keep her from rushing through the meal before she even had the chance to enjoy it and risk making herself sick from eating too fast, Colleen turned her attention to the man sitting before her. Once again, as she had the moment she noticed him standing in the saloon doorway, she gave his impressive form a once over; only this time, she was able to get a closer inspection. Now she saw the deep green color of his eyes. She made out the small scar over his left eyebrow.

Colleen stopped herself from reaching out to touch it, silently wondering how he had gotten it. Her curiosity would have to go unanswered for now as she doubted he would appreciate a stranger asking too many questions. He was a secretive man. In her experience, those who wanted to learn the secrets of others tended to not want their secrets known. Either way, she would not risk losing such a valuable client, especially when her clients were so few and far between. If she ever got to know him better, earned his trust some, she would ask the questions that her tongue itched to speak. She would ask him about the scar. Why he was so interested in Dowes. What it would take to get him interested in more than just her basic services.

This last thought caused Colleen to look the man before her over for the third time. She was unable to take her eyes off of him for more than a few moments at a time. After all, he was gorgeous. And, from what she saw so far, his beauty seemed to be greater than skin deep. No, she had no real idea of what he was like as a person, but from the short time they spent together, she was certain he was better than the other men who came through the saloon. He knew the truth about her and still treated her kindly. That was more than could be said about the monsters she met since arriving in this backwater town.

He may not have wanted her, but he did not treat her like garbage as others before him did. He was strong. He was powerful. Ezra was everything she ever wanted in a man, at least outwardly. She hadn't exactly had time to get to know who he was inside, but all that mattered to her at the moment was his appearance anyway. Colleen wasn't in love with the man, so what did she need to know about who he truly was on the inside? What good would knowing his inner strengths and weaknesses do?

Why bother learning anything more about the beautiful man before her when he would probably be gone in a day or two? It wasn't like she would ever see him again anyway. Her gaze moved back to his eyes; Colleen realized she had been caught staring. She graced him with a seductive smile before turning her attention back to the food. As she continued to eat, he stared at her in silence with a strange expression marring his handsome face.

She laughed softly. "What, Sugar? What do you want to ask me? Don't be shy now."

"Why do you do that? Flirt with me even when you already know I have no intention of being one of your customers? Why? What do you hope to gain when you know you will not get what you want?"

Unable to help herself, Colleen laughed. It was light and fluttering, but it was genuine. The first real laugh she'd had in a long time. "Don't worry your pretty little head, Sugar, I ain't laughing at you. It's just that, just because you don't want to have fun, it doesn't mean I can't have a little bit myself. Most of the men, if you can even call them that, that come through here are dirty, disgusting, smelly, slobs. You are a cool drink of water on a scorching hot day. And you, Sugar, will keep me warm on many a cold night. Or at least the memory of you will. Every time one of those nasty excuses for a man puts his grubby hands on me before taking from me what they paid for, I will imagine that it is you sweating and panting above me."

In her mind, Colleen saw his sweaty, naked form perched over her as she lay on her back, her breath catching in her throat as his heated hands touched her thighs. "Every time one of them enters me, either unable to discover the truth or not caring, I will pretend it's your big, thick cock and not their pathetic little stubs. And no, I do not need to see or feel yours to know what it is like, I can tell just by looking at you." Licking her lips, Colleen made a point to glance down to where she saw the outline of his manhood pressed against his pants.

He was not hard, but the way he was seated caused the material to be pulled taut against his groin, leaving very little, and way too much in her opinion, to her imagination. "Now don't get me wrong, Sugar, I would, of course, prefer the real thing to keep me warm at night, and all day long, but I will settle for what I can get. I won't pressure you into giving me what I desire—and oh do I desire you Sugar—but I will take every ounce of verbal foreplay that I can squeeze out of this encounter.

"Because a man like you, someone who can make my pulse race, make my breath catch in my throat, make me throb for your touch without even laying a single finger on me, does not come around often. Hell, there has never been a man like you before, and there probably never will be again. This encounter may mean nothing at all to you, but it means everything in the world to someone like me who has nothing." The image in her mind of his naked form was replaced by the others who came before him, each one a pale comparison to what she imagined him to be.

"So do what you came here to do, Sugar. I will be here, and I will keep what you do and say a secret. I am more than happy to help you in any way that I can, but like all things in life, Sugar, it comes with a price. The price is my flirting. I already know you are here for the man next door, and not to listen to his activities with Katherine. He so happens to be a man I have seen speaking to the sheriff on more than one occasion when he has come through town. It would be easy to announce your presence to him, but I won't. You have my silence, my word that I will repeat nothing of what you do or say. Surely you realize my price could be much stiffer than a bit of harmless flirting. And you would pay it too, I can see it in your eyes. No matter what I demanded as payment for my help, you would give it to me.

"If I threaten you, blackmailed you into sleeping with me to prevent me from going next door and telling him you are here, you would, but you needn't worry none about that. All I ask is you let me flirt. Nothing more. Surely you can allow me that," she insisted with a soft smile before turning her attention back to the meal in front of her once more, not bothering to point out that there was always one other option. He could always kill her to ensure her silence, but something in his eyes led her to believe it wouldn't come to that. While she was speaking, Ezra finished his meal, leaving only her share of food on the tray. Finishing her last few bites of food, Colleen stacked the plates back on the tray. When she went to stand to bring them back to the diner, Ezra grabbed her wrist.

"Flirt as you like, but that will be as far as it goes. I cannot allow for any distractions or attachments to hinder me. I will pay your price, but know this Colleen—if you become a hindrance, you will be removed like all other obstacles." Once she nodded, he released her wrist. Colleen rubbed it before picking up the tray. "Prepare a bath for me and then see to the dishes."

She nodded and headed into the bathing room, where she added another log to the dying fire. With the door being closed since they were last in the room, it was warm and would be perfect for stripping naked. Silently enjoying the thought of seeing him without any of his garments obstructing her view, Colleen grabbed a large pan and filled it with water from the tub. Placing it on the fire to heat, she made her way over to the washing bucket and checked the temperature. Deciding it was too cold, as she did not want anything to shrivel up, even if only temporary, she dumped the bucket over the drain that led to the dirty barrel out back.

Taking the pan of water off of the fire, she dumped it on one side of the tub and grabbed another pan from the opposite side. As the first had been, she placed the second above the fire before turning back to see what else needed to be done. Filling the washing bucket with some of the water from the warmer side of the tub, she put it back in its place. The thick towels she left within the chest, as it would force him to have to ask her for one, giving her a few more moments to look upon his natural state. She added another log to the roaring fire, ignoring the bead of sweat that slid down her spine, knowing the extra heat would not only help him to relax, but it would cause his muscles to glisten enticingly.

She finished filling the tub and hung the pan above the fire before returning to the bedroom. He was gone. A quick search found him out on the balcony. He was resting his arms on the railing and staring out into the darkness. Except for the saloon, the diner, and the jailhouse, every building was dark, their blinds closed and the candles snuffed for the night.

For a moment, she thought about letting him be, but there was something about the hunch of his shoulders that told her whatever he was thinking about, was not a good memory. "Bath is ready when you are, Sugar." He turned to her in confusion, as if he'd forgotten where he was. Colleen wondered what he had been thinking about that took his mind completely out of the present.

EZRA MADE HIS way into the bathing room, shutting himself off from her. For a moment, she waited, listening to him wash, before she returned to the hallway, grabbing their empty dishes on her way. She glanced around to make sure no one was near before heading over to Dowes' room. Certain Ezra was doing the same, she strained to hear anything coming from inside the room and soon picked up a few muffled noises.

Pressing her ear against the wooden door, she heard Katherine giggling and water splashing. A squeal of delight after what sounded like the slapping of bare flesh. The muffled sound of footsteps echoed on the stairs; Colleen quickly stepped away and walked downstairs. Ignoring the girl and her client who passed by her, she continued on and soon stepped outside into the dark. With the light from a sliver of the moon and the torches that were lit around town to guide her, she made her way to the diner and returned the dishes without a word exchanged between her and the sisters.

As she headed back toward the saloon, she easily heard the noises coming from inside long before she got anywhere near the front door. The laughter and squeals from the girls. The loud ruckus the men were creating over them. Some were accusing others of cheating at cards. Others were calling out for the girls to join them. Still others were shouting for another drink which they certainly didn't need, judging by how loud they already were. Deciding she did not want to deal with all the noise right now, she changed directions and walked toward the side door.

Like many saloons, this exit was used for quick access to the outhouse. Not the most pleasant of places to pass, but most of the time it was her only real option for coming and going. Though if she was on an actual errand for a client, the others wouldn't dare to interfere with her. Unfortunately, more often than not, she was not working for a client. Stepping through the entryway into the saloon, she went to close the door behind her but was pushed up against it. Grunting in pain against the wood, Colleen turned around to face her attackers, finding three of the saloon girls standing there glaring at her.

She was about to question what they were doing when the one in the middle began to speak. Etta was a tall, big-breasted woman with luscious long blonde hair that she allowed to flow freely down her back. "Did you really think you would be allowed to service one of the expensive rooms? You should have turned it over to me the moment you realized what kind of room he wanted. We want the rich customers to come back, not run away disgusted by you." She spat at Colleen before nodding to the two girls that flanked her.

Before she realized what they were doing, they relieved her of her coin purse and the key to Ezra's room and handed them to their leader. As Colleen stared at her in silence, debating her chances of getting her money back and away from them without future repercussions, she remembered this woman was the number one when she first arrived at the saloon.

Not long after, Katherine came and knocked her off of her throne, and Colleen took some silent comfort in that fact. It was always nice to see these women, who treated her so horribly for simply being different from them, be knocked down a notch or two. Realizing she had a small opening, as the girls turned their attention to counting the money in her purse, she spun around and reached for the doorknob. But before she got it open more than a few inches, Etta called out for the other two to grab her.

A moment later, her head was bashed against the closed door with enough strength to knock her off her balance. They dragged her into the storeroom and threw her inside. She cried out in pain as her leg scrapped against a loose nail on the floor before the door was slammed and locked behind her. Throwing the closest thing she found, which ended up being a can of beans, at the door, she growled in frustration before wincing at the throbbing pain in her head.

Gingerly touching the spot where she had hit her head, she was relieved to find her fingers did not come away covered in blood. It would bruise no doubt, a perfect match for the one forming on her cheek, but it would heal soon enough and not leave any unsightly scars to make finding customers that much harder. She glanced down at the wound on her leg but found herself unable to assess the extent of the damage with the little light that came from under the door. Outside she barely made out Etta saying something about going up to Ezra's room.

There was nothing she could do about that for the moment, and she knew, after what happened the first time she was locked in this room, that the barkeep would not take kindly to her causing a ruckus trying to get out. No, she would have to wait patiently, and quietly, until the next time he needed to come get something from the storeroom. Unfortunately, that would most likely prove to be hours from now as she already heard the commotion out in the main room settling down for the night.

Like he did every night, the owner would pour himself a glass of the good whiskey after the last customer had left and settle in for the night. It wouldn't be until the next morning that he came in to replenish whatever bottles they emptied the night before. If it was a slow enough night, he might not even bother coming for more liquor.

Her thoughts turned to Ezra up in his room; Etta had probably already joined him in the bathing room by now. For a moment, she wondered if he would end up taking the other girl up on her offer, but quickly dismissed that thought with a smug smile. He was far too focused on whatever it was he wanted from Dowes to waste his time with her. While she did not delude herself with the hope that he would come to her rescue, she took satisfaction in the fact that Etta would be turned down as she had been.

The woman who was once first would prove to be no better than Colleen when it came to enticing Ezra. Allowing herself a quick laugh at Etta's expense, she turned her attention back to her own predicament. No hero on a white horse would ride in to save the day—to save her. She would have to be her own hero for the umpteenth time in her life. As always was the case, there was only herself to rely on, but the knowledge did not hurt as much as it had when she was a child; the truth no longer cut quite as deep as it once did.

# Chapter Four

EDGEWOOD 1830

The sounds from the other room died down a few minutes before, but still, Ezra continued to lay in the tub, finding no reason to bother getting out. As much as he hated to be doing nothing, especially when it came to the Twelve, there was nothing to be done until the man Dowes was meeting arrived. Though he did not know his name or who he was, something one of the men said led him to believe he was there that night. He tracked down Dowes' most recent lackey in a small town, not unlike the one he was in currently, hustling the locals out of their money at the card tables.

It was easy to get him drunk enough to spill some information without remembering the encounter the next morning. He had lost five dollars that night in order to throw the game to ensure he kept the man's attention; it was easy to part with, even with as little money as he had to his name. Five dollars was a small price to pay to lead him to one of the men that were actually there that night. Perhaps even two.

While they played, the man admitted to being a member of the gang, albeit he was a low-level one. He spoke about working his way up. How he planned on joining his cousin's operation once he had gotten a little more experience. His cousin who happened to be Dowes. It was easy getting him to open up once Ezra convinced him he was part of the same gang.

Though he did not know specifics—what the operation consisted of, who all his cousin worked with, dates or times—he knew that Dowes always met with one of his partners when he was visiting his saloon girl. That he would be heading to see her soon, barely giving Ezra enough time to get there before him. He intended on taking off the moment the man passed out. He would have completely forgotten the night before when he awoke, but a fight broke out with another one of the players.

He accused the man of cheating, and his target was taken out in the ensuing gun fight. The other man was felled by a deputy at another card table. His loose ends already tied up, Ezra made his way out of town and came straight here. The second man he was waiting for, who Dowes' cousin said worked with him on everything, was apparently in no hurry to arrive. Without him, Ezra couldn't risk making a move on Dowes.

The plan was to listen in on their conversations, make note of the direction the man headed in once he left and deal with Dowes. The moment he was finished, he would head off after the second man. If he got lucky, he could catch him when he was far away from a town, lessening the risk of being caught. As he would with Dowes, he would get information out of him about the other members of the Twelve and about De Voe before silencing him permanently.

But for now, he needed to wait for the man to arrive. Reminding himself to be patient, Ezra opened his eyes and decided to get out of the tub. The sound of the door opening behind him caught his attention, and he turned, about to ask Colleen to hand him a towel, when he found another girl standing in the entryway, completely naked. His eyes scanned over her body, taking in her large breasts and long blonde hair.

He vaguely remembered seeing her when he first arrived. He glanced past her, searching for Colleen. Worry pricked at the back of his mind upon not finding her.

"Where is Colleen?" he demanded, his voice hard and cold. She took a step back at his tone but gathered her courage. She smiled seductively at him and stepped forward.

"That freak isn't anywhere near good enough to serve such an important client as yourself. Rest assured, I will be taking over your care," she promised, her eyes taking in his naked form beneath the water.

For a moment, Ezra remained silent, allowing her to move closer as he tried to determine if she was more than she appeared to be. Was she simply just a saloon girl viewing him as nothing more than a meal ticket? Had someone figured out that he was after the Twelve and sent her here to kill him? Distract him so someone else could? No, he decided as he appraised her once more. He would not let himself become paranoid without reason. She was as she appeared to be—a thief. She was trying to poach him from Colleen, probably because he paid for one of the expensive rooms. As that thought crossed his mind, he realized she should have returned by now.

He stood up to his full height so he towered above her. "Where is Colleen?" he demanded again, his tone now icy. She stammered something about a storeroom. Ezra brushed past her, grabbing his pants from the chair. Pausing in the threshold to pull them on quickly, he called over his shoulder, "Get out," before leaving. He didn't look back.

Grabbing the key from the dresser, he made his way downstairs, taking them two at a time. He was certain he made for a strange sight— shirtless, still dripping wet from the bath, barefooted—but at that moment he didn't care. Dowes was upstairs where he would not see him, and he was unsure what the girl might have been willing to do to Colleen to get his key from her. She wouldn't have handed it over willingly.

Turning down a small hall, he stopped at the first door in the corridor and tested the handle. It was locked.

GIVING UP AFTER being unable to find a way out of the room, Colleen collapsed to the floor and held one of the cold cans against her forehead; she hissed as it came into contact with her injury. After she got out, she would be certain to find the master key she knew the barkeep kept in his room. She would hide it in the storeroom somewhere so she could escape on her own the next time she was locked in here.

Colleen chastised herself silently for not having done so before. She should have learned her lesson the first time she was stuck in the room overnight, but it did not matter now. She could not change the past, but she would ensure that she did not have to go through this again.

Though being locked in there wasn't all bad, if she was honest with herself. In fact, the only reason why she even cared was because she actually had a paying customer today. Most nights she slept in the storeroom anyway and, so far, none of the other girls came there looking for her. They never imagined her finding comfort here when they used it to punish her, but that was what made it so perfect.

It was undisturbed by them. The only time any of them even came near this room was to lock her within it. It was here that she slept each night. Here that the small amount of money she managed to save up was hidden. It wasn't much, only fifty cents, but she kept it for when the time between her meals became too long, and she feared she would starve. Today she had been able to more than double her money, but Etta stole it from her.

Colleen smiled as she reminded herself that she had filled her belly for the first time in a long time and would not have to dip into her funds for a while. The smile disappeared as quickly as it appeared as she thought about the smug look on Etta's face when she locked her in this room. She needed to be knocked down a peg or two and Colleen was determined to be the one to knock her down.

But she needed to be smart about it. She couldn't openly attack them, as it would only result with her getting kicked out or worse, but she was certain to find little ways to make their lives hell without them realizing it. She might hide a dead rat in their tubs or under the beds they slept on when no one rented them.

Colleen's plans for childish revenge were interrupted when she heard the doorknob jingling. Someone was trying to get in. Part of her was happy that the barkeep needed to restock the shelves after all, while the other half worried Etta had returned to take out her failure on her. Colleen stood up and prepared for the worse, tightening her grip on the can; she was ready to hit whoever crossed the threshold with it if they tried to attack her.

Much to her relief and surprise, it was Ezra that forced the door open. He stood panting in the entryway, his bare chest heaving with each breath. She felt a strange flutter in her chest, and she couldn't stop the smile that threatened to split her face. "You came to find me," she whispered, her words sounding more like a question. Even with him standing before her, she scarcely believed he actually come for her. Nobody ever had before.

"I have no desire to deal with people who would stab someone in the back like that. I despise thieves." He stepped back to allow her to walk past him. As she stepped back out into the hall, she told herself that it did not matter that he came simply because he did not like Etta's actions or because he didn't want anyone else to find out he wasn't really there for the entertainment. She knew the truth, but the other girls did not.

As far as they would ever know, he chose her over them. They would think this time, she was more desirable than them. It would no doubt end in them retaliating even more, but there was always some excuse for them. If it wasn't this, it would be something else. At least with this, she'd be able to give them a smug look or two to rub it in their faces.

"Well if you hate thieves, you did right choosing to not go with Etta. That two-bit strumpet stole my coin purse," Colleen told him as she followed him back down the short hallway. For a moment, Ezra stopped walking, causing her to almost crash into him before stopping at the last second. Without a word, he continued on.

A QUICK SCAN of the main room was all Ezra needed to be certain the girl from before— Etta, Colleen called her—wasn't attempting to entice another man out of his hard-earned coin. Assuming she was upstairs, Ezra was about to mount the stairs when he spotted the woman he was looking for making her way back down.

Blocking her path by stopping in front of the last stair, Ezra managed to tower over her even though she remained above him. "Return it, now," he commanded. He hoped she would do as he instructed, but she seemed reluctant.

He stood even taller. "Return it at once. You will not like it if I have to take it back by force."

For a moment, she seemed to debate whether she could get out unscathed while holding on to Colleen's money. Her eyes darted first to the barkeep who was too busy cleaning the bar to notice what was happening, before they turned to the three men still in the main room.

They were obviously too drunk to care. And, even if they weren't, she had to realize they would not be of much use in her defense. She removed the stolen coin purse from her own and threw it at Colleen. "You will regret this, boy." She rushed past them to the safety of the barkeep.

As she retreated, he wondered if her boss would protect her. He hadn't even bothered to look up when she collapsed into one of the bar stools over-dramatically. Glancing toward Colleen long enough to make sure she was following, Ezra made his way back upstairs.

Not a word was passed between them as they returned to the room. Opening the door, Ezra stepped aside, allowing Colleen to enter before locking it behind them once more. As he turned back around, he was surprised to find her standing a foot away, a soft smile gracing her face. Before he thought to ask why she was looking at him in such a way, she placed a gentle kiss on his cheek.

"Thank you, Ezra. I know you only turned her away and came to my rescue because you do not want anyone else around to put whatever it is you are doing at risk, but even still, you are the first person to stand up for me—ever. This is certainly not the first time something like this has happened to me, but it is the first time things ended in my favor."

Ezra did not bother to correct her as she wasn't completely wrong. He turned the saloon girl away partially because his plans were already at risk enough with Colleen being near him, but, at the same time, he had no interest in her either. He went to find her because she was helping keep his cover while he waited to make his move, but his concern for her also drove him out of the cover of his room.

He could have easily stayed inside, waited until Etta and the others went to bed to find Colleen, let her out of the storeroom when there was no one else around to witness his concern for her, but the thought was dismissed from his mind as quickly as it formed. But he would not be telling her that. He had no idea what it meant, if anything, but he was certain it would complicate matters, and that was the last thing he needed.

Instead of admitting this to her or commenting on her admission, he almost unconsciously reached up to touch the new bruise forming on her forehead.

BEFORE SHE REALIZED what she was doing, Colleen leaned into his gentle touch, the warmth of his fingers dulling the throb behind her eyes. She felt the beating of his heart; there was something so peaceful about the sensation that it lulled her to sleep right where she stood. Coming to her senses, Colleen stepped back, breaking the contact.

Mumbling an apology, she glanced down to break eye contact, only to land on his bare, well-toned chest. Her heart skipped a beat at the sight in front of her before finally noticing his state of undress. "Did you want to finish your bath?"

He shook his head. Had there really been a moment between them? If there had, it was broken now. "Mind if I use it then, Sugar? It's not every day I get to have a hot bath."

"It's all yours," Ezra assured her, unmoving from his spot by the entrance. For a moment longer than was necessary, his hand lingered in the air when she broke contact. For a second, she wondered if she had not imagined the moment between them after all, but soon decided it did not matter. All that she cared about right now was a nice, long soak in a hot bath.

Colleen gave him her best flirty smile. "No peeking," she said with a wink before heading toward the bathing room. Closing the door, she rested back against it for a moment as she shut her eyes and took a deep breath. Opening them once more, she headed over to the washing area, stripping off her clothes as she went. They landed forgotten on the floor as she quickly washed in the cold water before making her way over to the tub, ignoring the pinkish water that went down the drain.

The warm, inviting water called to her. Colleen moaned as she stepped one foot in, and then the other. As she slowly sank into the water, she hissed in pain and shot back up. Glancing down, she found a red, angry scratch on her leg and, for the first time since it happened, she remembered injuring herself when she was thrown into the storeroom. In better light, she realized now that, while it was rather deep, it wasn't enough so she would need to seek the doctor.

EZRA SHOT TO his feet at the pained sound coming from the bathing room. He opened the door enough to see inside, careful not to make a sound. The sight before him caught him off guard as she stood naked in the tub, her back to him, and gently touched her leg. The large red scratch along her leg was impossible to miss even from a distance.

He stepped forward, intending to inspect the wound, but he stopped as Colleen lowered herself in the tub, hissing in pain once more as the warm water washed over her leg. She leaned back against the edge of the tub and cried. The soft sobs were barely audible from where he stood—clearly, she didn't want to be heard. Ezra gave her some privacy. If she wanted him to know, wanted him to see her cry, she would have done so in the other room. She could have used it to gain his sympathy, perhaps even extra coin if he felt sorry enough for her, but instead, she chose to bare her pain to an empty room.

The strength she showed both amazed and angered him. Never in his life, with the exception of his parents, had he ever known any to show true strength. They would give up when life got too hard and show themselves as the cowards they truly were. They would run scared, hide away until the trouble passed them by, leaving them unscathed while others around them weren't so lucky.

Once, when he faced off against Morton, he saw the true face of man for perhaps the first time in his life. He was ambushed, outnumbered by five-to-one, yet no one jumped to his defense. None of the men he worked alongside with stood against Morton, even without knowing who Ezra truly was. All they knew was he was a man who rode with them for almost six months. That he was the one who had their backs when they ran afoul of gunslingers.

They knew him as their brother, as never giving them any reason to be anything but loyal as he stood with them and made his way up the ladder to get closer to Morton, yet they acted if they never met when he faced off against the leader who treated them all like they were less than what his horse left behind. He saw them that day, peering out from around the buildings that surrounded him or through the windows.

They remained safe for their cowardice and showed Ezra who they truly were. Who everyone truly was. There were none in the world that would show him the bravery his parents shown the night they were murdered—of that he was beyond certain. Yet, almost as if she was trying to prove him wrong, here was this woman showing strength he had not seen since he was a young boy. Instead of using her pain to her advantage, or at least using him for a shoulder to cry on, she held in all that she must have been feeling and waited until she was alone to let her emotions show.

With such a simple action, she showed him a strength he thought didn't exist anymore, and he found himself amazed by her. But, sadly, that strength also told him something that made him so angry he was actually a bit startled by his own reaction. She was more like him than he realized. She possessed that strength because she needed to.

As she said, no one ever stood up for her before and, though she did not say as much, Ezra was certain that included her own parents as well. What happened to them for her to have never been defended by them? For her to have ended up here, in a job women only took when it was this or starve. It put a roof over your head and food in your belly, unless you were Colleen it seemed, but it was not the life one would dream of having when they were young.

She was strong because there was no one to be strong for her. She held in what she felt, her tears and pain, because there was no one there to lend her a shoulder. She grew up without a family to watch her back, to protect her from the hardships of the world, as Ezra had, but he wondered if she had not at least gotten a few years of peace as he did with his parents. When was she abandoned to the cruel world? Why was she so alone? Why was she the woman put in his path when he was so close to another rung of the ladder?

Any other woman he was certain would not even give him a moment's pause. He would not abandon his cause, not by any means, but what of her when he was gone once more? What would happen to her when Dowes was dead, and he was not there to answer for his actions? Would they believe she was involved, if they realized he was, and punish her for his actions?

As she feverishly scrubbed the evidence of her tears off of her face, he vowed that he would not leave her to the wolves when all was said and done.

He would not risk his mission, but neither could he risk her. Before he left, he would give her what money there was in his coin purse and insist she left for her own protection. Perhaps he would send her toward his grandmother's home. Though he had not been back in the five years since he learned of McKinley, he was certain it still remained empty. There was nothing there worth having.

A splash coming from the tub brought Ezra back to the present—she was coming up for air. Not wanting her to find him standing there watching her, he backed out of the room and closed the door as quietly as he had opened it. Grabbing the room key on his way out, Ezra forgot his shirt, as it remained in the bathing room with Colleen, and made his way downstairs once more.

# Chapter Five

EDGEWOOD 1830

Taking her time to get dressed, Colleen stared into the flames of the dying fire, knowing she should add another log before it went out completely, but unable to find it in herself to care. Crying wore her out, and all she wanted to do was curl up on the floor and go to sleep. She was so tired of dealing with the crap the other girls put her through each day. Tired of going hungry and cold. Tired of having to sleep on the storeroom floor when the others always managed to find a warm bed.

She was tired of the looks she got from the men downstairs; from the girls as well. She was a woman, just the same as any of them. Why must they treat her so cruelly? She took on the men that would have beaten or abused them. She took the punches, the kicks that would have been aimed at them if not for her. She did the dirty work none of them liked to do. The work that paid so little. All of this she took on and yet they couldn't even find it in themselves to be neutral to her. She didn't expect their gratitude, never asked for a single "thank you." Colleen just wished that they were not so openly aggressive toward her.

Was it really so much to ask to not have to look over her shoulder constantly for their next attack simply for being who she was? So what if she was born different from them? Who cared if she sometimes felt like a woman and other times as a man? How did it affect them any? It didn't in the least, and yet they behaved as if who she was, was a slight to them personally. As if being the way she was, was an attack on them.

It made little sense to her, their reactions to finding out she was more than one gender, but she would never understand them or their reasons. They were as foreign to her as she was to them. It was better that way. As much as she would have loved to have even a single ally in the saloon, she knew it would never last. Nothing ever did. Eventually they would have turned on her as her mother did, and she never wanted to experience pain like that again.

So here she was and here she would remain, surrounded by those far closer to enemies than friends, even as she wondered again why she did not leave this place far behind. She never intended to stay for long, just to make some money to afford traveling more than a few miles before starving to death. Instead, she found herself unable to save any money at the end of each day to put toward her future. If she was able to, she would have left long ago; live as a man who stood a better chance of finding work at some low man's labor than Colleen did at finding any other work than what she currently did.

Who she was as Colleen was nothing like who she was as a boy. Their personalities, their behaviors, even their speech were so different that they might as well have been two different people. But for now, with her male half being seen as too weak to work at the mines and there being little else for him to do in the area even three years later, she was forced to stay as Colleen full time even though she would prefer to spend her life equally between the two.

Perhaps one day she would feel safe enough to breathe life back into her second half, but that day was a long way off. If she found a man to love her as she was, as she was meant to be loved, perhaps that day would come much sooner, but if the years at the saloon taught her anything, it was that such a man didn't exist. Only two ever came close, and neither was interested in her as she might have been in them.

The first was the man who saved her life. He taught her how to defend herself when the men crossed the line between abusive and deadly in exchange for room and board. His name was Hemsworth, and he was a simple rancher having a run of bad luck. His horse got bit by a rattler, and he used what money he had on him to buy another. He, much like Ezra, did not want her the way she wished to be desired, but he treated her as the closest thing to a friend she had ever known.

He stayed two nights until his new horse was ready, teaching her everything he knew about self-defense as she used up what little she saved to buy his meals and a bed to sleep in. Though he shared both his food and tiny bed with her, their relationship was completely platonic. Before he left, he told her to come visit him if she ever headed out west. She had yet to leave, and he never returned, but still, she felt as though he was the one friend she had in the world. Until Ezra arrived and became the second.

He too did not want her the way she did, but it was okay. He treated her like a person, and that was already more than she hoped for. To the others she was dirt, gunk on the bottom of their boots to be wiped off, but to him, she was Colleen. She was a real person who mattered, who deserved to live. It would be harder for her when he left, much harder than it was with Hemsworth, but she refused to keep her distance to save her some pain later.

Colleen needed the same human contact as everyone else, and she was going to draw as much strength from this encounter as possible. Hold on to the memory of the time they spent together, bring it to mind when the nights grew too long and cold, when days turned into weeks without the touch of another. It was a pity though that he was not interested in her comfort as that would be a much better memory to keep her warm.

EZRA GLANCED UP as Colleen entered the room, fully dressed. Silently he waited as she closed the door before turning back around, noticing him for the first time. He was seated on the bed with bandages and cloths to clean her wound scattered around him. She gave him a confused look. "I figured you would have more injuries than the one on your face," he said, hoping she wouldn't realize he'd been spying on her.

She tried to smile, but she was clearly still in pain. "Colleen, your injuries need to be tended to. The last thing you would want is for them to fester and put you out of work completely. Show your wounds to me so I can dress them." He patted the bed in front of him.

She exhaled in a huff, causing the bright hair that framed her face to fly up. "I can't show you. My only other injury is on my thigh."

He shrugged—its location mattered little to him. He already knew what to expect when she raised her skirt. "It's nothing I haven't seen before," he tried to assure her, but it seemed to be the worst thing for him to say as Colleen glared at him. Unsure of what he did to anger her, Ezra kept his mouth shut lest he make it worse.

"Nothing you haven't seen before? Oh, so you have met another who would live their life half as a man and half as a woman? You met another born in the body of a man, but who felt they were meant to be a woman as well? You have seen another reduced to living in a whore house because they found no other work as a woman? Have you spent time with another who has a serpent between their legs and yet does not wish for a burrow to bury it in? Nothing you haven't seen before? *I am something you have never seen before, Ezra.*"

"I meant no offense, Colleen. I simply meant your thighs were nothing I hadn't seen before. I have seen naked women before." He kept it to himself that Etta was the first and her the second. He patted the bed in front of him again. "Sit down, Colleen." He grabbed her wrist and pulled her toward him; she ended up half in his lap.

"If you wanted me in your lap, all you had to do is say so," she said lightly.

Rolling his eyes, he helped her to sit on the bed in front of him. "Lift your skirt." Seeing her begin to shake her head in refusal, he added, "Either you lift it, or I do, and I won't know where to stop."

Huffing once more, she raised her skirt high enough that he had unobstructed access to the scratch on her leg. Without another word, Ezra dried and dressed the wound.

Once he was satisfied, there was nothing more for him to do, he set the leftover medical supplies down beside the bed. "It's time for me to get some sleep." As she rose from the bed, Ezra climbed under the covers and added, "Put out the candle and lay down."

A few moments later the room was cloaked in darkness, and he waited in silence for the bed to dip, indicating she joined him, and instead he heard her settling down on the floor.

"There is plenty of room in the bed, Colleen," he called out into the darkness softly. A heartbeat passed, and then another without her moving. "Unless you prefer to sleep on the floor, that is. Just because I don't plan on sharing your bed doesn't mean I can't share mine," he joked, knowing she would understand the double meaning to his words.

Judging by the giggle that floated up in the darkness, she had. A moment later, she was crawling over him and laying down on the empty side of the bed. "I would prefer to share my bed with you, but if you sharing yours is the best I can hope for, I would gladly accept." She laughed, sweet and genuine, at their strange banter.

"Every day should end with a laugh," he whispered to himself as he heard his mother's words echoing in his mind. Even without seeing her, Ezra knew she was looking at him confused; her unasked question almost audible in the silence. "It is something my mother used to say. Every day should start with a smile and end with a laugh. You should greet each day excited by the possibility of what good things it might bring and bid farewell to the bad before going to sleep so they would not haunt you in days to follow."

"In that case, Sugar, I will make certain my bright smile is the first thing you see in the morning."


AS THE NEXT morning dawned, Ezra was awoken by the warm rays of the sun on his face. When he rolled over in an attempt to get a few more minutes of sleep, he noticed the bed beside him was empty, though the sheets still felt warm. Colleen got up not long before him. A quick glance around the room found her standing in the balcony doorway, her entire body haloed by the sunlight.

For a moment, Ezra was mesmerized by the sight before him. She seemed to glow in the morning light and, a moment later, when she turned to find him awake and graced him with a smile, his heart skipped a beat. Shaking his head, blaming the strange feeling on being half asleep still, he sat up in bed before turning his attention back to her when she spoke. "I will go see to breakfast, Sugar. You'll need to pay for the room again if you want to stay another night."

He nodded. "I will get the money while you deal with the food," he told her as he rose from bed, throwing the covers over to her side.

"What's wrong Sugar—don't want me to see where you hide your coin purse?" He was not surprised when she laughed at his agreement. When she walked passed, he grabbed her wrist.

"How is your wound doing?" he inquired, his eyes trained on her skirt covered thigh.

She giggled. "Want to kiss it and make it better, Sugar?" For the third time in as many minutes, he found her laughing at him when he rolled his eyes, but it did not annoy him. If she was well enough to be joking with him about it, the injury must not be bothering her too much. He released her hand. She smiled once more before making her way out of the room.


OUTSIDE OF THE room, Colleen braced herself against the door as she tilted her head back and smiled. Shaking her head, she thought it was a pity he did not desire her as she would have liked. She desired him even more with each passing moment—each word, every look drew her in even more. The look of concern that filled his eyes was enough to make her heart flutter.

Biting her lip in frustration, Colleen shook herself to clear the thought of him running through her mind and went downstairs to procure the meal tickets. The other girls glared daggers into her, but she'd ignore them for now. This was not the last she would hear from them, she was sure, but there was little to do about that.

She would have to stay in the room as much as possible, hopefully give them a chance to calm down a bit. Considering it meant that she would get to spend more time with Ezra, it wasn't much of a sacrifice on her part. Her thoughts were so consumed by him, she didn't notice when she collected the tickets or retrieved the food from the diner. It wasn't until she was stepping into his room that she realized she had been so lost in her mind. Shaking her head, she shut out the rest of the world once more before glancing around.

Spying the morning light streaming in through the open balcony door, she set the tray of food down on the dresser before heading into the bathing room to heat the water for his bath. There were a few still warm, red coals at the bottom of the hearth, making the fire easier to rebuild, and soon she placed a bucket of water above the now blazing fire. Hearing a startled, slightly muffled voice coming from the other side of the hearth, Colleen strained to hear what she was saying.

"...watching us!" Though she only made out the last two words, it was not hard for Colleen to figure out who she was referring to. There was only one place within the saloon where anyone was able to see them with their front door closed. Gathering up her skirt in one hand, she rushed back into the other room, unable to recall a time when she ever ran so fast. Dropping to her knees in front of a very startled Ezra, she quickly shushed him before grabbing hold of his hips.

Keeping her eyes locked on his, she bobbed her head back and forth as though she was servicing him right there on the balcony, gesturing behind him with her eyes. Though she couldn't see him from her position, she heard him the moment Dowes stepped out onto the balcony. It was not hard to figure out her ruse worked when he called out, "Take it inside," before laughing perversely.

The sound was enough to creep Colleen out, but it seemed to petrify Ezra completely as he tensed up beneath her fingers. Confused by such a strong reaction, she rose to her feet, confirming Dowes went back inside, before turning her full attention to his frightened expression. She grabbed his hand and dragged him back inside. After locking the door behind them, she gently pushed him back against the bed until he was forced to sit. Cupping his face, forcing him to look at her, she whispered, "You look as if you have seen a ghost, Sugar. Are you all right?"

"Not seen. Heard," was all she got out of him before he startled mumbling something about "he was there" repeatedly. Worrying her bottom lip, Colleen stared at him in silence for a moment, unsure of what to do. Sitting down beside him, she pulled his head into her lap and stroked his hair as she whispered any reassuring words that came to mind. She couldn't remember any of what she said afterward, but her soothing voice calmed him enough that he was able to fall asleep.

FOR THE FIRST time since he was a young child, still small enough to sleep beside his parents, Ezra woke in the warmth of another's embrace. Confused by the warmth beneath his head and the gentle fingers running through his hair, he searched his mind for memories of what got him to this point. Slowly, thoughts filled his mind as each one gave another piece of the puzzle.

He saw himself standing on the balcony, trying to catch a glimpse of what was happening on the other side of curtains in the room next to his.

Colleen had come up behind him. To his shock, she'd dropped to her knees and pretended to pleasure him orally. He was about to question her actions when he heard the laugh from behind him. He realized two things in that very instant, both terrified him to the point where he found himself unable to move.

Dowes was mere feet away from him standing on his own balcony. Close enough to turn around and shoot him dead before the man realized what was about to happen, but even if Ezra found the will to move, he would never do that. I would cost him any chance of getting information about the others from him. The second, perhaps more terrifying realization he came to when he heard the laugh was that he heard it before.

The sound haunted his dreams for many years, and he hoped to never hear it again. He froze like he was the scared little boy he was all those years ago hiding in the bushes while his parents were killed in front of him.

Colleen had whispered something to him, but all he heard was white noise in his mind as if it was protecting him from hearing anything else he would be unable to handle. She had guided him back inside the room, and somehow, after they crossed the threshold, he found he heard her voice once more. Though, in all honesty, it was hard to hear anything over the pounding of his own heart.

She had said something about him seeing a ghost, but he remembered nothing after that. He did not even remember if he answered her before passing out from the shock. Opening his eyes, feeling her fingers falter for a moment before continuing to stroke his hair, he glanced around without actually moving and soon discovered he was laying in the fetal position with his head on her lap.

Turning his eyes to hers, he found her smiling softly at him, nothing but concern showing on her face. As he lay there in silence staring up at her, Ezra wished he was able to tell her everything. Tell her about the men that killed his parents. Tell her about those he found before. Tell her about how he accidentally killed McKinley. About the shootout with Morton that earned him his first bullet wound.

He wanted to tell her about Dowes being there that night, laughing that horrid, disgusting laugh. That even though he was out of Ezra's line of sight, he would recognize the sound anywhere. Dowes thought it was funny when the leader suggested his mother bedded Godfrey de Voe before and his laugh was easily the creepiest sound Ezra ever heard.

But, no matter how the laugh affected him as a child, it was no excuse to freeze up the way he did. Ezra was a grown man, someone who had taken the lives of others. He was no longer a small child needing, wanting to hide in his mother's skirts. He was not about to hide in Colleen's. And as much as he would have wished to tell her everything, find an ally after so many years of being alone, he couldn't risk everything. As he sat up, Ezra chastised himself for losing control as he did, even though he knew he should cut himself at least a little slack. Dowes was not the first of the twelve he came across, but he was the first he actually remembered being there; even if only by sound.

Of McKinley and Morton's involvement, he was certain—they even admitted as much to him before he was done with them, but he was unable to actually place them there that night. Dowes he could. Ezra knew he was directly connected to the murder of his parents with his memory alone. But that did not matter to him. There was still too much left undone, too many men still yet to be held accountable for their part for him to freeze up like he did and risk everything.

What if he had been in the room with Dowes when he heard that laugh? What if he froze when he had his gun pointed at him and given Dowes an opportunity to get the upper hand? It would all be over in the blink of an eye simply because of a mistake like that, and as he turned to find Colleen staring at him in concern, Ezra silently vowed that he would never make it again. He would not let the memory of his parents down like that again.

"WHAT IS IT, Sugar? Who is Dowes to you? What caused you to freeze up like that?" Colleen asked in a soft, concerned voice. Right away, it was easy to tell Ezra would not answer as he stared at her in silence. Sighing, she smiled softly before continuing. "It is your choice if you do not wish to tell me, Sugar, but as someone who has never had it before, let me assure you that things have to be easier when you have help.

"I have had to go through my entire life without help from almost anyone, but you do not have to go through whatever this is alone. I may not be able to do much, but I can at least lend you an ear. I would never betray you or anything you tell me, and I am here to listen when you finally understand and believe that." Giving him another smile, she stood and made her way over to where she left the tray.

The food had long since grown cold, but she was certain he would be too hungry by now to care. Placing the tray before him on the bed, she started back for the bathing room, intent on finishing preparing the bath, when he called out and stopped her. "Thank you, Colleen, for saving me. How did you know to come out anyways?"

"I heard Katherine calling out that she saw you looking at them when I was filling the tub earlier. They had a fire going in the hearth, or at least forgot to close the vent when they were done. Not everyone realizes you can hear each other as we rarely have more than one expensive room occupied at the same time. Make sure you keep quiet when you are in the bathing room or if the door is open, and they may never realize they can be overheard."

"Thank you," he said.

"Anytime, Sugar," she promised before disappearing into the other room.

A FEW MINUTES later, Colleen returned and told him his bath was ready. She took the five dollar bill on the dresser and told him she'd go pay for the room.

Once she was gone, Ezra stepped into the bathing room, closing the door behind him. He stripped out of his clothes, letting them fall into a crumpled pile on the floor, and washed before stepping into the tub. Almost without blinking, he watched the dancing flames as he listened to the sounds coming from the other side of the wall.

"On your knees, girl," he heard Dowes order the saloon girl, Katherine. Clearly, Dowes would not be discussing anything important right now. Ezra allowed himself to sink into the warm water around him, drowning out their voices. Resting on the bottom of the tub, he stared up at the ceiling, the image blurred by the water. When he need for air was too great to stay under any longer, he surfaced enough to breathe without allowing his ears to drain of water.

As he lay there, silently staring up at the ceiling without actually seeing it, he heard only the splashing of the water around him and the sound of his heart beating. He had no idea how long he lay there, but even as the water grew cold, he still did not rise. Closing his eyes, he leaned his head back further, ignoring the shiver that coursed through him from the chill, before opening them once more to find Colleen standing above him, her face marred by concern.

# Chapter Six

EDGEWOOD 1830

"It's time to get out of the bath, Sugar, before your skin shrivels up permanently," Colleen insisted as she stood over him. He rose from the water without a word. She stared at him, enjoying her unobstructed view, before realizing he needed a towel. Grabbing one from the linen chest on the other side of the room, she returned to his side, but instead of handing it to him directly, she used it to wipe some of the water off of his chest and arms.

As much as she enjoyed the feel of him beneath her fingers, she did not touch him for her own benefit, but because he still seemed to be a bit dazed, staring past her shoulder instead of directly at her. Not certain he could do it himself, she dried him, respectfully keeping her hands above his waist, before wrapping the towel around him and helping him step out of the tub.

Following him as he made his way back into the bedroom, Colleen grabbed a second towel before closing the door behind them. She waited until he sat down on the bed before crawling behind him. Without a word, she dried his hair, gently massaging her fingers into his scalp through the towel. It did not take long for his short hair to dry, and she tossed the damp towel aside.

For a moment, she ran her fingers through his hair before resting her hands on his shoulders and beginning to massage his strong muscles. He tensed at first, but as she continued, he relaxed.

When she was sure he was as relaxed as possible, she climbed off the bed. She turned back to him with a smile before covering him with the blanket. He opened his mouth to protest, but Colleen silenced him with a single, stern look. "Rest, Ezra. Whatever it is you are doing will no doubt require a great deal of stamina and strength.

Right now, you have neither.

Though Ezra gave her a look that made her think for a moment he might still plan on objecting, he closed his eyes. A few moments later, his breathing evened out. Satisfied, she returned to the bathing room and gathered up his discarded clothing.

Kneeling beside the long cold tub, she scrubbed his shirt and socks before hanging them over the fire to dry. Turning back to the bath once more, she began the painstakingly slow process of emptying its contents into the drain. Bucket after bucket of cold water was dumped out until the tub was empty. Careful to be quiet, she headed into the common bathing room to retrieve some fresh water.

The tub full once more, she stared down at the drain in annoyance. By now, the barrel outside that collected the dirty water from the expensive rooms would be full, and experience taught her that Katherine would never empty it herself. It would be up to Colleen, as usual.

But that would have to wait until morning as she was too tired to deal with it at the moment. Grabbing his pants on her way out of the room for the umpteenth time that day, she draped them over the end of the bed before quietly climbing into bed beside him. It was still a bit early, but she was not about to refuse herself extra sleep.

THE NEXT MORNING, before the sun even rose, Colleen carefully climbed out of bed, making sure not to wake Ezra, and headed into the bathing room. Folding and setting his now dry clothing off to the side, she built the fire back up from its last embers before heading back out of the room. Careful not to draw any attention to herself as she walked downstairs, Colleen headed outside.

The only ones inside the main room were the owner, who was currently handing out cups of coffee, and the men that paid for beds the night before. Before long, a few others would arrive for a cup before heading over to the mines.

Making a quick stop by the outhouse, she made her way toward the balconies, spotting the barrel that the water from the expensive rooms drained into. As her stomach growl, Colleen decided to see about breakfast before dealing with it.

After acquiring the meal tickets and fetching breakfast from the diner, she headed back to the room. Not wanting to disturb Ezra if he was still asleep, she set the tray down on the floor to unlock the door. Picking it back up, she went inside and found him exactly where she left him less than fifteen minutes before.

Deciding against waiting for him to eat, as her stomach grumbled at the thought, she quietly set the tray down on the dresser, opting to eat her share at the shaving table instead of the bed as usual. When she was finished, she stacked her empty dishes before sitting down once more. Grabbing the small sewing kit from the drawer, she flipped her skirt up enough that she reached the hole in the material that matched the one on her leg.

Mending her skirt hadn't been her top priority, but now that she had little else to do until he woke, she took the few minutes it required to patch it up. As she worked, she felt the stitches brushing up against her leg where it wasn't covered by Ezra's bandage. She pulled up the bandage—the wound was no longer bleeding, a thin scab already starting to form above it. She tightened the bandage before letting her skirt fall back into place.

Ezra still slept soundly, leaving her with little to do. If he hadn't been there, she would be taking a sponge bath right now while the girls were too busy breaking their fasts downstairs. She couldn't do it in the bathing room, as they left one girl there while they ate to make sure she couldn't "taint" their water. Usually she'd be forced to bathe out back using the freezing water directly from the pump.

But she wouldn't have to resort to that; she already had a hot bath the night before. She decided to see if there were any small chores she could do for the owner. Though he looked at her strange when she asked, considering she already had a client upstairs, Colleen joked about not being able to make any money from a sleeping man and accepted the barkeeper's offer of two cents for feeding the horses hitched outside.

"Extra nickle if you clean up after the mess they left as well," he added. Though it wasn't much, it was half the fee of a meal, and Colleen never turned down money that came her. Even though she was currently doing better than she ever did before, the buck twenty-five she made off of Ezra so far would only last her twelve meals.

And that was only if she didn't need to spend it on anything else, including the meals she got them this morning, and if Etta didn't try to steal it again the moment Ezra left the saloon. Twelve meals would not keep her from starving from too long as she might go a week, or more, without finding a single client. No, Colleen learned long ago to never be picky about how the money was earned or how much you were paid. Every single cent helped keep her alive, and that was all that mattered.

Making quick work of feeding and cleaning up after the few horses hitched up outside of the saloon, Colleen gathered her hard-earned seven cents and went back upstairs, more than a little surprised to find him still sleeping. Doubting he would want to stay asleep for too long, Colleen woke Ezra before bringing the tray of food over to him. His meal was eaten in silence before he made his way into the bathing room, though she realized he was not bathing as she had yet to hear a single splash of water.

She made the bed and gathered up the dishes. She considered poking her head into the bathing room to let him know where she was going but decided against it. She headed over to the diner, noticing the sisters' annoyed glares at her having returned the dishes so late without washing them.

"Won't happen again," she promised as she headed back outside without waiting for either of them to respond. She was already pretty sure they wouldn't say anything anyway. They never spoke to her, but Colleen long ago decided not to take it to heart once she realized they never spoke a word to any of the other saloon girls either. It wasn't who Colleen was that caused their rude behavior, but where she worked. As strange as it may have sounded to anyone other than herself, she was actually perfectly happy to be lumped with the other girls, even if it was in a negative way.


UNSURPRISINGLY, EZRA OVERHEARD nothing of interest while eavesdropping on Dowes after breaking his fast. He was pretty sure Dowes and the girl were still asleep. Either that or they closed the vent to the hearth making it so he couldn't hear anything coming from their room. Giving up for now, Ezra returned to the bedroom. After putting his newly cleaned shirt back on, he retrieved another five dollars, knowing he would need to pay for the room again for the third day in a row, as soon as Colleen returned from wherever she was.

Noticing the dishes were no longer where he left them and figuring she went to return them, he placed the money on the dresser and decided it was time he got out of his room for a bit. Other than to find Colleen last night after Etta entered the room and to relieve himself during the night, he had been cooped up in the room since he arrived. He wanted to keep a low profile, and staying in his room all day would draw unnecessary attention. Even if that was exactly what Dowes seemed to be doing.

He ran into Colleen in the hallway. "Money is on the dresser for today," he said. "Going to stretch my legs. You can wait for me in the room if you wish, but lock it whenever you leave." He left without giving her the chance to respond.

When he reached the mostly empty main room, Ezra made sure no one was paying any attention to him before slipping out through the backdoor. Fortunately, the few men that were sitting at the tables were either nursing their hangovers or simply trying to wake up still before having to go to work. The girls were on the opposite side of the room from the men, talking only to each other as they finished up their breakfasts.

It was a stark contrast to how everything was when he'd arrived. He'd never stayed the whole night in a saloon, usually leaving as soon he got the information out of the men he hunted. How strange it was to be in the same spot for so long.

Being stationary was not a feeling he expected to get used to any time soon. Once he dealt with Dowes, he would leave Edgewood immediately to follow after the man was waiting for. If he caught up with him when he was in the middle of nowhere, it would only take a couple of hours before he was on the move again with as much information as he was ever going to give him. Pain, or even just the threat of it sometimes, got men talking, but it was far too risky to try and wait for Dowes to get away from town to deal with him.

The man never seemed to stop moving, much like himself, and his nomadic life made it almost impossible for him to track him down again if he was to lose him. No, he would have to finish dealing with Dowes before leaving town. Sighing heavily, even though he was resigned to what he decided on, Ezra glanced around, taking his first good look at the side exit from the saloon.

Looking up, he spotted his own and Dowes' balconies, both their rooms equally hidden by their closed curtains. There was only about a foot between the two, allowing for him to step across to enter Dowes' room from his balcony. His biggest problem was making sure no one outside saw him.

There wasn't any cover for him to hide behind on his own balcony, even less than that when he stepped from one to the other. If anyone happened to be outside at the wrong moment, they would see him easily from almost any building in town. He would have to be careful on his way there, but even as Ezra made his way toward the front of the saloon, he knew he wouldn't have to worry about the way back.

The moment he killed Dowes, the entire town would be made aware from the sound of the shot. Perhaps, if he was far luckier than he ever was before, he could kill him with his knife instead of the gun, but even then, he would most likely scream. And, even if everything fell into place perfectly and he managed to kill him and get away without being noticed, it would not be long before they figured out who killed him.

If he figured out how to use the balconies to his advantage, he was certain the lawmen would figure it out pretty quickly as well. All of this added up to his plan being his best bet; he would leave as soon as it was done. Depending on how things went, he would either jump from one of the balconies or make the short trip he just made to his horse. Patting him gently on the nose, he pulled a carrot out of his saddlebag, feeding it to him.

Moving to give him a bit of hay, he was a bit surprised to find the feeding trough connected to the hitching post already been refilled. Did Colleen realize this was his horse and took care of him as part of her services? Glancing around at the other horses on the other side of the stairs, he realized they were fed as well. Most likely, whoever it was, simply fed all of them. And cleaned up after them by the looks of things.

He glanced back the way he came a minute before. If he had no time to escape, he would take the riskier exit. However, if he was given the chance, he would prefer the second option. He would go back into his room, get his stuff, and walk right out the side door. He would remain calm and draw as little attention to him as possible. From there, he would simply ride away as if nothing happened.

The second option was how he left after contact with underlings, but if Ezra was honest with himself, it wasn't how things ended with the men from that night. With McKinley, he needed to get out of town fast as he hadn't come up with a real escape plan before going in his house. He figured he would knock him out and walk away. His unexpected death threw him off, and he rushed out, probably drawing more attention to himself than he should have.

With Morton, he pushed his horse as fast as it would go to get as far away from the rest of his gang as possible. Though they had not come to either Morton's or his defense during the gunfight, there was no way for him to know if that would change once Morton was dead. Given the choice, Ezra definitely preferred the calmer retreat. Only time would tell which way his luck would go when the opportunity to deal with Dowes finally presented itself.

LATER THAT DAY, after eating their lunch in relative silence, Colleen decided to stop delaying the inevitable and deal with the water barrel outside. Though she didn't need to dump any more water down the drain for the moment, there was no way for her to know when Katherine might empty hers. Making a quick stop in the bathing room to relight the fire, she walked back downstairs, grabbing the lunch dishes on the way out.

After returning them to the diner, Colleen headed back to the saloon, this time stopping at the barrel beneath the balconies for rooms two and three instead of going inside. A quick inspection of the barrel informed her that more water had not been added since the last time she checked, and she set to work removing the water a bucket at a time and dumped it into a well-used ravine behind the saloon. It was a slow process.

As she grew bored by the mundane task, Colleen allowed her thoughts to wander to the man above her. Though she saw his balcony door from where she stood, the curtains were drawn, blocking her view. If she closed her eyes, she might picture him standing in the tub as he was the night before, completely baring himself to her. She remained respectful, as much as she would have liked to have gotten a better look at all he had to offer, and kept her eyes averted, but it hadn't mattered.

His well-muscled, glistening chest caused her heart to beat a little faster. She licked her suddenly dry lips at the memory before abusing them as more images came to mind unabashed. She saw herself drawing her tongue slowly across his chest, languidly licking the drops of water. Felt his cooled skin warming beneath the touch of her fingers as she massaged his pecs, her blunt nails digging slightly into his skin.

She swore her feet felt damp as she saw herself stepping into the tub, pressing her chest against his as she reached up to pull him closer. His lips mere inches from her, she need only rise a little higher to reach him... The vision was shattered before she ever knew the taste of his lips by a sudden, sharp pain at the back of her head.

Before she had the chance to figure out what was going on, she cried out in pain as she was struck on the back of her head once more, the force of the blow sending her forward into the barrel. Grabbing on to the edge, trying in vain to ignore the fierce throbbing in her head, Colleen tried and regain her balance only to find herself being spun around. A wave of nausea swept over her, threatening to knock her off of her feet, and she fought back the desire to purge her last meal.

Through blurry vision, she barely made out the forms of two large men standing far too close for her comfort. One still held a hard, shapeless object in his hand that she was certain was what he used to hit her. Probably a branch from one of the nearby trees or scrap wood left over from when they repaired the porch. Whatever it was, she was certain she would not be able to remain conscious, let alone standing, if she was hit with it a third time.

There was no way for her to know for sure if they were there to beat or rape her until they made a move toward either. Trying to recall what she saw outside while she was emptying the water, in case something was usable as a weapon in her defense, she was startled when a woman began to speak. "You will pay for daring to keep such a rich client to yourself."

Focusing her attention on the direction the voice was coming from, Colleen made out the outline of her silhouette through her blurred vision. She was standing behind the men, close enough to taunt her without being in any danger herself. Colleen would have to make it passed the two large men before even trying to reach her. Not that she would even be able to put up much of a defense with as dizzy as she was; let alone launch an offensive.

Knowing a physical altercation would not end in her favor, and that she would never be able to outrun them, Colleen bought herself some time. The clearer her vision became, the less her body fought against her, the better her chances of coming through this encounter without any serious injuries. Once she was certain the sudden moment would not cause her to be sick or more disoriented than she already was, she would figure out a way to slow them down and run to the safety of the saloon.

Though the barkeep wouldn't care if they beat her as long as they paid first, he did not tolerate the girls attacking each other as she was. If they were busy fighting amongst themselves, they were not making him the money they should be. Thoughts of safety would have to wait until she actually stood the chance of getting away.

"Nice try, but there is no rule saying I have to share anything with the likes of you!" she spat. "Y'all never share with me. Hell, y'all never even share with each other. Katherine has kept Dowes, and his coin purse all to herself since his first visit here, and he is a guaranteed expensive room."

"We don't have to share with you because unlike you, we are real women. Hit the freak again," the girl said to her goons. Colleen's sudden laughter took them all by surprise, herself included, causing the man holding the unknown wooden weapon to lower it once more as he moved to step toward her at the command.

"A real woman? If you are a real woman, Sugar, then how come you got turned down by my client? Why do you always come in second to Katherine? Weren't you supposed to be the number one before she arrived? Sure didn't take long for her to knock you off your throne," Colleen mocked, knowing it would only further enrage the girl. It wasn't much, but she knew getting her too angry to think straight might be her only chance to get away without further injury.

"It don't matter none if I am second or tenth in this saloon. At least I ain't nothing like the sorry excuse for a man you are," she threw back at her, and though Colleen still couldn't make out any real detail, she realized her vision cleared slightly, allowing her to see some of her larger features.

"Oh, you poor thing, I ain't a man right now. No, right now, I am more woman than you can even dream of being. Do you know why that is, Sugar? Cause I can bring a man to complete pleasure with nothing more than my tongue." It was true; she learned that useful talent when one of the rougher customers, who were sent her way, liked tying her hands. "The pleasure I can bring to them on my knees, brings them to theirs," she continued before running her tongue across her upper lip seductively as she turned toward one of the men. "I would be happy to show you what I mean, boys. Free of charge." She bit her bottom lip as she glanced to one man and then the other.

The growl of frustration coming from Etta pulled her attention back to her, and she hid the fact that she startled her behind a flirty giggle. "Beat that freak, and I will give you both a free ride tonight for your trouble," she screamed, and Colleen knew her time had run out. There was no way the two men would give up an opportunity like that; it was unlikely they would ever get a free ride from her or any of the other girls again.

Knowing she had mere moments before they would be on her as the men charged toward her, Colleen turned and dumped the mostly emptied barrel, causing a wave of dirty bath water to splash over their feet. Instantly the ground around them became a swampy mess, and the men were soon slipping and falling into the mud. In the same moment, she dumped the barrel over, Colleen was already running, though she barely saw the ground in front of her through her blurry vision.

Lady luck was not in her favor, as she rarely was, for she only got a few feet away before being yanked backward, as Etta grabbed a fistful of her hair, and pulled her down into the mud she created. Her hair flying loose haloed around her head as she fell, only to be caked in mud a few moments later as Colleen fought against Etta's hold. Not giving her the chance to break free, her attacker climbed onto her stomach and pressed her further into the mud. Try as she might, Colleen was unable to get a grip on the other girl as the mud on her hands caused her fingers to slip, only succeeding in dirtying the other girl.

"Get over here!" Etta called out above her and, realizing she must be having problems holding her down if she was calling for help, Colleen bucked as hard and as quickly as she could. Unfortunately, she was unable to throw her off before the men were on her.

As one of them grabbed onto her arms and held them into the mud above her head, pulling her down at a painful angle, the other took Etta's place straddling her waist as the saloon girl moved to give him room. Colleen drew a breath to scream out, only to have the wind knocked out of her when the man above her suddenly punched her without warning. The searing pain was enough to let her know he split her lip, but she was given no chance to worry about the injury as she felt another punch connect with her face.

The more she struggled, the harder the man holding her arms held her down, the harder the punches felt. The abuse leaving her drained, Colleen was about to stop fighting it, to just accept the beating in hopes that they would not be as brutal if she didn't piss them off anymore, when one of the men ripped at her clothes. Though she wasn't sure if they were planning on humiliating her or something far worse, she wasn't about to lay there and take that. Finding her voice once more, she screamed, "Get off of me!" as she fought against him with all of her strength.

"MAMA!" EZRA CRIED out as he woke suddenly. He rubbed his face—just another nightmare. His parents' cries still echoed in his head—would he ever be free of them?

Shaking himself as though it would chase the nightmare away, Ezra sat on the edge of the bed as he glanced around, startled to find the room empty. For as long as he remembered, he always hoped to wake up to an empty room. It would mean he was safe, and the men did not know he was hunting them. But now, somehow, he became accustomed to her being there. It felt odd to him to be alone in the room.

Stretching out the kinks, Ezra rose to his feet and removed his shirt, figuring a nice warm bath would do him a world of good. He wondered how long he'd been asleep, as he couldn't even remember falling asleep in the first place. Where was Colleen? Had she returned from dropping off the dishes and found him asleep, or was she still out? Dropping his shirt on the edge of the bed, Ezra remembered her saying something about emptying a water barrel.

Ezra decided to check if she was visible from his balcony. Breathing in the fresh air, Ezra was about to look for her when he heard a scream coming from below. "Get off of me!"

Instantly recognizing her voice, Ezra glanced down over the railing to find Colleen flailing about in the mud with two men holding her down and beating on her. A few feet away, he saw the woman who tried to steal him away from Colleen. Without a thought, Ezra leaped over the railing and dropped to the muddy ground below. He grunted as the impact caused a wave of pain to course through his legs.

He grabbed the man on top of Colleen by the back of his shirt and tossed him aside with more strength than he knew he possessed. He punched the second in the jaw, causing him to fall back into the mud, and pulled Colleen to her feet, only to have her fight against him. Pulling her tight against his chest, he wrapped his arms around her as he whispered, "You are safe, Colleen. I've got you."

Instantly, she relaxed against him. For a moment, Ezra wished he had his gun with him, to pay these men back for what they did, what they were about to do judging by the state of her clothes. But at the same time, he was thankful he did not have it. Firing his gun would only draw more attention to his presence and possibly put her in more danger if the two men had friends nearby.

"Get lost," he spat at the others before effortlessly lifting her into his arms and carrying her back inside. He paid no attention to the gawking of the others. He knew they must have made for a strange sight with her being covered in torn, muddy clothes, but none of them was worth even a passing glance.

All that mattered to him in that moment was getting Colleen upstairs and cleaned up to assess her injuries. He was certain she was beaten pretty badly as the man that was hitting her did not seem to be holding back his punches and, though he had no idea how long it was going on before he woke up, he was sure it did not just start moments before he walked out onto the balcony. Worried he would find her covered in cuts and bruises, Ezra quickened his pace.

Just as he arrived at their room, about to chastise himself for not having the key, he glanced down at Colleen's grunt of pain and found her holding it out for him. Smiling softly, he took the key and unlocked the door without releasing his hold on her. Kicking it shut without bothering to lock it, he made his way toward the bathing room. Silently he dared anyone to be stupid enough to come into the room uninvited. At least that way, he might work out some of his anger without raising suspicions and, for the moment, he couldn't even care less if the intruder had anything to do with the attack on Colleen or not.

Kicking the bathing room door closed as well, he led her to the cleaning area before heading over to the hearth. Finding an already roaring fire was a blessing twofold. It meant that he would not have to start the fire himself before heating the water for her bath, but even more than that, it also meant that she had not been out of the room for very long if the fire was still going so strongly.

Without a word to Colleen, not confident his voice wouldn't crack under the strain of his anger or regret, he heated the first bucket of water before turning his attention back to his equally silent companion. He couldn't look her in the eye—he should have prevented this from ever happening. Ezra drew a deep breath before peeling off her soiled, tattered clothing carefully. Dropping her shirt, corset, and skirt into a pile, leaving her in her slip, he grabbed the bucket of water and washcloth.

Drenching the cloth, he gently drew it down her face, washing away the mud that dried in places where it wasn't too thick. Streaks of red ran down her face with the dirty water. Rinsing out the cloth, he ran it down her face once more to assure himself that he removed all the mud. Now all the droplets that streaked downward were red, but there was nothing to be done about her cuts for the moment.

As he went to rinse the cloth out once again, Ezra realized the muddy water in the bucket wouldn't suffice. Dumping it down the drain, he grabbed the bucket off of the fire and dumped it into the tub, before using it to refill his own bucket. He filled it once more and put it in back in the hearth. Testing the water to make sure it wouldn't be too hot, he tossed the cloth aside before grabbing a clean one and making his way back to Colleen. He dunked the washcloth into the clean water and gently dragged it across her chest.

Though she did not make a sound, other to hiss in pain every so often when the cloth came across a cut, Ezra felt Colleen's eyes on him the entire time he was washing her. But as he worked, emptying and refilling his bucket two more times and added a couple of heated buckets to the bath, she never said a word. It wasn't until he was about to remove her slip, which would leave her completely bare before him, that she finally gave any indication that she had any idea what was going on. As she placed her hand on his to stop him, she whispered, "You don't need to do that. I will wash myself."

Certain she did not stop him because she didn't want him to touch her, but because she was worried about his reaction to seeing her completely nude, Ezra smiled softly at her and stopped her when she tried to step away from him. Holding her pained, scared gaze with his own confident one, he instructed, "Stay here," before making his way over to the linen chest and grabbing another towel. He handed it to her. Without a word, she took it and held it in front of herself.

Once he was certain he would not be able to see what was under her slip, he blindly reached behind the towel and removed her last article of clothing. Using the outside of her legs as his guide, Ezra washed away the mud from the lower half of her body, making sure to not touch anything he wasn't supposed to. Once he rinsed her off, he led her over to the chair and sat her down.

Stepping behind her, he removed the twigs and large clumps of mud before taking out her hairpins. They only held up about a third of her hair still, allowing it to flow down over the back of the chair. For the first time, he was able to see how long her hair was when it was down, but its usual fiery red color was dulled by the dingy mud and water that saturated it. Here and there, he still caught glimpses of her natural color.

Bit by bit, he washed her long tresses until there was little sign of the mud that once caked each strand. Dumping the contents of the latest bucket of water down the drain, he tossed it aside before turning his attention back to Colleen and helping her to her feet. He led her to the tub. Pouring in the water that was heating over the fire, he used the bucket to churn the water, mixing the boiling water with the rest so she would not burn herself.

Adding another bucket full to the fire, he turned back to her once more before holding out his hand for hers and helping her into the tub when she grasped his. As she turned to face him completely, her towel still protecting her modesty, Ezra finally took a good look at her face. Judging by the amount of damage he already saw, he was certain her face took the brunt of the attacks. Reaching up, he caressed her split lip.

Beneath his touch, she tilted her head to the side. Smiling softly at her, Ezra helped her to sit in the tub. She hissed in pain when the water came into contact with her injuries.

He squeezed her hand in reassurance. "Stay here where you will be safe." He left before she could object. Fists clenched at his side, he headed back out of the bedroom, locking it behind him.

He took a few deep breaths in the hall, hopelessly attempting to calm the anger inside him. He wanted nothing more than to make them pay for what they had done to her, but could not risk the attention on himself. No matter how much he felt as though he was failing her after she saved him on the balcony, he could not let his parents down again.

Dowes was low on the list, he was certain, but each man he found brought him one step closer to his ultimate goal: De Voe. He would simply have to find another way to make it up to her without going after the men that attacked Colleen, but that would have to wait as there were more pressing matters to attend to. Ezra made his way back downstairs and headed straight toward the bar.

"Need two meals and a change of clothing for your girl in room three," Ezra told him instead of asking politely. He was certain the barkeep saw the state Colleen returned in, or at least told about it from the others he was serving, but he did nothing to even see if she was okay. Whether he knew about the three outside or simply figured Ezra did the damage to her, he couldn't have cared less.

Though the man behind the bar eyed him strangely, he pulled out two tickets before calling out for one of the saloon girls to go pick them up. Without waiting to see if it was the girl from before, Ezra grabbed the tickets from his hand. "I need fresh air. I'll get them myself." Barely hearing his assurance that a change of clothing would be waiting outside his door when he returned, Ezra turned and made his way toward the front door without another word.


THE MOMENT COLLEEN heard the outer door lock, the usually soft sound seeming to echo in the silent room around her, she allowed herself to sink under the water, letting loose a scream the moment she was submerged. For as long as she had the breath to continue, she did just that, the sound of her scream muffled by the water. Forced to draw another breath, Colleen pushed herself back up to the surface and breathed in deeply.

Choking back a sob, she drew her knees to her chest and laid her head upon them, allowing the tears to fall down her cheeks unencumbered. The fact that this was the second time in as many days that she cried in the tub did not go unnoticed by her, but for the moment at least, she did not have the strength to care. There was no one to try to take advantage of the state she was in.

As she gazed at the fire, she allowed her mind to replay the events that left her in this state. It wasn't the first time one of the girls attacked her, not by a long shot. Nor was the first time one of them had gotten help from their clients, but every other time she was attacked by one of them, it always happened within the walls of the saloon.

She always knew that, at the very least, she could call out for the barkeep if her life was in danger. It might end up costing her place at the saloon, but she would be alive. If nothing else, she was sure the barkeep would not allow them to kill her; there was no money in that.

This time, however, she had no such hope. She was attacked outside of the saloon, and it had been a long time since she been so afraid that someone was going to kill her. She knew the barkeep would never go against two of his customers, let alone his number two girl, for her sake. She did not make enough money to make her worth the trouble to him. He made that much completely clear by sending the abusive men straight to her.

If Ezra did not come to her rescue like he did, then she would have died that night. And no one would have batted an eye at her death. if they even realized she was gone. But even as the thought crossed her mind, Colleen realized that it was no longer true.

Ezra cared. He risked his own life, risked whatever it was he was here for, for her. He saved her because he thought she was worth saving. For the first time in her entire life, someone thought that she, the abandoned, the unwanted child, deserved to live.

# Chapter Seven

EDGEWOOD 1830

Balancing the tray of food in one hand while unlocking his room with the other almost proved too difficult for Ezra, but he managed to get it open without spilling more than a few drops of their soup. He set the tray down on the dresser and grabbed the clothing that was left in the hallway for him before locking the door. He glanced down at the clothing in his hand and, for the first time, took a good look at it.

Though the deep red shirt and skirt was embellished where Colleen's own was bare, he spotted where patches of the fabric faded or were repaired. No doubt the clothing belonged to another of the saloon girls at one point, but, judging by their state, he was certain they had not been used in a long time. It was doubtful any of the girls there would take offense to Colleen wearing them.

Ezra entered the bathing room and froze in his tracks at the sight that greeted him. He watched in stunned silence as Colleen rose from the tub, droplets of water cascading down her naked flesh. He chastised himself for not knocking first.

Perhaps at any other moment, Ezra might have averted his eyes and apologized for barging in unannounced, but now he only stared, mouth agape, at the countless cuts and bruises that were already beginning to form across most of her body. Though most were minor and would heal quickly, there were so many that he would almost swear they covered more of her flesh than they didn't.

Her split lip and blackened eyes and jaw were only the beginning of what the men inflicted upon her. Down both of her arms and legs were smaller cuts and scrapes, most likely caused by whatever rocks and sticks were in the mud with her. Though he did not see her back, he was certain it would look much the same as her legs as it had at least been protected by being underneath her. Her stomach and chest were not so lucky.

Upon her chest, where the man who was pinning her down had ripped at her clothing, there were deep scratches caused by his nails digging into her flesh. Here and there were clusters of forming bruises. Unable to stop himself, he hissed at the sight before him, wishing to take away the pain he was certain she must be feeling, and drew Colleen's attention to his presence. Even without her having to say a word, he knew by her frightened expression as she turned toward him that she expected the others returned to finish their job.

Something in his expression must have led her to believe it was the sight of her fully nude that caused him to react as he did as she apologized and tried to cover herself up with the towel. Ezra stopped her hand, preventing her from covering herself up.

"My reaction was to the sight of your injuries and nothing else," he assured her before caressing a large bruise on her arm. For a few moments, Ezra stared at it in silence before finally sighing and wrapping a dry towel around her shoulders. Assisting her out of the tub, he set her clothing down on the chair. "Get dressed and join me for dinner."

Heading back out the way he came without waiting for a response, he closed the door behind him even as his hands fisted in anger. His nails dug into his skin deeply as he silently blamed himself for not being able to help her. It was his fault that she got hurt. They attacked her because she got a wealthy client over the others. He was the cause of every single scrap, cut and bruise that covered her body and, much like with his parents, he was unable to protect her. He failed her when she had saved him.

WITH SOME EFFORT, he calmed himself down. She still needed his help. Ezra set up the meal and waited for her to emerge from the bathing room. A few minutes later, she came out dressed in the 'new' outfit. Ezra gasped at the sight of her.

The deep red of the dress brought out the almost fire-like hues of her hair. The bright ringlets framed her face and fell to the middle of her back. Her skirt flowed across her legs like silk gliding in the wind with each step she took, while the shirt billowed in all the right places, making her appear to have more curves than she had naturally.

"See something you like?" she teased with a flirtatious grin that was made less effective by her split lip. She winced in pain. Ezra shook his head before gesturing for her to join him on the bed. It did not take long for them to finish their meals, each too busy eating to bother with much conversation. Once they were finished, Ezra set the dishes back onto the tray on the dresser.

He turned back toward Colleen. "Get into bed. You need to get some rest." Waiting until she had done as he bid, he closed the curtains and climbed in beside her. He pulled her shivering body to his. "It's to warm you up," he assured her. "Seems you stayed in the bath long enough that the water turned cold. Sleep now. I will wake you when it's time for lunch." Though her body remained tense against his for a few more moments, she eventually relaxed.

Knowing she was doing it for the warmth and comfort he provided, he decided not to draw attention to how firmly her backside was pressed against his groin. As he lay there in silence, waiting for her to fall asleep before drifting off himself, he practically heard how her eyes remained open through her shaky breaths. Without having to see her face, he knew she was staring at the wall in front of her without really seeing it.

He knew because he did the same many times over the years when he feared the nightmares to come would be too much to bear. Eventually she would succumb to sleep, as he always had, but the countless hours of worry would neither help her mind or body any, nor would it prevent the nightmare to come. She would have one, he was certain, after what she just experienced. They would have killed her if he had not gotten to her when he did.

How could nightmares not plague your dreams after almost being killed? Even the strongest of minds would succumb to the terrors in the night. All Ezra could do was be there for her when she awoke in a cold sweat, as she was bound to do, and lend her the strength of his arms as she slept. Perhaps if she felt him during the nightmare still holding her tightly against him, it would give her the courage to face whatever it was that she saw within her dreams.

Hoping she might be more willing to sleep if he was, Ezra purposely slowed down and evened out his breathing, making it appear as though he was asleep. Almost instantly he felt Colleen relax further in his embrace, though it took her another few minutes to fall asleep. Once he was certain she was out, Ezra slipped from the bed to go check on Dowes. The sound of splashing and a woman's giggle floated in from the other room.

COLLEEN SCREAMED, THE sound echoing off the walls. On instinct, she tried to rise only to find herself pinned down by strong arms wrapped around her. For a moment, she did not remember where she was or who she was with, but the sound of his voice brought the memories of the day before.

"You are safe within my arms," Ezra assured her in a muffled voice. Glancing over at him, as well as she could in the dark, she saw that his face was half pressed against the pillow beneath him, his eyes still closed. Before she could come up with a response, he pulled her closer to him and tightened his hold. She laid back down and allowed herself to be pulled against him once more.

She sighed, content to stay exactly where she was forever. His statement was the truest thing she ever heard. She was safe here in his arms, locked away in his room where no one could touch her. Where there was no threat lurking in the shadows. Right there, at least for the moment, she did not have to worry about anyone or anything else. She was safe. She was protected. For what had to be the first time in her entire life.

No one else ever cared about her or her safety. Not her mother, who abandoned her when she was a child. Not the father she never knew who abandoned her mother the day she told him she was pregnant. None of the adults at the orphanage, where she spent most of her life, ever gave a damn about her. Even the barkeep she worked for never tried to protect her. Hell, he sent abusive men straight to her to protect his other girls. "Thank you," Colleen whispered to her companion, certain he had already fallen back asleep and would be unable to hear her.

"Always," Ezra mumbled, half asleep, and Colleen couldn't help but smile, even knowing he had no idea what he was saying. It was the one thing she wanted all of her life, the one thing everyone denied her. Someone to be there for her and protect her for always. She should have had that in her mother, but instead, she was born to a retired saloon girl who spent more time drinking than caring for her child.

When she should have been there to feed her, she was gone for hours at a time, returning home only when she had no more money, and there were no more men willing to pay for her drinks or time. When she was supposed to be tucking Colleen in at night or showing her love and affection, her mother would be gone for days at a time.

In her entire life, Colleen's mother never did a single thing for her, to help her, to love her. She hadn't even bothered to give her a name. It was a man at the orphanage who named her when she was four years old. For four years, she was only ever called "bastard" or the thing "that ruined my life," by her mother. And that was before she ever found out about what made Colleen so unique. Back then, she was her mother's baby boy. It was when she discovered the truth about her that she finally abandoned her for good.

But that woman no longer mattered, or if she was honest with herself, she did not matter at that moment. All that mattered was she felt safe and protected for the first time in her life, and Colleen felt an unfamiliar warmth coursing through her. With a smile on her face, Colleen closed her eyes and allowed herself to drift off to sleep once more, this time certain the nightmare would not return. At least not that night.

MORNING DAWNED EARLIER than Ezra would have liked, but he did not mind the early rising so much when he opened his eyes and found an amazing sight before him. Colleen was resting on her side, now facing him, smiling softly.

"Good morning," she said. There was something so sincere about her smile that caused him to smile back at her. Right now, just the two of them lying in bed, there were no hidden agendas—she was simply happy to be there when he woke up.

For a moment, his mission disappeared. The moment was shattered as he noticed the jagged cut still marring her lips. He touched the wound gently before he realized what he was doing, pulling back when she hissed in pain.

"I'm sorry, Colleen," he said. "I want to make them pay for what they did to you yesterday, but I cannot draw attention to myself. If there was anything I could do, I would in a heartbeat." He glided his fingers over the bruises on her arm, his eyes refusing to meet hers. Ezra felt ashamed by his lack of actions. There *was* something he could do to avenge her; it would simply cause him to let Dowes slip through his fingers. Even after everything she had done for him, he would not do that.

"It is all right, Sugar. I know what you are doing is important, even if I don't know the details. I would not ask you to risk your chance for me." She smiled and laid her head on his pillow so she was close without actually touching him. Ezra heard her breathing him in before sighing contently. His smile went unnoticed as did the pained expression in his eyes as he glanced down at her before finally laying back down once more.

As he moved, Colleen's arm draped across his chest. He pulled it back when she tried to remove it. Holding her hand with his, resting them both over his heart, he stared up at the ceiling in silence for a minute or two before finally sighing himself. "Dowes is connected to the murder of my parents." Though he did not say much, Ezra found himself wondering if he said entirely far too much when the silence seemed to draw on around them.

"I am so sorry, Ezra. I cannot imagine what kind of pain you have been through." Colleen laid her head upon his shoulder. Before she finished speaking, he felt her hot breath washing over his skin. The spot tingled for a moment before Ezra put the feeling from his mind. He was beginning to enjoy her company, the feel of her skin against his, but this was not the time to get distracted by the new sensations.

Not even if she was the first real contact he had since burying his parents. He could not recall the last time another person actually touched him, but he was certain that was all his reaction was. An automatic response from having been denied contact for so many years. "I do not need you to feel sorry for me, Colleen. I need you to help me."

"I would do anything," she whispered.

He smiled. "I am beginning to believe that you would, Colleen." He rested his head against hers. "For now, there is nothing to be done but to wait. I am waiting for his partner to arrive and cannot approach Dowes before then or risk losing the opportunity to learn more about the second person. What I need from you is to wait and aid me when the time comes."

She turned on to her stomach. "I can think of a few ways to pass the time," she said, smiling seductively at him. Ezra was only slightly surprised. The expression had even less effect on him than usual as the movement caused her to cry out in pain as she reopened her split lip.

Rolling his eyes, he gently brushed away the drop of blood that pooled at the corner of her mouth. "For now, my dear Colleen, you are to pass the time healing."

THOUGH SHE DID not remember falling asleep again, Colleen wasn't all that surprised when she found herself waking again hours after her conversation with Ezra. Judging by the position of the sun that she saw through the closed balcony curtains, it had to be somewhere in the afternoon. She remembered talking to him for an hour or so before they decided it was time to break their fast. Ezra left to get their meals and to pay for the day, not wanting to risk the chance they would attack her again.

Though she wanted to object, she silently had to admit it was nice to have him protecting her. Even more so that he wanted to protect her. Deciding not to fight him on it, she waited in the room, locking the door behind him until he returned with the tray about ten minutes later. She felt no fear for his safety—he could take care of himself. She was another matter altogether. Each sound she heard, Colleen was certain was the men from the night before coming back to finish what they started. Each time she heard one of the girls' voices out in the hall, she would clench her hand around the chair she planned to attack Etta with if she dared to enter the room. It no longer mattered to her, at least not while she sat there alone and afraid, if she was kicked out of the saloon with nowhere to go. She knew now with certainty that almost anywhere would be better than where she was. She couldn't go back to the orphanage; she aged out long ago, not that they would have allowed her back in after what happened before she left. The insane man she spent a few nights trapped with, who dressed her up like his long-dead wife, was certainly the only place worse than the saloon.

Everywhere else, however, was looking better by the moment. Though she only possessed bad memories of a terrorized childhood there, even her mother's homestead seemed appealing to her. She had no idea if it was still standing, but she knew with certainty her mother did not go back to it after she abandoned her. If the woman was even still alive, she would never risk going back as she had no way of knowing if Colleen was still in the area.

But even if she was there, at the very least, Colleen might get a little closure before leaving her childhood home for good. She was starting to wonder where else she could go when Ezra knocked and called out for her to open it. Her fear from moments before completely forgotten, she let him in, and they shared another meal in comfortable silence. That was the last thing she remembered before falling back asleep.

When she woke again, Ezra and the tray were gone. Positive he would have returned long ago from bringing the dishes back, she glanced around the room and found that the door leading to the bathing room was partially open. Silently making her way over, she opened it and peered inside to find Ezra crouched near the hearth, listening to what was happening on the other side of the wall.

It was not hard to figure out the moans and grunts coming from the next room were ones of pleasure. Katherine was earning her keep again—did she ever bother closing the door?

Colleen grabbed a bucket of water from the tub and placed it above the roaring fire. She knew better than to speak lest they be overheard.

She smiled at his confused expression when he turned and found her standing beside him. Gesturing to the tub, Colleen waited until he shrugged and turned his attention back to their loud neighbors before turning back to her task. Getting a fresh towel and washcloth out of the chest, she placed them on the back of the chair before sitting down to watch him.

Sitting in silence, Colleen found herself torn. On the one hand, she wanted to help him in any way possible; on the other, she was happy that whoever he was waiting for was taking their time getting there. The longer they took, the more time she got to spend with Ezra. Each hour that they passed waiting was another hour she was alone with him.

It was selfish, she knew, but it wasn't as if she was working against him. She was merely enjoying the blessing that she received by their tardiness. And while she was on the subject of enjoying what was given to her without hurting him, she decided, as she switched out the buckets of water in the tub and turned back to his shirtless form, Colleen was not about to point out to him that he did not need to bathe as often as she prepared the bath for him.

It wasn't her fault he didn't realize it himself.


HAVING FORGOTTEN SHE was there, Ezra was a little startled when Colleen tapped on his shoulder before gesturing to the tub. Nodding his head to confirm he knew his bath was ready, he gave one last listen to Dowes, finding the sound had muffled quite a bit, and assumed they had moved their activities to the bedroom, before turning and making his way over to the other side of the room. He shucked off his rawhide pants, unabashed by his complete exposure to Colleen, and tossed them on the chair before walking toward the washing bucket.

Grabbing the washcloth, he dipped it into the bucket of lukewarm water and dragged it across his well-toned chest. Behind him, he heard Colleen switch the pan above the fire once more but paid her little mind as he continued to wash. The water dripped from his body, mixing with perspiration.

As he bathed, Ezra's thoughts turned to the woman silently preparing his bath behind him. It seemed strange to him, as a man who always kept his defenses up, who was always on alert watching for some unknown threat to cross his path, that he was completely at ease in her presence. Well, if he was totally honest with himself, not all of his defenses were down. It was true that he was completely exposed, unarmed and with his back to her, but he already knew he could trust her with his life.

She proved that when she saved him out on the balcony. It may not have seemed like much to her, or to anyone else had they been there to witness it, but to him, it meant more than he could ever explain to her. Katherine had caught him spying on them. Ezra wouldn't have had a good excuse if Colleen had not shown up.

So he allowed most of his defenses down in her presence. He trusted her with his life. With his safety. Even with a bit of the mission he was on to avenge his parents, but he did not tell her about Godfrey de Voe or the other men that were there that night. He did not tell her about the two he already killed before getting to this point. And more than that, he did not open himself up emotionally to her. He knew Colleen wanted more, but he could not let himself let go and fall into her desires. He could not, would not allow himself to form any more attachment to her, for it would make leaving her that much harder in the end.

And what would happen, heaven forbid, if she was to be injured or killed during his time here because of him and the path he was on to avenge his parents. If something was to happen to her because of him, he needed to be able to walk away unaffected by it. He needed to keep her at arm's length, but at the same time, he needed to keep her protected.

He wouldn't leave her to the wolves—he couldn't. He knew what it was like to live with those who treated you with hatred for simply being who you were, who you were born to be. He could not imagine what she went through in her life, but he knew it must not have been good if she ended up here. As she was still willing to stay here with women who openly despised her and tried to kill her, her life outside of the saloon must have been much worse.

Perhaps when this was all over, and things had gone his way, he would find a way to repay her for her help. Something that would help her get out of this dead-end town and start over somewhere where no one would know of his connection to Dowes or hers to him.

Dunking the rag back into the bucket once again, Ezra watched his strange companion out of the corner of his eye. If she knew she had his full attention, she gave him no indication, so he allowed his gaze to wander over her even as he halfheartedly cleaned himself.

From what he saw of her, not accounting for the time he had seen her completely nude, she appeared to be a soft, sensual woman that was willing to do anything to pleasure him in ways he couldn't even begin to imagine. Perhaps if he was anyone else, a random traveler passing through in search of a permanent job or if he was one of the miners that worked the veins nearby, if he had not been on a quest to avenge the death of his parents, he might have actually been tempted to partake in what she wanted to offer.

In truth, it did not matter how or where she was endowed as he never took an interest in women, or men for that matter. Encounters of a sexual nature never crossed his mind. All that was on his mind for as long as he remembered was finding the men who killed his parents. When he was going through puberty, and his eyes should have been turning toward girls, he was stuck alone at his grandmother's without anyone to tell him he was supposed to be interested in someone else in such a way.

When he should have been courting young women, he was hunting down the men from that night, one after another. Instead of breaking the hearts of beautiful ladies, he was breaking the bones of the men that would lead him to his parents' killer. He had been on their trail for five long years, and that was all that he ever thought about.

He would give anything to live like a man and enjoy the physical pleasures she would give him, but to lose himself now would be to lose the war. Even without looking, Ezra knew the moment her eyes traveled over his form unabashed, taking his unhurried actions as permission to gaze upon him. Something about the thought of her liking what she was seeing caused Ezra to react in a way he would not have expected possible.

Startled by the sudden sensation swelling between his thighs, Ezra decided it would be best to keep her from discovering the effect she was now having on his body—it would only cause her to be more aggressive in her attempts to get him to do more than just sleep in their bed. He tossed the washcloth to the floor before picking up the bucket of now cold water and dumping it over his head.

Even though the chilly water had the desired effect on himself, cooling his arousal and calming his heart rate, it had the opposite effect on Colleen. As the cold water cascaded over his well-toned chest and the sudden drop in temperature caused his nipples to harden into little beads, he heard Colleen suck in her breath before licking her lips. "You know, Sugar, you make it very difficult to keep my hands to myself when you're quite literally dripping wet. Keep it up, and you won't be the only one," she teased, and he swore he felt her eyes roaming over all of his naked flesh once more.

Something in the husky tone of her voice caused Ezra to shiver in anticipation and, against his better judgment, he played along with her flirtations. He turned toward her fully, not bothering to hide his impressive girth. He needed to keep her off balance, though he could not begin to imagine why he wanted to.

Almost as if his body moved on its own accord, he felt himself give a self-satisfied smirk when she nearly fell over. He made his way toward the tub, keeping his eyes locked on hers. As slowly as possible, Ezra stepped over the edge of the tub with one leg and then the other, submerging his body in the warm water completely before finally breaking eye contact with her as he rested back in the tub.

"You, Sugar, are one hell of a tease," she purred. "Oh, the wonderful things I would do with that body of yours. To that body." She crossed the room to the fire once more and emptied the pan into the tub, making certain to not burn him. Silently he told himself he should stop things before they went any further, but for the first time in his life, Ezra wanted to ignore the logical and just experience something as any other man would.

He would not allow himself to have feelings for her, not even platonic ones, and he certainly would not give in to her desires completely as it would give her too much hold over him. But for the moment, for the short time he remained in the tub, he would indulge in her fantasy. One he was reluctant to admit he was starting to share himself. It had little to do with the woman standing mere feet away from him, he was certain, but more to do with the fact that he craved human contact as any other would.

Deny yourself something for too long, and your body would seek out what it needed as if of its own accord. Refuse to eat, and your survival instincts will always overrule your wishes. That was all this was, his body craving another's touch, a connection to another. As long as it was just his body wishing for her touch, he would not be putting his mission at risk.

"Really? And what would that be, Colleen?" he finally inquired as he relaxed back into the tub and closed his eyes. She sucked in a breath. He smirked once more. One thing he admitted to himself was that he was thoroughly enjoying causing the seemingly confident woman to be off balance.

AS COLLEEN STOOD there in shock, wondering why he was intentionally teasing her, she couldn't help but think about the amazing view he graced her with for the last few minutes. While he was washing, Colleen stood beside the hearth, gazing at his muscular form uninhibited. Since he did not ask her to leave the room, she took it as a sign he didn't care if she saw his naked body and proceeded to memorize every line, every muscle, every last inch of exposed skin.

She allowed her gaze to trail downward, not at all surprised by what she found hanging between his strong legs. It was exactly as she knew it was going to be—long, thick, and very appealing. And that was when it was completely soft. She imagined how much bigger it would get once he was aroused. But that also meant that he was immune to being completely naked in front of her. Honestly, she was a bit disappointed by this realization, but it was completely forgotten when he startled her with his teasing.

"What would I do to you, Sugar, when given the opportunity to touch that magnificent body of yours? I would kneel behind you and massage your shoulders," Colleen began, speaking in an alluring whisper, as she followed her words by kneeling behind the tub, raising her hands so they were hovering a mere inch above his shoulders and imitated a massage. Leaning down so her lips were beside his ear, making sure to not actually touch him, she licked her lips before exhaling her hot breath.

"Once you began to relax from the massage, your body melting into the warm water surrounding you, I would allow my hands to travel lower, letting my nimble fingers rub circles around your pert nipples." As she spoke, her fingers followed her descriptions, keeping the inch of empty air between them. Even as her index finger drew circles in the water above his chest, she saw his body starting to rise involuntarily toward her; before submerging once more before he came into contact with her fingers. "Then," she breathed into his ear, smirking in satisfaction when he shivered, "I will allow my hands to trace your strong muscles down even further.

"They would caress your stomach, featherlight touches that would cause you to squirm beneath my hands. Silently begging me for more. While they teased your stomach, I would lay a trail of soft kisses down your neck before sucking at your pulse." For each pretend kiss, she bestowed him with a breath of hot air blown on to his neck until she reached the spot where she knew she would feel his pulse beating if she moved her lips an inch closer. "I would tease you here for a bit as my hand dipped even lower, finding your impressive manhood and running my fingers across it." She mimicked the motions with her hand; causing the water to churn slightly.

"I would take you in my warm hand, stroking from base to tip and back again as I sucked at your pulse. I would run the fingers of my free hand into your hair; massaging your scalp and causing you to purr beneath my touch. You would beg for me, buck into my hand as I refused to give any more than a light touch," Colleen insisted even as he did as she predicted and bucked into her hand; his slightly erect penis pressing against her hand for a moment before he lowered himself into the tub once more.

A bit startled to actually find him reacting to her words when he was completely unaffected moments before, Colleen felt emboldened and decided to take her teasing to a new level. Removing her hand from the water, she allowed the water to drip onto his bare chest. "I would trail light kisses down your chest," she continued, repeating her earlier actions on his neck. Though her lips never touched his skin, she knew he felt her breath fanning over his cooling skin. She lifted her head and locked eyes with his. "Sit on the edge of the tub."

Though Ezra was following her command, the glazed look in his eyes told Colleen he wasn't aware of what he was doing. Keeping his gaze,

Colleen reached up to where her new skirt gathered at her waist and untied it, letting the material pool on the floor at her feet. Pulling her shirt over her head, it joined her skirt. Dressed only in her corset, slip, and stockings, she stepped into the tub in front of him, ignoring the water that was soaking and weighing down her slip.

Kneeling before him, she reached her hands back up until they were just shy of touching him. "Next I would massage your hip with one hand as I held you with the other," she continued, her phantom touches acting out what she was not allowed to. "As I stroked you, I would kiss the tip before running my tongue across it." The miming of her tongue was almost enough to cause Ezra to break his resolve as her breath fanned over the tip of his penis. Though he refused to give in, it was not hard for Colleen to figure out certain parts of his anatomy was begging him to.

She saw it bobbing instinctively trying to move closer to the heat from her mouth. Smirking arrogantly to herself, she breathed on to the tip of his penis once more and heard him tighten his grip on the edge of the tub, no doubt trying to keep control of himself. "Then, I would take you in my mouth." Colleen opened her mouth wide enough to take him in without actually touching him. Breathing down the length of his shaft, she waited for a moment before pulling back off of him completely, even as her own body begged her to close her lips around him. "That, Sugar, is what I could do to your body if you would but let me touch you."

Rising and backing up, ignoring the water splashing over the sides at her sudden movement, Colleen's cheeks flushed as she glanced up and found him panting. "Colleen," he growled as his knuckles turned white from his grip on the tub. Instead of answering him, she climbed back out of the tub and opened the trunk that contained the towels.

"You need but remove your no touching rule, Sugar, and all that, and so much more, would be yours. But for now, it sounds like your friend has company," she whispered, gesturing toward the loud knocking coming from the other room before holding open the towel for him. As Ezra rose from the tub, Colleen wrapped him in a towel before backing away so he was able to step out of the tub and make his way over to the fire.

# Chapter Eight

EDGEWOOD 1830

Hearing a knock sound at his door, Gill Dowes buttoned his pants before heading toward it. Ignoring the still half-naked woman on his bed, he opened the door and stepped back to allow his guest to enter the room. "Katherine, see to our dinner. You can rejoin me as soon as I am done here." She walked out while still pulling her corset closed over her ample bosom. Once she was out of sight, Dowes closed and locked the door, turning his full attention to the man before him.

Claiborne Sedden stood nearly as wide as he was tall and at almost six feet, that was an impressive feat. His sandy blond hair was thinning in more places than it wasn't, and dark spots of perspiration stained his once white shirt. Though he had never been a lean or handsome man, the last few years has aged him. Dowes wasn't sure what caused the premature aging and excessive weight gain, but in their line of work, he wasn't surprised to see such a drastic change. Their jobs tended to be extremely stressful and, while he relieved his stress by coming to Katherine, Sedden apparently relieved his through food.

"When is the next shipment of guns scheduled to be transported by train?"

Sedden pulled a paper from the lining of his hat and handed it to him. As the heavier man was completely uneducated, he always delivered his information in such a way. The man that sold the guns, Hector Backus, would send a simple message that meant absolutely nothing to anyone who did not know what it referred to.

Even Sedden himself remained unaware of what the message actually contained. It was a very simple arrangement, and it had been working for months. Backus would sell a shipment of guns to a sheriff in a far-off town having problems with local gunmen. Their gunmen. Then he would send word to Dowes to let him know when and where to attack the shipment. Dowes would get the guns back, and they would resell them to another sheriff in another town.

The con was fueling most of the money they needed for their operations in the area. And there were quite a few currently in effect. Besides the gun heists, there were three mining camps—including the salt mine outside of town, a silver mine a few days ride to the east, and a copper mine a day and a half to the northwest—countless saloons and brothels, a few ranches where they put the cattle they rustled, and a few other smaller operations scattered about.

Dowes never paid much attention to the other branches of their gang as they never overlapped with his own. He received his instructions about the train, robbed it, and then delivered the guns back to Backus. By the time he arrived back in town to wait for the next shipment, as it took Backus time to set up another sell, weeks had already passed since he was last there. It was no wonder Katherine often complained about how little he spent time with her. Glancing down at the paper in his hand, he silently read each line of the note.

*April 5th.*

*4:30 a.m.*

*12th*

The date and time were obvious—he would simply board the train when it came through a few towns over and wait until the designated time to rob it. This was done so the robberies couldn't be linked back to him or connected, as they were always in different areas and at different times.

The final line was simply the number of the car the guns were stored in—twelfth from the front. The heist would go off without a hitch, he was confident, as all the others had before it. He would make his way toward the car, pretending to be lost, when the one or two deputies who were sent to pick up the guns from Backus, would tell him the car was off limits to passengers. He would draw one toward him, and Sedden would shoot the other from behind after coming in through the opposite door.

So far, it was a fail proof plan. And he was certain it would remain that way for a very long time to come. He crumpled the paper. "Head out tonight. I'll spend one more day with Katherine and then join you."

COLLEEN BARELY HAD the chance to close the bedroom door behind them when Ezra startled her with a frustrated "Damn it!" He sounded angry enough to throw things around the room. Maybe if they weren't worried about the man next door, he would have.

She watched helplessly as he paced the room. What was wrong? How could she fix it?

After a few minutes, he apparently noticed her concerned expression as he explained, "Nothing of use was said between them. Hell, never even heard the second man speak! That means I will have to interrogate him. Doing so increases my risk of getting caught. And there is no guarantee there isn't even a place to take him to force more information out of him if I do manage to get him out. Which means I have to interrogate him in the room. But that other girl doesn't leave him for very long. I need to find a way to separate them for a while."

He sat down on the bed with a huff of annoyance before letting himself fall back until he was lying with his legs still dangling over the edge. Colleen wondered if he even realized how much he had said to her.

Sure, she knew the man had something to do with the death of his parents, and he was waiting on the second man, but if he needed to interrogate him, that must mean he was looking for more than the two of them. Were others involved in the death of his parents? If so, how? Did he trust her enough to tell her how he was planning to interrogate him? Did he not realize she could simply go next door and sell that information to him?

If it was anyone else with him, Colleen was certain they already would have turned him in. After all, who was he to her, a struggling saloon girl that starved more often than she didn't? He was another customer, a chance to make a few bucks and even though he earned her the most money of any of her other clients, by far, she knew with certainty that Dowes would pay good money for the information as well. Perhaps even more than she made off of Ezra.

But standing there in silence, Colleen knew without even having to think about it that she would never turn the man before her in. Just the thought of making Katherine lose one of her main sources of income was enough of a reason to not betray him, but even more than that, Colleen had to admit that there was a strange connection to this man she only met a few days before. More than the fact that he decided she was worth saving, even at the risk to himself, more than once.

More than her obvious attraction to him. Ezra was a kindred spirit. He was all alone in the world just as she was. He was willing to risk everything to take a chance on her, how could she ever do anything but the same? He saw her as more than an abomination, as almost everyone else before him including her own mother had, and if given the time, Colleen was certain he would come to see her as a friend.

It went without saying as far as she was concerned, but she would never betray him; she would do anything to help him. For Colleen, an actual connection with another human being came so few and far between that she knew she needed to hold on to this one by any means necessary. For as long as possible. But wanting to help and being able to, was two completely different things. Having no idea what was actually going on made it difficult for her to be of use to him.

"I don't expect you to tell me all of your secrets, Sugar, I realize we have not known each other long enough for you to know with certainty that you can trust me. But I do need to have some idea of what is actually going on to be able to help you. You said Dowes had something to do with the death of your parents, yet your words make it seem as though there were others as well.

"What do you hope to learn from him by interrogating him? If you already know he killed them, or at least helped to, who else are you looking for? What happened to your parents, Sugar?" She sat down next to him on the bed. For a moment, Colleen suspected he wasn't going to answer her as he turned his gaze toward the ceiling. Eventually though, he turned toward to her, and she was graced with an enticing sight as the towel around his waist to parted slightly, exposing the well-toned muscle where his thigh met his hip.

As Colleen held his gaze with her own, she swore he was searching her eyes for any sign of an ulterior motive but was unconcerned as she knew he would find nothing but her honest curiosity. She remained silent, knowing it couldn't be easy to share your history with another person. Colleen had never told a soul about the horrible things that happened to her. From the way he looked at her, emotions dancing in his eyes, she was certain he hadn't either.

"When I was a child, my parents were killed in front of me. Men came to our home one night, just past midnight, and for reasons I still do not completely understand, they murdered my parents. By some freak twist of fate, I learned the name of one of the men who was there that night and tracked him down. Dowes is the third man whom I found, and he must lead me to the next, no matter the cost." Ezra's eyes grew hard as he spoke of the man in the room beside them.

It was the bare minimum of information, Colleen knew, but it was a start, and it was enough to convince her to help him. What she wouldn't give to have that kind of love for her parents, to want to honor them by avenging their deaths. She wasn't even sure she would bat an eye if she ever learned her parents were already dead. Ezra, on the other hand, would go to the ends of the earth, would risk his own life for parents long dead.

She may not have known how many men were actually there that night, only that there were more than three. She may not have known who these men were or why they killed his parents, but she was certain she knew which side of the law they fell on. Judging by the kind of man their son became, she knew his parents were not all that bad. Besides that, there was no way Dowes was ever the good guy in any scenario.

"He will meet the same fate as the other two..." Ezra vowed, though she was not sure who she was speaking to, himself or her, drawing her attention back to him. As she sat there in silence, he began his tale.

"YEARS AFTER MY parents were killed, I was living at my mother's childhood home when men came to rob it. By pure chance, their leader mentioned the gang that killed my parents—the Pine Box Crew—and the name of the man who was in charge of them, McKinley. I tracked him down and managed to get the name of Thomas Morton from him. I was planning on simply knocking him out once I had all the information I needed from him, but there was a struggle, and in the darkness, I accidentally stabbed him. It wasn't planned, but I do not regret his death now. I learned the hard way with Morton that I cannot afford to leave any of them alive.

"I spent six months being a part of a low-level group controlled by Morton and eventually worked my way up to his inner circle. He was never alone, so I could not just ambush him as I had with McKinley, and instead, I tried to get information out him during our regular interactions. I must not have been as careful as I thought, and he realized something was going on. He ambushed me one day, with four of his men, and I was the only one who walked away.

"I managed to get Dowes' name out of him. I tracked him down through other low-level grunts and found my way here. I set out to bring the men who killed my parents to justice, but I learned along the way that it was not true justice that I was after but revenge plain and simple.

"All that matters to me is completing my mission, no matter what it takes. It may make me ruthless, but I cannot afford to let any of them find out about my plans. I will never find all the men responsible if they do. Know this, Colleen, if it turns out my trust in you is sadly misplaced, and you put what I am doing at risk, you will suffer a fate to rival theirs."

Though his threat hung heavy in the air, Colleen realized it did not frighten her. Thinking back over all he told her, she realized he spoke nothing of the future. Ezra mentioned nothing about anyone past Dowes even though she knew there was at least one other still to be found. It did not matter to her. She did not need to know what came after this as she would only be there to help him with Dowes.

"Well, Sugar, it may not be much, but I can at least help you with tonight; I know the perfect way to keep her out of his room for a while. In fact, the opportunity to distract should be presenting itself in a few minutes. Just in case you have to get out of here quick afterward and we don't get a chance to see each other again, it was a pleasure to meet you, Ezra. I hope you find all that you seek and that you don't lose yourself in the process."

He put his hand over hers. "After tonight, you should leave here too. Tonight can only end in death, and it would be best not to be around when others realize what has happened. I will find you and a way to repay you one day for your help, no matter how long it takes."

She pulled her hand away and stood. Any words of gratitude she thought of in that moment sounded hollow in her mind. Instead, she chose to lighten the mood. "I can think of a few good ways for you to pay me back the next time we meet, Sugar." Colleen smirked. She turned serious once more. "Give me about five minutes before you head to his room. If I am unable to distract her as I have planned, I will come back here within five minutes to let you know."

She slipped out of the room without waiting for him to say good-bye. Colleen closed the door, pressed her back against it, and sighed. There was something about that man who had her heart pounding just being in the same room with him. Her sweaty palms, dry mouth, and nearly throbbing heartbeat were new sensations for her, and although she knew what they symbolized, no man ever caused such a reaction in her before.

No one ever even come close to making her feel like a giddy, young girl experiencing her first crush, even if that was exactly what she was. Even the men she found herself attracted to, making her job that much easier to perform, never came close to making her feel something real. Now that she finally found someone, she had to watch him walk away.

# Chapter Nine

EDGEWOOD 1830

After tonight, Ezra would most likely be unable to return. He would be off following whatever new lead he found, and Colleen would be left behind once more. Startled by the sudden, unexpected connection to her mother, Colleen shook her head and pushed herself off the door; making her way toward the bathing room. She did not have time to stand around feeling sorry for herself. Ezra would only be waiting for five minutes before he made his move, and if she didn't hurry up, she would not be able to distract Katherine before she returned to Dowes' room.

Making her way down the hall, clearing all thoughts of Ezra and her mother from her mind, Colleen almost instantly heard the sound of giggles and inane conversations coming from the girls within the room. A quick glance at the sign hanging outside confirmed her earlier assumption that it would be bathing time for the saloon girls. 'Enter only if you wish to pay fifty cents per girl currently bathing inside' was usually enough of a deterrent to keep the men away.

Before today, it was enough to keep her away too; not wanting to risk their wrath or them stealing her money to pay for the 'show.' Fortunately, Katherine tended to use this time to give her body a break from Dowes instead of just bathing in his room. Taking a deep breath, Colleen pushed open the door and stepped inside; ignoring the blast of hot air that greeted her. It was not hard to figure out, based on the immediate silence that followed her entering the room, that the girls were aware she was there, but she paid them no mind.

Tossing her towel over one of the empty chairs nearby, Colleen pulled off each of her stockings slowly before placing them on the chair. Purposefully ignoring the startled gasps coming from behind her, she untied the strings of her loose corset before removing the constricting garment and tossing it on top of her stockings. Steeling herself for what was going to come, knowing it was only a matter of time before they lost their patience, Colleen allowed her final pieces of clothing to fall to the ground.

Tossing her skirt and slip on to the growing pile of clothes on the chair, she turned toward the others with a soft, innocent smile on her face as she approached one of the empty tubs. "What the hell do you think you are doing?!" Katherine demanded and Colleen had to fight the urge to laugh when she covered her chest with her hands. Modest women they were not. "You need to leave this room right now unless you plan on paying each of us a dollar for the show. Freaks get charged double," she insisted as some of the other girls rose from their tubs and wrapped themselves in towels.

Apparently, even the thought of making money was not enough of a reason to keep them in the same room as her. Ignoring their treatment as it was nothing new, she turned back to Katherine with a smile. "I'm taking a bath, silly," she explained with a slight chuckle as she waved her hand dismissively before stepping one foot and then the other into the warm water. "And actually, I checked, that sign doesn't exclude me from being included with the girls. I work here, so I am afforded the same protections as the rest of you."

It was a lie. The barkeeper told her, soon after she arrived, that she was not on the same level as the other girls and that he would always choose them over her. It made sense, seeing as they made him a lot more money than she dreamed of making, so she did not fault him for his obvious favoritism, but that didn't matter at the moment anyway. She was only saying these things in order to piss the girls off and, judging by Katherine's screech, it was working. Colleen barely had time to submerge her lower half into the water before a very wet and naked Katherine was climbing out of her tub and stomping her way over.

The attempt to be intimidating fell rather short as her bare, wet feet barely made a sound on the floor and Colleen didn't bother trying to suppress a giggle as she relaxed back into the water. "You planning on joining me, Sugar? If you are, it's fifty cents," Colleen mocked, knowing she was pushing things too far, but refusing to stop. It felt good to piss off the woman standing before her after everything she put her through in the last few years.

At least this time, when they beat her to within an inch of her life, she would have actually done something to warrant their wrath. Unlike all the other times before. "Not much room in here for two, but you're welcome to sit on my lap," Colleen offered even as she ran her hand up her leg; letting it dip into the water where it covered the juncture between her legs before drawing it up to caress her chest. She put on her most seductive expression, biting on the corner of her bottom lip, tilting her head to the side and glancing up at her through her long eyelashes.

The effect was instantaneous. Katherine screeched once more as she lunged forward, grabbing hold of Colleen's hair and started pulling her backward out of the tub. Not wanting to risk her pulling out her hair in an attempt to get her all the way out, Colleen pushed up from the bottom of the tub, forcing herself up and over the edge. The two landed on the floor in as a pile of twisted, naked limbs with Colleen crying out as her head smacked against the unrelenting floor.

Katherine disentangled herself and punched her in the face before she had the chance to react. For such a tiny woman, she packed one hell of a punch, made worse by the bruises that had yet to heal from Etta's ambush, but Colleen didn't dare try to fight back. Though she was pretty certain she could defeat her easily, fighting her off meant the other girls would join in. She knew she had no hope of defeating all of them.

So, fighting against her most basic instincts to save herself, Colleen took the beating from the extremely pissed off woman that was now straddling her stomach, pinning her arms down with her naked thighs.

Not wanting to risk any further damage to her face, Colleen was about to buck her off when a sudden shot boomed from across the hall, startling them both. Apparently realizing which room it came from before Colleen did, Katherine cried out. "Gill!" even as Colleen felt her weight lifting off of her. Katherine jumped to her feet and rushed toward the door, startling Colleen by using his first name. She only ever heard Katherine refer to him by Dowes in the many times that he visited.

Boots pounded on the stairs. Though it was impossible to know how many there were for sure, Colleen guessed there were at least three men heading in the direction the shot came from. She followed them as they rushed toward the room, a still naked Katherine not far behind. A moment later, a second shot rang out. The men pulled out their guns.

Afraid for Ezra's safety, she dared not even breathe his name in case he managed to get away, and they had no idea who was in there with Dowes. If he was lucky enough to escape without being injured before they were able to break into the room, Colleen was not about to put him in more danger by announcing who he was. Instead, she grabbed a towel on her way out of the room and wrapped it around herself as a half a dozen men busted down the door.

There was a muffled commotion coming from the room before two of the men returned, dragging a body from the room as they left.

ONCE THE FIVE minutes had passed, Ezra made his way toward the balcony once more. Stepping out into the near complete darkness, Ezra silently closed the door behind him before turning his attention to the balcony across from him. Taking a deep breath, he stepped up to the railing climbed up onto the edge.

As he assumed before, traveling from one balcony to the other proved to be easy. Climbing down, Ezra stepped silently on to the balcony and made his way over toward Dowes' room. The door was locked. Pulling out his knife, he lifted the latch as he had on his own door and slowly pushed it open. Though it made a slight squeaking noise, the hinges apparently not accustomed to being used, he breathed a sigh of relief when the sleeping occupant on the bed continued to dream on unaware. Closing the balcony door, but leaving it unlocked for an easier escape, he closed the distance between them even as he put away his knife and pulled out his gun from the belt around his waist.

Ezra watched the man sleeping peacefully on his bed as though there wasn't a problem in the world. Caressing the butt of his gun, he released the breath he did not know he was holding before pressing the barrel up against his cheek. For a moment, Dowes continued to sleep on, but as Ezra pressed harder, his eyes fluttered open. The instant they did, Ezra felt him pulling away and shook his head, pressing the gun more firmly against his cheek.

"Where is Godfrey de Voe?! Tell me where he is, and you might live through the night." Instead of answering, Dowes sneered at him before turning and glancing up at the ceiling, acting as though there wasn't a gun pressed up against his cheek.

Certain he did not have time to play games, as there was no telling how long Colleen could keep the other woman busy, Ezra flipped the gun in his hand so he was holding on to the barrel, cold-cocking Dowes with the handle before righting it once more. "Where is Godfrey de Voe!?" he demanded again, the gun once again pressed against his flesh.

"You have no idea who you are messing with, kid. I will kill you," Dowes promised. "I ain't tellin' you shit, kid. He'd kill me in far worse ways than imaginable."

Looking into his eyes, Ezra knew he was speaking the truth. That would not bode well for Ezra, either that night or in the long run. If the men he was hunting feared De Voe more than him, he would get no information out of them. At least not about Godfrey de Voe. But, if he was able to find enough of them, perhaps he would be able to find something they feared more than their boss.

"Around ten years ago you ran around with a group of twelve men. Where are they now?" Ezra demanded. Even though Dowes opened his mouth to speak, perhaps to tell him off again or maybe give up one of the men he was searching for, Ezra would never hear what he had to say.

At that same moment, Ezra heard a woman cry out in pain and, instinctively knowing it was Colleen, he turned toward the closed door for only an instant. Even as his head began to turn, he knew he made a mistake and whipped back toward Dowes; finding those few seconds were enough time to turn the tide. Time seemed to slow before him as Dowes pulled his hand out from beneath his pillow.

Ezra knew without a doubt there would be a gun in his hand. An instant later, he heard it cocking and knew he would not be able to raise his gun quick enough to get out of this unscathed. No other course before him, Ezra did the only thing he thought of to do at that moment and dropped to the floor. Not a second later and a shot rang out above him, causing his ears to ring.

Taking aim at the bed above him, as he was unable to see Dowes's form, Ezra tried to plan his next action, but the decision was made for him as a shadow rose on the wall behind the bed. With a mind of its own, his gun raised and took aim at the bed, his finger already itching at the trigger.

As he exhaled, Ezra pulled the trigger and a second shot echoed in the room, followed closely by a cry of pain. Before he got the chance to make sure the wound was fatal, Dowes's body fell forward off of the bed, landing on top of him and pinning him to the floor. Though he heard the feet pounding up the stairs and men banging just outside the room, he was trapped and unable to get away.

# Chapter Ten

EDGEWOOD 1830

As time seemed to slow down, Colleen tried to make out anything that would identify who they were carrying, but the deputies blocked her view. She couldn't tell who they were dragging from the room.

From where she stood, it was impossible to tell if the man was dead or alive. A scream drew her attention away from the mystery man to the room where Katherine was standing in the entryway, obviously upset by what she saw inside. Moving a bit closer, Colleen was able to make out Dowes' lifeless form on the floor and breathed a sigh of relief. The other man was Ezra, and he must be alive. Otherwise, they would have left his body with Dowes'.

One of the deputies grabbed Katherine and turned her away from the horrifying sight in the room. Unfortunately, that brought Colleen back into her view. "This is all your fault!" she screamed as she fought against his hold, trying to get to her. "Your disgusting client did this!"

"Maybe you should leave, miss," the deputy suggested sympathetically as he glanced toward Colleen without breaking his grip on Katherine. The laugh that came from her was not unexpected, but the sound sent a shiver down Colleen's spine. In that moment, she knew the woman across from her was capable of far more cruelty than she ever imagined.

"That isn't a miss. That is a disgusting abomination, and I am going to kill it!" Katherine vowed as she struggled anew. Worried she might actually be able to break free of his hold, Colleen turned and fled, grabbing her clothing from the bathing room before heading to Ezra's room. Knowing she would be safe there for the moment at least, as she held the only key, she locked the door behind her and rested up against it once more.

Hearing Katherine bang on it behind her, Colleen jumped before pressing back even harder to ensure it couldn't be opened. After a few tense moments passed, realizing her banging was not going to bust it open, Colleen stepped away and took a quick glance around the room. Everything was as she left it about ten minutes before, other than Ezra not being there.

She went to the balcony and glanced over at the room beside it. Through the curtains, she saw the deputies that remained behind standing over Dowes' body. Turning her attention away from them, she looked to the street below, barely able to make out the forms of the two deputies dragging Ezra between them.

THOUGH THE BLOW the deputy had landed on Ezra's face hadn't knocked him unconscious, he sure wished it had. His head was pounding, and he wouldn't be surprised if he bruised a few ribs when Dowes landed on him. Though he did not have long after the second shot before the deputies busted into the room, he at least got the chance to confirm he died.

That alone was some consolation. If he was to die soon, at least he took out three of the men he was searching for. It was nowhere near what he would have wished for, but it was better than nothing. At least those three would never be able to hurt anyone else again; cause another poor child to become an orphan. Perhaps someone else, who hated them as much as he did, would finish what he started.

Not wanting to risk getting hit again, Ezra continued to feign unconsciousness and allowed himself to be dragged all the way to the jailhouse. The moment they stepped crossed the threshold, the scent of stale urine and dried blood assaulted his senses. Fortunately, his stay there would most likely prove to be a short one.

Ezra grunted as he was thrown unceremoniously into the first cell, and heard it lock a moment later. Picking himself up, he dusted off his pants before glancing around at his new, albeit temporary home. Within his cell, there was a small pile of straw apparently meant to be used as a bed, a bucket for waste and nothing else. Glancing toward the cell beside his, he found it was exactly the same except for the fact that it was empty.

The sheriff approached the cell. "Don't get comfortable. You're set to hang at dawn. We take murder very seriously in this town and, unfortunately for your sake, we are too small to have our own judge. We don't bother to wait the week it would take him to get down here to give you a trial.

"You were the only one in the room, your gun was used, and you were quite literally buried under the evidence. Consider yourself tried and found guilty. Make peace with your maker." The sheriff turned to one of the deputies. "Stay here and watch the prisoner while we deal with the aftermath at the saloon." Without waiting for a reply, the sheriff stepped back out of the jailhouse with the second deputy following close behind.

Grumbling to himself about being stuck babysitting, the deputy turned his back on Ezra and sat down at the desk nearby. Sighing softly to himself, Ezra glanced around his cell once more and tried to determine the best, and hopefully cleanest, place to sit down. With very few options, one to be exact, he made his way over to the straw bed and collapsed unceremoniously.

It would be a long night alone in the cell, but at the same time, Ezra knew the morning would come far too quickly. If this was to be his last night alive, he would make the best of it instead of sitting there feeling sorry for himself. But stuck in this cell, there wasn't very much for him to do with his last few hours. Perhaps sit around thinking about the last few years and everything he had done or hadn't done.

Or wonder about the strange woman he met recently. Try to figure out what caused her to come to such a place and work as a saloon girl. Or why she was still here when no one seemed to want her. Wonder what kind of a childhood she must have lived to lead her life to what it has become? But as he had no way to get the answer to any of his questions. Doing so seemed as fruitless as counting the strands of straw in his bed.

That only left him with one option; come up with a plan to escape before sunrise. Though judging by what he saw in the cell and jailhouse around him, there was little to work with. Glancing outside the bars in front him, Ezra spotted the keys to both his cell and the one next to it hanging from the guard's belt.

There were two desks in the middle of the room, one that was cluttered with wanted posters and other law enforcement reports. The other was clutter free and organized. The second Ezra was sure belonged to the sheriff. A half dozen pegs were lined up on the far wall; four of them had hats or coats hanging from them while the other two had gun belts. The first he recognized as his own and the second likely belonged to the deputy that was left to guard him.

If he somehow managed to get the deputy to come close to the cell, maybe he'd be able to grab the keys from his belt. Naturally, he would have to knock him out somehow to give himself enough time to unlock his cell door. That shouldn't be too hard to do though, the old "grabbing the shirt and pulling him into the bars" should work nicely.

The only problem with that idea was the fact that the deputy seemed to be currently sleeping with his feet propped up on the desk. But, with a little luck, that might actually work in his favor. If he decided to wake him suddenly once he was in a deep enough sleep, he might be groggy enough to make him easier to knock off balance. Giving the sleeping deputy one last glance, Ezra laid back on his bed to wait for an opportune moment.

COLLEEN WATCHED FROM the balcony, refusing to go back inside as Katherine was still pounding away on her door. The sheriff and one of his deputies made their way back over to the saloon after only being gone a few minutes. But at least with them being one deputy short that meant that they left one back at the jail to watch Ezra, and dead men needed no guards.

He was alive, perhaps only for now, but it was something at least. The men disappeared into the saloon; she could guess where they were going.

Colleen made her way to the connecting bathing room. Even though the fires would be long dead by now, she doubted anyone had the time to close the vents, allowing her the chance to hear what was being said in Dowes' room.

As she held her breath, afraid even the slightest sound might prevent her from hearing something important, she barely made out the sound of the sheriff whistling as he entered the room. "This is going to take hours," he complained, his voice barely carrying into the adjourning bathing room, let alone into the one Colleen was standing in.

"Send for the grave digger...prepare the hanging tree for sunrise... deal with the mess in this room..." Colleen only made out bits and pieces of his instructions. Not enough to even figure out how many deputies were in there with him. At least three, unless he was giving more than one task to a single man. Just to be on the safe side, she decided to count each one separately.

That meant including the sheriff and the deputy left at the jailhouse with Ezra, there were at least five lawmen. What good this information was to her, Colleen wasn't sure yet, but at least she had it if she ever figured that out. Hearing the voice of the sheriff coming through the wall again, she turned her attention back to him.

"I'm heading home for my wife's cooking. You can head home yourselves once you are finished. Meet back at the jail before dawn." As he spoke, his instructions became harder to hear, the sheriff apparently heading back out of the room. Colleen smiled to herself despite the current situation. There would only be one deputy guarding the jail all night. At the very least, she should have no problem getting in to say good-bye if nothing else.

Giving the men plenty of time to finish up their tasks and head home, Colleen stepped back into the main room and listened for any sign Katherine might still be waiting for her outside in the hallway. Hearing none, she quietly unlocked and opened the door. Sticking her head out enough to see down the hall, she listened for any sound that indicated anyone was still around.

Faintly she heard the men laughing and carrying on downstairs like nothing ever happened upstairs. It wasn't surprising—this wasn't the first time someone was killed in the saloon, and certainly wouldn't be the last. Though the men who were killed tended to be attacked downstairs—a game of poker getting out of hand or two customers fighting over the same girl. She listened for any sounds coming from the upstairs. Just barely, above the noise from downstairs, she heard the faint sobs coming from a few rooms down on the other side of the hall and the voices of some of the other girls trying to console Katherine. Knowing that meant there was little chance anyone downstairs knew of her connection to Ezra, other than perhaps the barkeeper who quite possibly was upset in the loss of a customer with a seemingly bottomless coin purse, Colleen decided to go ahead and risk heading down. Though she was a bit surprised that he had not come upstairs with the deputies, she supposed she shouldn't have been. If he left the bar unattended, it would make it that much easier for a thief to take advantage of the situation. He would never do anything that had even the slightest chance of hurting his income.

That, of course, led to a larger problem for her. There was always the chance that he would take out the loss of income on her. But, at the very least, she was certain he would not kill her for it. Katherine, on the other hand, she couldn't say the same for. There was no telling what that woman was capable of doing especially now that Dowes was dead. The only thing that Colleen knew for sure was that she needed to get away before Katherine had the chance to regain control over herself and exact her revenge. Only problem with that, was Colleen had little money and no horse to get away on.

As she walked downstairs, her beaten and battered appearance went unnoticed, and she headed toward the bar. "Can I get two meals? Thought I might take over a last meal for the man they dragged out of here and see if I can't get whoever is stuck watching him to part with some of his money," she lied, just in case he was not aware it was her client yet, as she handed over the money to pay for them. She needed to get into the little over three dollars she earned since Ezra arrived, most of which came from him, but, somehow she knew it would prove to be worth it. Taking the money, he reached behind the bar and handed her two tickets.

"Shouldn't you still be servicing your own client? I can hand the task over to one of the open girls, lost a few patrons tonight with all that went on so more than usual aren't busy. You should take him for all he has while you can, who knows if you will ever be lucky enough to get a customer wanting an expensive room and you again," he told her, though his expression and tone were angry, she realized that it was not directed at her.

Much like she was unable to, the barkeep had not been able to see who was dragged out by the deputies and, at least for now, he was not connecting his loss to her. Hoping Katherine would be too upset to fill him in, at least for now, Colleen decided to help keep him from putting things together on his own. "No need to worry none about that, Sugar, I already milked him dry before this unfortunateness happened. He made that clear when I refused to give him tomorrow's stay free of charge, and he beat me in response."

Gesturing to her face, knowing Katherine was likely to keep her mouth shut for that at least, as she risked getting in trouble herself for attacking another one of his workers, she decided to let the blame fall on Ezra for her current state. "The cur ran off at the sound of gunfire, puny tail between his legs, but his room is already paid for through the night, so I'm gonna take advantage of the hot bath and comfortable bed; if you have no objections of course."

As she paused, the look he gave her clearly indicated he did not care in the least, and she wasn't surprised. It did not look like there would be another rich customer wanting the room tonight, judging by those still scattered across the main room, and even if they did, the third room was still available. "Well, best be getting to the diner before they close for the night," she told him with a smile before taking the two tickets he held out and making her way outside.

GETTING IN JUST under the wire, Colleen managed to grab two meals, with instructions to clean the dishes herself before she returned them, right before the diner closed up for the night, and went to the jailhouse. Carefully carrying the tray in one hand, she knocked lightly on the door before pushing it open with her foot. "Hey sugar, Sheriff sent me over with a meal for y'all," she informed him, giving her best sultry smile while also giving him a quick once over to ensure he was not the one that was holding Katherine in the hallway.

If it was, and he believed what she said, things might not go as smoothly as she would hope. Satisfied he wasn't, and not recognizing him from any other time he might have visited the saloon, Colleen was confident that, even if he knew someone like her existed at the saloon, he would not actually know that it was her personally, she pressed on. "I thought you might get lonely all by yourself here with the other deputies busy over at the saloon. I'm sure he's not much for company," Colleen joked as she stepped further into the room and set the tray down on his desk. As she moved, she made sure to sway her hips as much as possible, knowing his eyes were on her.

"Not so lonely anymore with such a pretty thing to keep me company," he told her, confirming either his ignorance to who she was or his being one of the men that was unbothered by it, giving her what he must have thought was a charming smile. Though with his mouthful of rotting, half missing teeth, it mostly just turned her stomach. As he slapped her on the ass, she giggled softly before handing him his meal and grabbing the other, making her way over to Ezra's cell.

Leaning down to push his plate through the small opening on the bottom of the cell door, she glanced over her shoulder to make sure the deputy was preoccupied with his own food to pay attention. "The sheriff plans to hang you at dawn. Any suggestion on what to do now?" she whispered as he reached out for the plate.

His hand touched hers briefly. Smiling softly at the unintentional action, Colleen was so busy staring at his hand, almost as if willing it to touch her again, that she almost missed what he was saying. "In my room under the wardrobe there is a loose floorboard, my coin purse is under it. There is not much left, less than twenty bucks in fact, but it's yours. Thank you for all your help," he whispered with a soft smile.

Before she got the chance to explain that wasn't what she meant, the deputy banged on the bars above their heads, startling both of them. "Stop harassing the lady you scoundrel," he demanded before reaching his hand down to grasp hers, helping her rise to her feet. Kissing the back of her hand, he released her and led her back to the front door.

Tilting her head to the side like she was blushing, Colleen allowed herself to be guided back, stopping in the threshold to turn back. Glancing up through thick, batting lashes, she trained her eyes on Ezra though the deputy was none the wiser as he was too busy staring at her forced cleavage. "If you have no objections, I think I might come back and visit you later. I'm sure I'd make for much better company."

Without waiting for his reply, Colleen turned and made her way back into the night, a plan already forming in her mind. There were a few kinks to work out certainly, but she knew what she needed to do now. Though strange and perhaps a bit sudden, Colleen had never been so sure of anything before in her life. She knew, had known from almost the moment she met him, that there was something about this man that would change her life forever.

What it was or why she felt it, she honestly had no idea, she only knew that he was the only thing that mattered at the moment to her. What she was about to do would change her entire life, but nothing ever felt more right. She now knew the reason Ezra was brought into her life. Perhaps even the reason why she stayed at the saloon in the first place. Somehow fate put her in the path of this incredible man who was trying to avenge the murder of his parents.

They were connected, their lives intertwined even if she never saw him again after tomorrow, and for the first time in her life, she had the chance to do something of real meaning. Ezra found her to be worth saving and she knew in her heart, with such certainty that it actually frightened her a little bit, that he was worth risking everything for. Steeling her shoulders and making her way back toward the saloon, Colleen couldn't help but smile at the single thought that was flowing through her mind at that moment.

Before sunrise, before the sheriff returned to hang him, she was going to bust him out of jail.

# Chapter Eleven

EDGEWOOD 1830

As unnoticed as she was when she left about ten minutes before, Colleen returned to the saloon the same way. Only this time, it wasn't because the men were too busy drinking their whiskey or playing poker to pay her any mind, but that they had all gone home, or upstairs for those that could afford it, to retire for the night. She hadn't thought it was so late already, with the diner closing not that long ago, but as she still heard a few of the deputies upstairs, perhaps the sheriff told the barkeeper to close up early.

Colleen quietly climbed the stairs, putting on a polite smile to any deputy whom she passed. Making her way toward Ezra's room, she waited outside, listening for any sound to indicate the other girls were still awake. Hearing nothing but the noise the deputies were making in the other room, Colleen moved to unlock the door; only to realize it already was. Stepping inside the room, she locked it behind her before glancing around the room and instantly noticed everything was out of place.

The sheets and blankets were thrown off of the bed, piled up on the floor beside it. The wardrobe was open, the few items the saloon keeps in there for the customers scattered on the floor. Ezra's Stetson hat tossed across the room with what looked like a boot print collapsing the center. Apparently, the barkeeper opened the room with his master key while she was gone as she still had the only customer key still on her. That also meant he already knew the man that shot Dowes was her customer or, at least, that the sheriff believed it was.

Why was he not waiting downstairs to call her out on her lie about him taking off when the gunfire happened? Why was he not threatening to take the loss of business out on her? Or at least sending one of the deputies to talk to her? None of those she passed seemed to be aware of her connection with Ezra. Perhaps, by some strange luck that she was not accustomed to having, the saloon's owner did not put things together yet.

Though, even if that were the case, Colleen was certain it was only a matter of time. Deciding she needed an excuse for her lie, she decided it would be best to tell them the truth; half of it anyway. She would simply explain to any who asked that she was in the bathing room at the time of the gunshots and assumed he ran off when he heard them. Even if the girls decided to deny she was there, hoping to either cover up for what Katherine did to her or attempting to get her into trouble, the deputy that held Katherine back was sure to remember the encounter.

Turning her thoughts away from outside of the room, she walked into the bathing room, and found it to be pretty much untouched other than the fact that the few items in the room, such as the chair and washing bucket, we're in slightly different places than they were the last time she was in this room. On the far side of the room, there was a bit of soot from the fireplace scattered on the floor, the deputies probably searching for whatever they thought he might have hidden there, before tracking it across the room in the form of dark, filthy boot prints.

In case her plan failed and she was forced to deal with the consequences in the morning, Colleen decided it would be best to clean up as she was expected to do after a customer of hers used it. She needed to find a way to waste some time anyway, and cleaning was as good a way as any to pass the time. Making her way to the bucket of cold water, its contents already slightly dingy as the deputy apparently used it to wash his hands after rooting around in the ashes, she stripped down to her corset and stockings, not wanting to risk getting her only dress covered in soot, and began scrubbing the floor on her hands and knees.

As she worked, a thought popped into her mind suddenly, and she was imaging Ezra walking into the room behind her, finding her bare ass waving back and forth as she cleaned. She imagined him coming closer, his hand already cupping his impressive manhood through his pants, his hungry eyes trained on her bare flesh. Shaking her head, she cleared the stray thought before turning her attention back to her task. Once she was finished up with the floor, she straightened up the room and headed back into the other room. him coming closer, his hand already cupping his impressive manhood through his pants, his hungry eyes trained on her bare flesh. Shaking her head, she cleared the stray thought before turning her attention back to her task. Once she was finished up with the floor, she straightened up the room and walked back into the other room.

She made the bed using the rumpled pile of linens the deputies left on the floor after their search. As she reached across the bed to tuck in the sheet on the far side, another image popped into her mind; startling her into stopping for a moment. Closing her eyes, she barely smelled Ezra's unique, masculine scent on the bedding, and it was almost as if he was standing right behind her. Moaning softly at the thought of him walking up to her, as naked as she was, his hands caressing her backside.

Sighing in annoyance at herself for getting distracted again, Colleen turned back once more to her task. Finishing up with the bed quickly, least she got distracted again, she moved on to his Stetson. Pushing the center back out into the proper position, she dusted it off before tossing it onto the bed. She gathered the scattered items and returned them to their places.

It did not take long to have the room back in order, and Colleen glanced around to see if she missed anything on her first search before turning her attention back to the wardrobe once more when she was unable to find anything else out of place. Getting down on her hands and knees, she crawled over and reached her hand under to search for the loose floorboard Ezra mentioned. The first three boards she tried held firmly in place, but the fourth gave with only a slight tug. Pushing it to the side, she reached into the hole and felt blindly for the coin purse; pulling it out once she had it in her grasp. One more quick search assured her that nothing else was hidden there and she replaced the board.

After getting dressed, she retrieved the hat from the bed, hid the coin purse within her own, and made her way back out of the room. Certain everyone was asleep by now, she locked the door behind her and headed downstairs again; dropping the key off at the bar. She wouldn't need it for now, and she did not want to risk it dropping out and the deputy seeing it; in case he knew the rules about the rooms here and connected her to Ezra's. Heading to the hearth, she rebuilt the fire a bit before putting on a kettle of water. Silently making her way outside, deciding to confirm one last thing before making her way back to the jail for what she hoped would be the final time, she walked over to the hitching post.

Though he did not mention owning one, Colleen would have been surprised if Ezra had managed to get to town without riding a horse. They were pretty cut off from the surrounding towns in any direction. It took only a quick glance to know which one of the three horses belonged to her strange new companion. The two on the right were without their saddles, they were hanging from the hitching post beside them, which the men who arrived planning to spend the night often did. The third and only one on the left, however, was still saddled; showing the owner wanted to be able to leave at a moment's notice.

As it went with him having only two items in his room, less to repack, and the saddlebags being quite full, it wasn't hard to deduce the owner. Stepping silently over to the animal, Colleen whispered in her most calming voice, "I am a friend of Ezra's. Our boy got himself into some trouble, and I'm gonna need your help to get him out of it. Will you help me, big guy?" Without waiting for a response, Colleen reached out and gently rubbed the spot between the horse's eyes.

He neighed in response before stomping his front leg. "I'm gonna take that as a yes, Sugar. Come with me. I just need to get you a little closer," she explained as she unwound the reins from the post and lead the animal toward the jail. Searching for a spot that would be close enough to the jail for Ezra to reach quickly without the horse being spotted before they were ready for him, Colleen found a small patch of trees about ten yards from the front door of the jail and loosely tied him to one.

"Be back soon," she promised, patting him on the rump as she walked away. Making her way back to the saloon, she stepped quietly inside and walked over to the hearth; finding the water already starting to boil. Removing the kettle from the flames, she headed over to the bar and grabbed some coffee grounds and cups. Putting them all on a tray, she retrieved the kettle and headed out of the saloon for the last time.

The distance to the jail seemed to be greater than ever before as Colleen went over her plan again in her mind. Though she was there a little over an hour ago, she had gone without any real ulterior motive. Sure, she went to see Ezra, but she wanted to bring him food, and she did so openly. This time, she did not have such innocent thoughts in mind. She would do what she needed to in order to fix what went wrong, but as she walked with thoughts of harming the deputy on her mind, her footsteps seemed heavier than usual.

Almost as if they were weighed down to give her time to talk herself out of what she was planning, but it would take far more than a guilty conscious to stop her from saving Ezra from being hanged. Stepping up to the door, Colleen knocked with her boot and waited for the deputy to let her in. It only took a moment before she heard him shuffling around as he made his way over to answer. Putting on her sweetest smile, she glanced up at him, batting her lashes before gesturing to the tray in her hands with a slight tilt of her head.

"Thought you might like a little pick me up," she offered, her voice sultry as he stepped back; leaving enough room for her to pass in front of him. She set the tray down on the cluttered desk and poured him a cup. Pouring a second, she made her way over to the cell and passed it through the bars. "Be ready to run," she whispered before turning away before he got the chance to respond. Certain he would try to talk her out of what she was about to do, she was not about to give him the opportunity. She dropped her hands to her sides and allowed them to caress her from her breast to her hips. The deputy's eyes followed their path.

"I hope you don't mind, I've always wanted to have an audience," she explained, certain he would be questioning her giving coffee to Ezra if his mind was on anything other than her body at the moment. "Besides, poor boy should become a man before he is sent to his death. Don't you think?" She reached down and undid her skirt, letting it fall to the ground.

Stepping out of it, she raised her slip a bit as she moved slowly across the room, allowing her ankles to show. Again, his eyes followed her movement as she allowed it to continue rising inch by inch until her strong, yet soft thighs were exposed. Stopping before his chair, she knelt before him, carefully making sure not to expose more than she wanted to. A quick glance toward Ezra assured her that he saw everything she was about to do. Giving the deputy in front of her most of her attention, keeping a bit on Ezra to make sure he was still watching her, she reached out and cupped his manhood through his pants.

It wasn't an impressive size, not like Ezra's, but she wasn't surprised. Nearly all the men who paid for her services were merely average, if not a little smaller. Not about to let his lack of impressive girth stop her, Colleen undid his pants with one hand as she continued to massage his member with the other. Once he was free of his confines, she glanced up at him and licked her lips before lowering them over the tip.

He groaned as she pleasured him in ways she wished to do to Erza, and soon his body began to tremble. Hearing him begin to grunt above her, his release approaching, Colleen turned her gaze to Ezra even as she increased pressure and speed. Locking eyes with him, she imagined it was him she was engulfing with her hot, wet mouth, as she felt the deputy shuddering beneath her. Mentally readying herself for what she would do next, she increased her pace once more, and a moment later, the deputy cried out in pleasure, releasing his seed into her mouth. Moving before he realized what was happening, Colleen released him even as she grabbed the empty coffee pot and hit him over the head as hard as she could.

Unfortunately, it wasn't enough to knock him out, and he jumped to his feet, roaring in pain, but the sudden movement along with the blow to the head was enough to incapacitate him for a moment. Using his dizziness to her advantage, Colleen barreled into him; pushing him back into the cell. The sound of his head hitting the bars caused Colleen's stomach to lurch, and she spit out his release into a nearby spittoon before checking to make sure he still lived. Reassured by his strong heartbeat, Colleen grabbed his keys and unlocked the cell door. Turning back to Ezra for the first time since she assaulted the deputy, she found him standing there staring at her in stunned silence.

"You did not need to do that to save me. You owe me nothing. You should have left me to the fate I created by my own actions," Ezra insisted as he continued to stand unmoving in his cell. Laughing at the thought, Colleen headed to the other side of the jailhouse to retrieve Ezra's gun belt. "I'm serious, Colleen. Why did you lower yourself like that for someone you barely know? Why would you risk your life for me?"

"Sugar, considering I saved your life and all, please don't insult me by implying I am lowering myself by pleasuring a man. You may not be attracted to men as I am, but I wear who I am as a badge of honor. Even if it is not what is expected of me, what everyone else is, I take great pride in being true to myself. If you have a problem with that, you can save your own ass next time." Colleen turned her back and began walking away.

Ezra stopped her with a hand on her shoulder, turning her back around to face him. "You misunderstand me, Colleen. I only meant you were lowering yourself because it was someone you didn't even know. You shouldn't have to pleasure a stranger for my sake."

Smiling softly, Colleen cupped his cheek before handing his gun belt and retrieving her skirt. As she stepped back into it and secured it in place, she turned back to him, "Sugar, did you already forget how I make my living? Pleasuring him was an easy price to pay for your life. Now I suggest we get you out of here before he comes to or the others return to hang you." As she started toward the exit, Colleen thought better off it and turned back to the unconscious deputy, grabbing hold of his feet as she gestured to his head.

Waiting until Ezra understood what she wanted and grabbed him under his arms, she led the way into the cell before unceremoniously dropping the unconscious man on the floor. Locking the cell as the left, in case he came to before Ezra had the chance to get away, Colleen led the way back outside, checking to make certain the coast was clear before letting him cross the threshold. "Your horse is over here," she whispered even as she headed toward where she left it.

Sighing in relief when she spotted it, she unwrapped the reins as Ezra mounted the animal. "I hope you stay safe and I wish for our paths to cross once more, Ezra," Colleen told him as she handed him his hat and coin purse before stepping away to allow him to leave. Instead, Ezra sat there, staring at her in silence. "Go, Ezra. You do not have long before dawn and the return of the others."

"What are you talking about, Colleen? You're coming with me. They'll hang you for helping me as soon as that deputy comes to and tells them you knocked him out."

Colleen furrowed her brow. "Are you serious?"

Ezra laughed despite the dangerous situation they were currently in. "I could no sooner leave you here to your fate than you'd leave me to mine. Now get your ass up here," he demanded, reaching out his hand to help her up.

Settling her into the saddle behind him, he gave the reins a quick flick causing the horse to take off. Behind them, Edgewood grew smaller, closing the first chapter of their lives.

# Chapter Twelve

WEST OF EDGEWOOD 1830

Ezra and Colleen rode in silence, the small town of Edgewood long since faded from the horizon behind them. Time seemed to pass slower than usual while very different thoughts were running through their minds. Ezra barely noticed the surrounding scenery as they passed, or the second passenger on his horse, instead only one thought occupied his mind—*What now*? What was he supposed to do now that his only lead died before he gave him any real information about the man he was searching for?

Though it was not the first time the trail went cold on him, he never had to deal with the law chasing him or an extra unexpected companion. Now he had no idea where to go next and more complications than he knew what to do with.

No, that wasn't fair—Colleen was not a complication. Truthfully, she was the only reason he was still alive at that moment, and he knew he would never be able to repay her for everything she did for him.

He only met the woman a few days before and yet she risked her life, continued to do so, in fact, to save him from certain death. And why? Because he saved her from the men who were beating her? Because he did not turn her away when he realized that there was more to her than meets the eye? Sure, that might have been enough of a reason to keep quiet about his spying on Dowes, but to break the law for him? To risk her own neck to save his from the hangman's noose?

How horrid her life before now must have been for her to go that far for him, to give up her entire life, no matter how low it might have been, for a man she only knew for a few days. Granted, they developed a connection over the last few days, coming to each other's rescue as they did, but was it enough to behave as she had? And, if it was, what must that have said about her life before she met him. If the little kindness he showed her had been enough for her to react as she had, did that not mean that she saw little of it before?

What about her parents? Obviously, they were not still around, considering how she ended up, but surely they must have shown her love and kindness when she was a child, mustn't they? Like his, did hers die when she was still young? Was she on her own since then? Ezra knew his own history was horrible, bringing him to where he was in his life, how much worse must hers have been to bring her to where she was?

While Ezra tried to figure out what he would do next and how to explain the strange woman behind him, Colleen had a very different train of thought. She did not wonder where they would go from there or even what she would do once they split ways. The thought never even crossed her mind that she should be looking toward the future. There was only one thing on her mind as they rode north across the plains in silence; Ezra. The way his strong waist felt with her arms wrapped around it.

The heat radiating off of his skin seeping through his clothing and causing her own flesh to tingle in anticipation. She was already imagining his strong arms helping her to dismount the horse before pulling her flush against his chest as he looked into her eyes; getting lost in the violet orbs. Her breathing hitched as she envisioned him caressing her cheek with the pads of his fingers, leaving a trail of warmed flesh from her temple to her lips before finally lowering his eyes to them as she licked them unconsciously.

She saw his face growing ever closer to her own as he finally closed his green eyes and prepared to kiss her. In mere moments she would feel his warm lips pressed against hers, putting to rest her question of if they were as soft as they looked. Inch by inch he grew closer, teasing her with his slow pace. Just as she was about to imagine herself grabbing hold of him and pulling him the rest of the distance, the horse jumped off a slight hill, causing her to be jarred from her fantasizing.

Growling softly under her breath, Colleen turned her attention back to the real man of flesh and blood before her, saving the fantasy for later. This close to him, she smelled the same masculine scent she found on his bedding and breathed it in deeply before she knew what she was doing. No matter what tomorrow might bring, Colleen knew she would never regret throwing her old life away to ride off with this man. Even if she only got this one day with him, it would still be worth it.

A SUDDEN YELP startled the nearby townsfolk, causing the hustle and bustle in the town square to pause momentarily as they turned toward the noise, finding a young man on his back; his piercing blue eyes glaring through the settling dust. It took them mere moments to realize what happened and, unconcerned, they turned back to their previous activities. A patron being thrown out of the local saloon was such a common occurrence that it no longer held their attention for more than a moment.

For the man, however, it was one of the worst affronts he ever experienced, and it certainly had his full attention. Tossing him out of the saloon on his backside was adding insult to injury. It added fuel to the already burning fire in his belly. "That lowdown no good barkeeper dares to have his lackeys cheat me at cards and accuse me of being a swindler? You will pay…" the young man began as he rose to his feet, dusting off the dirt from his pants, before glancing up and finding the barkeeper already went back inside.

"You cheated the wrong man at cards you scoundrel! You will rue the day you accused me of cheating you rotten son of a whore!" he continued as his eyes glared fire at the closed doors before turning around. The barkeeper would pay for what he did, he would make sure of that, but there was no sense in doing anything about it in broad daylight. He would only end up getting himself thrown in jail again, and he was not looking forward to such an experience.

No, he would wait until that night after all potential witnesses had gone to sleep to exact his revenge on those in the saloon. As far as he was concerned, they were all as guilty as the barkeeper was. Some of the men were in the card game with him and the others knew that they were cheating, it was far too obvious to not be noticed, and did nothing to warn or help him. They would all pay before the night was through, he would make sure of it.

For now, he needed to lay low and wait for the right moment. As he made his way away from the saloon, already trying to figure out where to spend the rest of the day since his earlier plans to play cards well into the night were now off the table, he heard a strange splash behind him a moment before he was drenched in cold water. Growling as he turned back around toward his attacker, pushing the long strains of wet, dark hair out of his eyes, he found the barkeeper was already making his way back inside once again, the empty bucket hanging unhidden in his hand.

Shivering in disgust at the thought of the dirty water, fresh from some filthy slob's bath judging by the smell, that was dripping down his body, the young man gritted his teeth so hard they threatened to crack under the pressure. "I'd give a snake the first bite," he growled to himself, recalling his father's expression of anger. He only heard it once in his life, the day that lead to his parents' deaths, but it was something he knew would never leave him.

The thought of being mad enough to let a snake bite you before fighting back seemed funny to him when his father said it, but at that moment, it summed up how he felt perfectly. Unfortunately for the barkeeper, he was not a snake, and he was not about to give him the first bite. No, he would strike first and he would strike last. When he was finished, there would be nothing left of the barkeeper or his pathetic saloon.

"A STORM IS coming. We should seek shelter for the time being," Colleen called out over the wind that picked up only a few minutes before. Ezra barely heard her words. Glancing behind them and spotting dust clouds on the horizon, he nodded in agreement. Considering the clouds weren't there fifteen minutes before when he checked for pursuers last, he knew it would not be long before the storm overtook them.

As much as he hated the idea of having to stop so early, the one consolation would be that the lawmen following them would have to do the same. "Should be a town coming up. There was a sign a good ways back," Ezra called back over his shoulder even as he urged his horse to go faster. At least the storm would give them the perfect excuse to spend the night in an actual bed, take an actual bath. Though they only left the saloon two nights before, being on the road made it seem a lot longer when you had to sleep on the hard ground and scrub your face clean from a freezing stream in the morning.

"Ezra, follow this road to the right. Think I saw something down there that I need," Colleen called out after a couple of minutes, startling him, but he followed her instructions nonetheless. Confused, but curious, Ezra led his horse down the narrow dirt road, finding it led to a lone house once they crested a hill. Though he glanced back at his companion in confusion, he stopped as requested and helped her to dismount the horse.

"Stay here. I'll be right back," Colleen promised before heading toward the small homestead that appeared to be empty. As Ezra waited, torn between wanting to do as she requested and needing to make sure she was safe, she disappeared behind the house; heading back in the direction they came from. Keeping an ear out for Colleen, Ezra turned his attention toward the road behind him.

With the hill so close to where they stopped, there would be no warning before anyone on the road was upon them. Not liking the disadvantage, Ezra was about to call out for her to return when he heard footsteps coming toward him. Turning toward the sound, he grabbed his gun and pointed it at a strange man making his way toward him. "Where is she?!" Ezra cried out even as he glanced around, searching for his companion.

The stranger chuckling brought his attention back to him and, about to threaten him if he did not tell him what he did with her, Ezra was silenced when he spoke. "Look closely, Ezra. You'll see she's fine," the stranger assured him, his voice sounding oddly familiar though there was something off about it. Confused, he stared at the man before him, taking in his appearance for the first time.

The tan britches tucked into the nearly knee-high black boots, the vest over the button-up shirt and the ankle length overcoat seemed a bit old fashioned, meant for someone decades older than the man standing before him, but did little to explain who he was or how he knew his name. Did he hear her speaking when they approached? No, she did not mention his name since before they turned down this road, and if he was following them for that long, he would have spotted him long before then.

Even more confused, Ezra turned his attention back to his inspection of the stranger and found himself glancing from the unremarkable Stetson that hid his hair, to his unforgettable violet eyes. "Colleen," he whispered before he could stop himself. "But how?" he mumbled. It was like looking at a completely different person other than his eyes and the few strands of red hair he now noticed peeking out from beneath the hat.

"It's Cole, actually," he explained. Ezra couldn't believe the stark differences in the two halves of the person before him. Judging by their differences in appearance, he was sure he would quickly learn that his behavior would prove to be different from Colleen's as well.

As it was, Cole was already standing taller than Colleen did, and he was certain it had more to do with his posture than it did to the boots on his feet. And that was not all he noticed even after only being exposed to the second half for a few moments. Where she was soft, he was hard. Where there were poise and grace behind her step, there was purpose and strength behind his. Had he not have known better, he would have sworn they were two completely different people.

"It takes some getting used to, I know, but I figured two men traveling together would draw less attention to you traveling with a saloon girl," he explained, apparently completely unconcerned by the gun that Ezra had yet to lower. Staring at him in silence for a minute longer, Ezra finally blinked before mounting the horse after holstering his gun. Cole stepped forward and tucked something in the saddle bag. Helping his companion back onto his horse, finding the man to be even stranger than the woman who dismounted only a few minutes before, he turned the animal back toward the narrow road and headed away from the house.

There would be plenty of time to try to understand the sudden change in his companion later when they did not have the law on their trail. Perhaps once they settled in for the night Colleen, or Cole, might explain his two sides to him and maybe even explain how he ended up living the life he had.

# Chapter Thirteen

THOMASVILLE 1830

Things seemed to be going their way that evening as not only were they able to procure the last available room in the saloon, but all the town's lawmen were currently away from town. The day before, a group of outlaws robbed the bank, and the sheriff formed a posse to go after them. Deciding to take advantage of not only the storm slowing down those following them, but also not having to worry about the lawmen of this town, Ezra made his way to the saloon's community bathing room and was about to find someone to fill one of the baths for him when he spotted Cole pouring hot water into the only tub slightly hidden from the view of the entrance.

Though he knew from the beginning that the saloon girl he met was born male, he grew accustomed to the woman Colleen. It would take him a while to get used to the man Cole was turning out to be, even with them being the same person. But maybe that was what made it so difficult to get used to, the fact that they weren't the same person. Same physical body, sure, but mannerisms, body language, even the way they spoke seemed to be completely different.

It certainly did not go unnoticed by Ezra that Cole did not call him 'sugar' even once since changing into the stolen clothing. Ezra wondered if he intentionally acted differently depending on how he was dressed or if each persona came naturally for his two halves. Perhaps, if they were able to stay there without anything interrupting them until the storm broke, he would get the chance to question him. The last two nights of constantly staring into the darkness looking for the law did not leave much time to get to know each other better.

Apparently noticing his arrival, Cole smiled before gesturing to the tub in front of him. "I was about to come get you and let you know it was ready. Go ahead and bathe. I will see to some supper and be right back."

Cole moved toward the door when Ezra's hand on his arm stopped him. Catching his eyes with his own, Ezra was graced with a polite, normal smile, unlike Colleen's usually flirty one.

"You don't have to give up your bath to me, I'm not your customer anymore," Ezra reminded him only to be startled a moment later when Cole laughed, sounding more masculine than the feminine giggle he grew used to back at the saloon. Not sure what he found to be so funny, Ezra simply stood there crossing his arms as he waited for him to explain.

"I drew the bath for you in the first place. You're right, you're not my customer, but honestly you never really were. We only know how to be two things, Ezra, a saloon girl and an unwanted child. It is all we have ever known. I realize you are not interested in Colleen's many talents as entertainment, and I don't fault you for that, but for the short time you allow me to follow you, let me do the small amount I am able to. If not, what is the point in me being here?" Cole questioned before continuing on his way out to see to supper as he said he would.

Ezra waited until he was out of sight before making his way over to the tub Cole prepared for him and scrubbed off the dirt he accumulated on the road. As he washed, Ezra thought about the questions Cole's words brought to mind.

What exactly was the point of Ezra continuing to allow him to follow? Of course, he insisted Colleen left with him, certain her life would be in danger if she stayed at the saloon. The deputy would no doubt remember who it was that attacked him, and even if by chance he didn't, the barkeep would be angry with her for Ezra's actions. From what he saw, she seemed to be on a very thin rope at the saloon, and he doubted it would take much more to get her kicked out onto the street.

It hadn't just been for her sake that he insisted she come with him, though, as she knew enough about what he was doing to put his mission at risk if the man Dowes was talking to returned. Or if another of his friends showed up after hearing what happened to him. She'd probably make a good amount of money selling the little bit of information he gave her. And, if he was completely honest, he couldn't blame her if she did.

It wasn't possible for Colleen to have enjoyed her time at the saloon, not with the way the other girls and customers treated her. In the short time he was there, he saw her punched in the face by a potential customer, attacked and locked in the storeroom with another girl trying to steal the client she managed to get, and he saw two large men beating her outside. And he wasn't there that long. If such interactions were a usual occurrence, he doubted she would have lasted much longer.

Hell, he would not be surprised if she got killed if Etta decided to try again after he left or when Katherine attacked her for what happened to Dowes. For both of their sakes, it made sense for her to leave with him, but that was Colleen. Same person or not, he was no longer dealing with a saloon girl that broke the law for him and had others wishing her harm. Now he was faced with Cole, a young man he doubted anyone in the area even knew about. Except for the stolen clothes, Ezra was certain he was completely free and clear of the law.

So now he needed to figure out what to do with Cole. Originally, he simply planned on dropping him off once they arrived in a town of Cole's choosing, yet he had not even broached the subject with him. Neither during the two nights they stayed outside or in the few hours they traveled after Cole appeared, making it easier for him to blend in with the locals if the sheriff did catch up to them, did Ezra bring up the idea of splitting up.

He knew they needed to. It would make his own escape that much easier as he would be able to travel much quicker with his horse only having to deal with one rider, but something inside him insisted that having a companion would make some things easier on him as well. Cole seemed happy to be seeing to his basic needs, such as the bath Ezra was currently submerging into, but more than that, he knew it would come in handy having Cole with him.

If ever they came to a town where word of him being wanted had already reached its borders, he could send him in for supplies or to uncover information about the others. Having someone with experience as a saloon girl working for him might even have its own advantages if he needed to get the men alone or to talk. If Colleen had no problem continuing with that line of work anyway. And Ezra must admit, more than any of that, it would be nice to have someone to watch his back. The only problem, Ezra decided as he dunked his head back into the cooling water, was he had no idea if Cole was even able to fight or shoot a gun.


A FEW MINUTES before, after stepping out of the bathing room and making sure he was no longer in Ezra's hearing range, Cole stepped into a dark corner of the hallway and allowed himself to slide down the side of the wall that separated them. A few stray tears made themselves known, and he angrily wiped them away. He was Cole and Cole did not cry, he reminded himself, shaking his head to clear his thoughts before banging his head back on the wall, softly muttering to himself that he was being an idiot.

Though the other man did not seem to notice his slip up, Cole chastised himself for allowing his exhaustion to get the better of him. He never referred to himself as an 'unwanted child' before, at least not out loud to someone else, and he certainly did not want Ezra to think of him in such a way now. It was only a matter of time before they went their separate ways, as he was slowing Ezra down, and he did not want what little time they had left to be marred by his horrible childhood memories.

Resting his head back against the unyielding wall, Cole closed his eyes and drew a deep breath. For the first time since they left Edgewood, he was finally able to breathe. He was exhausted, mentally and physically. He had no idea what he was doing, if he was honest, following after a man he barely knew that killed at least three people that he knew of.

Sure, he said the men had something to do with his parents' murder, but what did that matter if Cole had no idea who and what his parents were? They could have been bank robbers for all he knew, Dowes and his men the lawmen that brought them to justice. Though he doubted that was the case, there was no way for him to know anything about the man he was following blindly. Colleen was the one to follow after him—hell she chased after the man they found extremely attractive.

Ezra saved her, more than once, but that was Colleen. Honestly, there was no connection between Ezra and Cole, and once he figured that out, Cole was certain he would find himself abandoned once again. After all, their arrangement was only temporary as it was only a matter of time before having him around became a disadvantage to Ezra.

For now, Cole decided as he scrubbed his face to clear any evidence of his weak moment, he would do everything possible to be of service to Ezra. Not just because of how good it felt to see to his needs as Colleen, and he was excited to see if it would feel the same as Cole, but because he knew the more useful he was, the longer he would be able to stay with him. It would end, he knew, but considering he had no idea where he would go with his life from here, Cole was in no hurry to be on his own again.

Colleen had already been for far too long. The last time they had actually been *wanted*, was one of the worst encounters in their life, but it was also when Colleen was born. As much as he wished for those few days that he was trapped with a man using him to replace his dead wife, to have never happened, he would not want to lose what they learned about themselves when he was there.

Forcing him to dress in women's clothing showed him how much he enjoyed the feel of them on his body. Looking at himself in the mirror, he realized the person looking back at him was not a stranger as he thought they would be. They fit, matched well with his masculine half.

It was almost as though he was only half of a person his entire life before that moment and connecting the two halves of his life was like lifting a giant weight off of his shoulders. No longer did he feel out of place in his own skin. No longer did he feel like something important was missing, a feeling he chalked up to missing his mother before that moment. He was whole. He was complete.

He was female, and she was male. Together they made themselves a complete person. It was not something they could ever explain to someone else and get them to understand completely, but as far as they were concerned, it did not matter. They would never be alone again. No matter how many times they were abandoned in their life, no matter who turned their backs on them, they would always have each other. Even if they were the same person.

Though Cole did his best to forget about the few days he was trapped and at the complete mercy of a horrific man whose mind seemed to die along with his wife, he knew they would forever remain an important part of his memory—of their story. Because of that man, and the horrible things he put him through, he found Colleen, and he would willingly suffer a hundred lifetimes with him if it meant he would have her in his life.

At least now he had a few dollars to his name after working for Ezra the last few days at the saloon, but that wouldn't last him long if he was forced on his own again. Leaving thoughts of the future passed that night in the hallway, Cole made his way downstairs to see about dinner. If he timed things right, he'd get his own bath in before dinner was ready and be able to serve Ezra his meal once more. There was something about sharing a meal with someone that made him think that that was what it was like to belong.

Like you were home, with family. Very few other meals in his entire life were eaten with someone else and he doubted he would have many more once the two went their separate ways. Arriving downstairs, Cole spotted the barkeep and put in his order for two meals, which he was informed would need to be picked up at the bar himself. Unlike the saloon he worked at before, this one actually had regular sleeping rooms and its own cooking hearth but did not appear to have any working girls.

Heading back upstairs, Cole made his way back to the bathing room as Ezra was making his way out into the hallway. "I'm going to take my bath now. I'll bring supper up to our room once it is ready," Cole informed him before stepping past and making his way into the room. Though Ezra looked like he might be about to say something, it went unnoticed by Cole who was too focused on cleaning the grime of the road off of his body.

AFTER STRIPPING OUT of the strange clothes and scrubbing himself off once he heard the door close behind Ezra, Cole made his way over to the tub and climbed in. Already the water was much cooler than he made it for Ezra, but heating it up seemed like too much work at that moment and would certainly make him late for dinner. Hissing slightly as the water covered the newest set of scratches Katherine gave Colleen, he realized they did not hurt as much as he was expecting. Fortunately, the time on the road gave them the chance to heal slightly. Closing his eyes, Cole brushed away the thought that Ezra was naked in the very same water only a few minutes before.

He needed to keep himself under control; he couldn't allow himself to get worked up or flirt with Ezra with the way he was now. He would draw too much attention to them and might even annoy Ezra to the point that he abandoned him sooner. It was one thing to flirt with him openly when they were secluded in their room and while they were Colleen— there he had to accept it as he was unable to send her away without another girl trying to take her place and drawing more attention to him.

Etta already proved that on her own. But here, as Cole, Ezra had no reason to keep him around if he became a nuisance. No, soon enough he would be on his own for the third time in his short life, but Cole was not about to bring their time together to completion any faster than it already would be. At least, he realized making his future seem a little bit brighter, this time he would actually be mature enough to be able to fend for himself.

He would not fall into the same trap he did after leaving the orphanage and, even though he was still a bit more daintily built than most men, he would probably be able to get a job as Cole. It was probably best that he didn't try a saloon again for a little while. After all, how many male-born saloon girls could there be in the area? Surely something like that would get back to the lawmen that were certain to be after Colleen as well.

And even if he would stay under the radar, Cole had enough of the Katherines and Ettas in the world to last him a lifetime. Perhaps one day he would return to Colleen's life, but for now, he would no doubt be better off as Cole. Deciding he was in the cold water long enough, Cole wrung the water from his long, red hair; even as he tried to figure out how to style it to hide its length for the foreseeable future without actually having to cut it. Colleen couldn't exactly get away with having short hair if she needed to make a return before it had the chance to grow out again.

AFTER DROPPING THEIR food off in their room, Ezra made his way back to the bathing room to let Cole know he would not have to retrieve it after all. Walking into the room as Cole was standing up, Ezra was startled by his own sudden intake of air. The last time he saw his naked form, his attention was on the cuts and bruises that littered his body. Though the now healing wounds did warrant a quick glance, he was surprised to find his own gaze was on the nude form instead of its injuries.

Something about the way the water cascaded down his thin, yet muscular form caused a strange sensation in the pit of his stomach. It was certainly not something he was accustomed to, but he did not have the time or desire to figure out what it meant for the moment. He refused to allow Cole to become a distraction; just as he wouldn't let Colleen. Blinking away the image of the naked man, that seemed determined to imprint on his mind, Ezra cleared his throat to announce his presence.

Apparently unabashed about being seen completely naked by him this time, Cole simply glanced over his shoulder toward him for a moment before grabbing the towel hanging nearby and wrapping himself in it. Ezra thought to draw his attention to the fact that he wrapped it around himself as a woman would, but a lone drop of water slipping down his collarbone and disappearing into the towel caused him to lose his train of thought for a moment.

Shaking his head, he explained, "Supper is ready in the room. Join me whenever you are ready. There are a few things we need to discuss," before making his way back out of the room without waiting for a reply. Unconcerned by looking rude, Ezra knew the only thing that mattered was getting out of there before the droplets of water slowly making their way down Cole's exposed shoulders caught hold of his attention and refused to release his gaze as they were already threatening to do.

COLE STARED AFTER his new companion for a moment, wondering about his strange behavior. He shook his head and turned his attention to his towel. It was only then that he realized he covered his chest as well. He redid the towel around his waist. "Funny how this is what seems strange to me now," he commented softly to himself as he stepped out of the tub and began dressing.

Once he finished, he made his way to their room. Ezra was waiting for him beside the untouched tray of food. Just as Cole was beginning to think how that was so sweet, he realized it was the first time it ever happened for him. Never before had anyone waited for him before starting to eat. Usually, he was stuck off in a corner somewhere because no customer requested his presence during a meal. He might have been in the saloon completely alone for all the company he had while eating.

Realizing Ezra was staring at him while patiently waiting, Cole gave him a gentle smile before seating himself on the other side of the tray from him. When he put the first morsel of food in his mouth, Ezra took the opportunity to speak. "I do not know if you have decided what you want to do yet, but I want to give you an option to think about. I want you to come with me. I have been at this long enough to know I could use someone to watch my back, especially now with the law after me. And you have proven to be worthy of my trust."

Stunned, Cole sat there staring at him in silence for a minute while he tried to wrap his mind around what he said. Ezra wanted Cole to go with him? Somebody wanted him? Someone actually wanted his dual-gendered, man-loving self when his own mother abandoned him as a child? He who was attacked, beaten and nearly killed by another teenager simply because that boy couldn't handle his own attraction to him? He was wanted?

Before Cole could stop himself, he felt the tears come for the second time that day, but this time he did not angrily wipe them away. Instead, he allowed them to flow unchecked.

Ezra's confident, calm expression quickly turned to one of concern. "What did I do? Why are you crying?" His worry was unmistakable in his voice. Though he reached to wipe away Cole's tears, he stopped short of touching him and allowed his hand to fall back to his lap.

"You did nothing, but want me, Ezra. You want my company, my companionship." For a moment, Cole paused to take a deep breath before deciding it was time to tell him the truth. As much as he would love to never again be known as the 'unwanted one' that he was his entire life, he needed Ezra to understand exactly what his words meant to him.

More than that, Ezra said that Cole earned his trust. Trust went both ways. And, if he was completely honest with himself, he needed to know if he would still be there. Would Ezra be able to hear the horror story his life was and still be there? Would he walk away, abandon Cole as his mother had even after being the one to ask him to stay? If anyone was able to handle the truth, Cole was certain it would be Ezra; after all, he barely blinked after finding out the truth about his genders.

Putting the tray of mostly untouched food to the side, certain neither of them would be eating for at least the next few minutes, Cole finally wiped the tears from his cheeks before turning his attention back to Ezra. "There are many things you do not know about me, Ezra, but I think you should know everything that brought me to this point before you decide if you want me to continue following after you. I will not blame you if you rescind your offer, but we cannot have true trust without honesty."

Taking another deep breath, Cole closed his eyes for a moment before opening them once again to find Ezra waiting patiently for him to speak. "As you've already noticed, I am both male and female, though only mentally. I am not sure if people like me have a name, or if there is anyone else like me, but I referred to myself as being dual-gendered. I did not discover this truth about myself until I was seventeen and was trapped in an insane, violent man's home where he forced me to wear the clothing of his dead wife, Becky.

"That was when I discovered the other half of me, Colleen, but it was not the first time I acted different. Even from when I was a young child, who I would one day become was noticeable. The only family I have ever known, I have never really known, if that makes any sense. My mother abandoned me for good when I was about four years old, but in all honesty she was never there, to begin with." Seeing Ezra was about to speak, Cole held up his hand to stop him.

"Please, let me finish. If I don't get this said, I may never." Once Ezra nodded his head that he would remain silent, Cole continued, "My mother, much like myself, was a saloon girl which is where she met my father. I have no idea who he is other than the fact that he abandoned my mother when he found out she was pregnant with me. I believe he was married to someone else. For this reason, my mother hated me even before I was ever born.

"I do not remember much from that time, being as young as I was, but I remember she was never there, and I would go for many days at a time with no food or water. My only companion was the cow my mother bought to feed me. One day, after she was gone for so long and I was barely able to get out of bed, she came home to find me lying on a pile of her clothes and holding a doll that looked like her. I put on her clothing because they smelled like her, but apparently, she assumed that I liked wearing them."

Cole couldn't help but sigh at the irony. "I supposed she was correct in that assumption, it just would be many more years before I figured this out for myself. Having a son that liked dresses and dolls was the last straw for my mother as she walked out of our tiny home and never came back. I would have starved to death if not for a thunderstorm that caught our barn on fire. The smoke must have attracted the sheriff because he arrived one day to find me right where my mother abandoned me. Since no one had any idea where to find my mother, he dropped me off at the local orphanage."

"I am sorry to interrupt, Cole, but I do not understand why you think any of this will change what I think about you. Your mother abandoning you as a child does not make you any less of a person," Ezra insisted. Cole couldn't help but shake his head with a smile. There was still so much he didn't know, didn't understand. Gesturing that he wanted to continue, he waited for Ezra to nod his head to assure him he was finished interrupting.

"My time at the orphanage was, if you can believe it, even worse than the time I spent with my mother. Hell, I would even prefer the cold nights that I lay frightened in my bed with the coyotes howling outside my door to my days with the other children. From day one, a group of boys decided to harass me, though I am still not sure what exactly started it. It began small. One of them would knock over the water bucket I was washing the floor with and knock me down into the dirty water.

"Another would push me down the stairs or step out from around the corner to punch me, taking off before I even saw who it was. As we got older, their attacks became more aggressive, especially from one boy in particular. Though I did not know it at the time, by the end of my stay at the orphanage, I realized all of the most brutal attacks were committed by this one boy." Shuttering at the memory, the boy's face clear in his mind as though he saw him yesterday and not three years ago, Cole shook his head to clear the image.

"When I was thirteen, I awoke to find someone spewed their release on the pillow next to my head. Then when I was fifteen, I found myself being pulled into a dark corner and punched in the face and stomach until I could barely stand. Once I was too weak to fight him, he forced himself into my mouth. I reported what happened to the headmaster, but even with my body being covered in bruises, I was told there was nothing to be done because I did not know who it was. When I insisted he do something to protect me, I was punished for my disobedience by being forced to sleep outside.

"The next year, there was a bad storm, and many of the bedrooms were unusable due to water and roof damage. The remaining rooms were jammed packed with boys, resulting in me being put in a room with the five boys that tormented me since day one. I often wondered if the headmaster did that in punishment for my complaining so much about them. That night, while the others were sleeping, I found myself suddenly awake when he forced himself into my mouth again. I was unable to see who it was in the dark, but I was sure it was the same boy as before.

"Again, I went to the headmaster and again he did nothing. This time, I asked to be allowed to sleep outside until the repairs were finished so I would not have to share a room with them. Naturally, he agreed. The following year, when I was still months away from aging out of the orphanage, the boy attacked me for the last time. I awoke to find him trying to force himself inside me from behind and for the first time in my life, I fought back.

"During the scuffle, we drew the attention of the others and the boy claimed that I was watching him while he bathed, and he was teaching me a lesson. That was the first time I realized he had a knife. It was also when I realized the headmaster was standing right outside the room and doing nothing. I told him I now had proof of who my attacker was for all those years, yet again he did nothing. The boy said something about me knowing better than to spy on him next time, and I shot back that he was too ugly for me to watch.

"Unsurprisingly, the insult pissed him off, and he attacked me again. I got away with nothing more than a cut to my arm, he, on the other hand, was not so lucky. At some point during the fight, he was stabbed with his own knife. His friends moved to attack me, but I held them off with his knife until the headmaster got others to get them back to their rooms. Then he told me to pack my things and get out within an hour.

"He said that he did not allow violent offenders to live with the other children. I think I actually laughed at him, telling him he never seemed to have a problem when I was the one being attacked. I walked away that night with the clothes I had on my back, what few pieces of food I found and the boy's knife." Cole stopped for a much-needed breath, and he waited to see how he would react.

He was more than a little surprised when his only reaction was to raise his eyebrow in question. "Again, I do not understand how this is supposed to make me change my opinion of you or cause me to trust you less. Cole, you being abandoned, abused, and attacked does not reflect on who you are as a person, but on who they were. You are no more at fault for the things that happened to you in your life than I am for those that happened to me."

"I killed him, Ezra. The boy died that night. And though he may have been the one that attacked me, I was the one that walked away. You cannot take another's life without it changing who you are, what you are capable of doing. Yes, I was protecting myself, but a life lost is a life lost. Can you honestly tell me you can look at me and see me exactly as you did a few minutes ago before I told you I was capable of ending another's life?"

For a moment, Ezra regarded him in silence before finally giving him an odd kind of smile. "You're right, Cole. I do not see you exactly the same as I did before. Now I am amazed by you. Now I am even more confident in my desire to have you come with me. You did not kill him, Cole, he killed himself with his own actions, but knowing how you will react to the taking of another life gives me more confidence in you. In case you have forgotten, I too have taken the lives of others, only I took some of them intentionally.

"You worry about me changing my opinion of you and rescinding my offer for you to join me, but you do not realize exactly what it is I am asking you to do. There is pretty much a guarantee where I am going will put us in danger and force us to take the lives of others, even if you never have to actually pull the trigger yourself. But even that, I cannot guarantee." Ezra rose and paced the small room for a moment before finally turning back to Cole.

"You want complete honesty? Can't have trust without honesty, right? The night my parents were killed, there were twelve men there. I call them the Midnight Twelve, and I have killed three of them so far. I will not stop until they are all dead and so is their boss. The man that ordered the death of my parents; Godfrey de Voe. I have very little information to go on to find them, especially with Dowes giving up nothing before I was forced to kill him.

"It can take months, if not years, to follow the clues I uncover back to one of the men that were there that night. I do not know their names, and most times, I don't even know with complete certainty that they were even there that night. Dowes I knew, I would recognize that disgusting laugh anywhere, but the other two I mostly guessed their involvement. My whole crusade to find them started with the smallest connection I found when men robbed my grandmother's house.

"As I mentioned before, the leader said something about trying to join the Pine Box gang. The night my parents were killed, the man who spoke said 'no one leaves the Pine Box Crew except for in one.' He was referring to my parents trying to leave their gang. Who my parents truly were, I will probably never know, but for whatever reason they left, they did not deserve to be gunned down like that. For revenge and no other reason, I search for the men, that were there that night, so I can kill them."

He paused for a moment to draw a deep breath. "I am not a good man, Cole. I am not the hero in my own story. I will kill anyone I have to in order to avenge their deaths, even you. I contemplated killing you back at the saloon if you became a hindrance to me. I have never been so glad that I didn't. I am only still alive now because of you. They would have hung me if you did not help me to escape. The question isn't whether I can see you the same as I did, if I would still want you to come with me. The question is would you want to join me?

"Can you continue to follow me knowing that nothing but death waits for us on the path I am on—either ours or theirs. Would you be okay with intentionally taking the life of another if that was what it came down to? Would you be able to lure men to their deaths or stab them in the back, literally or figuratively? Are you all right with being the outlaw, the villain in your own story? Would you be willing to spend possibly the rest of your life running from the law with me?"

"I would follow you anywhere, for however long as you will have me. You do not understand what it means to be wanted for someone who has spent their entire life being told they were not. I have never had a friend before, even the customer who taught me how to defend myself did not stay around long enough for us to become real friends. I will go anywhere, do anything if it means I can keep you in my life. But I must ask, I know why I would follow you, but what do you see in me that makes you want me to?"

"Honestly? I see myself in you. I see a young man, at least for the moment, who has nothing and no one in the world. Who is desperate for someone who will not judge him for who he is and what he does. I see someone who will have my back and not sell me out if anyone comes looking for me. Someone who is willing to risk their own neck for me before you even really knew who I was. You ask me why I would want you to come with me, but I think the better question would be, why wouldn't I?"

For an entire minute, the two stared at each other in silence, both a bit overwhelmed by what they shared with each other when they never told another soul so much about themselves before. It was a lot to take in and process, but neither of them had even the slightest regret of opening up so much to the other. It was strange, for two who were completely alone their entire lives, without anyone else to depend on, to put their trust so completely in another person they only met a week before.

But perhaps that was what it was; they saw themselves in each other, and that kinship was enough to break down the walls they built around themselves. Finally breaking the silence between them, Cole gestured toward their forgotten meal. "We should eat before it gets any colder," he insisted softly, before following his own advice and taking a small bite.

Giving him a moment to take a bite of his own, Cole wondered, "What exactly do you plan on doing now? You said Dowes did not give you any information, so where do you go from here?" At first, he only received a shrug from Ezra in response, though he was not sure if he did not know what his next move was yet or he simply did not want to speak with a mouthful of food. Deciding it was better to finish their meals before trying to speak, Cole turned his attention to his own plate and quickly downed the cold contents.

Though he was certain they would have tasted much better while they were still warm, Cole went hungry far too many nights to ever be picky about what he ate. Ezra, on the other hand, only finished about half of his plate before pushing the cold food away. Shrugging at his loss, Cole grabbed his plate and finished off his remaining food, much to the surprise of Ezra. "What? The amount of food I have managed to eat since meeting you is more than I usually get in an entire month."

"Well, that should not be a problem anymore. I may not be rich, nowhere near it in fact, but I usually have enough to my name to keep me fed and give me a bed to sleep in. We're running a bit low now, barely over twenty bucks combined, but without the five dollars a day draining on it, it will go much further. In fact, if we continue to share one bed and do a little trapping to supplement our meals, we should be able to live off of the same amount I do alone without going hungry. As far as where we are going from here," Ezra sighed as he leaned back against the headboard, crossing his hands behind his head.

"Honestly, I have no idea. Backtrack, I guess. Revisit the towns I went through when following the lead to Dowes. There were a few of his lackeys that I left alive either because I was unable to kill them or because I got the information without them realizing what I was doing. As I am sure you know, you can get a lot of information out of people simply by getting them drunk. I wish I did not have to go backward. It already took me so long to find those three. If I end up having to start over from scratch, it might take another five years."

Cole watched him in silence for a moment, enjoying the way the position of his arms caused his muscles to bulge under his sleeves. Biting his lip, he was more than a little tempted to climb on top of his prone form, kiss away the worry lines his pout was causing around his lips, but he shook his head and thought better of it. As much as he was sure to enjoy doing so, such actions would only serve to annoy Ezra. Best case he dumped him on the floor and told him to knock it off. Worst case, it might cause his new friend to punch him.

He was able to get away with a lot when he was Colleen, but Cole doubted the same could be said for their masculine half. Perhaps though, if he was lucky, the need might arise for him to take on his feminine form sooner than he anticipated, allowing him to cross the friendship line a bit. So instead of acting as his body desired, Cole sat down on the edge of the bed beside Ezra; he was close enough that if either of them moved slightly, they would touch.

As Ezra regarded him silently, Cole wondered, "Well, since the people you are looking for are part of a gang, why don't we check with the local sheriff's office?" Seeing the confused expression marring Ezra's face, he explained, "Well the lawmen are out hunting down the bank robbers, right? It didn't look like anyone stayed behind to guard the empty cells, so it wouldn't be too hard to break in. Especially with the dust storm keeping most people inside. Maybe they have some wanted posters on the gang or something else of use."

Ezra jumped up, causing Cole to fall into the spot he vacated. "That's a great idea. Why didn't I think of that?" He hurried to put on his boots.

Cole rolled over onto his side and watched as Ezra hopped around on one foot and then the other as he fought to put on his boots.

"Don'tcha think you'd be better off waiting for dark to go breaking into the jail?" Cole gestured toward the bright sunlight that was still streaming in through their window. Though the dust storm was making visibility more difficult outside, he could still see buildings in the distance.

Ezra laughed, embarrassed. He leaned back against the wall as he pulled his boots back off once more, tossing them to the side.

"I know a way we can pass the time..." Cole began as his eyes trailed over Ezra's body before catching himself. "Sorry, force of habit."

Ignoring his flirting, Ezra sat back down on the bed beside him. "What exactly do you find attractive about other men? I guess it makes some sense as Colleen, but what attracts Cole to men? If you don't mind me asking, that is."

For a minute, Cole stared at him in silence, wondering how he didn't realize the same things attracted him as both Cole and Colleen, before finally smiling and standing up, gesturing for him to do the same.

"Take off your shirt," Cole instructed, rolling his eyes when Ezra stood there stunned. "I'm not going to do anything, silly. You want to know what attracts me to other men? Then take off your shirt." This time, Ezra slowly unbuttoned his shirt before pulling it off and tossing it on top of the bed. "Now we'll skip the more obvious attraction to what's between your legs since I doubt I would be able to explain that one anyway.

"Do you see this?" Cole gently ran his finger down the line that separated the muscles of his neck and shoulder, tracing it down his chest to where it ended at his navel. "This line. And these ones," he continued as he caressed the lines that ran along his hips, stopping once he reached the top of his pants. Lifting Ezra's arm up at an angle, causing his muscles to flex slightly, Cole traced the line that cut across his bicep.

"These lines are what attract me to men," Cole explained, not missing the confused expression on Ezra's face. "These lines—" He allowed his fingers to fan out over his chest, running them down Ezra's hardened muscles before resting them on his hips. "—they signify strong, well-toned muscles. Muscles, in turn, indicate strength. That is what I am attracted to. Your strength—your ability to protect. Perhaps I can explain it better if I show you."

Turning his back to Ezra, Cole wrapped his strong arms around his slender frame, crossing his own in front of his chest to hold him in place. "Ignoring sexual attraction, or lack thereof, what do you feel when you wrap your arms around me? What does someone being in your arms make you think about?" Receiving nothing but silence in response, Cole glanced over his shoulder in question. Ezra only shrugged his shoulders.

"You've never held someone, have you?" Cole questioned without a hint of mockery. Still, Ezra moved to pull away, slightly embarrassed, but Cole tightened his hold and refused to let him retreat. Instead, he turned around in his arms to face him; though he did take a step back so they wouldn't be quite so confined. "What I feel, wrapped in your arms, is protected. I feel your strength, your power. I feel as though no one can touch me, no one can hurt me as long as I stand here.

"I am attracted to men—to you because of your strength. To be honest, the more I get to know you, your strength, the more attracted I find myself to you. It is only a matter of time before I cross a line with you. Even now, it is taking every ounce of strength that I have not to taste your lips," Cole admitted, his voice husky from lust, before growling at himself and pushing back away from Ezra, breaking their connection. "As

I said, only a matter of time. When you see me crossing that line, just remind me to back off. I may end up letting my lust get the better of me one day, but I would only kiss you.

"Of that, you can be sure. I would never force myself on you, Ezra. I would never do that to someone else. When that happens, when I can no longer be around you, when I feel my control slipping, I will walk away. For your sake and for mine."

# Chapter Fourteen

THOMASVILLE 1830

Outside, as dusk was beginning to settle over the town and the dust storm provided a hazy cover, a young man chuckled darkly to himself as he stalked the shadows surrounding the saloon, taking notice of the comings and goings of those inside. Though there were only a few he was truly seeking to punish for their treatment of him, he would not risk one of the others interrupting his plans. It was a rather simple plan; setting fire in the wooden saloon would take little work and should be easy enough to make it look like an accident.

Embers from the hearth escaping, a drunkard knocking over a candle. No one would be able to trace it back to him, and the bastard would be ruined. It was the perfect plan, as long as no unexpected complications arose. The cheat would lose his saloon and his life before the night was through, as would the men working for him, but he would make certain the others only walked away a little sooty.

Almost time to set his plan in motion, he made his way over to where he hid his last few belongings to his name. Before going into a saloon, he long ago learned to always hide them somewhere others couldn't find them in case he passed out or some bastard tried to rob him. Both of which happened on more than one occasion. Truthfully, there wasn't much left to speak of: a single change of clothing in desperate need of mending, his lucky horseshoe which failed to bring him any good fortune in quite a while, and his mother's necklace.

It was never meant to be his, but there was no one left besides him to have it. He turned his thoughts away from the jewelry and back to the men he was about to exact his revenge on. They cheated him out of the last few dollars he had to his name. Money he was forced to mine from dawn to dusk down in some dark, dank hole just to earn and he was not about to let any of them get away with it anymore. Money that cost another their life; almost cost him his. It was time they learned to regret messing with him.

You do not screw with someone who has nothing left to lose for they are willing to do anything to pay you back. Those bastards were about to learn what it meant to have him as an enemy, but it was unlikely they would live long enough to have the chance to regret their mistakes. Perhaps they would not even know who it was exacting their revenge on them; he might not be the last thing on their mind before the excruciating pain made it impossible for them to think anything at all, but that was all right.

They did not need to know who it was that was taking their lives as long as they paid their price. Reaching for the necklace, he stared at it in silence for a few moments, trying to recall the image of his mother's face, but everything about her had long since disappeared from his mind. He did not remember what she looked like. What she sounded like. Not even her name. He only remembered the day she died, how she died, but all he saw in his mind when he thought of them was the blurry images of his parents being hung.

Carefully clasping the necklace in place, he decided to abandon the rest of his belongings where they were. He would be unable to return for them once he was done, certain he would need to get out of town as quickly as possible, and they would only hinder him if he tried to bring them into the saloon with him. Wasn't anything worth worrying about anyway, besides her necklace of course, so they could sit and rot in the hole he left them in for all he cared. Righting himself, he turned and made his way back toward the saloon.


ONCE THE SUN sank behind the horizon, certain the men downstairs would already be too long in the bottle to notice him, Ezra made his way over to the small window in their room and glanced out at the jailhouse across town. From their vantage point, they could see well enough to know no one was there and Cole would be able to warn him if anyone did start making their way toward him. Though the storm helped provide him cover for what he was about to do, it was starting to die down so their visibility from the bedroom window was better than it had been just a few hours before.

"Just leave the curtains open as long as everything is okay and so you can keep an eye out," Ezra said. "If anyone comes too close to the jailhouse or if you see the lawmen returning, close the curtains. I will look out the window every minute or so, so I should be able to see the warning pretty quickly," Ezra explained before making his way over to the dresser and retrieving his gun belt. Settling it back into place, he double checked his gun before putting it in the holster and turning back to find Cole staring at him in silence, his apprehension clearly evident on his face. "You can't come with me, Cole. You have a much better vantage point from here. If you were watching from the jailhouse itself, you would only be able to see a few feet in each direction before the other buildings got in the way. Possibly even less with this storm."

"And what happens if you don't look up fast enough to see the curtains? What if something goes wrong, and you need back up down there?" Cole demanded, crossing his arms in front of him and blocking Ezra's path to the window. For a moment, Ezra stood there staring at him in silence as he wondered if the lighter man thought he would be able to stop him if he wanted to get passed. To prove his unspoken thought, he lifted Cole into the air and moved him to the side.

"Cole, do you even have a gun?" Ezra inquired, continuing without giving him the chance to answer as he already knew what he would say. "No, you do not have a gun. You would have to engage anyone that attacked in hand to hand, and they would most likely have a gun. If they return and I can't get out in time, I can simply tell them I was looking for the sheriff. That I wanted to report something was stolen. This part I can handle, Cole, I have been doing this for over five years. If you want to watch my back and help me, then I need you here where you will have a better vantage point."

"Fine, but you will regret it if you end up getting yourself shot," Cole warned him before huffing and retrieving a chair from the other side of the room. Placing it under the window, he stepped back to allow Ezra to climb out the window. Though tight, the window was wide enough for him to slip through. "Remember, fifteen minutes, and you come back. Get in and get out," Cole instructed before turning his attention to the curtains and tying them back.

"Yes, sir," Ezra promised with a salute. He made sure there was no one else around before he quietly climbed down off of the awning. He made his way toward the jailhouse, keeping to the shadows in case anyone happened to look out their windows. Having no choice but to step out of the shadows once he approached the jailhouse, Ezra glanced up toward the saloon to confirm his solitude with a subtle nod from Cole. Returning it, Ezra stepped up to the door and tested the handle, unsurprisingly finding it locked. Reaching down for his knife, which was thankfully returned with his gun belt, he carefully slid the blade between the lock and the doorjamb, where he was able to pop it open with a bit of maneuvering.

Another quick glance around to make sure no one saw him and Ezra ducked into the jailhouse before closing the door behind him. Making his way over to the nearest window, he signaled to Cole that he was in before turning his attention back to the dark room. Though there was a little light coming in through the windows, things would be a lot easier to search through with some candlelight. However, he did not want to risk someone seeing it.

Taking stock of the otherwise unoccupied room, Ezra found it to be not much different from the one he was in not that long ago. This one housed three cells instead of two and were perhaps a little better maintained, but still contained little more than a straw bed and a bucket. Though, judging by the smell, or lack thereof in this case, these cells were cleaned sometime before the posse went after the bank robbers.

Turning his attention away from the cells, he made his way over to the other side of the room which housed three desks and an empty gun rack. Unlike the other jail, it was a little harder to tell the deputies' desks from the sheriff's as they were all organized properly. Shrugging his shoulders, Ezra turned his attention toward the first desk and went through the papers; he made sure to put them back exactly as he found them.

A quick search of the wanted posters he found made no mention to himself or Pine Box. Another stack of papers yielded nothing but minor complaints made by the townsfolk, mainly pertaining to saloon brawls and noise complaints. Ezra made a quick trip to the window to ensure the curtains were still open before making his way toward the second desk.

A lot of what he found was similar to the previous desk, leading him to believe the two belonged to the deputies. Though the wanted posters were of different men and the complaints were filed by different townsfolk, they essentially amounted to the same useless information.

Ezra checked the window once more before turning his attention to the final desk.

Unlike with the first two, this one's stack of wanted posters had X's draw across them. Apparently, all of these men were already dead or brought to justice. A quick search assured him there were none from Pine Box and he turned his attention to the other stack of papers. Where the other desks had complaints, this one held what seemed to be evaluations on the people in the town. They listed whether they drank or were often drunk, if there were any issues with the other townsfolk, with the law, if they owned any property in the area, and if they had any outstanding tabs at the saloon or general store.

He turned to the last paper and found it almost completely blank. All that was written was a name, Carlee Pepper, and the fact that he owned the saloon. There was nothing else listed on his paper, not even the questions posed on the others. Finding that more than a little odd, Ezra returned it to the stack before searching the room once more in hopes of having missed something.

Disappointed when nothing popped out at him, he made his way back toward the front door and quickly checked to make sure the coast was still clear. Seeing Cole still standing in the window, his head tilted slightly in question, Ezra shook his head no before making his way back outside, locking the jailhouse behind him. Indicating to Cole that he was going for a walk, as the storm was nearing its end, Ezra waved off his concerned look before heading away from the saloon. He simply needed to clear his head for a few minutes; he would update Cole on his finding nothing when he returned.


SIGHING TO HIMSELF, Cole stepped away from the window and made his way over toward the bed. As much as he wanted to talk to Ezra about what he found, though he doubted it was much judging by his behavior, he would have to wait for him to return. Knowing he didn't need him to keep watch anymore since he wasn't breaking the law and was now out of Cole's line of sight anyway, Cole lay back on the bed and closed his eyes.

Though he doubted he would be getting much sleep, he actually managed to slip into a fretful slumber pretty quickly. At first, his dream started out how most of them did lately, the lawmen on their trail catching up to them, he soon found his dream changing to one he did not have in quite a while. Cole remembered the day as if it just happened, but even as the images played in his mind, he did not understand what was happening.

Or why things seemed to be different than he remembered. All around him, a strange scent seemed to fill the air, and he found himself walking outside the front door of his childhood home. Only he knew he never went out that night, that he stayed curled up in his bed. But there his feet were, leading him away from his house and toward the barn. His feet were not as they were when that night happened; instead, he saw his larger adult feet walking barefoot in the dirt.

Confused, but unable to stop himself from continuing on in the dream, Cole silently allowed himself to be pulled closer to the barn. The scent, which was becoming stronger with each step he took, threatened to suffocate him. Staring at the barn, his feet stopping him a few inches from the entrance, the image almost seemed to wave in front of him, becoming a blurry mess. Before he figured out the cause, a blast of hot air and smoke hit him straight on as the door was blown open.

Even through the smoke and flames, he saw the inside was not of the barn from when he was a child but was the main room of the saloon they stopped at the night before. He was given only a moment to wonder what that meant as the air from outside caused the fire to flame up. Screaming out as he felt the flames rushing toward him, Cole sat up in bed panting and choking on the smoke he inhaled in his dream.

Only, he realized, as he breathed in what should have been safe, clean, saloon air, actually caused his coughing to worsen. More confused than he was in the inaccurate dream, he glanced around the room, trying to make sense of what was going on. It was then that he noticed the strong scent he smelled within the dream had not yet left him. In fact, it only seemed to be even stronger here, and Cole soon found his eyes stinging from it and the strange smoke that filled the room.

Jumping to his feet, he rushed toward the door, testing it with the palm of his hand and finding it far hotter than it should have been. Terror rising up from the pit of his stomach, Cole forced it back down as he clenched his fists and gritted his teeth. He survived far worse than this, and he was not about to let his fear put his life at risk, especially not that he finally found something worth living for.

Testing the knob and finding it far too hot to touch barehanded, Cole glanced around the room searching for something to protect him, even as he shouted, "Fire!" hoping the others around him would wake up if they weren't already awoken by the smell as he was. "The saloon is on fire!" he called out loudly, soon hearing screams of panic coming from the other rooms, as he gave up on going out the front and turned his attention to the window.

About to climb out as Ezra did, and instruct the others to do the same, he soon found that plan was useless as the awning below him already caught on fire. Screaming in frustration, he tried the door again, only to find it refused to budge.

EVEN BEFORE HEARING Cole's shouts of fire, Ezra was already rushing back toward the saloon, having seen the smoke from where he was sitting on a hill overlooking the town. From all around him, he heard people shouting. Some were cries for help from those trapped inside, others were instructions from those outside calling for everyone to help put it out. Ignoring them and their calls to come back, Ezra rushed into the saloon, holding his arm across his face in an attempt to block some of the smoke.

Ignoring the rising flames coming from the main room, Ezra crawled up the stairs one-handed as he fought against his instincts screaming for him to run in the other direction. Practically on top of the fire now, he could not even see a few feet in front of him due to the smoke, and the heat was threatening to cook him alive.

Knowing he would not be able to find their room by sight, he called out, "Cole! Cole call out to me!" and soon heard his voice, along with the others begging him to save them. Ignoring them for now, knowing that two of them would have a better chance of saving everyone and he had no way to guarantee any of the other random men would stay to help, he followed the sound of Cole's voice back to their room.

Though it was nearly pitch black in the hallway, it was not hard for his hands to find where the door's shoddy craftsmanship caused it to warp into the doorjamb from the heat, causing it to create a seal. "Stand away from your doors!" he called out, giving Cole exactly two seconds to listen before kicking the warped wood as hard as he could.

Though it did not open, the creaking as the wood threatening to splinter was heard over the roaring fire that was quickly drawing closer to him. "Open damn you," Ezra swore as he kicked again and again until it finally busted open, giving Cole enough room to squeeze through the splintered remains of the door. Giving Cole a quick once over, only able to find burns on his hands and unable to tell the extent of the damage in the firelight, Ezra fought the urge to draw a deep breath in relief.

"I think the fire welded all of the saloon's doors shut. I need you to help me kick them open. I'll take the right side. Call out if you need any help," Ezra instructed, waiting long enough for Cole to nod before taking off toward the nearest door to his right. Even as he was instructing the occupants to back up, he heard Cole doing the same. Which each room he emptied, he felt the fire growing closer even as Cole moved further away.

At last, he reached the final door and busted it open before making his way back toward Cole. Finding him stuck on his own final door, the room closest to the fire received more damage than the others, he gestured for him to back up before attacking it himself. Once it was opened, he was more than a little concerned when no one came out. Every room was rented out, they managed to get the last one available, so there must be someone inside.

Already knowing what to expect, Ezra crawled in through the door that had been destroyed and searched the room. Through the heavy smoke and flames that were now climbing up the far wall, he barely saw anything and opted instead to crawl around on his hands and knees, searching the ground nearby with his hands instead of his eyes. Soon enough, he found the unmoving form of the room's only occupant and passed him through the destroyed door as best as he could to Cole.

The guy would surely have a few extra cuts and scrapes to go with any damage he suffered from the fire, but they would not kill him if the smoke he inhaled didn't. "Bring him outside, I'm going to go double check on the owner before getting out myself. Any idea where he would be?" Ezra questioned after coming back into the hall and beginning to help Cole drag the man toward the stairs.

"You should leave him, Ezra," Cole insisted suddenly, shocking Ezra into almost dropping the half of the man he was carrying. "Owners tend to sleep in a room behind the bar, Ezra. All of that liquor could go off at any minute plus he's the closest to the fire, it's unlikely he survived this long," Cole answered honestly as they reached the bottom of the stairs before gesturing for Ezra to release his side.

"Bottles haven't caught yet, and the fire hasn't reached the bar, I'll just do a quick check and get out," Ezra promised, resting his hand on Cole's shoulder for a moment before heading off toward the bar. The closer he got, the thicker the smoke seemed to become; causing him to cough and choke on it. Ezra jumped over the bar and searched along the wall for the room he was certain was there even if it wasn't visible through the smoke.

It took longer than he would have liked, but Ezra eventually found the door, only to find himself confused when he reached down for the handle only to find something stuck in the wood, sealing it even without the heat from the fire. Someone had jammed this door purposefully.

He kicked the door down and entered the room. There was no one there. Confused, he carefully made his way to the bed only to find it just as empty. Deciding to try the last place before giving up, before he ended up getting himself killed as well, he was about to search for open windows he might have escaped from only to realize he heard voices coming from outside.

Making his way toward the sound, figuring it would lead him to the window the owner escaped from, Ezra was surprised to find the sound was coming from behind a dresser that was pulled away from the wall. Stepping behind it, he felt along the wall until he almost lost his balance when his hand fell into an empty space. Assured the owner was already safe on the other side, Ezra got down on his hands and knees and squeezed through the small tunnel as he heard the bottles of whiskey exploding behind him.

EZRA STUMBLED OUT of the saloon. "Ezra!" Cole shouted. He rushed to him and wrapped his arms around his shoulders. Though it took him a moment, Ezra soon returned the hug, resting his head on his shoulder as he breathed in the fresh air. "I'm sorry, Ezra, I noticed the owner was already out here too late to get back in to warn you. Seems the coward was one of the first ones out and didn't bother to go back and help the others." Cole gestured to where the saloon owner was standing with a few men, an angry scowl on his face as he yelled at the others. He was a large, burly man with short black curls and hard brown eyes.

"Considering what I found, I am not surprised." Ezra stepped around Cole and making his way over to the onetime saloon owner, drawing his attention.

"Any idea why someone set your saloon on fire and barricaded your door so you couldn't get out?" Ezra demanded. The other people gasped in shock. The owner, on the other hand, seemed completely calm if not for the angry look on his face, which turned even darker as Ezra spoke. "Went to check on you and found someone stuck a piece of wood through your door handle. Lucky you had that escape tunnel in your room."

"Luck's got nothing to do with it. In my line of work, you tend to make enemies," he explained with a shrug as though it were an everyday occurrence, his anger from a moment ago seeming to disappear. "Not the first time someone tried to rob me. It's not hard to figure out a filled-up saloon brings in a bit of money. Guess whoever it was figured they would have better luck with the sheriff off chasing bank robbers."

About to call him on the obvious lie, as Ezra highly doubted anyone would set a building on fire to try to rob it, he was interrupted when another man approached and spoke to the owner. "Mr. Pepper, he was seen heading north after stealing one of the horses that were hitched outside your saloon," he explained, his words causing dread to creep up in Ezra's mind. Somehow, he knew his concern would prove to be correct.

Turning his attention to where someone moved the remaining horses, it did not take more than a moment for him to realize which one was missing. "He stole my horse," he growled as he turned toward Cole who glanced over to confirm for himself before growling out his own frustration. Turning back to Pepper and finding him instructing others to prepare to go after him, he announced, "I'm going with you."

Before Pepper got the chance to respond, Ezra felt himself being pulled back before Cole harshly whispered in his ear, "You should let him go, Ezra. It's not worth the risk." Knowing he was worried about him involving himself in something that might attract the attention of lawmen, Ezra smiled gratefully before patting his hand in reassurance. Though Cole released him, he did not make a move to back up.

"There is more risk in being reduced to walking," Ezra whispered back, careful to make sure no one else heard him, though the others were too busy listening to Pepper give out orders to care about the two of them anyway. "Besides that, Cole, he could have killed you. He may have only blocked Pepper in, but he started a fire that almost killed you and everyone else inside." Seeing Cole still wasn't convinced, he offered, "I will return in twenty-four hours if we are unable to find him by then."

"I'm going with you," Cole decided.

Ezra shook his head. "No."

"What do you mean 'no'? Weren't you the one that was just saying how you wanted me to watch your back? How am I supposed to do that if you leave me here? Who's going to watch your back out there? Pepper?"

"Actually, you will be watching my back by remaining here, Cole. If they return before I get back, I need you to put up a signal so I know not to enter town. Leave a piece of cloth hanging from the tree near what's left of the saloon.

"When I return, I'll remove it, and you can meet me in the trees nearby. Until then, I need you to stay here so I know where to pick you up. I will come back for you." He squeezed his hand before joining the others without waiting for Cole to respond. Finding them one horse short, he commandeered the only open one before its owner mounted up.

"I'm borrowing your horse. I'll return it when I get back," Ezra informed him instead of asking, grabbing the reins and turning the animal toward the others. About to object, the man was silenced when Pepper nodded his head to Ezra before signaling for his horse to begin heading north. Following along behind him, Ezra glanced back over his shoulder to find Cole watching him with concerned eyes.

Smiling reassuringly, Ezra tipped his hat to him before turning his full attention to the road ahead of him. Reminding himself that he only had twenty-four hours, Ezra sped up a bit to pull up alongside Pepper. "He's already got a pretty good head start on us, no sense in taking it slow, right?" Without waiting for a reply, he sped up once more and was soon leading the group north.

# Chapter Fifteen

THOMASVILLE 1830

Cole waited until Ezra and the others were out of sight before turning his attention to the small town around him. What exactly did Ezra expect him to do while he waited for his return? There was no saloon to sleep in, the diner would not open for hours yet though they were at least promised a free breakfast once it did, and the few other businesses that the town offered closed hours ago. Glancing around at the others that were now out of shelter for the night, Cole spotted a couple of card games going up as if nothing out of the ordinary happened.

Cole knew they were all faking their almost nonchalant attitudes; even with everything he went through, he barely kept his hands from shaking. Glancing once more in the direction Ezra had gone in, Cole realized he needed to behave the same as the others if he wished to wait for his return there without any problems.

Realizing for the first time that Ezra never had the chance to tell him how things went at the sheriff's office, Cole sighed once more before turning his attention back to the card games cropping up around him. Though he didn't have the chance to play before himself, his time at the saloon gave him plenty of opportunities to watch the others, picking up a few tricks along the way. Evaluating each of the four games as he glanced at their players, he dismissed the two whose dealers were cheating.

Though the others did not see the cards making their way into the hand of the person on the dealer's right, Cole had a completely unobstructed view. Turning toward the other two, he found one with buy-ins he could not afford, let alone the hands themselves and made his way toward the final, poor man's game. Though he was only able to claim a few dollars to his name, losing half of it might prove worth it if it kept the others from wondering about him or Ezra.

And, if he was lucky, one of them might be able to give him information that was useful to Ezra's cause. Sitting down beside the others, Cole pulled out half of his money, leaving the rest to pay for meals while waiting for Ezra to return, before handing it over to the dealer, who handed him a stack of chips.

After being told the chips were worth a nickel each, Cole tossed his ante into the pile and gathered up the cards he was dealt. A quick glance at them assured him it was going to be a losing hand; though judging by the faces of those around him, he wasn't the only one. He observed each man carefully as they went around either raising, calling or folding outright; it was not hard to pick up the tells on three of the men. The fourth, however, he was certain should have been in one of the other games judging by his skill and ability to hide his tell.

For the next few hours, Cole kept himself entertained with the game, making sure to never take on the man he couldn't read. He caught on to what Cole was doing, always folding when he started to raise the bet himself, but he did little more than smirk at Cole each time he did, assuming he was too chicken to take him on. As the others slowly faded out of the game, their chips ending in either Cole's pile or the other man's, they continued to watch the two of them continue to play.

When he began going all in early on a couple of hands, Cole was certain he was done playing and ready to end the game. Folding each time he did, knowing his hand would only beat his opponent if he was completely bluffing, he waited until he was certain he had a hand that at least stood a chance of winning. As much as he wanted to walk away, perfectly happy to take away only a third of the money in the pot, the dealer made it clear that they would play until one player won all the money.

Worrying his bottom lip, he waited until his opponent was all in again before 'suppressing a yawn' and giving up. Pushing in his own pile of chips, he waited silently as he turned over his cards. Ace of clubs. Ace of hearts. Ace of spades. Cole's heart beat a little louder in his ears than it was a moment before.

Queen of hearts. Queen of spades. Full House. He had a full house. Correction, Cole couldn't help but smile as he went over the order of hands in his mind, his hand was *only* a full house. Flipping over his own cards even slower than his opponent did, Cole watched his face for the moment he knew was coming, the moment he realized he lost. Jack of hearts. Jack of clubs. Jack of spades. Jack of diamonds. Six of diamonds.

"Four of a kind wins the pot," the dealer told them, and Cole barely contained his excitement as he reached out and pulled the chips to him. He was careful not to go overboard, having seen many men lose their temper after losing a game of poker and not wanting to set him off. For a moment, the man seemed as though he was going to get angry before sighing, nodding to Cole and walking away. Sighing in relief, he turned his attention to the dealer who seemed as worried about an outburst as he was.

Smiling softly, Cole handed over his chips; quickly counting the money before hiding it away in his coin purse and making sure it was out of sight. It wasn't much, five dollars and sixty cents, on top of his own buck forty that was returned, but it was way more than he had a few hours before. Tipping the dealer a dime, even though he took one from each of their buy-ins already, Cole tipped his hat before glancing around and finding the diner was beginning to open.

Knowing there would be a rush at first, with all the men from the saloon impatient to get their food, Cole decided it would be better to take a walk first instead of fighting the crowd. After making sure everyone else was occupied with the thought of food, Cole went in the other direction, careful to stay out in the light of the rising sun. No sense in standing in the shadows and putting himself in unnecessary danger in case one of them decides to try and rob him of the money he won.

AS THE FIRST rays of the sun peaked over the horizon, Ezra thought they seemed to be getting nowhere fast. Though they knew the general direction to follow the night before when they left the town of Thomasville, there were no further signs for them to follow. For all they knew, they could be going in a completely different direction than the man who set fire to the saloon and stolen his horse, having been unable to notice his change of direction during the night.

In fact, Ezra was about to suggest backtracking until they picked up his trail again when one of the men called out, "Mr. Pepper, he went this way. Perhaps an hour or so ago." As Ezra turned his attention to what the man saw to make him say that, he found no sign that anyone had been there himself. Though to be fair, he knew little more than to search for footprints and broken stems on plants, what his father showed him when teaching him how to hunt.

But where the man was indicating, Ezra saw neither. Deciding he had little choice but to take his word for it, he followed after the others as they continued on once again. At least this time, Ezra was forced to admit, they seemed to have some idea of where they were going, and that was more than they had a few minutes before. His curiosity from the night before still unsatisfied, he urged his borrowed horse to fall in beside Pepper.

"So why did this guy burn down your saloon, anyways? I doubt he was trying to rob you since it's kinda hard to steal money when you can't see two feet in front of you due to the smoke. And, no doubt, the money would have been with you, yet yours was the only door that was barricaded. I don't mean to pry too much anyways, but it's only fair I should know what I am getting myself in the middle of, no?" Ezra asked with a smile, pretending to have more respect for the man that he actually did.

It seemed to Ezra, the longer they were on this trip, the less he liked Pepper. Though he didn't outright do or say anything to cause Ezra's distrust, aside from the lying the night before about why his saloon burned to the ground, there was something about him that did not sit right with him. More than that, he was beginning to give Ezra the creeps. He seemed far too anxious to find the man they were chasing, and Ezra suspected it had something to do with him looking forward to punishing the man.

Ezra did not think he should get away with what he did, not when he almost killed all of those people, Cole included, but he knew the difference between justice and revenge when he saw it. Pepper was not out to bring the man to justice, to bring him back to the jailhouse to go on trial for his crimes—he was merely looking for revenge. Ezra was certain only one of the two men would be leaving their confrontation alive.

While that may not have been the most unusual thing, the man seemed to take far too much pleasure in the thought of hurting another man. Enough so that Ezra found himself wishing he gave the horse up for lost and stayed with Cole back in town, but it was too late now. If he went back, he knew he was leaving the other man to a slow, painful death. At least with him there, he would assure that it was quick.

And, perhaps more than that, Ezra needed to know what caused him to react in such a way. Nothing would make risking innocent lives like that okay, but Ezra himself put others in danger during a shootout with Morton. Perhaps, if he truly only sought to kill Pepper and his reasonings were sound, Ezra might let him live if doing so didn't put Ezra in any danger at least. "He lost at the card table. Accused my dealers of cheating, so I threw him out. Guess he took offense to the dirty bath water being dumped on his head."

"Did they?" Ezra questioned without a second thought, though he was pretty sure he already knew the answer. Judging by the smirk Pepper answered him with, his first thought was correct. His men cheated the man at cards. Still did not justify almost burning everyone alive, even with the added insult of dirty water being tossed on him, but he understood him a little more at least. Perhaps he would simply bring the man back to the jail himself after retrieving his horse.

"Mr. Pepper," one of the men called out. "He's headed into the valley. We can box him in if we take the high ground," he suggested as he gestured up toward the high-rise cliff above them. Glancing around, wondering if their horses would even handle the steep climb to get up there, Ezra turned his eyes toward the valley below them; just able to make out the form of a horseback rider getting further away from them.

"Two take the right side, two on the left in case he tries to escape. Me and the new kid will block this way," Pepper instructed before heading into the valley at full speed without bothering to wait to see if Ezra was following. Shrugging to the others, Ezra matched his speed, deciding not to bother pointing out to him that the others would not have enough time to get in front of the other man if they continued at this speed.

Going uphill would slow them down considerably, but that actually worked out in Ezra's favor. It would be a lot easier to assure the man was brought back for a fair trial if he only had Pepper to worry about. A quick glance over his shoulder assured him the others would be too far away to offer any help. Ezra smiled to himself before picking up his speed once more, leaving Pepper to follow after him instead.

With each minute that passed, Ezra found they were gaining on him, his own horse refusing to go as fast as he wanted him to. Smirking as a plan formed in his mind, Ezra whistled as loud as he could, the sound vibrating off of the valley walls around them, causing his horse to stop suddenly, throwing his rider forward before he figured out what was happening. "Good boy," Ezra praised as he pulled up alongside his horse and caressed his mane.

A quick inspection assured him he was unharmed, and he turned his attention to the two men as Pepper dismounted his horse and stalked toward their quarry. The other man, apparently injured when he was thrown from the horse, limped to his feet, trying to reach his gun in his gun belt, but finding it knocked from his hand before he could aim it. Getting his first real look at him, he decided his five seven stature and narrow, but muscular form was the same as countless others he saw.

However, his piercing blue eyes and long dark hair, worn in a low ponytail down his back set him apart. Though he couldn't exactly get a good look at it from his position, what he saw of the man's hair led him to believe it was almost as long as Colleen's, though his was straight when hers was completely curled.

"You picked the wrong man to mess with, boy," Pepper said. "Should have taken the loss and moved on, but no, you had to go and be stupid, setting my saloon on fire. I have my own fees that are coming up due, and De Voe will have my hide if I am unable to make my payment. Unfortunately for you, I don't handle failure well." He raised his gun at the other man, only to freeze at the sound of Ezra cocking his own gun. Ezra's heart pounded with each second that passed. Pepper's shock quickly gave way to anger. "Watch where you aim that thing, boy."

"De Voe?" Ezra questioned, his hands beginning to shake, "You work for Godfrey de Voe?" This was not supposed to happen right now. He had no chance to plan how to handle meeting up with one of his men, and he would be grossly outnumbered once his friends made it around the valley. Judging by the distance they were currently at, high above the valley, there were only a few minutes before they rejoined them. He would not waste any time on questions he knew he would never get the answer to.

"Did you use to run with a group from Pine Box that included a man named Dowes?" he demanded. Getting nothing but a chuckle in response from him, Ezra gritted his teeth before taking aim and shooting him in the hand, forcing him to drop his gun and the other man to dive out of the way. Forgetting about him and the gun he was now drawing from his hip, as it was pointed at Pepper and not him, he demanded, "What were the names of the others you ran with?"

The man just sneered in reply. Ezra took aim again and shot him in the leg. Though he was aiming for his foot, the shaking in his hands caused his aim to be off. Deciding to aim lower than intended in the future, not wanting to risk killing him before he got any information out of him like he did with Dowes, Ezra growled out his question again. "Their names! Now or you lose the other leg."

"Why do you care who I used to run with, boy? You're only asking for a very painful death if you go up against them," he taunted through clenched teeth as he tried to apply pressure to both his hand and leg at the same time.

Ezra glanced up toward the cliff face once more, realizing how much closer the men had gotten in the short time since he checked on them. Pepper was stalling for time.

"Maybe you should ask McKinley, Morton, and Dowes about just whose death was painful. You're dead one way or the other, Pepper, it's only a matter of if it's a bullet to the head or one to the gut. I hear they can be quite painful and take a long time for you to die," Ezra warned, though he already knew he would end Pepper with a single bullet to his head no matter how he answered. He could not risk letting him live long enough to inform the others of who he was or what he did. "Start naming them, Pepper or your legs are going to become a pair." The threat of a bullet in his other leg seemed to not be enough to convince him and, growing impatient, Ezra followed through on his threat.

"Clayton Hodge, Claiborne Sedden, Matthew and Michael Johnson, Hecktor Backus, Jake Wickers, Ervin Harris, and Arthur Granmil," Pepper hissed out after screaming in pain when the hot metal pierced his skin in his previously uninjured leg. As much as what he was doing threatened to turn his stomach, Ezra knew it needed to be done. He needed to get the information out of him any way possible; there was very little chance he would be this lucky again and happen to stumble upon another one of the men.

"Do you know the location of any of the men you used to run with?" Ezra questioned even as he took another quick glance at the others, realizing they would be within shooting range in a minute or two. Turning his attention to the odd man out, he found him still holding his own gun on Pepper, seemingly content to follow Ezra's lead.

"I ain't ran with them in years. You've seemed to know the location of more of them than I do. What'cha want with us anyway? What'd we ever do to you?" Pepper demanded through clenched teeth as he fought in vain to stop the bleeding.

Out of the corner of his eye, Ezra saw that his time was up, the others were already raising their guns in his direction and would be within range in mere moments. He had no time to waste, and yet something deep inside him demanded that he answered Pepper's question. He wanted to see the light dawn in his eyes when he realized why he was being killed before he snuffed it out forever.

"My name is Grayson," Ezra said. As Pepper's eyes grew wide in recognition, Ezra swore he saw his lips forming his father's name but gave him no chance to speak as he raised his gun and pulled the trigger.

A bullet to the head ensured that his parents were the last thing he ever thought about. "Take right," Ezra instructed even as he himself was turning left and raising his gun to the two that were approaching on that side. Shots echoed around the valley, the sound thundering in his ears as it drowned out the screams of those that were hit. At one point, a searing pain shot across his arm, but he barely even noticed as the adrenaline pumped through his veins.

After a minute, the firing stopped. As the dust settled, he saw his two targets were no longer a threat. Turning toward the other two, he found them in the same prone position as his attackers. Checking on his temporary ally for the first time since the fight started, he found him with his gun half raised though not actually pointing at him. It appeared he wasn't going to shoot him unless forced to defend himself. Ezra holstered his own gun with a sigh.

"As much as I want to shoot you for nearly burning my friend alive, not to mention everyone else in the saloon, you get a free pass just this once. If you hadn't done that, I would have never known he was one of the men I was looking for. So you get to live, and you can even have Pepper's horse, but I am taking mine back. His gun is mine too and any money on him, but you can have the others if you feel like searching them."

Ezra glanced up to find the other horses all scattered in the gunfight. It was too bad, they could have used a second horse since he needed to return the one he borrowed, but that would have to be a problem for another day. For a moment, he thought about keeping Pepper's horse for Cole but decided against leaving the other man completely stranded. Retrieving Pepper's gun, surprised that such a large man carried a small two-shooter, and his coin purse without bothering to check how much was in there, he mounted his own horse before leading it over to where his borrowed horse was grazing; strangely unaffected by the noise that was echoing through the valley a few minutes before.

As the other man mounted Pepper's horse, Ezra said, "I will be telling them you were killed in the gunfight. Stay away from Thomasville if you value your life." Without waiting for a reply, Ezra headed back south, spending the entire trip hoping he would return before the lawmen did. There were too many things to do now to be slowed down by their arrival. He may not have known where any of the others were, but at least having their names was a good place to start.

THE DAY DAWNED hours ago, so long in fact that Cole already broke his fast and eaten lunch at the diner, and he found there was little to do to keep himself busy while waiting for Ezra to return. His only real options were to walk around, make a quick stop by the jailhouse to ensure the sheriff had not returned and window-shop outside the few stores that were there. The only one to grab his attention was the dress shop, whose mannequins sported the most beautiful dresses he ever saw.

He knew the others might find it odd if they noticed him standing there, staring in the windows, but Cole didn't have it in him to care. It wasn't as if he was actually trying them on, and it would be easy enough to claim he was looking at them for his sister or a girl he was sweet on. The thought of him having a crush would cause most men to tease him relentlessly, or at least that was what it seemed based on what he saw at the saloon.

But it mattered little at that moment as no one passing by seemed to even notice his presence. The others from the saloon, except for the man waiting for Ezra to return with his horse, had all gone on their way after breaking their fast that morning as there was nothing to keep them in town now that the saloon was gone. The people who actually lived in Thomasville seemed too busy with their own lives to pay any attention to the two that remained in town.

Once the excitement of the fire died down, they went right back to their normal lives as though nothing happened. Though he found it a bit strange, Cole honestly couldn't blame them. They weren't actually personally affected by the fire, they lost no belongings, and no one was killed, and, more than that, time stopped for nothing and no one. They all still had their jobs to do, their families to feed, and their lives to live.

Hell, it was all Cole wanted to do himself. Instead, he found himself figuratively frozen in time as he waited for Ezra to return. He was unable to leave town, and there was nothing to do there to pass the time. Perhaps, if he was planning on being there longer, he might look for a bit of work doing side jobs for the residents of Thomasville, but Ezra promised he would only be gone for twenty-four hours. As it was, his time was only half up.

He would be on his way back soon, if he wasn't already, which left little time for him to even look for work, let alone get it done. Sighing as he took one last look at the dresses, Cole made his way around the town again, nodding politely to anyone he saw even if he barely even noticed them. Back to checking on the jailhouse before wandering around once more. Perhaps this time he would go right from the jailhouse, bringing him to the ruins of the saloon first instead of going left as he usually did; which would bring him to the diner.

FOR A MOMENT, Ezra thought to call out his name when he saw Cole standing in front of the dress store, but something caused him to hold his tongue. He caught sight of Cole's hand raising toward one of the dresses before he sighed and continued on his way without looking back.

Wondering how strange it must have been for him to want things as Colleen even when he was dressed as Cole, Ezra watched him disappear around a corner, heading in the direction of the jailhouse, before smiling to himself as he pulled out Pepper's coin purse. Frowning a bit when he realized there was far less in there than he was expecting, he shrugged his shoulders and made his way into the dress shop.

It would be more than enough to suit his needs, and that was all that mattered at that moment as he smiled at the shopkeeper and gestured toward the dress that captivated Cole. A few minutes later, it along with some undergarments were wrapped up. Ezra made his way back toward where he tied up his horse and returned the one he borrowed. So far its owner was the only one to care about Pepper's location, buying that he had been killed during a shootout with the man who started the fire.

The graze from one of the bullets on his arm helped convinced him easily enough, and Ezra was glad he did not take the time to stop and bandage it. After all, if someone witnessed the death of six men and was the only one to make it out alive and was wounded in the process, it stood to reason that he should be far too panicked to have the presence of mind to wrap his wound instead of rushing back to town as fast as possible.

The rivulets of crusted blood that ran down his arm caused the other man to shutter and silenced any questions he might have had. Judging by how fast he rushed out of town and the fact that Pepper did not object to leaving him behind, it was not hard for Ezra to figure out that he was not actually been a part of Pepper's crew, but instead was simply one of the men that were staying in the saloon the night before. Deciding it was best to get out of town before any others showed up looking for Pepper in case he had more men than the four that went with them, Ezra mounted his horse and approached Cole.

"Hey," he called out softly, startling Cole for a moment before his eyes grew wide in relief. "Be happy to see me later, we need to get going. We don't want to be here when someone figures out how badly things went." Ezra reached his hand down and helped Cole to climb on to the horse behind him, wincing when the strain caused the wound to reopen. Ignoring the new droplets of blood that leaked on to the dried ones, Ezra turned his horse and led them out of town.

"Ezra, you're bleeding," Cole hissed, his lips so close to Ezra's ear that he felt his hot breath fanning over his skin. Instead of waiting for his reply, Ezra felt Cole moving around behind him, searching for something in the saddlebag beneath his legs. Cole pressed a cloth tightly against the wound on his arm and glanced down to find him applying pressure.

"It's just a graze. Had already closed in fact. Don't worry too much about it," Ezra insisted before picking up the pace, wanting to get as much distance from Thomasville as possible. "I'll fill you in when we make camp for the night," he assured him and, catching Cole's nod of agreement out of the corner of his eye, he turned his attention back to the road ahead of them. With each passing minute, it seemed less and less likely that anyone was following them, and Ezra allowed himself to relax slightly.

A FEW HOURS after darkness settled over the surrounding land, Cole breathed a sigh of relief when Ezra came to a stop and announced that they would be making camp there. Unaccustomed to riding a horse, even after being on the road for most of the last few days, Cole found himself worn out and sore each day they rode, but at least it seemed to be taking longer for him to reach his limit the longer they were out. Perhaps one day he might even be as unaffected by the rough ride as Ezra seemed to be.

Either that or he was good at hiding his discomfort. Dismounting, Cole set about preparing the fire as Ezra grabbed what they would need out of their bags, as usual leaving the rest still on the horse in case they needed to make a fast getaway. So far, they were lucky, able to leave their camps at their own pace in the morning, but Cole was certain they were both waiting for the day that their luck ran out and they were happened upon in the middle of the night.

If only he knew how soon their luck would be running out. Sitting down beside the fire, Cole warmed his hands above the flames more from having nothing else to do than from actual cold. Glancing up when he noticed Ezra was sitting down beside him, handing him a hardened lump of bread and a slab of jerky, Cole found himself wishing they had the time to grab more food from the diner before they left. Deciding it was too late to worry about that now, Cole bit off a small chunk of the jerky as he turned his attention to Ezra.

"Pepper, the man that owned the saloon," he began, waiting until Cole nodded his head that he knew who he was referring to before continuing, "it turns out he was one of the men I was looking for." Shocked by the unexpected news, Cole sucked in his breath and the piece of jerky with it, causing it to become lodged in his throat. Even as he realized he was starting to choke, Ezra was already on his feet, slapping him hard on the back several times until the food became dislodged.

"Thanks," Cole whispered in a hoarse voice before taking a swig of water after Ezra offered him the canteen. Taking a deep breath to assure himself and Ezra that he was fine, he set the rest of his meal aside explaining, "Might be a better idea to wait until you are finished before trying to eat. Something tells me I am not done being shocked tonight." After a moment, Ezra nodded his head in agreement. Turning his complete, undivided attention to Ezra, Cole gestured for him to continue.

"When Pepper was talking to the man who started the fire, I never did get his name," Ezra realized, speaking more to himself for a moment before turning his attention back to Cole, "he mentioned the gang I am looking for. With a little persuasion, I managed to get the names of the other men I am looking for, though he did not know where any of them were. Or at least he claimed not to. Perhaps if I had more time to interrogate him, I might have gotten their locations, but the rest of his posse was closing in on us.

"After making sure he recognized my father, I put a bullet in his head. The rest of his group were taken out during the gunfight that gave me this." Following his gaze to the wound, Cole bandaged haphazardly while on horseback, he stared at it for a moment in silence before questioning what happened to the man they were originally after. "Honestly, Cole, I let him go." Without having to see his own face, Cole knew his shock was clear as day.

"As much as I wanted to kill him for what he did, he led me to one of the men, and because of that, I ended up with the entire list of names I needed. I understand if you are angry with me for my decision, but as I told you before, I will do anything to find these men. That is the only thing that matters. It has to be the only thing that matters, or I risk everything I have worked for years to achieve."

For a moment, Cole only stared at him in silence before finally smiling and shaking his head. "Relax, Ezra, I am not mad at you for letting him go. If you recall, I wanted to let him be in the first place. He was not trying to kill me, I just got caught up in his revenge on Pepper. Did you ever figure out what that was about?" Cole bit off another bite of jerky.

"From what Pepper said, he lost at cards to some of the men in the saloon. Pepper pretty much confirmed that his men had cheated. I think it was a part of his operation here. Apparently, he had to pay dues to the gang leader." Ezra explained before turning his attention to his own food.

For a couple of minutes, the two ate in silence, opting to wait until they finished before either of them spoke up again. "So, how was your day?" Ezra inquired jokingly, causing Cole to laugh.

"Definitely not as exciting as yours. Played a bit of cards, even won about five bucks, but I think you are right about Pepper being behind the cheating. In two of the four games that were going on, the dealers were cheating. Burning down the whole building with people inside was a bit much, but I can understand the desire to pay Pepper back, especially if that was the last few bucks he had to his name. You only have to go hungry once to realize how precious money can be."

"Well as I said before, that is not something you should have to worry about again as long as you are with me," Ezra told him with a smile, before breaking out into a large grin suddenly. "I almost forgot. I got you something," he continued before jumping up and making his way over toward the horse. Cole wondered why he was acting so strangely.

Ezra came back with a package wrapped in brown paper and tied with a red ribbon. "Well it's not actually for you, Cole. It's for Colleen," he explained before handing the package over. Cole stared at him in silence for a moment before finally turning toward his gift. Unwrapping the paper carefully, he found himself even more shocked than he was when he learned Pepper's connection to Ezra. Cole found it harder to breathe as he stared down at the light tan-colored shirt and skirt he saw in the window of the dress shop.

He ran his fingers along the delicate, tiny blue flowers that ran along the border of the skirt— they looked even more perfect close up. "How did you know? You didn't have to do that for me, Ezra." Cole looked up at him with watery eyes.

"I arrived back in town when you were standing in front of the window admiring it. I would have said something then, but I wanted to surprise you. Before you try to claim you can't accept it, you should know it was not an entirely unselfish purchase. There may be times during our journey where having a woman at my disposal might come in handy. You're less threatening and people tend to pay less attention to a woman looking at wanted signs or asking questions."

"Oh, don't you worry none, I have no intention of refusing this dress. In fact, I should probably double check to make sure it fits properly," Cole decided with a smirk. He set the package aside and retrieved the corset from the saddle bag. It was the only piece of clothing he saved from the saloon, but it was a lot harder to find one that fit Colleen's not quite feminine shape than the dresses were.

Making his way back over to the fire, Cole unbuttoned his vest and shirt until he realized Ezra was still watching him. "A little privacy, if you don't mind," Cole teased and, though he saw the confused look on Ezra's face, he turned his back as requested. Making quick work of his shirt and pants, Cole searched through his new clothes until he found the pair of silver pantaloons Ezra bought to go with them and pulled them on, pulling the string as tight as it would go.

Though Colleen would usually prefer a slip to pantaloons, as they were easier to pull up while still hiding certain aspects of her anatomy, Cole was forced to admit it would be much easier to escape on horseback in them if the need arose. The skirt could simply be pulled up, leaving the lower half still covered in the silver material of the pantaloons, instead of being completely exposed by having to pull up the slip as well. It was either that or the even less appealing prospect of riding sidesaddle.

It did not matter if it was Cole or Colleen that was doing the riding, they hated the 'preferred female' position equally. Wrapping the corset around his chest, Cole turned his back to Ezra before calling out, "Can I get a little help?" Though he did not see him, he heard Ezra rise to his feet and felt him beginning to tug on the strings to tighten the corset. "Tighter please," Cole instructed as he grabbed on to a nearby tree for support.

"That's one thing I do not understand. Why wear something that looks so uncomfortable if you do not have to?" Ezra wondered even as Cole felt him pulling the strings tighter as he bid. Unable to answer him for the moment, as he was currently sucking in his breath to allow the corset to be pulled even tighter, he indicated for Ezra to wait a moment, finally exhaling once Ezra finished tying the corset closed.

"It helps push up my breasts, Sugar, and gives me a more feminine figure," Colleen explained, having effortlessly stepped into her female self, gesturing toward the extra curves the corset created. Reaching down into the top of her corset, she grabbed her chest muscles and pulled them up, causing her 'bust' to be even more pronounced. Colleen knew from experience that people would notice if they looked hard enough, but most men tended to not look for more than what was so obvious in front of them.

Retrieving her new shirt, Colleen turned her back to Ezra once more, glancing over her shoulder at him as he spoke. "How do you do that?" Ezra asked. "Seamlessly switch from Cole to Colleen with nothing more than a change of clothes. I have to be honest, it throws me off a bit. How do I know who I am speaking to if I can't see your clothes?"

Colleen giggled as she finished dressing. She raised her skirt slightly as she sat down, resting on her legs instead of crossed legged as Cole did. "It's something about the corset, I guess. I just no longer feel like Cole the moment it's on, or as Colleen once it comes off. If you can't see my clothes? Planning on seeing me naked often?" Colleen teased, causing Ezra to roll his eyes at her.

"To be honest, I cannot imagine you will see me completely naked as Colleen often. I have always kept the corset on when I am her, even during my encounters with the men at the saloon who knew who I was.

Until I met you, I was never Colleen when completely nude, and during those times, I wasn't in the right mind to think about who I was at that moment. I have always bathed in my corset on the rare occasion I was able to do more than give myself a sponge bath as it is impossible to put back on myself and they weren't exactly lining up at the saloon to assist me.

"My mind grew to associate the corset with Colleen. But whether I am Colleen or Cole, I am still the same person, Sugar. I may speak, act, and even walk differently, but the core of who I am is the same. What promises I make as Cole will be upheld as Colleen. My attraction, what I feel as Colleen transfers to Cole as well. For example, I find you as tantalizing in this very moment as I did two minutes ago," she told him before licking her lips seductively.

"Sorry, Sugar, but in case you haven't noticed, Colleen is a bit of a flirt. You can pretty much expect me to be always flirting with you whenever I am in a dress. Not so much as Cole though, and I should spend the majority of my time as him. In fact, I will change back into him first thing in the morning. For now, I want to be able to enjoy getting to wear a proper dress since there is no telling when I will actually be able to wear it again."

Ezra shrugged; apparently her choice of persona for the night made no difference to him. Colleen bid him good night before rolling Cole's clothes up and using them as a pillow. Though she closed her eyes the moment she laid her head down, she heard Ezra settle in for the night after stoking the fire so it would not go out. No doubt it would wind down during the night, waking one of them up as a chill settled around their camp, as their campfires did every night they have been traveling together.

# Chapter Sixteen

NORTHWEST OF THOMASVILLE 1830

Ezra swore he was only sleeping for a few moments when he felt a strange pressure against his temple. A sudden chill crawled down his spine as he realized with a foggy mind just what was being held against his head.

Dread gnawing at him in the pit of his stomach, he opened his eyes to find the cold barrel of a gun pressed against his temple. Two thoughts crossed his mind in sequence even as his heart pounded in his chest. First was that he wished he remembered to give Cole Pepper's gun as he was planning. The second was concern for Colleen's well-being as he had yet to hear her make a sound.

Perhaps, he tried to reassure himself, she was still sleeping unaware, but somehow he knew he would soon discover that was not true. Sure enough, as he scanned their camp, he found her very much awake with a large, dirty hand of a second man covering her mouth. The burly man was quickly forgotten as he noticed a third who stood to the left of them; his gun out and pointed at Colleen.

Turning his gaze back to his companion once more, something in her eyes assured him she was not harmed—yet. Taking in the appearance of the three men, or at least as much of the one holding a gun to his head as he was able from his position, it was not hard to figure out that not only were they not lawmen, they had no intention of obeying the law. At best, they planned to rob them. At worst, kill them.

Before he got the chance to offer them their money, the man who wasn't holding on to one of them spoke, causing a much darker dread to creep up on Ezra. "Out and about looking for some easy pickings, and what do we find, but such a pretty young thing." He grabbed on to her hair and yanked her out of his own man's hands; causing a few curls to fall from her hairpin.

Staring down at her with unmistakably hungry eyes, he growled at her, his voice heated with lust. "You look like you would make for some fine entertainment for me and my boys tonight, girly. I'm sure we'd satisfy you much better than this boy could. What'd ya say, girly?"

Much to his surprise, Colleen put on a sultry smile before biting her lower lip even as she stood. The man released his hold on her hair, and the rest of her fiery waves cascaded down her shoulders. "Oh, I very much am, Sugar, but there is no reason to force the willing. Much more enjoyable with me working toward your pleasure, don't you agree, Sugar?" Though the man chuckled above her, Ezra couldn't take his eyes off of Colleen as she reached up and unbuckled his belt.

Realizing what was about to happen, Ezra fought against the man holding him in place, the threat to his life forgotten for a moment, drawing Colleen's attention to him. Holding his gaze, she shook her head before turning back to the man with an alluring smile. Torn between wanting to protect her and not wishing to put her in any more danger, Ezra gritted his teeth and clenched his fists, and he sat back down, waiting for a sign that Colleen wanted him to stop what was happening.

Colleen removed the man from the confines of his pants and stroked the length of him, causing him to moan. Once he began to rise from her attention, she lowered herself to her knees. Ezra refused to take his eyes off her even as she ran her tongue across the tip of his manhood before dragging it down its entire length.

As much as his mind screamed to close his eyes, begging him to not witness what was happening before him, Ezra knew he dared not risk missing a signal from Colleen. That alone kept him focused on her as she drew his entire length slowly into her mouth. He groaned again from above her as he bucked instinctively toward the warmth. Clenching his fists hard enough that his nails drew blood, Ezra took stock of the men who were invading their camp.

With the gun cocked at his head, he saw very little about the man holding him, but he was certain he would be quick to pull the trigger if Ezra tried anything. His hand did not so much as even twitch. Unlike him, the third man, who now held his gun trained on Colleen as the leader was busy, was currently rubbing himself through his britches. He should be easy to overpower as he was distracted, but the same could not be said about his own captor.

With no other choice than to let it play itself out, Ezra turned his attention back to Colleen. She picked up her pace with her lips and hands, causing the man to grab a fistful of hair as he matched her pace with thrusts of his own. As his grunting grew louder and more animalistic, Ezra breathed a sigh of relief that he was almost done only to find him pulling Colleen off of him before he finished.

Dread coursed through him once more as the man reached under her skirt before either of them could stop him. For a moment, he seemed confused before a large grin split his face as he squeezed her in his hand, causing Colleen to cry out in pain. Though he struggled against his captor, the leader paid Ezra no attention as he smiled at Colleen. "Is this why you were so willing, girly?" he questioned, this time the nickname sounded as though he was mocking her.

"Must get awfully lonely being a pretty boy such as yourself, must not get many to warm your bed. Lucky for you, makes no difference to me and my men. After all, a hole is a hole as long as I can stick my cock in it." He chuckled darkly before flipping her over onto her hands and knees. Apparently getting tired of his attempts to escape, the man beside Ezra cold-cocked him with his gun.

ONCE THE MEN were finished with her, Colleen drew her knees into her chest and wrapped her hands around them. She refused to cry as they were still there and, after all, it would do her no good. Though she watched them out of the corner of her eye, just in case they planned to kill them after all, she barely had the time to realize what they were doing before one of the men grabbed on to the reins of Ezra's horse and tried to mount it.

Instead, the horse reared up and knocked him on his ass, though he made no further attempt to get away. "Leave the animal. Pretty boy won't be walking for a while," the leader taunted as he mounted his own horse. He headed away from their camp without bothering to make sure his man followed his instructions. He stared at the horse for a few more moments in silence before finally rising and making his way over to his own.

Colleen waited until they were no longer visible before turning her attention back to Ezra's unconscious form. After assuring herself that he would be fine, she closed her eyes against the tears that threatened to fall.

They were simply clients, she tried to convince herself, men that grew rough once they realized the truth about her and refused to pay for her services afterward. She needed to see them this way as the truth of what happened would only make her feel even worse.

Unable to do anything while she waited for Ezra to regain consciousness, Colleen finally let go and allowed the tears to flow freely down her cheeks. It was not the first time she was treated like trash by another, but once again, she found herself praying that it was the last. Usually she loved the feel of a man's strong body behind her own. The way their well-toned muscles pulsed with each thrust of their hips. The heat and friction that was caused when their callused hands slid across her smooth skin.

Honestly, she did not even mind having to lay with a man she was not actually attracted to. At least with them, she had the chance to feel the pleasures another body had to offer, and she always imagined that it was someone else with her. Usually she would envision him as whoever was the least repulsive in the saloon that night. Or when that failed to work, she would imagine him faceless; some unknown man she had yet to meet that would one day sweep her off her feet.

The unknown man now wore the face of Ezra, but she refused to imagine him in the place of the men that assaulted her that night. There was no pleasure in being taken like that and she never wanted to think about Ezra when the nightmare she lived through came back to haunt her, as she knew it would. Turning her thoughts from what she went through, she turned her watery eyes back to Ezra as she watched his chest rise and fall.


AS EZRA FOUND himself being drawn back to consciousness, his head was pounding and his stomach was threatening to revolt. Groaning in pain, he held his head in his hands for a few moments; hoping the heat from them would help calm down his throbbing head. Though his mind begged him not to, Ezra slowly opened his eyes; he needed to check on Colleen. The early morning rays of the sun were near blinding; forcing him to close his eyes once more against the assault.

Rubbing his eyes with the base of his hands, he opened them once more, slower this time, and found himself adjusting to the unexpected light. Blinking away the moisture the bright light caused, Ezra turned his attention to the last spot he remembered Colleen being in. He found her sitting there, her hands wrapped around her knees, as she stared unblinking into the distance. Climbing to his hands and knees, afraid standing upright would cause the throbbing in his head to worsen, Ezra crawled over to her.

Having no idea what he was supposed to do after what happened, Ezra decided it would be best to tread lightly, lest he scare her any more than she already was. It was the gentlest of touches on her shoulder, but it was still enough to cause her to cry out in fear. "It's just me, Colleen. You are all right," Ezra assured her, though, if he was honest with himself, he was not entirely sure she would find him nonthreatening at the moment or be reassured by his presence.

After all, he did nothing to stop the men from attacking her. Whether she gestured for him to not interfere or not, he should have done something. Perhaps if he remembered to give her the gun he took off of Pepper's dead body, she would have been able to defend herself, and none of this would have happened to begin with. If he never gave Cole the dress for Colleen in the first place, he doubted the men would have thought to use him in such a way. As he watched her, silently chastising himself for his role in what transpired, he saw the recollection dawn in her eyes and found himself sighing in relief when he was not met by hatred.

Wiping her eyes with the back of her hand, Colleen smiled softly at him before resting her head once more on her knees. "I'm all right, Ezra," she assured him, though Ezra knew by her shaking and the fact that she was currently curled up in a ball that this was not entirely true. Deciding it was best not to point this out to her, he was about to suggest they head out in case the men came back, when Colleen's words stopped him cold.

"This is not the first time I have gone through something like this. I simply need a few more minutes to collect myself, and I will be ready to go." Though she indicated before that she met with unsavory men in her past, she never mentioned anything like what happened. Did she mean to say she dealt with more than one attacker at the same time or did she simply meant it was not the first time she was raped?

Though he was far more worried about his friend than he remembered ever being before, Ezra knew better than to ask her to elaborate. If she wanted him to have the information, she would share it with him as she did with the rest of her story. As Ezra thought back on what she told him before the fire consumed the saloon, he realized he already had his answer. Desperate to do something, anything for his friend even if it only stood the slightest of chances of making her feel a tiny bit better, Ezra offered, "Is there anything I can do for you, Colleen? Anything at all, just name it."

He knew by offering her anything she could take advantage and ask for something he normally wouldn't be willing to give, something he already refused her, but he knew it would not matter to him even if she asked for something sexual in nature. Though he doubted being touched was something she wanted at that moment, he knew that if it was what she needed to feel even an ounce less of the pain she was going through, he would oblige in a heartbeat.

Colleen stared at him in silence, obviously startled by his offer. He practically saw the questions, she was no doubt wondering, in her eyes. Did he not know that giving someone permission to ask for anything was never a good idea? Didn't he know that she might ask him for something that he was not comfortable with? In response to her unspoken questions, Ezra simply smiled at her, knowing she would see nothing but a confident, determined look in his eyes.

He would hold true to his promise no matter what it was she asked of him and he would do so without complaint, without repercussions later on for her. Holding her gaze with his own, he was a bit startled when she got a teasing look in her eyes, but instead of being intimidated by the possibilities, Ezra simply smiled back at her. "I want a kiss," Colleen informed him after a moment, her eyes trained on his for any sign he was backing out.

"Very well," Ezra agreed without hesitation before leaning forward to close half the distance that was between them, closing his eyes. Even with his eyes closed, he felt her gaze on him as she continued to sit in silence. Forcing himself to sit still, as much as he wanted to open his eyes and ask her what was taking so long, Ezra was more than a bit surprised when he felt her soft lips being pressed gently against his forehead.

AS EZRA'S EYES flashed open, Colleen knew he was startled by the location of her kiss and couldn't help but smile at his confusion. "Why didn't you really kiss me, Colleen? I wouldn't have agreed to it if it was going to make me uncomfortable, if that is what you were worried about,"

Ezra assured her, causing her smile to grow wider at his obvious lie. She was certain, if she asked for him to be with her the way she wanted since the moment she met him, he would have agreed to it to alleviate his own guilt.

She did not blame him for what happened or for the fact that he did nothing to stop it as she herself was the one that told him not to. If they would have fought back, they would probably be dead now or, at the very least, the men would have been far rougher with her than they were. As it was, they were not even as rough as most of the men she managed to snag as a client. The men were monsters, that much was certain from the moment they abruptly woke her with a hand over her mouth, but they were, at the very least, not completely barbaric.

"Yes, you would have, Sugar. If I asked you to make love to me, you would have done so if only to make me feel better, all the while feeling worse yourself. But it does not matter for your offer alone was enough to make me feel a little better. And besides, Sugar, I never said the kiss needed to be on the lips," Colleen teased before resting her head against his shoulder, nearly knocking him off balance by the sudden movement.

"I just need to relax for a little while and being in your arms makes me feel safer than I have ever felt before. I hope you do not mind, Sugar," Colleen said, though she was not entirely sure she would have been able to move on her own if he did take issue with her resting against him. Her legs felt too weak to support herself, and she was not quite ready to try and move yet. Though other encounters were more painful, it took far more out of her body to accommodate three instead of one.

At least, she told herself to hold on to at least one slightly good thought, they took turns. Though it was rare at the saloon, considering the cost associated with it, there were occasions where more than one man would pay for use of a girl at the same time. The girls always took a while to recover after such an encounter even though they claimed to have enjoyed it even though they usually hated the ass service requests.

As her thoughts returned to the women she left behind at the saloon, Ezra settled himself into a more comfortable position and wrapped his arms around her; practically pulling her into his lap as he moved. Comforted by his presence and the warmth of his body, Colleen closed her eyes as she pressed up against him and breathed in his scent deeply. There was just something about the smell of him that both helped calm her heart and cause it to race at the same time.

It was a strange feeling, to say the least, but one she thoroughly enjoyed and hoped to be able to experience it again many times in the future. After a few minutes passed between them in silence, Ezra spoke softly as if he was trying not to startle her, "I think it would be wise for us to begin heading toward the next town soon. I would very much like to sleep on a real bed, and I am certain it would do you some good as well."

Rising to his feet, he helped Colleen to hers before continuing, "Besides, we still need to stock up on the essentials since Thomasville was a bust. If not, we'll be out of food and a few other things in a day or two. No telling when the next chance we get to stop would be." Nodding her head in agreement, Colleen did not bother to tell him she wanted to suggest the same thing herself. No sense in being on the road when she needed to recover, but she did not want to slow them down either.

At least with it being his suggestion, she need not feel guilty about them being held up in another town right after being delayed in the last. Packing their belongings, which the men scattered while searching for anything worth stealing, Colleen put them back into the saddlebags as Ezra made sure the long-dead fire was completely out. Waiting until he mounted the horse, Colleen allowed him to help her up, biting back a grunt of pain as she came in contact with the saddle.

This would prove to be a very painful ride, she was certain, but at least there was a town not that far from where they were. She remembered seeing a sign the night before that indicated one only a few miles away from where they broke off of the road to camp. Reminding Ezra about it, she waited until he nodded to indicate he heard her before turning her attention toward the passing scenery. Though it was as boring as it was the day before, the unremarkable plants allowed her mind to go blank as she watched them pass by without actually seeing them.

THE TWO RODE in silence, making the trip that only took a few hours seem like it took much longer. As much as he wanted to check on her throughout the trip, Colleen chose to remain silent, and Ezra wanted to respect her decision. She would be the one to break the silence, or they would continue on as they were; he decided soon after starting out. At least while they were on the road anyway. As they pulled into the next town a little after noon, Ezra glanced around the tiny western village of Glendale.

It was like countless others that were littered across the frontier, some of which he saw with his own eyes and many of which he hadn't. There were a saloon, a barber and a general store.

Ezra called for his horse to stop in front of the two-story boarding house. Unlike with Thomasville, the lodgings were provided in a different location than the saloon. Quickly dismounting and helping Colleen down, Ezra couldn't help but wonder if it would not have been better for her to change into Cole before entering the town, but it was too late to do anything about it now.

Reaching into his coin purse, more than a bit surprised that the men did not steal it or his guns while he was unconscious, Ezra handed her a few coins. "Head on in and get us a room for the night. Just tell them we are brother and sister as that might draw less attention to us, though in a town like this I doubt they will care one way or another. I'm going to make a stop by the blacksmith and have him check out his shoes; one feels like it might be coming loose." Petting the horse's mane, he glanced around, searching for said blacksmith.

Finding one not far off, he smiled to himself before turning his attention back to Colleen. "I will probably be gone for a few hours, so don't wait for me to eat or sleep. I want to search around for any clues about the names Pepper gave me, but I will keep a low profile. I'll grab the supplies at the general store as well in case we need to get out of here quickly." Seeing Colleen was about to object to him doing all the work, Ezra cut her off.

"You need to rest, Colleen, I know that ride was not easy on you, and there is no telling when the next time we will be able to sleep in a bed is. Rest now, you will be no good to me later if you are in too much pain to move." Without waiting for her to reply, Ezra pulled something from the saddle bag before turning back and handing her Pepper's gun handle first. "I doubt you will need it in there, but I will take no more chances," Ezra informed her. She nodded her head before hiding the gun in her boot.

Without another word, Ezra pulled on the reins and led his horse away. Behind him, he heard Colleen sigh before turning and making her way into the boarding house, the squeaky door giving away her entrance. Glancing over his shoulder, he watched through the window as she made her way toward the front desk and booked a room for the night. The bright smile she'd shown to the man behind the desk threw him off for a moment, but he soon realized she was pretending to be completely fine in order to draw less attention to herself.

Once she was out of sight, following the proprietor upstairs to their room, and knowing she would be safe for the moment, Ezra remounted his horse and turned away from the blacksmith, heading back in the direction they came from. What he hadn't told Colleen, knowing she would try to stop him, was that he saw the tracks the men left the night before. Though a bit surprised that he was putting his own quest on hold if only for a few hours, Ezra never gave his decision a second thought. After all, they would not be leaving town until the morning anyway so as long as he was back before then, he wasn't actually wasting any time.

# Chapter Seventeen

JAGGED VALLEY 1830

Once he was far enough away from the boarding house that he was certain Colleen would be unable to see him no matter which direction their room was facing, he urged his horse to go faster, not wanting to give the men any more of a head start than they already had. Now that his horse was burdened with one less rider, he was able to travel much faster, and Ezra soon found the breeze blowing through his hair as he raced back toward where their path diverged.

When they were traveling that morning, Ezra followed the trail as far as he could, beginning to wonder if they were heading to the same town as he was, but after a mile or two the men left the main road, opting instead to follow what seemed to be a wagon trail leading into the uninhabited wilderness in the northeast. Turning on to the road, nearly hidden by the sudden forest that seemed to pop up out of nowhere, he estimated that they had about a half a day's lead on him. If he was lucky, they would not be traveling with any real speed.

There was no reason for them to suspect that he was on their trail and they did not even bother to hide their tracks leaving the camp. Ezra couldn't help but wonder, as he followed the narrow trail deeper into the trees if their lack of caution was due to ignorance or arrogance. Though he knew it would not matter in the end and either one would make his hunting them down just as easy as the other.

Urging his horse faster still, ducking beneath a low-hanging branch that appeared in his path moments before he would have hit it, Ezra reminded himself to pay attention. He would not let his anger and desire for revenge to cloud his mind; it would only put him in unnecessary danger. He justified tracking the men down by the fact that they would not be leaving the town until the next morning anyway, but if he was not careful, he would end up getting injured. That would certainly put his mission in danger.

Ahead of him, Ezra saw the trees parting; opening up to rolling plains that seemed a stark contrast to the landscape on the other side of the forest. Though there were plenty of small bushes and even a few scattered trees, he did not remember the last time he saw grass; especially not this green. Apparently cut off from the world as this area was, it kept others from tramping over and killing the land.

As he slowed his horse, Ezra took a better look around only to realize they were steadily rising since leaving the forest. Understanding the reason for the thriving plant life, as the higher you went up the mountain, the more rainfall you seemed to get, he put the matter from his mind as he continued to search for any sign of the men. Though the rolling hills gave him some cover in each direction, there was no telling when he would suddenly find them on the other side of one of them.

They would not see him until he was right on them, but that meant that he couldn't either. Searching for their trail, which he lost in the lush grass, Ezra decided it did not matter when there didn't seem to be one. There was only one way for the men to have gone as the path seemed to lead them into a valley between to large mountainsides, much like the one he traveled to with Pepper. Only this time, the sides were far too steep for them to have climbed as the rest of his posse did.

Toward the end of the valley, as the lush grass gave way to a rockier path, Ezra was forced to dismount and continue on foot. Leading him by the reins, he continued on, kicking many of the rocks out of their path. Though annoyed he was forced to go at such a slow pace, Ezra was relieved to see the multiple sets of boot prints imprinted on top of each other in the dirt.

Not only did it confirm that he was going the correct way, as the piles left by their horses seemed to be only a few hours old judging by their 'freshness,' it also meant that they were forced to slow their pace even further as well. Wondering what exactly he was going to find once he finally crested the hill he was climbing, Ezra continued on, keeping his ears open for anyone who might be on the other side.

Though dusk was still many hours away, Ezra found it to be much darker than he was expecting as he reached the peak and took his first look at the valley below. The large mountain to his right seemed to be completely blocking the sun now even though it was bright as day a few minutes before. As he glanced around at what lay before him, Ezra saw a mountain rising up on three sides of the valley, cutting it off completely except for the trail he followed in.

Smiling to himself in satisfaction, he almost felt sorry for the men as it meant that they were within an hour of him at most and there was nowhere for them to go. Almost, but not quite as now they would know what it felt like to be trapped and unable to escape. Beginning to make his descent with the horse following along behind him, Ezra moved slower than he would have liked as he dared not risk spooking the horse and causing him to alert the men to their presence.

As he glanced out in each direction, in case the men were closer to him than he was expecting, Ezra noticed something in the distance; squinting his eyes as he tried to make out what it was. Though he couldn't make out any of the finer details from where he was, he saw a small house nestled in the farthest corner of the valley. From his distance, he barely made out the smoke rising from the chimney, but he knew they were there even if he hadn't seen it.

There was simply no other place for them to be. Realizing the ground evened out again, Ezra remounted and made his way toward the house. The open valley left little cover for his approach, but he managed to keep a large boulder in front of him for most of the trip, making it at least a little more difficult for anyone in the house to see him coming. Riding as close as he dared, not wanting to risk them hearing the hoof-beats, Ezra dismounted before hiding the horse behind the boulder.

Though he found its presence to be a little odd, there were, in fact, a few large boulders scattered around the valley, no doubt deposited there during some rock-slide. The only problem was, the jagged edges of the rock left little room to hitch the horse who he worried might bolt at the sound of gunfire. Though he was usually pretty good and staying with him even through his battles, he had the feeling that the echo in the valley would prove deafening.

Finding a thin, but seemingly strong vine crawling its way up the side of the rock, Ezra decided it would be his best option and threaded his reins through it. Patting the horse on the head, he took his face in his hands to make sure he had his attention. "Stay here, boy. If something happens to me, go back to Colleen. She will be waiting in the town we left her in," he explained, not entirely sure he even understood a word he said, before removing his coin purse and hiding it in the saddle.

No sense in risking it making noise and if he didn't make it back to the horse to retrieve it when it was all over, he wouldn't need it anyway. Better Colleen get the money than the men in the house. Not that he was planning on dying; there were far too many men that still needed to pay with their lives before he lost his own. After checking to make sure his gun was fully loaded, Ezra made his way slowly toward the house.

With little effort, he made his way over toward one of the dusty windows, glancing in to find two of the men he was searching for sitting down beside the fire. From his vantage point, he saw most of the living room, but there was no sign of their leader. A photograph resting on the mantel above the fireplace caught his eye, and Ezra realized the elderly man picture with his wife was not one of the men inside.

Already knowing what that meant, but hoping he was wrong, Ezra searched around outside, needing to know if there was a risk of hostages inside that might make things more complicated. It only took him a few minutes to discover the freshly dug grave behind the outhouse.

Hatred seethed inside him. Ezra silently prayed they at least buried them together in an unmarked grave. The alternative was not something he wanted to think about. It was not hard to figure out they never would have kept the man alive if they were planning on being there for an extended amount of time, and if she was still alive in there with them... Ezra refused to think about what that would mean for her. He doubted the elderly woman would have been able to handle it as well as Colleen had.

As odd as it sounded, Ezra prayed that she was dead, killed at the same time as her husband. Perhaps, if they were lucky, the men stumbled upon them after they already died of natural causes. Putting the couple's fate from his mind after promising to give them a proper burial when this was all over, Ezra turned back toward the house and made his way over toward the woodpile a little way away from the front door, knowing it would provide the best cover for him.

Taking a deep breath once he was in position, Ezra went over his own disadvantage in his mind. He was outnumbered three to one. They had the safety of the house to hide in while he was exposed with nothing to hide behind other than a medium sized pile of firewood. Once the leader joined the others, Ezra took another deep breath before deciding it was time. Hoping to draw them out to give himself a slight advantage, Ezra called out, "Get out here, you yellow-bellied dogs!"

The men jumped to their feet, nearly tripping over themselves as they rushed toward the front door, guns drawn. His hand shaking despite his attempts to keep himself calm, Ezra held still for a moment as the leader shouted for the men to spread out, paying their instructions little mind. He did not intend on giving them enough time to discover where he was and flank him.

Clenching his fist to stop the shaking, Ezra cocked his gun, raising it to aim at the leader's chest. At the same moment, he was spotted, the man's eyes widened a fraction of an inch as he realized who he was before sneering at him. A moment later, the first shot echoed around the valley.

LONG AFTER NIGHT arrived, bathing the land in near darkness with not but a tiny sliver of a moon and a few scattered stars to see by, as most were covered by dark clouds threatening rain, Colleen tossed and turned on her bed, her sleep haunted by unrelenting nightmares. One after another, they came, her unconscious mind finding no reprieve between them. Her dreams were haunted by images of what the men did to her. By the first man to take her against her will.

By Cole's last night in the orphanage. Each one changed from what actually happened to a nightmare far worse than they have ever imagined. Instead of being told to leave the orphanage, as he was in reality, the boy lived. He and his friends imprisoned Cole in the cellar as they, and other men that shown up, bought him for the night. At the end of each night, he would be whipped until he lost consciousness to ensure he was unable to run away while they slept.

The men from her nightmares were far crueler than she remembered anyone ever being to her in the waking world if that was even possible, and she breathed a sigh of relief when she finally sat up in bed, the cold sweat she was suffering from the only reminder of what haunted her sleep moments before. Desiring the comforting touch of Ezra's arms, or at least the calming effect of his presence, she turned toward his side of the bed to see if he was still awake and, in the mood, to talk.

Instead, she found his spot empty and unslept in. Concerned he had not returned yet, Colleen glanced out the window to find she saw the first rays of the sun appearing on the horizon. Dawn would break soon, and Ezra never entered their room during the night. The town grew quiet before she went to bed herself so she could not imagine he was out trying to gather information from the others.

Few explanations crossed her mind for his absence, and each was less appealing than the last. He might have been recognized by someone who saw his wanted poster or chased out of town during a gunfight or turned over to the nearest lawman. Or killed during the fight. Reminding herself she would have been awoken by the sound of gunfire did very little to reassure her. Though it was less likely he was killed without putting up a fight and getting at least a shot off, it was still possible for him to run off or be captured if they caught him off guard.

But his insistence on her remaining there caused Colleen to worry more now than she did the night before. Had her greatest fear come to pass once more? Had she been abandoned again? No warning, no reason, just waking up to find he was already gone? It was the story of her life, but Colleen thought, hoped it was in the past. Certainly Ezra, at the very least, would have given her the chance to say good-bye.

Once again, Colleen realized with a heavy heart, she completely misjudged someone; misjudged her own importance to them. At any other point in her life, it would not have mattered so much to her as she had already grown used to it being as it was the only thing she ever knew, but that morning was the absolute worst time for her to be left behind. After what she suffered and the nightmares that followed, she needed a friend to talk to.

Someone to find comfort in. Someone to hold her and assure her the worst was already over. Instead, Colleen found herself left wanting once again. For the first time, since their mother abandoned Cole as a child, Colleen realized she actually cared that she was completely alone, that she was unwanted. The people in her life always turned her life to garbage so being rid of them was only seen as a blessing, but Ezra was different.

Or at least she thought he had been. He did not make her feel like she was worth less for simply being who she was. He did not treat her like garbage, was not disgusted by her attraction to him. He said he wanted her, if only as a friend, but he abandoned her all the same. His leaving hurt far worse than her mother's ever did. The woman who gave birth to her never treated her with kindness or respect; she missed what the woman was supposed to represent more than she ever actually missed the woman herself.

Ezra was her friend, the only one she ever had, and he turned his back on her during one of the worst days of her life. Later, she would hate him, breed resentment for him deep within her soul, but at that moment, the only thing Colleen could do was curl up into a ball and cry herself to sleep. It took longer than she expected, her eyes red and bloodshot by the time the nightmares returned in full force.

This time, as her unconscious mind returned to the campsite from the night before, instead of Ezra being held at gunpoint, unable to do anything to help her as the men attacked, he shook his head before turning his back on Colleen when she needed him the most. As she tossed and turn in her sleep once more, she called out for him, begging for him to return. Begging him not to leave her.

CERTAIN SHE HAD only slept for a few hours at most, Colleen was startled to find herself being awoken by a strange sensation. A quick glance toward the window assured her the darkness was simply caused by an overcast day, and she was about to go back to sleep when she remembered what had awoken her to begin with. The strange sensation pricked at her mind, causing dread to freeze her in place as she realized what it was.

She was not alone. There was someone in the room with her. As much as she might wish for his return, she knew it was not Ezra that entered their room while she slept; he would have announced his presence. Worry crept into her mind that the men followed them there, waiting for Ezra to abandon her before attacking again. Or perhaps a guest of the boarding house saw her and waited until they were certain she remained alone before assaulting her.

But it did not matter what the truth was about the intruder—she would never let them have the chance to hurt her again. Glancing toward the door where she barely made out a lone figure moving toward her in the darkness, Colleen slowly reached down under her covers, her fingers following her pantaloons down until she reached her ankle. Just beneath the cloth, she found the two-shooter Ezra gave her; strapped to her ankle by a thin piece of cloth she re-purposed from a pile of scraps she found downstairs.

Raising the gun before her intruder got close enough to grab her, Colleen took aim in the darkness.

# Chapter Eighteen

GLENDALE 1830

"Take another step, and I will drop you, Sugar. Whatever you were planning isn't worth getting shot over. Leave now, and I will let you live," Colleen warned in a hard voice that was usually reserved for Cole, even as she cocked the small revolver. She received a groan in response as the man continued toward her. It dawned on her in that moment that she was about to answer the question Ezra put toward her before, not that it mattered any longer.

It would seem she was, in fact, able to kill someone intentionally. Aiming as best she was able to in the dark, Colleen pulled back on the trigger as the clouds parted briefly enough to let enough light into the room for her to see who was standing there. "Ezra!" she cried out, as she quickly pulled her finger off of the trigger, uncocked the gun and set it down on the nightstand beside the bed. Turning back to him, she was equal parts ready to yell at him for scaring her and thankful she was not abandoned by him after all.

About to demand to know where he was and why he did not announce himself, Colleen noticed how he seemed to be staggering toward her. "Ezra?" she questioned concerned before striking the flint and tinder, causing a small but powerful enough spark to light the candle on the nightstand. Turning back to him now that she could see, it did not take long for her to see what was causing him to behave so strangely; dark blood soaked through his shirt at his shoulder.

Before she was able to question what happened, he pitched forward, and Colleen practically flew off of the bed to keep him from hitting the floor. Grunting at the force of his dead weight landing on her, Colleen realized he lost consciousness and would not be answering any of her questions any time soon. Glancing over to their beds, Colleen took a deep breath before beginning to walk backward, dragging him with her, the strain of his weight, causing her to grunt with each step she took. It took every ounce of strength that Colleen possessed to half carry him all the way over to the bed, and it was all she could do not to drop him once she reached it. In their current position, she was left with little choice than to fall backward herself before rolling them over so he would be underneath.

At any other time, thoughts of what they could be doing would have been teasing her, but at that moment, their position never even crossed her mind. Instead, she was focused on pulling him into a better position for her to reach his wound once she climbed off of him. Though it was almost as difficult as it was to get him to the bed in the first place, she finally got him so he was lying on his back, his injured shoulder at the edge of the bed where she stood.

She confirmed he was still breathing before turning her attention to the mess that was his shoulder. The thick pool of blood was already beginning to dry, meaning he was shot some hours before he returned. Where was he at that it took him so long to return to her? Who shot him and why? Would he survive?

Her increasingly morbid thoughts went unanswered as she reached her fingers in through the hole in his shirt caused by a bullet and tore it open. Once the ruined shirt was out of her way, Colleen raised the candle above her patient to get a better look at the damage he sustained.

The small, roundish wound confirmed her suspicions of what weapon caused it, and she tentatively reached under him to check for an exit. Though there was plenty of blood, now that he was on his back, she did not find any injury to his flesh. That was not the news she was hoping for. No exit wound meant that she would have to dig the bullet out herself and it was certainly nothing she ever did before.

She saw it once or twice at the saloon as there was no real doctor in town to treat the occasional bullet wound, but it was always from a distance. The barkeep insisted she stay close in case they needed extra bandages or fresh water, and the other girls refused to go near the sight of blood, but she never had a good vantage point before. It was certainly not something she wanted to try on her friend for her first time.

But neither would she let him die, and she dared not risk alerting the proprietor as it would cause them to ask too many questions. Drawing a couple of deep breaths to calm her nerves, Colleen reached into Ezra's boots and grabbed the two knives she knew would be there. Building the fire, she set one of the knives in it before heating the second in the flames for a few moments.

Certain it was as clean as she was going to get it, she walked back over to the bed to find him unchanged. Silently praying he remained unconscious for what she was about to do, Colleen steadied her hand and drew the heated blade toward his wound. The moment the knife touched inside him, he thrashed around cried out in pain. Worried his frantic movements might cause her to injure him further, Colleen stopped what she was doing for a moment to climb on top of him, trapping his arms at his side between her legs.

Though it made it much harder for her to reach his wound in a comfortable position for her, there were far fewer chances of her doing serious damage to him that way. Checking to ensure he was still unconscious once more, Colleen slowly dug around inside the wound for the missing bullet, all the while praying she was not doing him further damage.

Feeling the tip of the knife brush against something hard, silently hoping it was the bullet, she dug it out slowly. Fortunately, it did not take long for her to confirm her suspicions as she stared down at the bloody bullet that was resting in the palm of her hand. Setting it and the knife aside, she headed back toward the fireplace and retrieved the second blade.

Glancing down at her shaking hands, Colleen whispered soft assurances to herself before making her way back over to the bed. She grabbed hold of the headboard to steady herself and pressed the hot blade against his wound to cauterize it. The moment the searing metal touched his skin, Ezra let out an ear-piercing scream. Worried he would wake the others, Colleen quickly placed her hand over his mouth to muffle the sound only to bite back a scream of her own when she felt his teeth sinking into her palm.

Knowing it was nothing more than his instincts reacting to his pain or perhaps fear, she simply bit her own lip and pressed the blade harder against him. She pulled it back after a few moments. After assuring herself that the bleeding stopped, she turned toward Ezra even as she prayed that he would release her now that she was finished. Much to her relief, he unclenched his jaw after a moment, and she was able to pull her injured hand away.

Unsurprisingly, as she pulled her own hand toward the candle to inspect the damage, she found his teeth broken the skin and caused her to bleed. As her own wound was small in comparison to his, she turned her attention back to him. A bit startled to find his pain-filled eyes staring up at her weakly, she gave him a soft smile before assuring him, "I got the bullet out, Sugar, but you need your rest. Sleep now."

His eyes fluttered closed a moment later, and soon his breathing evened out. Setting the knife down on the nightstand beside the first one she used, she decided it was time to deal with her own wound.

Making her way over toward the water basin, she gently cleaned her hands as she tried to remember if she saw the pump to refill it on her way in the day before. She could not leave bloody water in the room for them to find when they came to clean, but she was certain, even though she did not remember passing it on her way in, that it would not prove too difficult to find.

She headed toward the fireplace. Now that her hand was clean, Colleen was happy to note that the bleeding already stopped. Apparently, he only broke through her skin enough to draw a few drops of her blood; the rest was his. Fortunately, she would not require stitches as she was certain she would be unable to do them on herself.

She flexed her injured hand for a moment to ensure the bleeding would not start up again with use, then went to the chest where they stored the extra linen. Hoping they wouldn't miss one blanket and making a mental note to leave an extra dime to pay for it before they left, she returned to the bed. After setting the sheet down on the bed, she grabbed the bloodied knives and quickly washed them in the already reddish water.

Drying them, she put one back inside Ezra's boot before using the other to cut holes in the sheet, making it easier for her to rip off a few thin strips. She awkwardly wrapped her own left hand, tying it as tight as she could using her teeth. Grabbing two of the strips, she wet them in the basin before returning to Ezra's side.

Wringing the first one out above his shoulder, Colleen gently wiped away a lot of the dried blood before tossing it aside and repeating her actions with the second strip. Once she was certain he was as clean as he was going to get without an actual bath, she folded up another strip of cloth and dabbed around the wound to dry it. Satisfied she did as good a job as she would be able to, she folded yet another cloth and placed it on top of the bullet wound.

Colleen couldn't help but wish once more that she had any idea what she was doing. She tore off a thicker strip than before and wrapped one end over his shoulder and the other under his arm. Pulling the ends together at the top of his shoulder, Colleen held them together for a moment, cocking her head to the side as she inspected her work.

Something did not seem quite right. Worrying her bottom lip for a moment, she pulled the ends apart once again and looped one of the ends under his arm again to ensure the wound would stay covered even if the bandaged moved. But as she drew the ends together once again, it was clear that it still did not look correct. Sighing in frustration, Colleen glanced around in an attempt to find something that would keep the bandage from slipping down his arm at the slightest movement.

As she glanced back at his unconscious form, her search unfruitful, the solution was right in front of her. Shaking her head, Colleen wrapped the two ends around his neck and tied them together. It was far from what an actual doctor would have been able to do, but it would do for now. Stepping back, she surveyed her work for a moment, making sure the blood wasn't seeping through the bandage before sighing in relief.

Apparently, she did something right after all. Smiling to herself, Colleen stretched her arms over her head to relieve the stiffness in her hand only to realize her hand was beginning to throb something fierce. Deciding she had no other option than to ignore it, as she currently did not have anything to dull the pain, she turned her attention to menial tasks that would keep her mind occupied with the mundane.

Checking to make sure Ezra was still unconscious, she grabbed the basin, the water tinged a dark pink from all the blood. Quietly making her way out of the room, closing the door noiselessly behind her, she made her way downstairs and outside, careful not to let any of the others staying there see her.

After tossing the contents of the basin into a small ditch that was dug for such things, she searched the area for the water pump. As she expected, it was not that hard to find. No doubt the dirty water ditch was dug close to the pump to make it easier for their lodgers. Placing the basin under the spout, she pumped the handle with both hands a couple of times before bending over to wash out the residue from the blood, as the water began to pour out.

Once she was certain it was clean, Colleen picked the basin back up and went inside. As she was about to head up the stairs, she was stopped by the cook calling out to her, "The first batch of lunch is about ready if you would like to wait a moment, Miss. Wouldn't want you to have to fight with men over when they come rushing in." Smiling at him in gratitude, she assured him she would be back after putting the basin back in her room.

After a quick check on Ezra to assure he was still unconscious, Colleen went downstairs once more, sitting down at one of the small tables to wait. Though it would not take long for it to be ready, she was grateful for the reprieve from her room. It was not as though she did not want to be around Ezra, in fact, quite the opposite, it was just that she was not accustomed to dealing with injuries that were not inflicted on her.

Her blood and bruises she handled well enough as she wasn't given much of a choice as no one else would help her tend to them after one of the men got violent with her, but tending to someone else's wounds, touching someone else's blood was an entirely different story. The last time she was forced to deal with blood that was not her own was the night Cole left the orphanage.

The memory still left a bad taste in her mouth, a haunting image in her mind, and Colleen doubted she would ever be able to see blood again without being reminded of what happened that night. It was not Cole's fault; the boy was responsible for his own actions even if the others hadn't agreed. They placed the blame solely on Cole's shoulder, and instead of giving him the chance to recover after what he went through, he was tossed out on the street.

Perhaps they might have thought differently if the boy survived, but Colleen didn't put much stock into such thoughts. Nothing could be done for what already passed anyway, and she doubted his friends, at the very least, would ever admit that being different didn't automatically make Cole responsible for everything that happened. Shaking her head to clear the darkening thoughts that were forming, she focused her thoughts on the man upstairs.

As much as the thought of him lying there bleeding for hours before coming to her, terrified her, worrying about her friend was safer for her sanity. The moment he awoke, she would have to get the answers to some very important questions. What happened? Who shot him? Where was he that his blood dried before he made it back? Was he held somewhere in town or, which would open up a whole other host of questions, did he travel out of town before being shot?

Shaking her head once more, Colleen turned toward the cook with a smile when he cleared his throat. "Thank you," she told him before handing over a dime, retrieving the tray and making her way upstairs before he questioned her odd behavior. Maneuvering the door open while balancing the tray seemed to be getting easier with practice, but Colleen barely noticed as she was too occupied with checking on Ezra the moment she entered the room.

THOUGH IT WAS late into the next night when Ezra finally regained consciousness, it would be a while before he realized how much time passed. As he awoke, the first, and for a while only, thought that entered his mind was wondering why his head was pounding so hard. He was groggy and had no memory of what caused so much pain, but as a minute and then another passed, the fog slowly faded, and he realized there was actually a second pain, a steady throb coming from his shoulder.

He was shot. As he focused on that thought, his mind slowly added in other pieces of the puzzle until the picture was clear. He followed the men that attacked Colleen to the home in the valley, and he was shot during their gunfight. Before he pictured what happened after that, Colleen's soft voice interrupted him. "I removed the bullet yesterday. You've been unconscious for quite some time. About a day and a half, I'd say. Managed to get some broth and water into you, but that was about it. You must be starving."

Opening his eyes, grateful to find the room was only dimly lit by the candle beside the bed, he glanced over toward Colleen to find her standing beside the bed, smiling down at him softly.

"Come on, Sugar, let's get you sitting up so you can eat." Colleen helped him to sit up against the pillows before sitting down on the bed beside him. She grabbed a bowl of soup from the tray on the nightstand and brought a spoonful of the broth to his lips. Though he was about to insist he was capable of feeding himself, the throb in his shoulder contradicted him.

Ezra swallowed one spoonful after another, grateful when she finally fed him the actual chunks of food instead of just broth. He glanced around the room before his eyes settled back on the tray once more, noticing half of everything was empty. Apparently, she ate while waiting for him to wake up and Ezra couldn't help but smile at the knowledge.

Though he was certain she was worried about him, it was a relief to know she continued to take care of herself.

Not realizing how much he ate until she set the empty bowl aside, Ezra fought the urge to smile when she grabbed a napkin and dabbed it around his lips. Accepting the chuck of bread, Ezra waited for the questions he was certain were to come. Sure enough, a moment later, she fired them off one after another. Where did he go? What happened? Who shot him?

"I lied to you when I dropped you off here. In truth, I wanted to go after the men, and I thought you might try to stop me. I saw their tracks leaving the campsite and simply headed back to where they changed directions from us. I followed them to a small house in the middle of a valley, seemingly cut off completely from the rest of the world, where I found the grave of the owners.

"I called them out and was shot in the gunfight that ensued, as were they. You never have to worry about them again nor will any other woman," Ezra assured her.

First confusion clouded her eyes, but it was soon replaced as they brightened in understanding. She worried her bottom lip for a moment before running her tongue across it to relieve the dryness. "You got shot avenging me?" she asked.

Ezra nodded. He bit back a smile at how drastically she changed from surprise to crying in disbelief. "No one has ever done something like that before; would ever do that for me."

Through the tears, her eyes softened. She leaned forward and gently pressed her lips against his for a brief moment before pulling away, smiling shyly. Her gaze settled on the empty tray. Realizing she was going to return it downstairs, Ezra grabbed her arm.

"What are you doing?" Colleen asked softly, her eyes transfixed on his as he pulled her closer. Shaking his head, as he honestly had no idea either, he pulled her even closer still until her daintier form practically fell into his lap. Before she could open her mouth to questions his actions further, Ezra pressed his dry lips against hers.

# Chapter Nineteen

GLENDALE 1830

As the first rays of the morning sun flittered in through the window, Colleen was roused from slumber by the heat on her cheek. Moving to rise, she found her limbs tangled up in Ezra's, unable to tell where she ended and he began for a moment. As she tried to figure out how they got into such a position, memories from the night before started to tease her mind. Watching his still sleeping face, Colleen remembered the moment he pressed his lips against hers.

They were softer than she would have imagined, albeit slightly dry, and if she closed her eyes, she still felt them. Even now, replaying the memory in her mind, she hardly believed she was kissed by him. But more than that, what she truly did not believe, was he fell unconscious midkiss, putting far too quick of an end on what was the greatest kiss in her life, refusing to release his hold on her.

Smiling softly at his sleeping form, Colleen decided it was time she stopped dwelling on the teasingly short moment from the night before and set about her day. Untangling their bodies as gently as possible, Colleen stood and was about to make her way out of the room when she noticed his beautiful green eyes were staring up at her. "I'm going to see about breaking our fast, Sugar. Get some more rest," she suggested with a smile before making her way out of the room without waiting for a reply.

Judging by how much he slept since he returned two days prior, it wasn't hard for Colleen to figure out that the wound he sustained, or the battle he got it in, completely wore him out. Closing the door behind her, Colleen couldn't help but wonder if he even remembered what he did the night before. Or if he'd actually been in control of himself when he kissed her.

She headed toward the cook, who was currently handing a tray full of steamy food to one of the other lodgers. "Yes, Miss?" he asked as he turned toward her with a smile.

Realizing all eyes were on her, she turned toward the others with a soft smile in greeting and was rewarded with many tipped hats in greeting. Being the only woman currently lodging at the boarding house, she grew accustomed to their attention rather quickly.

"Can I get breakfast for my brother and myself from the next batch of meals?" Receiving a nod of agreement, Colleen continued, "I'll be back in a few minutes to pick them up. Need some fresh air. Enjoy your meal, gentlemen." She graced them with one last smile and made her way out into the bright morning sun. Behind her, she heard one of the men wondering if they were really siblings, but decided to pay him little mind.

Let them wonder if they were having extramarital relationships. It was better than them figuring out the truth. She doubted any of them would care enough to stop them if that was the case. As she blinked her eyes to adjust them to the sudden assault of light, she was not surprised to find the townsfolk were already bustling about their day at full speed.

Colleen made her way around the town, enjoying the fresh air as she said she would. While taking care of Ezra over the last two days, she barely managed to leave their room, let alone actually make it outside. As it was, the town was still as foreign to her as it was the day they arrived.

Taking stock of everything she saw as she walked, Colleen was surprised to see a small, one or two cell, jailhouse. Did Ezra not notice it on the way in or had he simply decided it was worth the risk to avenge her? Would they be lucky enough for news of him not to have reached this far out yet? Sighing softly to herself, knowing there was only one way to find out, Colleen was about to make her way over to where she already saw the yellowed pages of old wanted posters, when a man stepped out into the sun and made his way over to add another.

Turning subtly toward the window of the nearest building, Colleen pretended to be interested in the Stetson hats that were showcased there until he went back inside. After counting silently to ten, she strolled over even though every inch of her screamed to hurry up. Taking a deep breath with each step, Colleen climbed the three stairs that lead to the jailhouse and turned toward the bulletin.

Across the top, etched into the wood of the bulletin, was the words 'armed and dangerous' and beneath that were numerous posters depicting men and the bounties on their heads, many of which long since yellowed with age. Whether they were captured over the years or not was not indicated, but Colleen paid them little mind either way and turned her attention toward the newest poster to be added. Instantly she saw the drawing bore more than a passing resemblance to Ezra.

AS COLLEEN STOOD there staring at the wanted poster in disbelief, her hand slightly raised as though she was reaching out to touch it, she was startled when someone cleared their throat behind her. Spinning toward him with a smile, and spotting the silver badge on his chest that announced he was a sworn deputy, she feigned embarrassment before fluttering her long lashes at him.

"You startled me, Deputy. Truth be told, I found myself wondering what he was wanted for. Mamma always told me my curiosity would get me into trouble one day. I do hope today isn't that day." Colleen said, using a flirty tone before caressing her neck with her fingers. She knew it would hide certain truths from him, which would be easily spotted at that distance, and it would keep him off balance slightly.

"No, Miss. You can rest assured it ain't that day," the deputy said with a bright smile as he tipped his hat and stepped up next to her. "This particular scoundrel is wanted for murder, jailbreak and assaulting a deputy." He tapped two fingers on the drawing of Ezra.

Before she realized what she was doing, Colleen muttered to herself that it "wasn't right." After all, it was her, not Ezra, who assaulted the deputy in charge of watching him.

Did the deputy not realize it was her that attacked him or hit his head so hard he lost the memory of what happened? Was he simply unconscious at the time the sheriff decided what happened? Or, and Colleen was certain was most likely, did he simply lie in order to not make a fool of himself for being attacked by a woman? Deciding it didn't matter either way, as her not being associated with Ezra meant that she was free to continue walking into any town they came across without trouble, she turned back to the deputy to find him staring at her in question.

"Oh, I mean that it wasn't right attacking a deputy. Can't blame a man for doing his job, now can ya? I hope you catch him soon. The fewer criminals we have on the streets, the safer I will feel in my bed at night," Colleen said with a smile before bidding him good-bye and heading back toward the boarding house. Behind her, she sensed the deputy watching her go; his eyes greedily following the movements of her hips beneath her dress.

As much as she found herself wanting to run again, Colleen knew it would not bode well to risk drawing even more attention to them and forced herself to walk at the same, even pace she was using before noticing the wanted poster. Once she finally stepped back into the dimmer lighting of the boarding house, she closed her eyes for a moment as she waited for them to adjust before making her way toward the cook when she noticed him gesturing toward her waiting tray.

She greeted him and the others still breaking their fast with a smile and a nod of her head. After paying for their meal, she returned upstairs. Ezra was sitting up on the bed as though he was waiting for her.

"Perfect timing; I'm starving." He reached for his bowl of porridge. Instead, Colleen set the tray down on the nightstand before beginning to gather up their belongings.

"We have a problem, Sugar. I saw a wanted poster of you going up at the sheriff's office. Thankfully it's so new I doubt many have seen it yet, but we need to get out of here before those that saw you when we first arrived notice the poster." Once she gathered up their things, Colleen turned her attention to the steaming hot food and began packing up what little would travel. "Take a few bites of your porridge, it won't be coming with us."

Though she felt his eyes on her while she moved, Colleen soon heard the spoon scraping against the bowl as she moved to the window. "You aren't going to like it, but I do have a plan to get you out of here unseen. Unfortunately, there are too many people downstairs, so you are going to have to jump out the window. It slants pretty low, so it won't be much of a drop, but the landing will be jarring on your wound."

Not bothering to give him the chance to respond, Colleen grabbed a clean shirt for Ezra and helped him put it on. His old one, with a ripped and bloody sleeve, had long since burned in the fire. "Once you are on the ground, head northwest behind the buildings and I will pick you up on the road just out of town. I'm going to see that we aren't disturbed for a while," Colleen assured him before opening the window and tossing their belongings out onto the roof.

"I will see you in a few minutes, Sugar. Be careful." She headed back out of the room. Knowing time was not on their side, Colleen hurried toward the owner with a soft, almost nurturing smile on her face. "I'd like to pay for another night. My poor brother isn't feeling too well. Can you make sure no one disturbs us?" she inquired with a quick batting of her lashes.

"Such a beautiful day today, isn't it, gentlemen?" Colleen inquired with a polite smile as she stepped passed the men, who finished eating and were now sitting around playing cards, before stepping back out into the morning sun. Barely noticing their agreements, she headed toward the stables to retrieve Ezra's horse, making sure to walk at a natural pace so she would not draw unnecessary attention.

Though she was a bit worried she might have problems trying to pick up a horse when she was not there when Ezra dropped him off, she was surprised when she realized luck was shining down on her for once. The blacksmith's helper, who seemed to be the only one around at the moment, was rather incompetent as he didn't even bat an eye when Colleen told him which horse she was there to pick up. If she was a horse thief, she might have taken a second one.

Luckily for the boy who was not much younger than her by the looks of it, she wasn't. He gestured to the fenced yard where the horses were currently grazing. Colleen made her way over and led the horse out of the fenced-in pen. Mounting side saddle as much as she loathed the position, she bid the boy a good day and headed north.

She urged the horse to go faster, and it was not long before they arrived at the road where she told Ezra to meet her. Only he was nowhere in sight. As she began to panic, thoughts of things going wrong and Ezra being caught by the deputy she spoke to running wild in her imagination, Colleen forced herself to calm down.

Reminding herself he was injured, and that it did not take her anywhere near as long at the stables as she allotted for, Colleen drew one deep breath after another. No more than a minute later, she realized how unfounded her worries were as Ezra stepped through the trees beside her. She dropped down from the horse, retrieved their belongings, and packed them in the saddlebags before helping Ezra to take his position on the front of the horse.

Though it was much harder without Ezra able to help or the stump at the blacksmith to stand on, Colleen soon climbed on to the back of the horse and held on, careful not to touch his injured shoulder.

"We need a place to hide out while I heal," Ezra said. "Even if no one sees the poster who remembers seeing me, word is catching up to me. Trying to move around when I am pretty much useless would not be a wise move." He gave the reins a little jolt, and his horse started moving.

"Well, provided no one has moved in since the last time I was there, I may know the perfect place. Head west," Colleen instructed, though she was not looking forward to visiting such a place again, she was certain it would still be abandoned, and it was more than far enough from the town that Ezra would not be spotted once word of his wanted poster made it that far out.

# Chapter Twenty

EAST OF SHADYNOOK 1830

It was early the next morning when they finally reached their destination, and Ezra found himself staring up at a small, rundown house that he could not imagine anyone having lived in for many years. Judging by the state of the old, barely legible sign that indicated the 'Warren' property was ahead, that he noticed less than a mile back, he wasn't all that surprised by what he saw. Dried up, long since browned ivy vines climbed up the walls while large, fist-sized patches of paint peeled off completely. The two windows were covered in a thick layer of dust and could no longer be seen through.

After dismounting, he helped Colleen down as best as he could without the use of his right arm. Ezra took a good look around the rest of the property. Weeds long since strangled out the life from any plants that might have once been there making the yard as unkempt as the house.

"Where are we, exactly?" he finally asked as he removed the saddlebags from the horse and hitching him up to the post. Giving the animal a much-deserved brushing, he was a bit startled when Colleen explained where they were.

"This was my childhood home; if you can even call it that." The sadness in her voice was impossible to miss.

He had no idea what to say, but it did not matter as she went inside without giving him the chance to respond. The moment she pushed the door open, its hinges creaking for lack of use, he heard her suffering a coughing fit when over a decade's worth of dust was unsettled.

As Ezra waited outside, not sure if Colleen was ready for someone to trespass on her childhood, he barely made out her words. "It's exactly the same," she said as she ventured deeper inside. "It's safe to come in," Colleen called out to him, turning toward him as he stepped inside to find her lighting a candle. "If the massive amount of dust wasn't enough to assure us that no one was ever here, my mother's clothing still on her bed would be," she told him.

Though the sky was brightening outside, inside the house was so dark even with the candlelight that Ezra almost missed the pile she was referring to. Deciding a fire was worth the risk, as they would be unable to cook anything without one, Ezra built one in the hearth from the logs still stacked up beside it. Behind him, he heard Colleen shaking out an old, dusty towel before attempting to wipe down the table.

Judging by her grumbling, it only made things worse. "We'll have to bring in some water soon," Colleen called over to him, and as he turned back to her, now that the fire was going, he found her setting the table with the last bit of food they left from the boarding house. The cloth she wrapped it in made for a makeshift tablecloth.

Not bothering to do more than shake the chair to loosen the dust, Ezra joined Colleen at the table. "I'm going to head into town once I finish eating and make a trip to the general store. We're going to need a lot of supplies if we are going to be here for a while and I highly doubt that anything can be salvaged after being here so long. Food would have been long spoiled if there was any. Can barely even tell where the barn once stood due to the overgrowth of weeds." Ezra realized he did not even see the burned-out remains of the barn himself. "I'll make a quick stop by the sheriff's as well to make sure the poster hasn't made it this far yet."

Once she was finished eating, Colleen retrieved Cole's clothing from the saddle bag. "What are you doing?" Ezra asked as she stepped behind an old dusty and ripped changing curtain, watching her silhouette as she removed the dress he bought for her. Instead of answering right away, Colleen appeared at the edge of the screen, her corset needing to be untied. Walking over to her, Ezra untied it, his fingers grazing her back as he pulled the strings loose.

"I can't exactly go claiming to be the owner's son if I am dressed like a woman, can I?" Cole's masculine voice called out from behind the screen as he pulled on his breeches and button-up shirt. He came back around the screen and finished buttoning his shirt before sitting down on the bed to pull on his boots, not bothering with his vest or overcoat.

"Being Colleen would only draw too much attention to us," he continued. "And that's the last thing we need if we want to be able to stay here long enough for you to heal. Wait for me here and stay out of sight just in case someone actually comes this far out." Cole headed outside and closed the old, creaky door behind him.

As Ezra sat there in silence after he was gone, he couldn't help but look around; wondering what there was to do inside while waiting. Deciding to deal with what little cleaning that was possible without actual water, he made his way over to the bed and gathered up the dresses; he coughed at the cloud of dust moving them caused. Noticing a small doll with the same fiery red hair and violet eyes of Cole among the dresses, he placed it on top of the dresser.

Returning the dresses to the closest so Cole would not have to look at them again once he returned, Ezra made a quick inventory of what else was inside and dismissed everything as being useful. Though some of the clothing was still wearable, if a bit dated, he doubted Colleen would want to wear anything of her mother's. Nor would Cole of his father's as he was certain that was who the two shirts and breeches in the back of the closet belonged to.

As he ran the fingers across the material, able to tell they were of much better quality than the dresses as they held up better over the years, he couldn't help but wonder what he would find if he ever made his way back to his own childhood home. Did it still stand exactly as he left it all those years ago? Were his mother's dresses and his father's shirts and pants still hanging in the closet as Cole's was? Did someone else move in once they realized no one lived there anymore?

Did the Pine Box crew return to burn it down in spite of his parent's memory? Shaking his head to clear such pointless questions, Ezra made his way over to the dresser and decided to have a quick look though he was certain anything it contained would be as useless as what was in the closet. Much to his surprise, when he opened the top drawer, he found an old shotgun and an almost empty box of shells. A quick inspection informed him that, though it would need a serious cleaning before it was usable again, the gun was built to last, and he found no reason why it would not fire.

Grabbing the cleaning supplies from the back of the drawer, Ezra made his way back over to the table and cleaned the shotgun. Though he hoped they would not need it, at least while they were there, he learned long ago to always prepare for the worst. An extra gun would certainly come in handy even if it needed to be reloaded after each shot. Once it was cleaned to his satisfaction, Ezra set the shotgun aside and turned his attention to the saddlebags, taking out anything he thought they might need over the next few days.

ABLE TO TRAVEL much faster with one less rider, it did not take long for Cole to arrive in Shadynook, only to realize the very moment he gazed around the town that he had absolutely no memories of the place. He assumed that somewhere in the deepest part of his mind, like it was with his childhood home, he would recognize it; at least subconsciously. Though, if he was honest with himself, it was what he should have been expecting.

After all, he never actually saw the town before. Somewhere over the years, he convinced himself that he imagined spending the entire first four years of his life trapped at home, certain he must have contact with someone else other than his mother as, surely, she could not have been that heartless; right? He was so young, so traumatized, surely his mind played tricks on him, and he remembered things incorrectly.

But as much as he would have wished that to be true, he reminded himself that the sheriff who found him wasn't even aware of his existence. If she never even spoke of him in town, why would she have brought him in and given him the chance to imprint it on his memory? Perhaps it was just his own wishful thinking, hoping to make his mother a little less evil than she actually was, but as his mind drifted back to his childhood, Cole realized he remembered nothing more than the inside of the house and the barn.

What was on the other side of the house? Was there anything else on the property other than the two buildings? Would it still be there after all these years if there were? Why did he never explore more of his home? That question, at least, Cole already knew the answer to. He was always so malnourished that he barely had the strength to milk the cow, let alone go exploring. Though there would be no way of knowing if it changed in the years that he was gone, Cole made a mental note to investigate the rest of his childhood home when he returned.

For now, with other pressing matters to attend to, Cole turned his thoughts away from his unresolved mother issues and went to the general store. Stepping inside the dimly lit room, the eyes of the few inhabitants turning toward him instantly, it was not hard for him to realize that something was off as soon as his eyes adjusted. The shelves were almost completely bare, dust long settled in the place of missing goods, and no one seemed to be able to find anything they were looking for.

Finding it odd, but deciding it was not the time for him to be worrying about other people's' problems unless that person was Ezra,

Cole rambled around the small store, collecting what few items on his list that were actually in stock. Flour, a few yards of thick cloth to make towels and such, sugar, lard and coffee was all that he found. No dried or salted meats, no baking soda or salt, no candles or dishes, no pots and pans.

No a lot of things. Deciding he would simply have to make do with the dishes he had back home, after a much-needed scrubbing anyway, Cole realized it made more sense in the long run. It would only have ended up a waste of money since he doubted they would be able to take them with them when they left, but he honestly hated the thought of using his mother's dishes. They didn't exactly hold any fond memories for him.

Fate seemed to not care about his feelings once again. Sighing, Cole made his way to the front of the store and set his items on the counter. He waited while the man behind it added the prices up in his head before ever turning his attention to him. "That'll be ten dollars. And we don't give credit," he practically snapped, and Cole forced himself to not take an involuntary step backward. Before he addressed the man's sudden attitude, the price he gave registered in his mind.

"Ten dollars?" Cole practically shouted as he glanced down at the few items he gathered, doing a rough estimate in his mind. *Buck eighty for the flour, a buck and a nickel for the sugar, forty cents for the lard, thirty-five for the coffee and maybe a buck fifty for the cloth.* "That's double the normal price," Cole insisted even as he glanced back down at the goods and did another mental count to make sure he did not miss something.

"That's what happens when the stagecoaches carrying my merchandise keep getting held up before they can get to town. We haven't had a shipment arrive in over a month. I gotta hire some protection just to get a small shipment in before the town starves to death and that costs a pretty penny. Take it or leave it, but consider yourself lucky I don't outright refuse to sell to a stranger," the merchant threatened and, not wanting to risk it and having no other choice, Cole forked over the ten dollars, silently hoping Ezra wouldn't be mad at him for spending so much on so little.

Gathering up his purchases, Cole made his way back outside, shielding his eyes against the sudden assault of sunlight. Without having to look at his coin purse, he knew the money they had left would not last long at this rate and something needed to be done so they didn't end up starving to death. With Ezra not exactly in top shape for hunting and trapping game, it would appear that it was time Cole learned how to himself.

But that would have to wait until he returned to their temporary home, and for now, he had more pressing matters to attend to. Spotting the sheriff's office, Cole made his way over to the wanted posters that were hung outside it. Breathing a sigh of relief when none of them appeared to feature Ezra, or were even newly added, Cole moved to step back when someone behind him cleared their throat. He whirled around and found a man with a gold star on his chest behind him.

"Pardon me, Sheriff, you startled me," Cole said with a chuckle before taking a deep breath to calm his racing heart. "Actually, I was just on my way to see you," he informed him honestly, though judging by the dubious look in his eyes, he didn't believe him.

Nonchalantly gesturing over his shoulder, Cole explained, "Apparently I was worried over nothing. We had the same poster back home, and I thought I saw the outlaw on the way here. Seems I remembered his face completely wrong. Can't believe I was getting worried over nothing." Cole laughed and changed the subject. "My name is Cole, and I used to live outside of town with my mother. I'm not sure if you remember me." The man was at least old enough to have been the same sheriff he met all those years ago even if he couldn't actually remember what he looked like.

The man before him had soft blue eyes, his face framed in salt and pepper hair and easily stood a good two or three inches taller than him, but there was nothing familiar in his features. Wasn't exactly anything unfamiliar either. "The little boy that was abandoned at Miss Warren's homestead? My goodness, has it really been long enough that you're a grown man now?" As the sheriff gave him a closer inspection, Cole only stood there stunned as his words slowly sank into his mind. "It's been so long that I nearly forgot all about'cha. What brings you back out this way? Did you just leave the orphanage?"

"My name is Warren?" Cole asked in disbelief before finally glancing away, blinking away the tears that threatened to fall. Shaking his head, he took a deep breath before turning back to the sheriff with a smile.

"Sorry, I never knew my last name. I've been out for a few years now, actually. I'm passing through on my way looking for work and figured I might as well stay at the old homestead while I was here. Dawned on me after I arrived though that I have no idea if Momma ever sold the place.

"You wouldn't happen to know, would ya? Or who she sold it to if she did?" He didn't want to risk angering anyone if they did own it now. The last thing they needed was for someone to show up suddenly with their gun cocked demanding to know what they were doing on his property.

"Actually, I know for certain that she didn't sell the place. Miss Warren tried to a few years back but couldn't get any takers. Folks don't have much money round these parts. Truth be told, too many bank robbers and thieves and not enough work for honest folk has left this town as dried up as an old creek bed. Course, it didn't help none that she never did nothing to fix the place up either."

"My mother...my mother came back here? When? Do you know where she is now?" Cole demanded desperately, not caring how he sounded to the man standing before him, or anyone else for that matter. It was the first clue he found to his mother's whereabouts since she abandoned him all those years ago. She was here. At some point, even if only for the briefest moment in time, she came home.

Did she think about him? Look for him? Did she finally want him? So many thoughts raced through Cole's mind, even as he tried to tell himself that the answers did not matter, that he didn't want to know as the truth would probably only hurt him more until the sheriff confirmed his worst fears with his next words. "It must have been about five years back that she came through town. Said her plan was to sell the homestead and move on again but was never able to sell it," he explained after thinking for a moment, before nodding his head to himself as though he was confirming his own thoughts.

"Where is she now?" Cole inquired, even as his heart clenched painfully in his chest now that he finally had the indisputable truth. All these years, she never once regretted leaving him as she did. She never intended to return for him, to finally be a family. Five years ago, he was still in the orphanage, she would have found him easily if that was her desire. The sheriff still remembered him even now, and Cole was certain he would have told her his location if she but asked for the information.

"Same place she's been since the grip came to town about five winters back. Right next to the church, but there is something you should know," the sheriff told him softly, but Cole did not bother waiting for him to finish as he took off down the steps the moment he had the information he needed. As he headed toward the church, he spotted on top of a hill when he came into town, he remained unaware that the man he failed to notice when he arrived was now gone.

# Chapter Twenty-One

SHADYNOOK 1830

Even without waiting to hear what the sheriff wanted to explain, Cole already knew exactly what he would discover when he finally found his mother. Very few things were ever built next to a church, certainly not a saloon though he was certain she was far too old for that line of work anyway. There might be lodgings for the priest that was in charge of the church, but Cole could not imagine his mother living with a priest, platonically or otherwise.

Occasionally extra hospital rooms were built during outbreaks or war, but there were currently no wars being fought, and the townsfolk certainly were not acting as though there was an ongoing outbreak. Strangers tended to be shunned, if not outright run out of town, during those times in fear of them being the ones spreading the disease. He doubted his mother would still be staying in one of those rooms since the grip the sheriff mentioned.

Rarely, a schoolhouse might be built beside the church if it wasn't used itself, but he doubted his mother ever even stepping foot inside of a school. And, of course, they would never allow an ex-saloon girl to educate their children. That only left one possibility to what was beside the church, one possible place for his mother to be and Cole did not need to hear it from the sheriff to know that was the only place she could ever be.

Stopping at the bottom of the hill, Cole glanced up at the church, long since fallen into disuse, and barely made out a fence he did not notice before. Taking a deep breath, he nodded to himself and began the short climb up the hill, stopping in front of the fence and confirming what he already knew. It was a graveyard. After all these years, countless sleepless nights of wondering what happened to her, he finally found his mother.

Only, she had already passed. As he stared down at the small gate that stood barely half his size, Cole realized that, more than he was upset to learn of her death, he was relieved to finally have an answer. He knew his entire life that he would never see her again, he simply never wanted to believe it was true. As long as she was alive, she might have changed her mind and go back for him; they could have been a family.

Clearing his throat, forcing his tears to remain unshed, Cole opened the old, weathered gate and took his first steps into the graveyard. Scanning each stone for his mother's name, much easier now that he at least had her last name to go by, it did not take long to find. A good deal of them bore the same year as hers; a good chunk of the town's residents lost during the same grip that took his mother. Stepping up in front of her crudely carved stone, he noticed it contained only her name, Anabel Warren, and the year she died—1825.

They didn't even know the year she was born. As he glanced around at the others, he realized two things almost immediately. The first was with all the others their birth years were listed, no doubt they had family members or friends around who told the stone carver what to write. His mother had no one by her own choice. She lived completely alone; died completely alone. The other was that some of the names and dates were carved by someone with a far steadier hand.

Apparently, the stone carver was taken by the grip as well, and someone else stepped up in his place. Turning his attention away from someone he never met, Cole focused on the woman he never really knew. Wringing his hands as he stared down at her grave in silence, he realized they felt empty. Glancing around once more, he realized some of the graves had flowers or, in some cases, a doll or small wooden toy placed on them by those that loved them.

Though most were weathered and aged, flowers little more than a hardened stem, a few were relatively new. It would seem some still mourned their loss; were at least still around to tend to their graves. "Sorry Momma, but I ain't got any flowers for ya. Perhaps next time," Cole told her as he turned his attention to her grave once more. "You know, Momma, all of these years I thought and planned what I would say to you the next chance that I got, but now that it's here, nothing comes to mind.

"What do you say to the woman who brought you into this world only to hate you? I'm not an abomination, Momma. I am your son. I am your daughter. The one you always wanted. I am your child, given to you to love and protect. Not to be disgusted by and thrown away. Not to abandon at the tender age of four, left alone to die because you were afraid of what people would think about you if they knew what your son was like.

"It wasn't even what you thought, Momma, I did not try on your clothes because I wanted to be a girl; I did not realize that I was one for many years down the road. They smelled like you, Momma. I only missed you. But did it really matter? Why were you so afraid of what Papa would think? Did you think he would blame you for how his son turned out? Why even care, Momma? He abandoned you like you abandoned me.

"He didn't want either of us, Momma, but we could have had each other. I never would have abandoned you, Momma. I would have taken care of you. I would have been there for you when you were sick. Did you truly hate me so much that you would rather die alone than send for me? I would have forgiven you if only to see you only last time before you were gone, Momma. I would have come if you but called me home, and I know that they would have been happy to get rid of me, just like you were." His voice cracked, and for a moment, Cole closed his eyes against the sight before him.

Knowing he would have to face her eventually, he drew a deep breath before opening his eyes once more. "I know you never tried to send for me, Momma, but I suppose I cannot truly blame you for that, can I? Why would you ever want to spend what was to be your last few days with someone who reminded you of your past? Of your failings. Of yourself... Did you see that coming, Momma? Did you know that I would one day follow in your footsteps? I was a saloon girl, Momma, just like you. I gave myself to men I did not know and would never see again.

"I let them use me and throw me away because it was all that I was able to do, but unlike you Momma, I did not fall in love with one of the faceless men to pay for my company. I did not end up sitting home every night, lonely and hopelessly waiting for him to come back. At least, Momma, I know that while my past might reflect yours in many ways, my future will not. I will never give birth to a child just to abandon it because its father was a bastard.

"I may never get the chance to be a mother, or a father for that matter, but at least I can take solace in the fact that I will never be a mother like you, or a father like him." Taking a deep breath, forcing himself to calm, Cole stared down at the stone for a moment, his heart hardening against her, no longer able to call her what he had longed to since he was four, before finally shaking his head. "I want you to know something, Mother, this is the end of the road for us. I know now where you are and what type of person you were to the very end.

"I wish, more than anything in the world, Mother, that I never knew you. I wish you abandoned me at birth. At least then I might have believed in some fantasy of my mind's own creation of how you were really such a wonderful person and mother, that you had to abandon me to protect me. That I was stolen from you and you were still out there searching for me. Perhaps you died saving me or bringing me into this awful world.

"That you had given up your life so that your only child might live. But the truth cannot be unlearned, Mother, it cannot be forgotten. Know that, from this moment on, you will no longer cross my mind. I will no longer search for a mother's love that never existed in the first place. Just as you have forgotten me, so shall I forget you," Cole swore as he defiantly wiped a tear from his cheek. Closing his eyes against the wave of emotions that were threatening to spill out, Cole opened them once more, noticing the empty spot in front of her grave.

Its bareness was the perfect metaphor for the spot in his heart that should have been filled by her. "Sorry, Mother, but it looks like you won't be gettin' those flowers after all."

Cole left the graveyard. More so than at almost any other point in his life, Cole felt an overwhelming desire to run. If it was not for the fact that Ezra needed to heal, he would have done just that and never looked back.

All of his life he remembered his desperate need to come back home, to find his mother, but now that he was there, Cole couldn't wait to get away. The place simply held too many painful memories and not a single happy one. It was one thing to simply say that he did not have a happy childhood, but the truth was that he did not even have a single happy memory of his mother. Not a single memory of the time he lived in his childhood home that he wouldn't rather forget.

Cole knew, without a doubt in his mind, that if there ever was a single moment in history that his mother loved him and shown him that she cared, he would have held on to that moment for dear life. One small glimmer of hope in an otherwise desolate existence was not soon forgotten. Unable to recall such a memory assured him that none existed.

Strangely enough, Cole felt as though this last moment with his mother, his one chance to tell her how he felt and to wash his hands of her, was the closest thing he had to a good memory.

AFTER RETRIEVING EZRA'S horse, Cole returned to the homestead, his mind clouded by thoughts of his mother.

As he was tying up his horse, the sound of approaching horses startled him. He spun around and reached for the gun Ezra gave him, but they already had their weapons drawn and trained on him. He held his head high, refusing to let them see they'd caught him off guard.

"You gentlemen are trespassing on my land. I will give you the benefit of the doubt and assume you did not realize this land belonged to anyone since I have been gone for so long, but now that you know, best be on your way."

Instead of heeding his warning, the man at the front of the group aimed his gun and shot off a couple of rounds at his feet, causing Cole to dance around as he tried to avoid the shots. "Finally decided to show your face? And here we were hoping a good for nothing cow pie such as yourself would have the good sense to die already," the man taunted from his saddle, giving no indication he planned on dismounting any time soon.

"What did I ever do to you?!" Cole demanded as he kept his eyes on his gun while mentally going over his recent trip into town. A quick rundown of his steps assured him he did not flirt or even smiled at them, or anyone else that was there for that matter, inappropriately. He gave no one the slightest clue of his being dual-gendered nor of his attraction to men. He was always careful, when he was Cole, not to give away any of his secrets as it would draw too much-unwanted attention to himself, and now to Ezra.

There was nothing he did during his trip into town to explain their behavior. Knowing they were not there because he was in his childhood home, as there was no one there in the years that he was gone, Cole thought about the last few days, but again he came up empty for an explanation. They were not in the last town they stayed at, and there was no one on the road between there and the homestead.

They paid their bill at the boarding house, so there was no reason for the owner to have sent men after them. The men that attacked Colleen, who Ezra assured him are dead, looked nothing like any of the men standing before him and even if they were connected to the men in some way, they would have been after Ezra, not him.

Though perhaps more concerning than the fact that he had no idea what might have caused them to fire on him without warning, even if it was just to taunt him, was the fact that Ezra was nowhere to be seen. The gunshots, which he was certain, were heard from every corner of the small piece of land the homestead stood on, should have sent him running, yet he was nowhere to be found. Did they somehow know where he would be heading before he ever left town and sent someone ahead of them to lay a trap?

Did they find Ezra there waiting, already injured? Turning his attention away from his concerns about his new friend and back to the more pressing matter in front of him when the leader spat at his feet with a sneer. "It has only been a few years since you murdered him, surely you couldn't have forgotten us already?" he insisted as he tilted back his hat so Cole had an unobstructed view of his face as though that would help jog his memory.

While it, in fact, did nothing of the sort, Cole didn't need it to. There was only one death he was involved in, before meeting Ezra anyway, so it was not hard for him to figure out the boys were at the orphanage with him. As he glanced at each of the boys in turn once more, he was still unable to picture them as youths, but he knew exactly who they were without having to. While no one else cared what happened to him, only one group of boys actively hated him.

The very same youths that tormented him, blamed him when their original leader's own actions got him killed, were now standing in front of him and there was little for him to do to stop them from exacting the revenge they've been waiting since that night for. Someone must have overheard his conversation with the sheriff and alerted them to his presence.

"Your friend was responsible for his own death. He attacked me in the middle of the night. He was killed by his own weapon. I did nothing but defend myself from someone who was trying to rape me!" Cole insisted, causing the man in front of sneer at him once more as the others shouted obscenities at him.

"If what you say is true, then you should have died with him that night as you are as disgusting as he was. You are lucky that I like it here in this town so much otherwise I'd risk losing it by killing you outright. I will give you to dusk to get out of my town, as I have no intention of sharing it with the likes of you." He spat at Cole once more before urging his horse to turn back toward town. Even though he knew his life was in danger, Cole refused to allow this man to scare him like he did when they were children.

"I will leave when I am good and ready to. It was your mistake to move into my town. If you have a problem with me being here, then you can simply leave," Cole insisted defiantly, deciding it did not matter that they only planned on being there a couple of weeks at most while Ezra healed. He was not going to be intimidated by someone who was barely a man, and waving a gun around as though simply having one made him tough.

"Either you are gone by dawn, or you will die when I return. Either way is fine by me." The man headed off in the direction of town with his lackeys following after him. The moment they were out of sight, the adrenaline that kept Cole standing dissipated and he sank to the ground with a shuddering breath. Before he got the chance to regain his strength and stand up, Cole heard the sound of rushing feet.

A bit concerned that they might have returned, and not at all in the right mind to realize he would have been hearing hoof-prints if that was the case, he turned toward the sound and found Ezra running toward him. He was barefoot, holding his pants up with one hand and holding his gun in the other, his hair slick with still dripping water.

# Chapter Twenty-Two

EAST OF SHADYNOOK 1830

Ezra glanced around and found no sign of who was there a minute before, other than the jumbled mess of tracks that were trampled on by each of the men who left in turn. He turned his attention to Cole. Helping him to his feet, he assured himself that he was not injured before he demanded, "Where are they?"

"They are gone, for now, Ezra," Cole assured him as he gestured in the direction the men disappeared in. Catching Cole give him an inspection of his own, it was not hard for Ezra to figure out he was concerned about his well-being. He did not blame him, even if he ended up being angry at him for taking so long, as in all honesty, Ezra had no idea how long the men were there before he finally realized it.

"I'm so sorry it took me so long, Cole. I was bathing and thought the gunshots came from the other direction. Took me a minute to hear the voices coming from the front of the house," Ezra explained, expecting Cole to be angry with him for leaving him in danger, only to be met with an understanding smile. For a moment, Ezra's breath caught in his throat at the sight but chalked it up to being surprised he was so lighthearted after such an ordeal.

"Worry not, Ezra, you shall get your chance to make up for it tonight." Cole retrieved the supplies from the saddles. Ezra waited for the flirtatious joke he was certain was going to follow, but Cole seemed serious. "I will fill you in on everything inside." Perhaps Ezra misjudged him, confused what he expected from Colleen to cross over to Cole as well.

"Now go finish getting dressed before you get cold," Cole insisted before starting toward the front door. Stopping at the threshold, he called over his shoulder, "Or I get hot." Nope there it was. Perhaps they truly had the same flirting tendencies and Ezra simply usually did not see it from Cole as he was not comfortable flirting with him while in that form. Did that mean he felt comfortable enough now, at least when he was alone with Ezra, or did Colleen simply poke through Cole's persona for a moment?

Shaking his head at his confusing companion, knowing he would probably never have the answer to such questions, he made his way back to the tub and threw on his boots and shirt, not bothering to button it. Sighing at the loss of the bath, as he spent most of the time Cole was in town scrubbing out the tub and heating the water, Ezra dusted off his hat and made his way back inside.

Blinking his eyes as he waited for them to adjust to the dimmer lighting inside, Ezra found Cole on his hands and knees, scrubbing at one of the lower cabinets. Even though the years of dust refused to disappear completely, he soon had enough of it removed that the shelves were usable. Ezra tried in vain to wring out the extra water that still dripped from his hair.

About to give up on it, he turned his full attention back to Cole as he placed all the supplies, sans cloth, into the cabinet and closed the front door before turning back to him as he stood. Something in his eyes made Ezra shiver as Cole gave his body an approving inspection, as though he never saw him before. Ezra practically saw the hunger Cole felt as his eyes follow a drop of water glide down his exposed chest, disappearing into the waist of his pants.

A bit startled by his sudden change in attitude, as he was wearing even less a minute ago and he was not as affected as he was now that he was almost completely dressed, Ezra stood there stunned until Cole finally shook his head. Whatever was going through his mind, Ezra was sure would have made him blush. Deciding to draw his thoughts away from his body, Ezra made his way over to the table and sat down. "So, what was that earlier?"

For a moment, Cole remained where he was, completely silent as he seemed to debate what to do or say next. Apparently making up his mind, he moved to sit across the table from Ezra and sighed. "You remember the boy I told you about who I killed? The one who attacked me in the orphanage and ended up getting killed by his own weapon?" Ezra nodded. "Well, the men who were here were his friends.

"Though they did not seem interested in killing me in revenge for their friend. Apparently, they realized he had the same preference as me, and their leader was not happy about me returning to town. It seems he moved here after aging out of the orphanage and refuses to share the town with me. Someone must have overheard me telling the sheriff who I was and realized they knew me from the orphanage.

"Only way they would have known to follow me out of town anyways. But it doesn't matter right now as he has given me until dawn to get out or they will be back to kill me. I need to get this place ready for an attack," Cole decided, seeming to speak more to himself than to Ezra. Ezra remained silent, figuring it would be best to stay out of his way until he asked for his help, Cole removed the old, dingy glass pane from the window.

"Can't afford to have that replaced," Cole admitted, though Ezra couldn't be sure who it was directed at. Cole began pushing the dresser in front of one of the windows; Ezra jumped to his feet to help. Though it was not perfect, it would at least offer them some protection when the shooting started. After bolting the door, Cole made his way over to the kitchen table and cleared everything off of it.

Turning it over onto his side, he rolled it toward the only door, and Ezra stepped up to help. The action apparently startled Cole as he stopped what he was doing and looked up at him. "Do you want to leave while you still can? This isn't exactly your fight," Cole pointed out

Ezra couldn't help but chuckle at the thought. Ezra's mission to avenge his parents' murder wasn't exactly Cole's fight either. Breaking him out of jail was not his responsibility. After everything they went through in such a short time, Ezra was not about to turn his back on him because of a couple of thugs. Instead of answering the ridiculous question, Ezra rolled the table once more, not missing the relief that flashed in his eyes. Once the front door was secured, Ezra watched as Cole made his way toward the dresser; reaching for the top drawer.

Already knowing what he was going for, Ezra explained, "It's on the bed. I cleaned the shotgun while waiting for you to return. It's in pretty good shape, considering how old it is." Turning back to stare at him for a moment, Cole smiled before making his way over to the bed. Cole inspected the gun before loading it with a carriage. Dragging one of the chairs over to the window he left open, Cole sat down before finally turning his attention back to Ezra.

"We should take shifts sleeping so we will have the energy to defend ourselves when they do come back. You can take the first shift since you are injured," Cole decided before turning back to stare out the window without waiting for him to reply. Deciding not to fight him, especially since a nap seemed like a good idea at the moment, Ezra made his way over to the bed and pulled the covers off completely.

Though those that were exposed to the air were covered in a thick layer of dust, the sheet that was underneath was left untouched other than looking darker than the rest of the bedding. Flipping the thin pillow over, Ezra laid down on the bed and turned his gaze back to Cole. He did not have to say it for Ezra to understand exactly what was going through his mind as he stared off in the distance.

Tonight would prove to be one of the longest nights of their lives, just sitting there waiting. Knowing the enemy was coming but having no idea when they would actually arrive. Each minute would pass as an eternity, fraying their nerves and causing paranoia to set it as the hours wore on. But it was more than that, more than knowing the night would pass impossibly slow.

They may have no way to know what the future might hold, it was impossible for even Ezra to not realize how that night would prove to be an important night in Cole's history, whether they won the battle or not. This day would change him forever before the sun rose once more. Either he would be dead, though Ezra had no intention of letting that happen any time soon, or Cole would have been forced to intentionally take a life.

Perhaps many lives depending on how many come and how many Ezra is able to take out himself. Ezra did not have to hear Cole's thoughts to know with certainty that he was reminding himself that it would have to be them or him; he saw it in the way his knuckles turned white from his grip on the rifle. Much like Ezra himself learned, Cole knew there was a huge difference between accidentally killing someone while defending yourself and making the conscious decision to take their life.

THE HOURS PASSED them in silence, other than the occasional word or two when they changed shifts or the soft snoring when one of them actually managed to fall asleep, but Ezra long ago grew used to going for days if not weeks at a time without talking to another person, so a few hours was no problem. Or at least, it should have been. Somehow in the short time he traveled with Cole, he got used to being surrounded by noise at nearly every waking moment.

He wasn't complaining, other than the fact that it now made it harder for him to sit in silence. He was simply surprised by how much they changed in his life since he met Colleen. Even as he wondered what any of this might mean, especially seeing how unconcerned he seemed to be by all the drastic changes he brought to his life, Ezra's thoughts were interrupted by the sound of approaching horses. Apparently, they decided dawn was too long to wait, or, more likely, they always intended on cowardly attacking in the dead of night.

Knowing it meant the men returned, as he doubted the property saw so many visitors since it was built, he made his way over to Cole and shook him awake. "They're here," he said softly, nodding toward the open window before helping him to stand in the dark. Though the moonlight shone in through the window, it was not enough to penetrate where they were, leaving most of the home in almost complete darkness.

Handing Cole the shotgun and removing his own from their holsters, he was about to move into position by the window when he noticed a shadow passing over it. Grabbing Cole's hand before he got the chance to move, Ezra pulled him deeper into the shadows, slipping his hand over Cole's mouth to prevent him from making a sound. His lips were so close to Cole's ear that he felt his hot breath fanning over it as he spoke. "We have company."

Cole gave him a quick nod, and they turned their attention to the man that was crawling in through the window. Even in the near complete darkness, he apparently made out the silhouette of the bed as he headed straight for it. Though they were hidden in the shadows, the moon at his back caused his entire body to be eclipsed in light, making him an easy target. Not wanting to risk putting themselves in more danger than they needed to be, Ezra held Cole in place even as the man took aim at the bed.

He shot the bed without a moment's hesitation and in the flash of the gun, Ezra saw his eyes widened in surprise when he realized the bed was empty. Releasing Cole even as their attacker turned in their direction, Ezra felt Cole taking aim from his position even if he could not see it. The nearly point-blank shot struck the man in the chest, throwing him away from them even as the kick forced Cole back into Ezra's arms.

The loud noise echoing around the small house caused his ears to ring, and he barely made out the voice from outside. "Is that abomination dead?!" About to call out in answer, Ezra was surprised when Cole mimicked his earlier actions and placed his hand over his mouth to silence him. Hearing a soft *shhing* coming from Cole, Ezra nodded against his hand to convey his understanding. Though he did not see it, something told him that Cole smiled at him before turning his attention back to the window.

"No, but your little buddy is. Just as the rest of you will be in a few minutes if you do not get off my property!" Cole called out to them, causing their leader to scream in outrage, making a sound Ezra wasn't even aware humans were capable of making. Without a word, or at least one that they heard, the men outside opened fire. Feeling Cole pull away from him, getting into position to defend themselves, Ezra followed suit.

Though it only took a few minutes for the gunfight to finish, it took them nearly a minute to realize they were the only ones still firing. Catching Cole's gesture for him to stop, Ezra did as he instructed and sat back, listening to the silence that surrounded the house. As strange as it still sounded to him, Ezra swore the silence that followed a gunfight was always louder than the battle itself. Cole carefully checked to make sure the coast was actually clear and the men were not lying in wait. Once he decided it was, the two hurried outside.

NOW THAT THE fight was over, Cole was assaulted by the scent of gunpowder and blood and fought the urge to gag. Still, Cole breathed a sigh of relief that it was over. Cole leaned against the wall and allowed himself to slide down it until he reached the floor. As he sat there, he heard Ezra moving around but paid him little attention until he noticed the room beginning to brighten suddenly.

Turning his attention to his companion, he found he started a fire in the hearth once more. Glancing around at his childhood home, it was impossible to miss the first man to die that night along with all the damage that was caused by the gunfight. Grumbling to himself about having to clean up the mess, Cole rested his head back against the wall, closing his eyes for a moment. A few minutes later, he felt a warmth on the back on his head.

Glancing over his shoulder, he realized the sun was beginning to dawn on a new day. "I need to inform the sheriff what has happened. Though I doubt anyone will happen this way and see this mess, I don't want to risk someone looking for them and drawing attention to your presence." Standing up without waiting for him to reply, Cole removed the table and unlocked the door before turning his attention back to the man who attempted to kill him in his sleep.

Kicking him in the side, both for thinking he would be stupid enough to fall asleep and leave himself completely defenseless when he knew they were coming and for being a coward, Cole grabbed under his arms, noticing Ezra grabbing his legs without having to ask. Grunting under the weight as he slowly walked backward out of the house, Cole led them to where the other bodies were scattered and literally dropped his burden on them.

"Stay hidden until I return in case they have friends waiting nearby as back up. I'm going to borrow your horse as theirs seemed to be as cowardly as they were," Cole told him after glancing around and realizing Ezra's horse was the only one to not run off after the firing started. Seeing Ezra's nod of agreement, Cole mounted the horse and returned to town for the second time in less than twenty-four hours.

# Chapter Twenty-Three

EAST OF SHADYNOOK 1830

It took Cole far less time to find the sheriff as he was anticipating that someone heard the gunshots and already alerted him before he made it into town. Instead, he found him on the road, about halfway to town, making his way toward the homestead. "Sheriff," Cole greeted, tipping his hat before greeting the deputies in the same manner. "Just on my way to see you—again. I had a bit of trouble on my property last night."

"So I have heard. Care to explain what happened exactly? Your nearest neighbor reported gunfire but had no idea how many or why," the sheriff informed him as Cole turned the horse back in the direction he came from. He silently prayed Ezra had enough time to hide as he began leading the men. Glancing back at the deputies, Cole realized one of them was pulling a small cart behind his horse. Apparently, they were expecting to transport the dead back into town to be buried.

"Last night four men attacked me and were killed during the gunfight. They were at the orphanage at the same time as me and blamed me for the death of another boy. His harassment of me went too far one night, and he was killed by the same knife he meant to hurt me with. Though it was his own fault, his friends still blamed me.

"Apparently, they saw that I returned when I went to talk to you yesterday but waited until I was way out here alone to attack me." Cole decided it was a better explanation than the truth as he pulled the horse to a stop not far from where the four men still lay. He did not need to know that they attacked him for being attracted to men and for refusing to leave his own property. "Should I be worried about repercussions from this, Sheriff?"

Even as he waited for the sheriff to answer him, who seemed to be preoccupied with staring down at the dead men, Cole dismounted and helped the deputies to load them into the cart. "Nah, I wouldn't worry none about that. If they have any family, I never heard of them, and all four of the boys are known to run together are here. Law's on your side too. They were trespassing on your land, and you had every right to shoot them whether they pulled their weapons on you first or not.

"Weren't exactly well liked in town neither. Been causing problems around these parts since they aged out of the orphanage. Truth be told, we suspected they might be behind the stagecoach robberies, but we got no proof. Guess we'll have it now if they suddenly stop," the sheriff tossed over his shoulders to the deputies causing them to chuckle even as they loaded the last man, the leader, into the cart. As Cole stood there staring at their unseeing eyes in silence, he couldn't help but realized he never knew their names.

Neither when he was a child with them at the orphanage nor since their return into his life. How strange it was to be so hated by someone when you didn't even know what their names were. In fact, the only thing he actually knew for sure about any of them was that they were at the orphanage the entire time Cole himself was.

"We'll bring them back into town and deal with their burial," the sheriff said. "Though I can't imagine that you would, but if you have any further problems, don't hesitate to come get me." He tipped his hat to Cole and remounted his horse. Bidding them good-bye, Cole stood there silently as he watched the group disappear on the horizon.

Certain they would not be returning anytime soon, he turned and headed back inside. Closing the door behind him, he called out, "They have gone, Ezra. It's safe to come out now," before sitting down at the dining room table. Apparently, while he was gone, Ezra straightened up the furniture and soon stepped out from behind the dresser he pushed back into its original spot. Ezra took a seat at the table beside him; it was impossible to miss the unasked question in his eyes.

What was he going to do now? Ignoring the unvoiced question for a moment, Cole stared off into the fire, watching as the flames danced on unconcerned by all that transpired, before finally turning his attention back to Ezra. "Not much I can do right now. The place should be safe enough to use while you heal as the sheriff assures me there should be no others around connected to those men, but I will be glad when we are gone from this place. There are far too many ghosts of days long passed echoing through these walls."

"What do you mean 'ghosts'? You don't expect the spirits of those men to haunt you, do you? Or do you mean the memory of your mother here?" Ezra wondered softly, and Cole knew he must have noticed the strange emotion that flashed in his eyes as he glanced around his childhood home. It was sadness, acceptance, and even a bit of defeat rolled into one emotion, though Cole was certain he did not have a name for it yet.

After all, what do you call coming to terms with your past yet being haunted by what you have discovered about it? Hauntingly content? Acceptance of horror? 'Old wounds that never quite heal' isn't really describable in emotions. Sighing softly to himself, Cole stood and made his way over to the open window, breathing in the fresh air from outside. Now, with the bodies gone, it only contained the slightest scent of death.

"With all that happened yesterday when I returned, I never got the chance to tell you that I found my mother in town," Cole began as he turned back to Ezra, the bright light from the morning sun haloing around him. "Apparently, she returned five years ago to sell the house, without ever stepping foot back in it by the looks of it, but was taken by the grip. I found her grave in a small cemetery next to the church." Hearing Ezra express his sympathies, Cole couldn't help but laugh.

It was devoid of humor, a dark unfeeling chuckle that echoed off of the walls that surrounded them and startled Ezra to the point he nearly jumped off of his chair. Cole couldn't blame him honestly, it was not exactly the response you would expect when someone tells you how sorry they are that you lost your parent, but it was so natural of a response to Cole that he wouldn't have stopped it if he was able to.

"I'm not sorry she's dead. Five years ago, I was still at the orphanage, and she could have come for me at any time. She consciously chose not to. She hated me so much that she allowed my life to become what it has. As much as I swore to her grave that I would never think about her again, I know that will never be true until I can let go of this anger, I have toward her. And until I can do that, I will never be at peace in this house.

"But it doesn't even matter, in truth, for as long as you will let me, I want to continue traveling with you. Perhaps, one day down the line, long after your mission is over, I will come back, and this place will actually feel like the home it never was. Maybe we can make new memories in this place by you coming back with me." Cole gave Ezra a bright, flirty smile, before laughing a true laugh when he rolled his eyes at him in response.

"We'll talk about that later," Ezra said. "For now, we have more pressing matters to attend to. If we want to be able to continue traveling together as we are, we're going to need to get a second horse. Having to carry both of us at all times is starting to take a toll on him," Ezra gestured for Cole to sit. As much as Cole would have liked to continue standing in the warm rays of the sun, he was beginning to feel the effects of how tired he was.

He plopped into the seat with a smile. "Actually I might have an idea about how to go about getting a second horse. I was planning on keeping one of theirs since they would not need them anymore, but unfortunately, all four horses ran off during the noise last night. I don't expect them to come back this way once they've calmed down. Will probably head straight back home, wherever that is.

"I'm not sure how much I mentioned about him, but quite a while back I had a customer a bit like you. Only wanted a bed to sleep on and a meal in his belly but did not have the money to pay for it. Instead, he offered to teach me how to defend myself in exchange. From what he told me, his home should not be too far from here and, while it may not have been a blood oath or anything, he did say that I should drop by if I was ever out his way and needed work as Cole.

"According to what he told me, he has a rather large ranch and would no doubt have an extra horse to sell. We may not have anywhere near enough money to pay for one even if we combined our money, but we should be able to work for him in exchange for one. Large ranches always need work done somewhere, right?" Without giving Ezra the chance to answer him, Cole continued," So we'll rest up here for a week or two until you feel well enough to work and then we'll head there.

"Can't stay here too long though, there is almost nothing for sale in the general store, and everything is twice the price due to stagecoach robberies in the area. Feel up to teaching me how to hunt and trap now?"

Ezra nodded. Cole made his way over to the shotgun, intending to take it with them, but Ezra shook his head and pulled out one of his knives from his boots, handing it to Cole with a smile.

"Not enough bullets to risk wasting them and the game in this area will probably be so small that the rifle will decimate what little meat they do have. We'll start with traps and hunting by knife. They require more patience and skill but are far safer than shooting a loud rifle and alerting everyone to your presence."

Shrugging, Cole hid the knife in his own boot and followed Ezra out the front door. As they stepped out into the bright sun, they had to shield their eyes, but it only lasted for a moment as Ezra led them to the back of the house, putting the sun behind them.

# Chapter Twenty-Four

EAST OF SHADYNOOK 1830

As the days blended one into another, the two of them hidden away at Cole's childhood home, Cole found himself anxious to move on. As much as he enjoyed playing house with Ezra, especially as they were not bothered by any other visitors in the week they were there, there was simply not enough variety in their lives. Each began the same; they would wake, break their fast, and go hunting. Cole even managed to get pretty good at setting the traps on his own though he still refused to be the one to skin the animals. That was left up to Ezra, though he did not seem to mind the bloody work.

By the time Ezra himself was strong enough to do the hunting alone, they were already planning on leaving the next day. Once the hunting was done for the day, the traps checked and emptied, the two would set about cooking or drying and salting the meat to save for later. Though they did not have much left over, with little more than meat and biscuits to eat at every meal, they were able to store enough to last them a meal or two if they rationed it.

Once they took care of the game, they would sit around the fire and talk, all day long. There was little else to do out there isolated from everyone else, that Ezra was willing to do anyway, except for their evening walk. With little to do to pass the time, the days seemed incredibly slow to Cole, and as much as he loved spending time alone with Ezra, he was desperate for a change of pace.

If he stayed there much longer, he was certain he would go stir crazy. Though occasionally their mundane routine was interrupted by an article of clothing needing mending or Ezra whittling a piece of wood away into nothing, each night would end the same as the one before. After supper they would crawl into bed beside each other, neither of them wanting to force the other to sleep on the hard floor, and Cole would end up being unable to fall asleep for hours with him lying beside him. His mind would wander to what he wished to do to his body, what Ezra might do to his own, if he but let him.

Each morning was met with frustration and a missed opportunity for release. With such tight quarters, there was nowhere for Cole to go to take care of his more personal needs that Ezra couldn't just suddenly stumble upon him. For a moment, he considered heading out into the small wooded area where they did their hunting, but the fear that Ezra might worry he was gone too long and come looking for him kept him from attempting it.

Each evening after supper, as he did in the saloon, Cole would prepare a bath for Ezra. In truth, it was to help pass the time as they had yet to do much to accumulate dirt. Their routine continued on, almost as if it were on a loop, until the night before they were planning on leaving. The evening started out as the others before it did; they ate their supper, and Cole headed outside to prepare the bath. As Ezra headed out to bath, Cole headed back inside as he usually did, the only difference was that he packed up their belongings while waiting for his turn instead of lying beside the fire and staring into the flames.

"Your turn!" Ezra called out to him a little while later as he did every night.

Making his way back outside, Cole found Ezra heading toward him, shirt tucked into the back of his pants instead of on and, though he found it a bit odd, Cole paid it little mind as he made his way over toward the bath. Testing the water with his fingertips, he found it was still warm. Ezra seemed to always make sure to get out of the bath fast enough that Cole wouldn't have to reheat water for himself. His thoughts on Ezra, he turned toward him, expecting to find him already inside the house to sit before the fire.

Instead, he found him retrieving the ax from the wood stump and setting up a log. Figuring he decided to test how well his shoulder was working before they left tomorrow, Cole paid him little mind as he stripped and stepped into the water. Startled by the sudden *thunk* of the ax against wood, even though he was expecting it, Cole turned toward him before leaning back in the tub to watch him work. Each time he raised his arms, the muscles beneath them seemed to ripple to Cole, causing his breath to catch in his throat.

With every downward swing, his muscles were pulled taut, showing Cole the very strength he was attracted by. Groaning softly, Cole bit his bottom lip as he slowly slid his fingers across his chest, teasing his nipples with a gentle pinch before continuing down toward his navel. Wetting his suddenly dry lips, his eyes glued on the sight before him, a sudden thought crossed his mind.

Could he? Out there in the open, within sight of Ezra? Did he dare? He trailed his hand lower until he felt his own heated member beneath his fingertips. Wrapping his fingers around the base, Cole applied the slightest amount of pressure before sliding his fingers forward at the same time that Ezra swung his ax down into the wood. The movement drew a soft gasp from him, but it was easily drowned out by the noise of the ax.

As Ezra raised his arms once more, Cole's fingers slid back down to his base only to thrust them forward even as Ezra swung the ax again. Holding the rhythm, stroking himself only when Ezra moved as well, Cole soon found both of them beginning to pant. Biting his lip once more to prevent himself from calling out as he increased the pressure at the sight of the sweat dripping down Ezra's back, Cole felt himself drawing close to release.

At long last, he would find his completion once again, allowing himself at least some relief. Just as he felt the pressure building up inside him, Ezra set the ax down, wiping the back of his hand across his forehead. Not about to go unsatisfied yet again, Cole continued to move his hand beneath the water even as Ezra turned toward him with a smile. Worried he was caught after all, he willed his hand to stop, but it seemed to have a mind of its own as it not only continued uninterrupted, but it actually picked up the pace and pressure.

"Looks like my shoulder is doing better. No pain no matter how hard I swung the ax," Ezra called out as he rolled his shoulder. Cole tilted his head toward the water to prevent Ezra from seeing him bite his lip. He silently begged him to not mention anything being 'hard.'

Ezra continued, "I'm going to head inside now and make sure we've got everything packed."

As he watched him go, his hand increasing in speed once more, Cole was torn between wanting him to hurry up and wanting him to stay outside a little while longer. Just the thought of Ezra being so close without realizing what he was doing, or who he was fantasizing was doing it, made the whole thing that much hotter.

"I'm coming in a minute!" Cole called out to him teasingly, assured that Ezra had no idea what he was doing inside the tub when he waved his hand over his shoulder in response.

Cole rolled his eyes back and groaned, sinking deeper into the tub as he stroked to his heart's content, causing the water to churn with such force that some splashed over the edge. A moment later, he forgot how to breathe as he felt his whole length tighten up before spilling his release into the water. Taking a shuddering breath, Cole rose from the tub and rinsed off before emptying the dirty water. After giving the tub a quick wipe down to ensure no evidence of his actions remained, he dressed and made his way toward the house.

EZRA SHUT THE door behind him before leaning up against it and letting out a shuddering breath. He could not believe what he witnessed, what Cole was doing to himself. Though he was unsure of what was happening at first, once he moved toward the front door, he had an unobstructed view of Cole. He saw his fingers each time they slid down his shaft. Heard Cole panting even over the sound of the churning water.

For a moment, he thought Cole knew he saw him but realized he thought he was completely hidden. Would he have stopped if he did know Ezra did see him? Would he simply have joked about him joining? Judging by his teasing choice of words before Ezra got inside, he was pretty sure there was very little that would have stopped him in that moment. Perhaps if Ezra would have asked him to, but what right did he have to ask such a thing?

Certainly, he could ask, demand even, that he wait to do that after Ezra went inside, but as Ezra thought about the last week they were there, he did not remember a time where Cole had the opportunity to do such a thing. There was simply nowhere for him to get away and Ezra was certain he did not do so in the bath before as even now he heard the churning of the water inside. Surely, he would have noticed such a sound before if he had.

Was this something he was used to doing regularly? Did he do so before while they were traveling without Ezra realizing it? Did he imagine it was Ezra's hand pleasuring him as he told him he would the first night at the saloon? His curiosity getting the better of him, Ezra made his way over to the window. Staring out into the fading sunlight, he saw Cole relaxing back in the tub as his hand moved unseen beneath the water.

He seemed to hold his breath for a moment before his entire body relaxed. Seeing the content expression on his face as he rose from the tub, Ezra gazed at his naked form for a moment before turning away. Making his way over to the fire, he added another log before sitting down to wait for Cole to join him. Contemplating whether or not to tell Cole he knew what he did, he was a bit startled when Cole came in and plopped down on the bed without a word.

Glancing over, it was impossible for Ezra not to notice the slight bulge in Cole's pants, informing him that he did not go completely soft yet. Ezra decided not to tell him what he witnessed, but instead to tease him a bit. After all, if he was going to fantasize about him, which Ezra was certain he did, he should at least give him something worth fantasizing about.

Removing his shirt, though he usually slept in it, Ezra slipped out of his boots before laying down on the bed beside Cole; he made sure he was close enough for them to touch slightly. "Good night," Ezra said, though he was certain Cole would be tossing and turning for a bit as he did every night. A little while later, once he was certain Cole would think him asleep, Ezra cracked his eyes open enough to make out his companion propped up on his elbow; his eyes were glued to Ezra's naked chest.

Smirking to himself, Ezra closed his eyes and pictured Cole once more in the bathtub. Only this time, it was Colleen teasing him back in the saloon, her body hovering above his without ever touching him. He remembered the sensation of her hot breath fanning over his skin. He felt the water churning around his shaft as her hand mimicked Cole's earlier actions to himself. This time, Ezra wrapped his fingers around hers, guiding them to close as he bucked up into them.

Though he only meant to groan in his mind, Ezra soon realized he, in fact, made the sound out loud as Cole sucked in a breath beside him. Knowing his thoughts were having the desired effect on his quickly rising member, he imagined her instructing him to sit up on the tub. Only this time, as he followed the instructions, it was Cole standing beside the tub outside of the house they were currently occupying instead of the one in his bathing room back at the saloon.

As his breath fanned over his engorged member, the appendage far harder than he allowed it to get previously, his lips just shy of touching the heated flesh, Ezra sank his fingers into his unbound hair and thrust himself into Cole's mouth. Instantly his lips closed around his shaft, and he was soon dragging them up and down the length before allowing it to plop out of his mouth to run his tongue across the tip, exciting a moan from Ezra both within the fantasy and without.

As Cole groaned beside him, he knew he figured out what was happening in his "dream" and decided to take it a little further. Arching his back off of the bed as he groaned once more, his hips thrusting into an invisible mouth, he fisted his hands into the sheets making sure his arm was close enough to Cole that it brushed up against his thigh. "Ezra," Cole groaned out beside him, his voice heavy with lust.

After a moment, he realized the cause. At some point, Cole began pleasuring himself once more, and though he thought to stop abruptly and prevent him from finishing, something at the back of his mind begged him to let him find his release. It was one thing to see it happen from across the yard, but if he allowed it to continue, he would actually be able to hear Cole find his satisfaction. Something about the thought of that spurred him on.

Ezra groaned out between clenched teeth as he arched up for one last thrust and imagined himself finishing in Cole's mouth. He had no idea what such an experience might actually feel like, but he was certain he would have enjoyed it. Judging by the sudden gasp coming from the bed beside him as Cole stilled, he was not the only one. Settling down into the bed, Ezra allowed himself to drift off to sleep even as he felt Cole rise from the bed to clean up.

# Epilogue

LATE INTO THE night, a silent figure hid in the shadows. He waited for prey he knew would soon be there. If anyone was there to see him, they would have seen his soft, joyful eyes turned sorrowful—full of hate. If anyone were there to hear him, they would have heard his usually calm voice turn dark and threatening.

But there was no one there, not anymore. Now he was alone, crouched in silence, patiently waiting with no other thought than the fact that he would soon be victorious once again. Though his plan had not yet brought the conclusion that he so desperately wished for, he knew it was only a matter of time before his actions drew the attention of the one he sought. He would pull him out of hiding, and he would end his miserable life for what he did.

Hearing the sound of hoofbeats getting closer, knowing it meant the stagecoach would be coming around the bend any moment now, he turned his attention back to the present and away from what the future would bring. He listened, unmoving from his spot, knowing it was not yet time. It was easy to tell the driver was urging the horses on faster than they usually would around the blind turn they were approaching.

He did not blame them, in truth, as they no doubt heard what he was up to and feared for their own lives. They would wish to be safe within the city as soon as possible, each crack of the Whip driving the man's horses faster, harder than the one before. It would not matter in the end, since it always ended the same way for them, but he had to hand it to them for the courage. Not everyone would continue to take up the reins after countless stagecoaches before them never made it to their destination.

But they would not give up, the man behind them would never let them. Each time as he heard them coming closer to the bend he was hidden by, he contemplated letting them live, as they were only doing their jobs, but such thoughts only lasted but a minute. They may have courage, but they still worked for him, and that was all that mattered. He would draw that man out if it was the last thing he did, and he was pretty sure it might prove to be, and their deaths helped make that become a reality that much faster.

They were not innocent, he would remind himself each time, not like she was. If that wasn't enough to convince him that mercy was not an option, he would simply remind himself he had no way of knowing if they did the same to others as the men, he was searching for, did to her. It was better that he took an innocent life than to let a single man get away with what they did. At least in his mind and his was the only one that mattered now. They saw to that.

Shaking his head to clear the thoughts of her beautiful smile, he turned his attention once more to the stagecoach that was appearing at the edge of the bend. Almost as if he read their minds, he knew exactly what went through the Whip's mind each time the coaches came around that bend and realized how exposed they were. It was the exact reason he chose this location for the ambush.

As they would come around the blind, they realized the disadvantage they were suddenly at. Once they reached that spot, the only place that provided any type of coverage was the short tree line to their left. Which, of course, offered far better protection to anyone lying in wait to ambush them than it did for them. It was exactly why he continued to use it, though he was not entirely sure why he never found lawmen waiting here for him.

He always left the stagecoaches a burning wreckage below him. Though it was always cleaned up by the local sheriff before his next ambush, they never used that knowledge against him. Perhaps, he decided as he aimed his first already loaded rifle, they simply had no way of knowing when the next coach was coming and did not have the manpower to watch the spot at all times. Perhaps he was simply too far away from the town, the only lawmen in the area, called home. Maybe the lawmen actually knew who these men truly were and couldn't be bothered with their protection. In the end, he supposed the reason didn't matter.

A quick glance around the stagecoach, taking his eyes off of the Whip for but a moment, he counted four men besides him before pulling the trigger. The loud blast echoed around him even as the man fell sideways off of the stagecoach, the horses running wild now that there was no one to steer them. Paying the animals little mind, for now, he tossed the rifle aside and grabbed a second loaded gun from the pile he set up against the tree he hid behind. Inhaling, he took aim as the men raised their own guns, searching for him in the trees. Exhaling, the shot echoed round him once more as a second man dropped from the stagecoach. The first gun was joined by the second and then a third as he fired every single shot before disposing of them.

Each rifle seemed to hit the ground at the same time as the man it dropped, but he barely noticed as he was already grabbing for the next before the previous even hit the ground. As the two remaining men fired in his direction, unable to find him but knowing he was in the area, he paid them little mind as they hid behind the carriage of the stagecoach; exposing only their arms as they shot wildly. Knowing he had only a few moments before they would be too far away from him to reach without exposing himself, he aimed his next shot at the animals leading the coach.

As much as he would have preferred to let them go free once he was done, as he did with the others, he took aim at the closest horse and fired his shot, quickly dropping the animal. As it fell, it tripped the other, causing the stagecoach, and the two men still inside, to go flying. As the large wooden carriage was crashing to the ground, shattering into hundreds of useless pieces, he grabbed his last preloaded rifle and made his way down the hill, making a mental note to prepare a few more next time.

Quickly spotting one of the men running away as fast as he was able to with a limp, he took aim and shot him in the back before reloading the gun without bothering to check if he went down. He knew he had; they always did. Making his way toward what was left of the stagecoach, he soon heard the painful groans coming from the last man and the frightened cries of the second horse. As he stepped around the wreckage, he found the horse was trapped under the one he took down but seemed unhurt otherwise.

Ignoring the animal, for now, he turned his attention to the last man who was pinned under a large chunk of the carriage, trying to reach his gun that was mere inches from his fingertips.

"You should know, laddie," he began as he stepped on his hand, preventing him from reaching the weapon. "You have Hodge to blame for your death." Without giving him the chance to respond, he took aim and pulled the trigger. Staring down at the remains of what used to be a man, he sighed softly before turning his attention to the only other being to survive the carnage.

Retrieving a knife from his boot, he cut away the horse's harness and stepped back as it climbed to its feet. He slapped the horse on the rump, and it darted off. Once the horse was gone, he turned his attention back to the scattered supplies that were thrown from the carriage. Retrieving his own wagon from around the blind, he gathered up what hadn't been destroyed, along with any guns the men were carrying and put them in the back of his wagon.

Turning back to the destruction he caused over the course of a few minutes, he set to work catching the carriage on fire. He climbed into his wagon and headed back toward his small, one room home he built with his own hands. Dropping the supplies off in the barn with the others he stole over the last few months, he locked the door and made his way inside his home. He kicked off his boots and fell back in bed. As he lay on his back, he held his wrist up and stared at the three thin bracelets made from human hair that were wrapped around it.

# About the Author

Hairann is the author of the Outlaw Seven series. She is an out and proud Pan who lives with her amazing family in Montreal. She's worked as a ghostwriter on Fiverr since 2018 and has an Associates degree in early childhood education. She invites you to follow @AuthorHairann on Twitter.

Email: Hairanntheauthor@hotmail.com

# Coming soon from Hairann

## Damned If You Don't

The sun had only just begun to rise as Erabus silently made his way through the thick forest, his footfalls inaudible on the damp leaf-carpeted ground, with his bow at the ready; an arrow notched and ready to fire. Navigating around one cluster of trees and then another, he allowed the sounds from the other hunters to fade into the background as he got further away from where they were making far more noise than they should be if they expected to be able to catch anything.

Putting the far less skilled hunters from his mind, he paused momentarily to sniff the fresh forest air; filling his nose with the strong scents of pine and moss. Smiling softly at the feeling of calm the scents had over him, he continued on in search of any deer that might have passed through the area recently. Though if the others continued to make as much noise as they were now, he doubted they would remain in the area for very long. Sighing softly at having been assigned to such an obviously inexperienced hunting group, Erabus tuned them out once more as he crouched to the ground and gently removed any debris from an indent in the dirt.

Tracing the imperfect print with the pad of his index, he thought to himself, Deer. Or perhaps a goat down from the mountain. The print didn't cause a deep enough indent to tell for sure which it. The only thing he was sure of was that the print was fresh. With any luck, the animal would still be in the vicinity and Erabus was determined to catch it before the others could alert it to their presence. Careful to walk only on the pads of his feet to reduce what little noise he made as much as possible, he followed the prints further into the forest until he heard the rustling of leaves coming from the other side of a cluster of trees that grew so close together he couldn't see through them.

Parting the branches as much as he dared, he waited only long enough to spot the horns before carefully releasing the branch and taking aim through the trees. Though he could not see his target from his current position, he knew roughly where it was standing and took aim to the right and down a bit from where he was certain its horns had ended. Inhaling softly as he put the string taut, he released the arrow at the same time as his breath; easily able to hear the whoosh the arrow made as it pierced through the air.

The gentle thud of the arrow striking wood came only a moment before a voice called out in alarm; startling Erabus and nearly causing him to drop his bow. Had another hunter made it out farther than I had realized? Even as he thought this, he silently reminded himself that he had seen the horns himself. Confused, he had just shouldered his bow to investigate when he heard a voice call out, "Watch what you are doing!" Horrified at what he had done, having almost injured another in his desire to not investigate closer and risk scaring off the game, he quickly pushed his way through the thicket.

"I'm so sorry, sir. I could have sworn I saw horns," Erabus insisted as he practically fell through the trees; taking a moment to right himself before turning his eyes on the man he had almost shot. Only it wasn't a man standing before him he quickly realized as he took in his appearance. Standing just a foot away from where his arrow had struck the tree, stood a creature with the body and face of a man, but the legs, hooves, tail, and ears of a goat. Most importantly, the horns of one too.

# Also Available from NineStar Press

# Connect with NineStar Press

Website: NineStarPress.com

Facebook: NineStarPress

Facebook Reader Group: NineStarNiche

Twitter: @ninestarpress

Tumblr: NineStarPress